Beauty and the
Wiener

Casey Griffin

St. Martin's Paperbacks

This is a work of fiction. All of the characters, organizations, and events portrayed in this novel are either products of the author's imagination or are used fictitiously.

BEAUTY AND THE WIENER

For information address St. Martin's Press, 175 Fifth Avenue, New York, NY 10010.

ISBN: 978-1-250-08468-2

Our books may be purchased in bulk for promotional, educational, or business use. Please contact your local bookseller or the Macmillan Corporate and Premium Sales Department at 1-800-221-7945, ext. 5442, or by e-mail at MacmillanSpecialMarkets@macmillan.com.

Printed in the United States of America

St. Martin's Paperbacks edition / February 2017

St. Martin's Paperbacks are published by St. Martin's Press, 175 Fifth Avenue, New York, NY 10010.

10 9 8 7 6 5 4 3 2 1

For Devin

Finally

Praise for
MUST LOVE WIENERS

"Paws down, one of the funniest books I've read in a long time. A lively romantic mystery with a quirky and relatable heroine, a sexy leading man, and adorable dachshunds. No bones about it, this book is a real treat!"
—Diane Kelly, author of the Paw Enforcement series

"A satisfying blend of romance and mystery . . . Add the appropriate amount of playful banter and dog shenanigans, and you've got the makings of a promising start to a new series. A delightfully adorable mystery-romance with a well-planned plot. And dogs!" —*Kirkus Reviews*

"A fun and charming series . . . *Must Love Wieners* combines humor and romance with a dash of mystery, all while showcasing the author's determined heroine fighting for her dream. Settle in and enjoy, and keep the puppy treats handy!" —*RT Book Reviews*

"Griffin's spirited, wholesome love story escalates into a deeper mystery offering playful comic relief en route to a revealing whodunit." —*Shelf Awareness*

"Who doesn't love a story with cute dogs, hot billionaires, quirky heroines, and a sweet HEA. I cannot wait for the next book in what is the start of a wonderful series to come." —*Harlequin Junkie (Top Pick!)*

"Griffin's debut and first in her new rescue dog romance series is definitely barking up the right tree. Perfect for the dog days of summer read." —*The Reading Frenzy*

Also by Casey Griffin

Must Love Wieners

Acknowledgments

I began writing *Beauty and the Wiener* at a time when the changes happening in my reality coincidentally paralleled the stories happening within my writing. While this novel is purely fictional, I owe the passion and inspiration found in its pages to my partner, Devin, for simply coming into my world and giving me the life I never knew I truly needed. Thank you for the love, the support, and the wieners. You had me at "*Firefly*."

To Rose Hilliard, my biggest cheerleader and the top dog of editors, thank you for believing in me. You're always there with the best advice and puns. You had me at "wieners."

A special thanks to Pat Esden and my amazing agent, Pooja Menon, for helping me make this wiener rock solid before I put it into the hands of the magicians at St. Martin's Press, the most incredible team I could have asked for.

1

Doggy Style

Fur flew through the air under Addison Turner's skilled touch as though she were born holding a pair of scissors, as natural as Edward Scissorhands sculpting purebred pooches into masterpieces. Her current muse came in the form of a fluffy bichon frisé named Elvis whose hair clippings were getting stuck in the glittering details of her black sequined dress. Stray dog hair sticking out of the tight number wasn't exactly the come-hither look she was going for.

Addison's assistant, Melody, noticed the wardrobe mishap. "Oh no. Your dress. How are you going to hook your man now?"

"It's okay," Addison said with a wink. "I can make anything look good. Even dog hair."

Melody grabbed a brush and began working any excess hair out of Elvis's coat. "You keep talking about this perfect guy, but I don't think you've told me his name."

"That's because I don't know it . . . *yet*," she added.

As Addison trimmed around the dog's face, her

normally steady hand shook. Not with nerves, but with irritation. Elvis's owner, Kitty Carlisle, hovered behind the two of them, twitching with each clip of the scissors as though Addison was going to accidentally slip and cut a jugular vein.

Kitty continued to pace back and forth across the stage they were working on. Addison tried to ignore her, but twelve pairs of eyes watched the woman's anxious movements with interest. Addison already had a full list of clients currently lounging on colorful bohemian pillows in various stages of her patented Pampered Puppies Program. She'd already completed puppy pawdicures, Shih-Tzu shiatsus, bow-wow bath and brushes, and hound hydrotherapy, all free of charge in order to promote her business.

That night's cocktail mixer was being held in the Grand Ballroom of the historic Regency Center on Sutter Street. The neoclassical surroundings created the perfect romantic ambiance for the elite dog lovers of San Francisco to rub elbows, not to mention size up the competition before the Western Dog Show in two weeks' time.

Addison sighed just thinking about it. The glitz, the glamour, the extravagance, the beauty. Nobody showered their four-legged friends with more affection and luxury than hopeful winners of the coveted Best in Show award. It was something she could certainly relate to—puppies were her passion. Now *that* was a client list she wanted to tap into. She was going to be the Coco Chanel of the four-legged world, and the next two weeks were going to make her or break her.

Unfortunately, Addison was stuck behind the scenes. Literally. She'd been allotted the ballroom's built-in stage to set up her portable grooming station and pamper the party's furry guests. While that should have allowed her the best view of the night's event, they'd closed the stage curtains. Apparently one of the guests had complained. Maybe they didn't like witnessing all the hard work being done while they enjoyed their escargot and champagne.

Kitty flinched again, looking ready to lunge for Elvis and protect him from Addison's abuse.

"Mrs. Carlisle," Addison addressed the nervous woman hovering over her shoulder, yet again. "Are you certain you wouldn't feel more comfortable out in the ballroom enjoying the cocktail mixer?"

The older woman shook her head stiffly, not a single white hair from her beehive stirring. She'd probably used a full can of hairspray on it. "I'm perfectly fine here with Elvis." She cringed as though Melody's brush was going to grow teeth and bite her dog. "You just never know who you can trust during competition season." Her puglike eyes bulged conspiratorially.

Addison bristled at the comment. Surely, Kitty wasn't suggesting that Addison would ever do anything to risk a show dog's chances. That would be the death of her business before it even had the chance to take off. She was only just beginning to break into the niche show dog market.

One last snip of the scissors and Elvis's traditional show cut was complete, resulting in his head looking like what Addison could only describe as a round ball of white cotton candy. Two black eyes blinked out from the sphere of fur. It mirrored Kitty's '60s beehive hairstyle almost perfectly. Or perhaps Kitty modeled herself after her dog.

For the pièce de résistance, Addison fastened a formal bow tie and tux collar around Elvis's neck. There was a hidden metal ring where a leash could be attached. *Fashion, meet function,* Addison thought.

The ensemble was one of her many creations she was giving away for free that night, a way to garner attention for her new line of designer doggy duds. At the stroke of ten o'clock, the curtains would part to reveal a small taste of her upcoming fashion line. She hoped it would have the owners begging to be placed on her fashion show RSVP list.

Wiping away the mounds of white feathery fur, Addison unclipped Elvis from the grooming arm above the table. She stood back and held her arms out Vanna White–style, to display Kitty's little white dog. "What do you think?"

Kitty reached out and straightened the bow tie. "How charming."

Was that an actual smile? Addison felt giddy, like she was on an ice cream sugar high.

"It's part of my premiere fashion line for four-legged fashionistas. It's called Fido Fashion." Addison whipped out a sparkly pink flier and held it up. "I'm launching the line on the same weekend as the dog show. You and Elvis should come check it out. In fact, I'm still looking for volunteers to model the designs. Maybe Elvis would like to be involved." She gave Kitty a hopeful smile, trying her best not to come off as a slimy used-car salesperson.

Kitty clung to Elvis like a mother on her kid's first day of school. "I don't know," she said uncertainly.

"He'll get to keep any outfits that he models," Addison offered.

Biting her lip, Kitty plucked the flier from Addison's hand. "I'll think about it."

Backing away slowly, like she wanted to keep an eye on Addison, Kitty finally made a break for it. She cradled Elvis to her chest and whisked him across the stage. His black eyes bored into Addison over Kitty's shoulder as they ducked through the heavy stage curtains and out to the ballroom.

The thick drapes parted, and classic jazz music drifted into their workspace, punctuated by the clink of glasses and murmur of voices. Wandering up to the front of the stage, Addison peeked through a gap.

People were dancing across the blond hardwood flooring, flirting on opulent camelback sofas, and showing off their sure-to-win purebreds near the cocktail bar. Men in tuxes, women in beautiful cocktail dresses, and most important for her business, some of Dogdom's most prominent authorities.

Addison assessed the state of her own cocktail dress, picking at the tufts of fur clinging to it. It wasn't the most sensible uniform for dog grooming—her high heels were *not* the most comfortable—but a good PR campaign for her business wasn't the only reason she'd been looking forward to this dog show for months. She'd also wanted to build a few *personal relations* of her own.

Addison's life was perfect. Her business was doing well enough that she could afford to hire an assistant, and she was about to launch her new fashion line. Everything was unfolding like a blockbuster Hollywood movie, except for one thing. Her leading man had yet to be cast. She was more like the makeup artist than the leading lady, but after the fashion show turned out to be a hit and her business reached a whole new level of success, that would all change. It was time for her Cinderella story to begin.

Addison could feel the night slip away as she hid behind the scenes. She'd been so busy, she hadn't had a chance to enjoy the evening herself. Maybe she could get away for a little while, she thought.

She glanced back at all her equipment waiting to be

dismantled and stored in her car, the fur that needed to be swept, the dogs that needed to be arranged for the big reveal. That's when she noticed her own object of affection saunter across the stage: a beautiful, longhaired, cream dachshund.

Like a movie star, the doxie strode imperiously down the length of red carpet rolled across the stage to join the lineup of other stars of the night. The beaded flapper-girl dress that Addison had designed especially for her glittered beneath the lights. As she passed each dog show contender, she eyed up the competition. Her ample chest swelled with confidence—which said much about her belief in her own beauty, as these particular pups were the crème de la crème of the Western United States.

Finding her adversaries wanting, the beautiful blonde huffed, and with a flick of her long, wavy locks, she returned to her pink velvet pillow embroidered with her name in gold: PRINCESS.

Addison walked over and scratched Princess behind the ears. "What do you think of our customers?" she asked her. "Do they pass your rigid beauty inspection?"

Princess yawned, seeming unimpressed.

"Of course they don't even come close to your caliber, your highness." Addison gave her a little bow. "You don't need to bother competing in the dog show. We already know you're the best."

"Woof," Princess agreed, and then bestowed a lick upon Addison's hand.

Addison took this to mean "You have pleased us."

But she didn't mention the real reason she wouldn't enter Princess, because despite deserving every award there was, in the end, she would sadly lose.

An angular limb deformity had left Princess with one leg shorter than the rest. Her previous owner had been devastated to discover her precious Princess would never be eligible to compete in a conformation show. So devastated, it seemed, that the first chance she got, she dropped Princess off at a shelter.

Addison recalled the day she met Princess at the San Francisco Dachshund Rescue Center where she volunteered regularly. Maybe the doxie's deformity was why she'd felt such an instant connection with the abandoned show dog. It meant they had something in common. Only, Addison's defect couldn't be seen by the naked eye. No one could see what was hidden beneath all that makeup, hair, and stylish outfits. To everyone else, Addison was perfect, and her life seemed perfect.

But beauty was only skin deep. It was what was on the inside that mattered, right? Although Princess would never reach the pinnacle of pooch perfection sought after by show dog enthusiasts, she was certainly number one in Addison's heart.

Now if only Addison could find that special someone who saw Addison the same way. Preferably one with two legs.

Addison scanned the collection of aspiring dog show champions lined up on the stage, all pampered and ready to be shown. "Well, I think they look pretty good."

"Good?" Melody said. "They look amazing! Everything's perfect." She gave Addison a reassuring smile. "You've outdone yourself tonight. I think everyone really took notice. Just wait. There won't be a seat left in the house at your fashion show."

"You think so?"

"I know so."

A Pekingese named King Winky Von Rainbow Valley, or Kingy for short, was wandering around Addison's supply bag. He'd obviously sniffed out her treat stash. Plucking him up into her arms, she carried him back to his pillow and snuck him a treat.

"Don't tell the others, okay?" she told him.

She fluffed the cubic zirconia–encrusted bow on his back. The elegant brocade was arranged in the traditional form of a Japanese obi, accenting the orange coy on the blue kimono nicely.

Addison picked up a half-inch barrel curling iron, ready to get started on a silky terrier's bangs.

Melody stopped her with a look. "Back away from the curling iron," she said. "Everything is ready for the reveal. Just go out there already and advertise a little, promote, rub elbows, and most important, enjoy yourself."

Addison looked around at all the equipment again. "But there's still so much to clean up."

"I'll get the stage ready for ten o'clock. Don't worry." Melody waved Addison away. "You need people to put a face to your infamous name and your work. Now go."

Addison sighed and put the iron down. "You're right. Thanks."

After checking on a Maltese whose nails were currently drying with Rainbow Frenzy nail polish, Addison brushed off what dog hair she could from her dress and grabbed the leash belonging to a pinscher named Rosie. She clipped it to the collar around her neck designed to look like a gold and ruby necklace. Addison created it for the pricier end of her line, and it was one she knew would blow her hot owner away.

As she prepared to leave, Princess pranced over, ready to shake her tail on the dance floor.

"Don't worry, I wouldn't leave you behind," she told the doxie. "Are you ready to go make some friends?"

In response, Princess spun in a circle, already getting her groove on.

Addison fastened Princess's hot pink lead to her Art Deco pearl collar and waved to Melody. "I'm going to return Rosie to her owner."

"Good luck. I hope he likes it." Melody gave Addison a wink that told her she didn't mean the grooming they'd done on his pinscher.

"Who wouldn't?" Addison threw her a flirtatious smile. She checked her hair in one of the mirrors placed around their makeshift salon, ensuring it was perfect, and whipped the thick curtains aside.

The moment Addison emerged, the smell of wet dog was replaced by expensive cologne, and the sounds of barking faded beneath the calming clarity of classical jazz floating over from the band in the far corner. From thirty-five feet above, teardrop chandeliers cast a warm glow onto the guests circulating the ballroom. It was as though she were Alice passing through the looking glass. It was an entirely different world.

Using the dog show circuit to promote her business was a two-week-long ticket to a parade of high-class events around San Francisco—and Addison had a VIP backstage pass. Sure, it wasn't a singles mixer, but it was a social event, nonetheless. Something she hadn't seen much of since she opened up shop two years earlier.

For two weeks, she would be surrounded by well-dressed, classy men. Men who held doors for ladies. Men in tuxes. Men who cared about grooming themselves as much as they did their dogs. Men with style. Addison was nothing if not stylish.

Her Prince Charming would be the perfect addition to her perfect life. Her happily ever after.

Now all she had to do was go out there and find him.

2

Beware of Dog

Addison descended the stage stairs like Cinderella at the ball. She escorted Rosie and Princess down to the floor level, or rather they escorted her. They were so well trained, there was no fighting, or sniffing, or barking like there would be with any other dogs. In fact, they owned the room, two hot chicks out on the town. *Make that three*, Addison added in her head.

Rosie was elegant in her necklace, and Princess looked ready to do the Charleston in her 1920's-style dress. They weaved their way through cocktail tables toward the bar located in the center of the room where Rosie's owner, Rex Harris, said he'd meet her. They strutted with confidence. Only, Princess's stride had the slightest hiccup. The little limp that you'd notice only if you were really paying attention. Addison liked to think of it as a swagger.

The lights had been dimmed, the mood accented by hundreds of candles scattered around the room. Their flickering light reflected off the gilded wall decor surrounding the upper balcony and off champagne glasses, diamonds caressing throats, gold Rolexes, and her own dazzling sequined dress.

The ambiance, the energy, the allure. It was all so romantic, like a real fairy tale. The perfect place to meet her Prince Charming.

Her eyes cast around the small groups of show dog owners and event supporters sipping their martinis and Pino Grigio in search of Rex. She spotted him on the other side of the bar, hair coiffed fashionably, svelte in his three-piece suit. The bartender passed him a drink across the counter as Rex leaned against the bar, one leg crossed over the other at the ankle.

He watched the room with a confident ease as he sipped his drink. Whiskey, maybe. No, a martini. Just like James Bond. Yes, he looked exactly like the secret agent—Pierce Brosnan style. Ooh, Addison liked that. Definitely five-star potential.

When Rex spotted her slinking toward him from across the room, his eyes drifted down the length of her curvy body appreciatively. Well, she thought so, until his eyes didn't roam back up. They remained fixed on Rosie. *Ouch.*

Second-guessing herself, Addison glanced down at her evening dress with its sleek black lines and revealing—though not too revealing—neckline. There was a fine line between saying "I'm your *one*" and "I'm your *one night stand*." But when she noticed the tall, dark, and sexy bartender flash her a lingering look over the bottles of top-shelf liquor, she knew it wasn't the dress's fault.

Never mind then. She'd dazzle Rex with her sparkling personality.

"Rex Harris." She smiled as she approached the bar. "Rosie is all ready for you. What do you think?" To let him know she didn't mean the grooming, she leaned against the bar to give him a better shot of that low neckline—okay, even Prince Charming probably needed baiting.

She toyed with Rosie's leash, wrapping it teasingly around her finger. But Rex's loving gaze was still glued to his pedigree pinscher. Oblivious to her efforts, Rex bent down and gave Rosie a pet.

Addison thought she heard a soft snort from behind the bar. When she turned to the bartender, he was studiously wiping down the glass counter, but she could have sworn that was a smirk on his lips.

"Oh wow," Rex said, drawing her attention back. "Rosie's fur has never looked so shiny. How did you do that?"

Addison beamed. "That's the yogurt and oatmeal rub."

"Yogurt?" He glanced up and seemed to notice her for the first time.

If she had a tail, it would be wagging. "Yes, the yogurt strips away the dirt and moisturizes, while the oatmeal treats the skin and softens the fur. It also makes for a good breakfast," she joked.

He smiled, standing back up to take in the full view. "I can think of better breakfasts to make. I know my way around a kitchen."

"You like to cook?" *Mmm*, she thought. Cooking skills were definitely worth a star.

"Only for someone special." He swirled his drink before taking a sip, eyeing her above the rim. "Maybe I could cook for you sometime."

That would make Addison *someone special*. She liked the sound of that. "Sounds delicious."

"Why don't you give me a call sometime?" He reached into his suit coat. "Here's my card."

"Thanks. Maybe I will." She took the card and traded it for Rosie's leash.

"Thanks again," he said. "Come on Rosie. Shall we go for a walk?"

The pinscher's nubby black tail shook in response.

Rex gave Addison a wink and turned to head across the ballroom, holding the leash aloft in true show form. Rosie trotted alongside him like she was already showing off for the judges attending the cocktail mixer that night.

Addison and Princess were watching him stroll away when a small wastebasket was thrust in front of her, obscuring her view. She flinched back and turned to find the sexy bartender holding it out. His dark eyebrows quirked up as he shook the basket expectantly.

She frowned at it. "What's that for?"

"For that card," he said.

"For Rex's card? Why?" She clutched the slip of paper protectively. "Maybe I'll give him a call."

"You and about ten other girls at this party tonight." He shrugged and put the wastebasket under the bar again. "But it's your call."

Her face fell. "Ten?"

In response, the bartender tilted his mop of dark curls across the ballroom where Rex was slipping another card from his pocket and flashing it at a young brunette waitress. *Maybe I'm not so special after all*, Addison thought. She picked Princess up, needing a little moral support from her girl.

"You think I'm special, don't you baby?"

Princess gave her a kiss on the neck in reassurance . . . or maybe it was because she was wearing coconut body butter.

"Don't feel bad," the bartender said. "I've got eyes like an Afghan hound. I see all. I know all. Most of all when it comes to slimeballs like him." He gave her a cheesy wink.

Addison gave the tall bartender the once-over. He had a certain tilt to his square jaw that spoke of confidence, or cockiness, she wasn't sure which. Being a bartender, she was sure he'd had plenty of conversations across a bar with a pretty girl to make it the latter.

She leaned against the bar with a wicked grin. "Is that right? Or does it just take one to know one?"

She'd been that pretty girl across the bar and had heard every cheesy pickup line there was—she'd certainly fallen for enough of them. And she wasn't about to fall for his.

He flashed a good-humored smile. "Can I get you a drink?"

"No thanks. I'm on the clock." She turned her attention to the rest of the room to resume her search for true love. Her head bobbed around, and it was all she could do to not climb on the counter to get a better look at her options.

"Looking for someone?" he asked.

"Yes. I happen to be looking for Mr. Perfect."

"Well, it's your lucky day," he said. "You've found him."

Falling for it, she glanced back at him.

He spread his arms outward, presenting himself. "Right here."

She snorted and rolled her eyes. "We must be talking about a different guy."

He chuckled, not deterred in the slightest. "Oh, you mean a different perfect guy. Sorry about that." He went back to wiping the counter with his cloth. "But I'll let you in on a little secret. There's no guy that's perfect."

"Sure there is," she said. "I just haven't found him yet."

"No, really. Trust me. I know people."

"People?"

"All people. Even your Mr. Perfect." He gestured around the room vaguely. "I'm in the perfect position to people-watch, to observe the human species, to understand what makes them tick. I have years of practice."

"That and the fact that if you ply anyone with enough alcohol they'll spill their guts." She used a dismissive tone, trying to send the guy a hint. She didn't have long before the clock struck ten and she had to be backstage again.

He leaned on his elbows, settling in for a long discussion—apparently observing people didn't make him an expert at taking hints. "Oh sure. People open up to a bartender. I've seen and heard it all. Nothing surprises me anymore."

"I can only imagine." As hard as she tried to ignore the guy, her curiosity was piqued. He was a good talker, engaging with an undeniably charming smile that bordered on devilish, the kind of smile that probably earned him a mint in tips.

He held her cornflower blue eyes with his own brown gaze, and she imagined he could sell a Jägerbomb to a nun. Maybe he had. She began to wonder what kinds of things he'd seen and heard.

But she didn't have time to get distracted by stories. She hadn't pulled out her best dress that night for nothing. Prince Charming was somewhere in that room. She could feel it.

"But there's more to it than that," he continued. "There's a difference between what people are telling you and what they're saying. When someone talks, at the same time an entirely different conversation can be going on. You just have to know how to tune into it."

"How do you do that?" She was only half-listening, scanning the room again.

"Watch, listen, read between the lines. It can be how

someone enters the room, in the way they dress, what drink they order, how fast they drink it, posture. Body language, you know?"

"Uh-huh. Is that so?" She was trying her best to block him out now.

"Take you, for example."

"Me?" Her attention suddenly wheeled back around to him, her man-hunt on hold. She narrowed her eyes. "What *about* me?"

He began rearranging the liquor bottles until all the labels faced out. "You walk in here like you own the place, yet you're practically the help—"

"I'm not the help." Her chin rose indignantly. "I'm an artist."

"An artist? And your canvas . . . dogs?" He gestured to Princess in her arms.

She ignored the rush of heat beneath her skin. "Well, I am an artist. Business is booming," she told him matter-of-factly, maybe even a little sourly. "Everyone in the doggy couture world will know who I am. I'll be a household name."

"What kind of house?" he asked with a sly grin. "A dog house?"

This guy was making fun of her. She wrinkled her nose at him. Who did he think he was? He didn't know the first thing about her. Arrogant son-of-a— She stopped herself before she lost her cool. What did his opinion matter to her anyway?

"Look"—she glanced down at his nametag—"Felix. Canine fashion is very popular, I'll have you know." She ran a critical eye over him. "Of course, what would you know about fashion?"

He wasn't even clean-shaven for the stylish event. And she could just tell by the way he let his loose curls flop around unchecked that he'd probably never heard of styling gel. Although she had to admit he did have a nice head of hair. Just long enough that the soft waves curled around his handsome face.

As though he noticed her scrutiny, he tucked a curl behind his ear. "Okay, okay," he relented. "I can believe that. I've been working the dog show scene for a few years now."

"Good. See? You don't know what you're talking about. And you don't know the first thing about me."

"You're right, *Addison Turner*. I don't."

Her mouth popped open. She was about to ask how he knew her name when he held up one of her business cards. "I assume this belongs to you. I've been finding them left all over the bar." He bit the inside of his cheek, clearly trying not to laugh. "I'm running out of garbage bags from cleaning them up."

Addison raised her chin, already turning to leave. She didn't need this kind of negativity. "Excuse me. But I have to look for someone."

She and Princess walked away, but he called out to her. "Wait! Wait. You didn't let me finish."

Addison hesitated. As hard as she tried, she couldn't seem to leave, especially once she saw the sheepish look he gave her. Cautiously, she returned to the bar, giving him a steady stare like he was a door-to-door salesperson and she was waiting for the catch.

"You're right. I don't know everything about you," he began. "But I do know that your posture is strong and proud, like you're six feet tall, not five-foot-nothing."

She scowled. "Five-foot-two." Why was she even bothering to argue with him?

"Five-two. Okay." He held up his hands in mock surrender. "So you're clearly very confident, gorgeous, intelligent"—she smiled—"but desperate."

Her face fell. "Desperate?" Her voice rose, then she

noticed an elderly couple with a Tibetan terrier shoot a look her way. She lowered her voice and hissed across the bar. "What do you mean 'desperate'?"

"Your eyes scan this room like laser beams. Your target? Any single man."

Her mouth fell open and a sound of complete and utter indignation came out, although she couldn't quite find an argument. Her mouth snapped shut. She didn't even want to dignify that with an answer.

Addison looked at Princess like *Can you believe this guy? Where does he get off?* But she couldn't ignore Princess's piercing stare. She knew Addison too well.

Traitor, she thought as she placed the dog on a stool.

Addison's shoulders slumped. Okay, well, maybe that's exactly what she'd come out there in search of, but was it really so obvious? The resentment his words created suddenly fizzled out of her.

"Is it so wrong?" she asked, at last. "I just appreciate someone with style. Grace. Good breeding."

"Are you talking about a man, or a dog?" Felix asked. "Look, I'm not saying it's a bad thing. You know what you want. But you're like a girl on the prowl. I can feel the anxiety oozing off you."

Addison rolled her eyes. "You cannot."

"In fact, you're getting it all over my counter." To prove his point, he picked up his cloth and shooed her away before wiping down the spotless glass.

"And I'm not anxious."

"Really?" His eyes dropped pointedly to her hands.

She followed his gaze and froze as she noticed the confetti in her hands. She'd shredded Rex Harris's card into a million pieces. Okay, so maybe she was a bit nervous. It didn't mean she was desperate.

Felix reached under the bar and brought out the waste-paper basket again. He held it up while she threw away the evidence.

He leaned against the bar, resting on his elbows like he was at home and not in a room full of San Francisco's high society. "Maybe you're not desperate. But you're coming off that way. You're a pretty girl. Let the guys come to you. Besides, what are you in such a rush for? You can't be more than twenty-four."

"I'm twenty-eight. And thank you." She liked how sincere he sounded, curbing some of her annoyance with him. "But if I've learned anything from running my own business, it's that you can't wait around for things to happen. You have to make them happen. Take chances. Put yourself out there."

"Well, just don't put yourself *so* out there." He gestured with his hands, like "out there" was an actual place to avoid. But where that place was, Addison couldn't be sure.

"What do you mean?"

He leaned in until they were close enough that she could smell his cologne. The kind of cologne you'd follow a man around a store just to inhale. Princess must have smelled it too, because she placed her front paws on the counter to get closer. Felix gave her a soft rub under her chin.

"You have to be logical about it. Choosy," he said. "You've got to hedge your bets. Make a wise investment of your time versus the effort you're putting in. Think of it like a numbers game."

"Love isn't logical." Addison laughed, wondering what cave this guy crawled out of. "Love is a dream come true. It's destiny. You can't explain it with numbers and odds. It's a feeling." She sighed. "Like when Meg Ryan hears her computer tell her 'You've got mail' and it's from Tom Hanks. Love is Julie Andrews spinning on a grassy knoll singing 'the hills are alive.' It's the wind beneath Rose's arms as Jack holds her at the front of the *Titanic*, and the orchestra builds to a climax and—"

"And don't forget lollipops, rainbows, and unicorns." There was a condescending smile on his lips.

Offended, she cocked a perfectly penciled eyebrow. "That is why I'm looking for a man with class and refinement. Clearly someone like you wouldn't understand."

His own eyebrows shot up, but he shrugged it off. "Fair enough." He moved to the other side of the bar and began stacking clean glasses onto the delicate pyramid of glassware. After a minute, a pretty waitress sauntered up to place a few orders.

Princess watched her chin-scratcher leave with a whine. Having made her point, Addison turned her back on the bar and continued the search for her Prince Charming. Princess followed her cue and turned around on her stool to face the dance floor. She jutted her chest out, acting all *I'm too good for you, anyway.*

When Addison noticed that she was anxiously tapping her manicured nails on the glass bar top, she froze. She snatched her hand back and leaned against the counter instead, the epitome of casualness. So totally not desperate. Nope, not at all. What did Felix know anyway?

Her eyes scanned the room, totally not like lasers, checking for wedding bands on fingers. But there were hundreds of people there that night. With all those expensive suits, finding Prince Charming was like trying to find a dachshund in a hot dog factory.

After a few moments, she picked Princess back up and began to inch her way around to the other side of the bar where Felix was talking with the waitress—shamelessly flirting, more like it. Not that she blamed him. She was pretty, if a little obvious, wearing a bright red bra under a thin white button-up shirt. Addison thought it was a cheap tactic for attention. Who was desperate now?

Setting Princess down on another stool, Addison took out a stack of business cards from her clutch and arranged them neatly on Felix's countertop while she waited. Finally, Red Bra left to do her rounds.

Addison leaned closer to the bar. "If I were to hedge my bets," she began hesitantly, "you know, filter some of the rainbows and unicorns out, where exactly would I start?"

Felix's brown eyes slid over to her, and he seemed to think twice about helping her before finally relenting. Throwing the white cloth over his shoulder, he leaned in and dropped his voice low. "Okay, you have to watch for subtle clues. Don't be too hasty. Just sit back and watch."

"What am I watching for?"

"General behavior. For example, if they're eyeing up every skirt that walks by, then you'll just be a number to him. Another skirt."

"Like Rex."

"Like Rex," he agreed.

While she was watching for clues, a customer strolled up to the bar with his English bulldog in tow. He was a bit older than Addison, maybe ten years older, salt and pepper starting to fleck his chocolate hair. His smile showed all his brilliant white teeth, and when he turned it on her, she found herself glancing at his ring finger. Finding it conveniently naked, she smiled back. *Not bad*, she thought.

Addison waited to the side while he ordered a whiskey on the rocks and left. Once he was out of earshot, she leaned across the counter. "How about that guy?"

"Married," Felix said.

She frowned. "But he wasn't wearing a ring."

Felix shrugged as he tucked a bottle of whiskey away with the others. "He took it off."

"How could you tell?"

"There was a faint white line around his ring finger where the sun couldn't tan it."

"Maybe he's recently divorced," she said.

He nodded. "Or separated. And if it's that fresh, do you want to risk being a rebound?"

"Okay, well let's try someone a bit younger. How about that guy over there?" She pointed across the room to the man tapping his foot to the jazz music.

Felix's eyes flitted around until he spotted the guy. He shook his head. "You're barking up the wrong tree. He's gay."

Her mouth popped open. "No way. I usually have pretty decent gaydar."

"Oh. He hides it well."

"Then how can you tell?" she asked, appraising the man in question.

Felix smirked. "Because he gave me his number."

Her head snapped toward him. "Are you . . . ?" She eyed him, searching for the clues he seemed to see in others, reading between his lines.

But Felix shook his head. "Considering what the sight of you in that dress does to me, I'd say I'm pretty straight."

Addison's mouth fell open again, but before she could respond to the comment, another man came up to the bar. She watched Felix mix a Bloody Mary for him, regarding him for a moment instead of the customer.

Felix held himself like he was the biggest, baddest dog in the neighborhood and he knew it. And big he certainly was. Broad-shouldered and muscular, he stood a good foot and a half above her—which wasn't tough since she was barely over five feet tall. But he wasn't the hard, ripped kind of muscular that meant his favorite topic of conversation would be how many grams of protein he'd eaten that day or how many reps he'd done at the gym. It was a comfortable kind of muscular. The kind that was made for working rather than looks and was perfect for snuggling. Not that Addison was imagining what it would be like to snuggle with him. Okay, who was she kidding? She totally was.

While Felix cleaned up his station, she nodded toward the customer leaving with his Bloody Mary. "How about him?"

"No."

Addison blew out a breath, her blonde bangs fanning out. "Okay."

She then went on to point out several more men circulating the ballroom. Felix wasn't wrong; the bar seemed the prime place for people-watching. If they weren't wandering up to it to order, they were congregating around it. But each time she found a potential Prince Charming, Felix shot them down for one reason or another: too rich, too flirty, too awkward, too good-looking.

"Too good-looking?" she asked. "Is there such a thing?"

"Do you want the man on your arm drawing attention away from your good looks?" he asked with a grin.

She flashed one right back. "No one could draw attention away from me."

"Touché."

"And besides that, what's wrong with being too rich?"

He shrugged. "I suppose if that's what you're looking for."

"I'm not out for someone rich. Not exactly. But it certainly doesn't hurt to never have to worry about money."

He relented with a tilt of his head. "I'll second that."

It was something she knew about all too well.

"There has to be someone you approve of," she said. "Do you always see the worst in everyone?"

"Occupational hazard," he said. "But your faith in people makes you an easy target for men. You need to be more discerning."

"At least I'm open to the possibility of love."

"Or an unrealistic ideal of some Mr. Perfect fantasy. It's delusional," he said, but not unkindly.

"I like to think of it as optimism," she said, her chin rising. "Well, are there any that you do like? You've rejected practically everyone at the party."

"Well"—his eyes dropped to the counter and he shrugged—"not everyone."

She just stared at him, suddenly realizing he meant himself.

The bartender was right up her alley, both physically and when it came to his sharp wit and certain brash charm. The kind of guy she'd snatch up like a cashmere sweater from a Boxing Day bargain bin. But that was just the problem.

Addison was famous for making bad choices when it came to men, which was why she was still single. But not anymore. She was done with men like him. Everything was going to fall into place, her career, her love life, her happily-ever-after. And that wasn't going to involve Mr. Bartender. She'd dated enough bartenders / struggling musicians / I-swear-I'll-call-you-later one-night-stand disappointments.

Felix was exactly the type of guy she'd normally go for. Which meant he'd be just another mistake like all the rest of them. She'd been there, done that. She'd been used enough times by the wrong kind of guy, and he was probably just another one of them. It was time for her to make a better choice, a smarter one.

It wasn't Felix's occupation that bothered her. Looking

for a man at a swanky event like this wasn't about nailing down a guy with money. It was about the manners, the courtesy, the civility—or maybe that was just too many rom-coms about wealthy love interests speaking.

Addison knew money wasn't everything, but it could sure make life rough if you didn't have it. In fact, she'd grown up watching a marriage fall apart because of it. The struggling, the bills, the bickering over money. It had finally all ended with a nasty divorce that left her father raising her alone when she was only seven years old.

Even to this day, her father still struggled to keep his corner store in business—something Addison fully planned to help him remedy once her business took off. It would certainly help him and his new wife, Dora, out. It was the least she could do after everything he'd sacrificed for her. He'd even put her through dog grooming school, and it was time she paid him back. And then some.

Ignoring Felix's hint, she turned her attention back to the rest of the room. That's when she spotted Thor. Okay, well, he probably wasn't the Norse god, but he sure looked like him—very Chris Hemsworth except with shorter hair. To add to his noble, dignified stature, he stood next to his English mastiff. The perfect picture of godliness. The kind of guy who should pose for canvas paintings.

Thor was tall and broad, his A-frame filling out his designer suit like it was an extension of his body. It was as though the chandelier's light had been created just to shine down on his close-cropped golden hair, to highlight his strong features. It was heaven's light sending her a sign.

"What about him?" Addison's voice was hushed, matching the reverence of that fated moment.

Felix followed her gaze and snorted. "Well, if you like that obviously rich and handsome act."

"You can't act handsome or rich," she said.

"I mean, what is he trying to prove with that chiseled jaw and those perfectly straight teeth?"

"So what you're saying is you can't find anything wrong with him." Addison stood there, breathing in the moment, committing it to memory so she could reflect on it for years to come. Could recall everything about it when she retold the story of how they met on their wedding day.

She sighed, maybe a little too loud.

Felix clicked his tongue at her. "Obvious much?"

"Threatened much?" she spat back.

"Threatened? Me?" He waved the accusation away. "I'm just looking out for you."

"I'm not entirely certain it's *my* best interest you have in mind." She glanced pointedly down at his crotch.

Addison turned to Princess. The doxie seemed to give her a nod, like *this is it*. She set Princess down on the hardwood floor and turned away, not bothering to glance back at Felix.

"Wish me luck," she said over her shoulder.

"I thought it was destiny," he called out after her, "not luck."

But Addison's focus was now on the owner of the English mastiff.

She felt as though she was walking in slow motion across the room, that this really was *it*. Her whole life, her search for the perfect man, had been building up to this one moment in time. She made her way across the room, and the crowd moved like they were parting for her, for them. Making way for destiny.

The red bra'd waitress passed by, the movement raising a breeze that blew Addison's golden hair like a wind machine. As though he sensed her, Thor looked her way.

His eyes were drawn to hers like it was scripted. Or better yet, predestined.

The jazz band in the corner seemed to drown out the clink of glasses, the occasional bark, the murmur of voices. It all faded away. It was just the two of them, hurtling through time and space, overcoming all odds to meet in this exact time, this exact place. Like it was meant to be.

She began to move faster and faster. At the same time, he lurched toward her. It was as if some unseen force was pulling them together. Then she realized it was in fact their dogs tugging on their leashes, closing the distance between them.

Addison's high heels skidded and clicked on the polished flooring as Princess urged her closer and closer to the English mastiff and his owner, out of curiosity to meet her new competition. Or maybe because she too understood how important it was for them to meet.

The heels made it difficult to hold Princess back, and since her soul mate's dog probably weighed two hundred pounds, Addison imagined he had a harder time. But it didn't look like he was putting up much of a fight. Not with that dazed grin on his face as they drew closer to each other—probably the same one she had on her face.

Addison's focus had been so fixed on him that she'd forgotten there were still other people in the ballroom. So it came as a complete surprise to her, and the waiter, when Addison bumped into a passing server handing out champagne glasses.

The silver tray went flying. Glasses smashed around their feet. The server tried to catch Addison as she stumbled forward, but Princess had stopped to lap up the champagne, and they both got caught in her leash.

Addison pitched forward. Unable to move her legs, she automatically threw out her hands.

The hardwood floor flew up to meet her. But she never reached it. Instead, she landed in cashmere-clad arms, staring up into eyes as blue as the heavens in which he fell from: Thor.

3

Doggoneit

Addison gazed up at the man of her dreams, conscious of his strong arms around her waist. "My hero," she said.

Thor's face lit up. Felix had been right; he really did have perfect teeth. "My pleasure, miss. Are you all right?"

She did a quick mental check. There was light-headedness, the heart palpitations, and stars blinking across her vision. In other words, she was as twitter-pated as Bambi. Addison reminded herself to breathe.

"I'm much better now, thank you."

Thor helped her to stand, steadying her as she untangled her legs from Princess's leash. His firm hands burned hot against her exposed arms, and the sensation ran through her like lava. When she looked up, his gaze was locked on her eyes, not her low neckline. But of course they would be; her soul mate was a gentleman.

He held out his hand. "My name is Phillip Montgomery the third."

"Addison Turner." She put her hand in his and felt the sparks fly, just like in the movies.

Instead of shaking it, he brought it to his lips and kissed the back of her hand lightly. Not many men could pull off the gesture. She would have rolled her eyes if it had been anyone else—especially a guy like Felix. But this wasn't just anyone. It was Phillip Montgomery III.

"It's a pleasure to meet you, Addison."

"Likewise." *Oh, this is going well*, she thought. She even sounded posh. Posh enough to date a guy that had a number after his name.

Addison could have continued to stare into those beautiful blue eyes all night long if someone nearby hadn't cleared his throat. Reluctantly, she pulled her attention away from Phillip to see the small group he'd been standing with staring expectantly, as though waiting for introductions. Princess bumped into her ankle, reminding her that she was there too.

Phillip gestured to the round man on his left. "Addison, this is Walter Boyd. He's one of the judges for this year's Western Dog Show."

"Actually, I've been a judge every year for the past fifteen years." His chest puffed up, causing his buttonholes to pucker from the extra strain. "I'm the longest-running judge on the panel."

"Judge Boyd has a very keen sense of perfection," Phillip told her. "It's almost like a sixth sense. It's uncanny, really."

"Hopefully that keen eye spots my little Lilly this year," said a short, balding man with a cane. "Not that I'm worried, of course. She hasn't let me down yet."

Phillip laughed good-naturedly. "She'll have a tough time stealing the attention away from my Baxter, here." He patted his English mastiff's wide head. "Addison, this is Alistair Yates." He gestured to the balding man. "He's been competing in conformation shows for, what is it now? Forty years?"

"Careful now." He shook the curve of his cane at Phillip teasingly. "You're aging me."

"Alistair has hired a handler this year to prepare his beagle for conformation," Phillip said.

"The old hip isn't quite what it used to be. But my Lilly is in good hands this year." He gestured to the tall, thin woman standing next to him. "This here is—"

"Penny Peacock." Addison's mouth popped open as she gaped at the woman's familiar face, one she'd seen in magazines, on dog food tins, etched into treats, and on pooper-scoopers. She closed her mouth when she realized how rude she was being. "I'm sorry. It's just, I've read all about you in *Doggy Digest*. You're the best handler there is," she gushed, feeling the rush of meeting a Dogdom star.

Princess barked, like she too recognized Ms. Peacock from the aisle in the pet store that was practically dedicated to her products. And to think, Addison was actually meeting her in person. If only she could get Penny to notice her designs that night. One word from her on social media and Addison would have no trouble filling the seats at her fashion show.

"Penny is the best of the best," Phillip said.

Penny's hooked nose rose an inch, but she looked pleased. "Oh, well, I wouldn't go that far."

Alistair leaned on his wooden cane eagerly. "She has never lost a competition. That's why my Lilly's a sure win."

"I'm only as good as the dogs I handle," Penny replied.

Addison thought that if she was a better actress, it almost would have sounded humble. But she supposed she deserved to be a little smug with a resume boasting a qualification like *I'm the best*. Besides, when your face is on dog food, you don't have to apologize for anything.

"Well, we'll see about that," Walter said. "That's a job for the judges to decide."

Now that the introductions were through, Phillip turned to Addison eagerly, or rather to Princess. "You have a beautiful dachshund."

Princess's floppy ears perked up, relieved the conversation had finally moved onto a more interesting topic: her.

"Oh, thank you," Addison said, picking Princess up so she could be involved in the discussion.

"Yes, she's quite the specimen." Penny's eyes seemed to narrow, like she was homing in on the competition. "Are you planning on entering her this year?"

"Unfortunately, she wouldn't get very far," Addison whispered, as though Princess might hear.

Judge Boyd laughed, or maybe he was just clearing his throat. It turned into a phlegmy cough and tapered off into a struggled wheeze. "She would have been a fine specimen. Of course, I could see the bitch was flawed from a mile away."

Addison cringed at the word. She didn't think she'd ever get used to the b-word used so flippantly in the show dog circuit—especially not when it came to her Princess.

"She's not flawed," she said, a little sharper than she'd meant to. "She's perfect."

"I'm sorry to hear you won't be entering," Penny said, shoulders relaxing. "But she's awfully lovely. Who is your stylist?"

"I style her myself," Addison said. "I own my own business in town. It's called Pampered Puppies."

"Oh. So you're the dog stylist everyone is talking

about tonight," Alistair said. "I'm looking forward to seeing what you've done for my Lilly."

Addison went through a mental list of all the dogs that
were dropped off in her care that evening. Melody must
have checked Alistair's dog in. "Lilly. Lilly. Is she the
tricolored beagle?"

"Yes, that's the one." His expression was that of a
proud father's.

"Best of Breed and Best in Show three years running,
you know," Penny said. "I thought since it was still two
weeks away from the show I would allow her to receive a
little TLC. It is a special occasion after all." She eyed
Addison sharply. "As long as you don't cut anything, dye
anything, or use any products that are not one hundred
percent natural-based."

Addison recalled the long list of demands and things
to avoid during treatment. She had the sneaking suspicion it had been Penny who dropped the beagle off. Her
heartbeat jumped in tempo to know she had styled one
of the dogs that Penny Peacock handles. God, she hoped
she liked her work.

"My assistant is just putting the finishing touches
on her pawdicure. Don't worry. She's in very good
hands."

"You're not giving the nails a trim this close to the
competition, I hope. You can never be too careful."

"No, definitely not," she assured the handler. "But if
you like the results of today, I'd be happy to be her stylist for the show." She automatically drew out a card from
her clutch like it was second nature.

Penny held up a hand. "No one touches my dogs but
me. Tonight was a special occasion."

"Of course," Addison said, a little miffed. To be fair,
Penny hadn't even seen her work, so how could she judge?
Famous or not, there was smug and there was pompous. "I

suppose a marathon runner wouldn't trade in his old, worn-out running shoes for new ones before the big race."

Addison regretted the comment immediately. She was trying to get on Penny's good side—if she had one.

Phillip snorted but covered it with a cough.

Penny didn't seem to notice she'd been compared to a pair of stinky, old running shoes, or if she did, she was too serious about show dogs to comment. "I not only train them, but I also groom them, exercise them, and make their own dog food from scratch."

"From scratch?" Addison said. "That sounds like a lot of work."

"Only the best for my dogs."

Addison returned the card to her clutch. "Well, I have other services available if you're interested," she suggested, altering her sales pitch to meet her customer's needs. "And there's always my upcoming fashion show."

Alistair looked up from his glass of port with an expression of mild interest. "Fashion show?"

"I'm launching my new fashion line for dogs the weekend of the show. I still need volunteers to help model the designs if you'd be interested in involving Lilly."

Alistair smiled. "Well that sounds—"

"Tasteless," Penny cut in. "My dogs don't wear clothing."

Addison frowned. Penny might have been the best handler in the world, but she seemed to forget Lilly wasn't *her* dog. She was Alistair's.

"Well, you can count Baxter in," Phillip piped up.

"Really? That's great. Oh"—she clapped her hands—"I have the perfect letterman jacket in mind."

"Sounds excellent. I was never on the football team. I'm more of a tennis man myself."

The others had sunk into a heated debate about the historical purpose of the ankle fur on a traditional poodle cut. Phillip took the opportunity to draw Addison away. "So is your schedule fully booked tonight?"

"Why? Does Baxter need some grooming? I'm sure I could fit him in."

His ears turned pink and he ducked his head. "I was asking more for myself."

Addison blinked, her one-track mind focused on work now, imagining a collaboration between Penny's dog supplies and her fashion line. Forget a whole aisle in the pet shop. They would need the whole store. "You need grooming?"

Phillip laughed and it sounded clear and musical. Oh, how she could listen to it all day long, maybe even record it and set it as her ringtone. "No. I was wondering if I might steal you for a dance."

"Oh." Addison wanted to slap herself for being so stupid. Sometimes she opened her mouth before her brain had caught up. Batting her eyelashes, she tried to hide the blunder with her best flirty look. "I'm sure I could spare a little more time."

"Good." He took her hand. "Because they happen to be playing our song."

Phillip led her to the other side of the historic ballroom where couples circled the dance floor to the classical jazz music. Although he was hidden behind his bar, she could sense Felix's eyes on them as they passed. She kept her gaze forward, fighting the urge to stick her tongue out at him like a two-year-old. He'd called her "delusional." Well, she thought, how was that for "delusional"?

At the edge of the dance floor, two dog minders approached them. They wore suits with red cummerbunds and bow ties, even the women, maintaining the elegant air of the evening. The minders took Baxter and Princess while Phillip swept Addison away. And the man could dance too. But of course he could. He was perfect.

Addison had learned how to ballroom dance as a teenager from online videos. Because what princess wouldn't be able to dance with her Prince Charming? While she realized a long time ago on some disappointed level that she wasn't, in fact, an undiscovered Disney princess, she'd obviously been preparing for just this night. For Phillip.

"So how long have you been competing in dog shows?" she asked.

"A few years now," he said. "It's something special Baxter and I can do together. It's a shame your doxie can't enter. She looks well-bred. Were you upset when you found out you couldn't show her?"

She shook her head adamantly. "Not at all. I knew she had the deformity when I brought her home."

"You did?"

"I adopted Princess from the San Francisco Dachshund Rescue Center where I volunteer. She was dropped off by her owner after she realized she'd never be able to win a competition because of her angular limb deformity. When she'd first been picked up at the breeder, there was no way to know. It surfaced as she grew older."

Phillip nodded and spun her in a circle, her dress shimmering beneath the chandeliers. "Even if I couldn't show Baxter, I would never give him up. He's like family to me."

Addison felt her heart swell until it left her lungs no room to breathe. Could Phillip get any more perfect?

"I enter him into competitions because I want to see him win," he said. "But many breeders and owners see it as their own win. It doesn't matter what dog they use to get there."

"We see a lot of purebreds come through the rescue center," Addison said. "People buy them because they're so beautiful, but they don't realize the work or cost that goes into them if they have health problems. And most of them do. Especially when they come from a puppy mill looking to make a quick buck."

"I'm surprised you're here supporting the dog show lifestyle after your experiences with Princess and your rescue center." Phillip's dancing became a little stiffer as he watched her expression. "Some people in your circumstance might look down upon dog shows."

It was a touchy topic for any show dog owner; the rescue-versus-dog-breeder debate. Those passionate about dog shows were sensitive to the accusations from the general public and of course the local group SFAAC, San Franciscans Against Animal Cruelty.

Addison's expression barely waivered. "I'm neither against nor in support of dog shows. I just support dogs in general. Purebreds and mutts alike. The only thing I'm against is disreputable breeders and puppy mills."

Phillip seemed to relax, and he spun her once again. "You must really love animals. I do a fair bit of fund-raising myself for SFAAC. In fact, I'm hosting an event next weekend, if you'd like to attend."

She beamed up at him with her pamplemousse pink lips. "I'd love to."

"I thought you might be interested. You follow the dog show circuit, you volunteer at a rescue center, you're a dog groomer."

"I prefer the term 'dog stylist,'" she corrected him. "My services encompass so much more than simple shampoos and trims."

"Excuse me." He flashed her a teasing smile. "Dog stylist. And by the looks of the dogs around here tonight, I'd say you're pretty good."

"I like to add my own special flair. Part of the Addison Turner experience. Hopefully after tonight, everyone in the San Francisco show dog world will remember my name."

His hold around her tightened a fraction. "I know I certainly will."

Addison smiled coyly and let him spin her around the dance floor a couple more times, while inside she was screaming *Weeeeeee!* like she was on the Tilt-A-Whirl. It was the perfect moment. She thought she could get lost in it forever—that is, until she caught sight of his Bvlgari watch.

Addison gasped, her waltz faltering.

"What's wrong?" he asked.

"Is that the time?" She stepped away from him. "I'm late."

"For what?"

"Some of the guests have volunteered their dogs as models for a sneak peek of my fashion line this evening. I'm supposed to reveal them." She started to back away to the edge of the dance floor avoiding the oncoming dancers.

"When?" he called after her. He tried to follow, but a couple bumped into him.

"In less than five minutes."

"Wait! I haven't gotten your number yet!" He gave chase, weaving in and out of dancers twirling under the chandeliers.

"I'm sorry. I'm late." Finding Princess's dog minder, Addison swept the doxie off the floor and into her arms. She waved at Phillip over her shoulder. "I'll find you after."

She scurried back across the ballroom as fast as her heels would allow. She'd been so distracted by Phillip that she'd almost forgotten the entire reason she was even there that night, the whole purpose of offering pro bono services, handing out free gifts, and working so hard—to promote her upcoming fashion show. She wasn't about to waste all that time and energy, even for Prince Charming.

Rounding the bar, she saw Felix eye her curiously. Perhaps curious of how things went with Mr Perfect. She took on the cocktail tables and settees like a slalom course. The event organizer, Darcy, approached her, seeming to slink from the shadows in his black suit, shirt, and tie.

"Excuse me, Miss Turner," he said. "Are you almost ready on stage?"

"Absolutely." She tried to catch her breath. Her push up bra was too tight—but so worth it. "Give me sixty seconds."

Melody would have prepped the dogs and positioned them all on pillows. However, this was Addison's moment to shine, to make a name for herself. She wanted to ensure everything was perfect. Every dog on its pillow, every hair in place, every bow fluffed.

She carried Princess up the stage steps and ducked behind the curtain, ready to make some last-minute changes. But there had already been a few changes made since she'd left.

All the pillows were certainly in place, arranged neatly in a semicircle to show off each dog's best features and, most important, her designs. Only, there was just one tiny little hiccup. Most of the pillows were unoccupied.

Nearly all the dogs were gone. There were only three out of the original ten left: a bull terrier in a black leather jacket with sunglasses on his head, the Maltese with the

Rainbow Frenzy nail polish and pink tutu, and a miniature schnauzer wearing a bowler hat and monocle.

Addison dropped Princess by her pillow and shot from one side of the stage to the other, as though the rest must have been hiding around there somewhere. But Melody had already cleaned up the stage. Addison's equipment was all packed away into her car. There was no place for them to hide. Not for seven dogs. And where on Earth was Melody anyway?

She checked her phone just as the clock struck ten. Addison stood frozen at center stage as the curtains began to part.

"No. Stop!" she cried out. "I'm not ready. I'm not ready!"

She darted to the front of the stage and grabbed both curtains, gripping them like she could keep them together, could prevent anyone from seeing before she could figure out what had happened. There had to be some mistake. Maybe they all needed to go for a walk at the same time, or all the owners happened to take them back or, she didn't know what. Alien abductions?

The motorized track whirred far above her, dragging the curtains apart. She dug her heels in, not ready to give up yet. She'd worked too hard. Her hands cramped, her muscles screamed out as she grit her teeth and pulled back in a tug of war, struggling to resist their draw.

The entire room full of guests turned toward her, watching with curiosity and expectation of the fashion show preview that had been promised. The owners of the models gathered the closest, eager to see their stars shine, including Alistair and Penny. *Oh God*, she thought. Penny Peacock.

Addison held the drapes for as long as she could, arms outstretched, heels slipping on the stage. The crowd began to chatter, laughing at her antics, but she wasn't kidding around.

Finally when the curtains threatened to tear her in two, they ripped out of her desperate grip. She was left standing alone in the middle of the empty stage. The floodlights poured down on her glimmering sequined dress, lighting her up like a disco ball.

The gathered dog lovers grew still, tense with anticipation. It seemed to her that they held one collective breath, like this was some kind of magic show and she could go "Alakazam," and the missing dogs would suddenly appear.

But she was not the Wizard of Oz. She was the fraud hiding behind the curtain, and she'd just been revealed.

As though searching for some explanation, some friendly face, her eyes roamed over the party, over the breeders and owners, the judges, the staff, Phillip Montgomery III, and even Felix. But they all just stared back. After a few hushed moments, the murmurs began, then the vicious snarling and growling—not from the dogs but from the human guests.

"Where are the dogs?" Judge Boyd demanded, succumbing to a coughing fit.

"My dog was supposed to be up there," a voice said, but Addison couldn't quite pinpoint who with the lights glaring down at her.

"What's happening!?" a woman cried. "Where did they all go!?"

Someone screamed. "My dog! My little angel! She's gone!"

Addison spotted Kitty Carlisle in the crowd, cradling her dog protectively.

The event organizer appeared at the bottom of the stage. "What's going on?" Darcy hissed up at Addison. "Where are they?"

"I . . . I don't know. Th–they're gone." Her answer was barely a shocked whisper, but a man nearby heard her.

"They're gone!" he yelled. "The dogs are gone!"

Addison recognized Rex Harris's smooth cadence. She squinted against the spotlights, peering at the faces, but instantly regretted it. Enraged expressions glared up at her, wide eyes, clenched fists. She wanted to close her eyes, make it all go away. It couldn't be real.

From the sides of the room large men in dark suits drew closer to the stage with placid expressions and purposeful movements. Security, she realized, getting ready to subdue the crowd if necessary. *Or maybe me.*

"How!?" one woman cried out. "Where did they go!?"

"She lost them. She lost our dogs!" a man with red hair screamed. He rushed the stage, maybe to come look for the dogs himself, or maybe to strangle Addison.

She stepped back, but the security guards took action before the irate man could get his hands on her.

The redhead shrugged the guards off and jabbed a finger in her direction. "You'll be hearing from my lawyer."

"Give me my dog," someone else was saying. "I just want my dog."

A man with a cul-de-sac of hair on his shiny head was arguing with security at the base of the stairs. She remembered his last name was Jackson. He climbed the stairs, security in tow to make sure he didn't try anything funny. But he completely ignored Addison, his focus consumed by the Maltese who trotted up to him, Rainbow Frenzy nails clicking on the stage floor. Jackson picked her up and held her close as he headed off the stage, clearly glad to be one of the few people lucky enough to still have his dog.

The other two owners followed his lead, coming up to claim their dogs. A woman stepped forward for her miniature schnauzer, silent tears streaming down her face.

"It's okay, Lemon Drop. I've got you now."

The bull terrier's owner glared at Addison as he led his dog off the stage. "You should be ashamed of yourself."

"Someone call the police!" Rex called out.

She wanted to find his ripped-up business card and jam it down his throat. They didn't need the police. Because the dogs weren't missing. They just couldn't be.

Addison adored dogs too much to let anything happen to them. She wanted to pamper them, love them, and show them that they mattered. Melody could vouch for that. Where was she anyway? Why would she leave the dogs so close to curtain call?

Addison wanted to step up, to act like the professional she knew she was, a professional who would never lose a dog. But her legs felt like bendy Twizzlers, so she sat down on a bohemian pillow, trying to pull down her dress so the entire room wouldn't see her underwear.

She couldn't breathe. The spotlights roasted her like an oven, but maybe not as badly as the angry, laserlike glares shooting at her.

Next to her, Princess sat up on her pink embroidered pillow. Barrel chest jutting proudly, basking in the attention from so many worshipers at once.

Alistair Yates pointed his cane up at Addison from the ballroom floor. "What have you done with my Lilly?" His lip curled and spittle flew from his mouth.

"Nothing," Addison panted, feeling faint. "I didn't do anything with her."

"Noooo!" a woman screamed. It drew out like someone was falling from a tall building. When Addison searched for the source, she saw Penny Peacock burying her hooked nose in her hands. "My Best in Show. My blue ribbon. My perfect streak. Gone. All because of you, Addison Turner!"

Addison sank deeper into the pillow and stared at her empty stage. She'd hoped to make a name for herself, but this wasn't exactly what she'd had in mind.

4

Thrown to the Dogs

"Addison . . . ? Addison . . . ? Miss Turner?"

The voice broke Addison's trance and she tore her gaze away from the stage to refocus on Officer Simpson.

"Sorry," she said. "I just . . . I can't believe they're gone." She held Princess closer to her chest, not willing to let her out of her eyesight.

Princess grumbled, probably annoyed that she hadn't been able to touch the ground in the last forty minutes. She shifted in Addison's hold and nestled in.

"I understand, ma'am," the officer said. "I just have a few more questions for you."

Addison nodded numbly, glancing at the middle of the stage floor where the dogs should have been and thinking that if she just stared hard enough, she would see a glimmer in the air, like there was a magic door the dogs had accidentally passed through.

Once the police had arrived and things started to sink in—the dogs were really gone—Addison could no longer deny it. She'd lost them. They were out there in the city somewhere, maybe wandering the streets. Or worse. In the hands of someone who wanted to use them for money or even illegal dog fights.

Officer Simpson scanned his notepad. "You said you were dancing when the dogs went missing?"

Addison cringed. It sounded so unprofessional when he said it. Why had she allowed herself to get so distracted on such a critical night?

"Yes. I was dancing with Phillip Montgomery the third."

The officer wrote down his name. "You never saw anything before you left? No one hanging around the stage?"

"No. Everything was normal. It was perfect, in fact. Melody was just finishing up the last of the grooming." Addison paused. "Actually, there was one person hanging around, way longer than any of the other dog owners. Kitty Carlisle." She recalled the way the old woman seemed nervous as she stalked backstage, but looking back, maybe she'd been casing the place, making her evil dog-stealing plans.

"Was her dog stolen as well?" he asked.

"No. In fact she seemed overly protective about her bichon frisé, hovering, making sure she got him back. I didn't see her after that until the dogs were already gone."

He made another note. "Can you think of anyone else acting unusual? Maybe someone might have said something alluding to the dogs going missing?"

"No. No one."

Beyond the thick stage curtains, she could hear the few remaining guests, or witnesses she supposed, talking to other police officers in the ballroom. Most of it was muffled murmurs to her ears, but every once in a while, her name rang clear. Probably because it was said with such ferociousness that it cut through the curtain, and her, like a freshly sharpened pair of trimming scissors. She closed her eyes and rubbed a hand over them.

"How long has Melody Butters been working for you?"

Her eyes flicked open and her voice rose an octave in surprise. "Melody?" Addison hadn't suspected her assistant for even a second. But of course she would be a suspect since she was directly responsible for the dogs when they went missing. The police were probably drilling her at that very moment. "About six months now. Part time."

"Do you know much about her personally? Who she hangs out with, any criminal connections?"

"God no. The only thing criminal about that girl is her addiction to ABBA. But I suppose I don't know her extremely well outside of work."

As he held his pen to paper, she added, "But we talk a lot at the spa, and I can't see her doing anything to these dogs. Not on purpose, anyway."

She thought back to the curtain call. Melody had been nowhere to be found at the time. Had she run to the washroom? Maybe Addison had taken too long to come back and she couldn't hold it any longer.

"So you think someone might have stolen them?" she asked the officer.

"We're considering all possibilities at this point. Some dogs were left behind, so it may just be a case of the dogs wandering off. It's too soon to tell."

"Is anyone out there looking for them? Has anyone called animal control or any rescue centers?"

"We're taking steps to look for them."

Addison's mouth turned down. That didn't exactly sound like they were scouring the city. It sounded like a generic police-y type answer to her.

"But seven dogs are gone. If you think they might have

run away, shouldn't someone be out there driving the streets looking for them just in case?" She sounded harsher than she'd meant to. No, actually she meant to sound harsh. It wasn't exactly hard to drive around a few blocks. The police were out there patrolling as part of their job anyway.

Officer Simpson glanced up from his notepad, keeping his tone level but firm. "We're doing what we can."

Looked like that "someone" was going to be her. She wanted to wrap things up, get out on the streets in her Mini, and search the neighborhood herself. Do something to help find those poor dogs.

She held Princess closer, thinking of how she would feel if her doxie was out there lost and alone. Her stomach flipped with nausea. Now there were seven dogs out there somewhere, and seven owners with flipping stomachs. And she was responsible for it. It suddenly occurred to Addison that she could be sued, by seven powerful and expensive lawyers.

Show dogs were pricey breeds to begin with, even before the cost of their training, grooming, and only the best products and food. But those deemed the best of the best were often used for their superior genetics. A stud fee was sometimes a thousand dollars or more. Over the lifetime of a show dog, sometimes hundreds of thousands of dollars are invested. And there were seven of them. Seven dogs, seven potential lawsuits. Addison didn't exactly have that kind of coin laying around.

Forget losing her business. Addison could be held criminally liable.

"Miss Turner? Are you all right?" Officer Simpson was watching her closely.

Addison's breaths were coming faster than a panting dog's on a sunny day. She felt dizzy; the room a little crooked.

Officer Simpson laid a hand on her shoulder, not comfortingly, but as if he thought he might have to catch her. "I think you should sit down."

She nodded and collapsed onto one of the bohemian pillows. Princess curled up on her lap and promptly fell asleep as though everything was perfectly normal.

"Am I going to jail?" Addison asked between panicked breaths.

Officer Simpson squatted down to her level. "Right now, we're just investigating. You're free to go. However, we'll need you to come down to the station tomorrow morning to answer more questions."

His response didn't make her feel any better. It wasn't exactly a "no."

"You're looking a little pale, Miss Turner."

"I'm okay. I'm okay." She held a hand to her forehead as though she could feel if she was pale. All she felt was cold, damp beads of sweat. "I just need a little sugar is all. I'll be fine."

The officer seemed reluctant to leave, but he eventually took a card out of his pocket and handed it to her. "If you have any questions, here's my contact info. Please stop by the precinct in the morning."

Addison took it, staring at Officer Simpson's name as he left the stage, his big boots clomping on the wood. He'd been very nice, even concerned for her, but all she could wonder was if he would be the one to clamp a pair of cuffs on her if the dogs weren't found.

She suddenly had a whole new reason for driving around the neighborhood searching for the dogs that night. It wasn't just the dogs' well-being she had to be concerned about anymore but her own as well. And what about her dad? How was she supposed to pay him back when her own business was on the line? And then there was Princess. Who would take her in when Addison was behind bars? And orange was so not Addison's color.

Addison's thoughts were flipping around erratically. She had to do something, but first she needed to find Melody and question her assistant personally.

Since she could still hear guests and police officers lingering outside the closed curtains, she chose the back door to the alley where they'd unloaded her car at the start of the night. It seemed so long ago now.

Carrying Princess like one of those owners who don't think their dogs can walk, she headed for the exit. The heavy metal fire door was propped open with an empty storage bin. When she pushed it open, she found Melody picking at her lip absently in the alley, a smoke in her hand.

Addison watched her suck back on the cigarette like a scuba diver would oxygen. "I didn't know you smoked."

"I don't," she said. "Well, I didn't." Melody took another drag, her hand shaking. "I quit a couple of years ago, but I started up again this week."

She didn't bother to flick away the long length of ash drooping at the end before she took another desperate drag. The ash escaped on its own and fluttered down the front of her work apron.

Addison nodded. She couldn't blame her. She'd already gone through four liters of her ice cream stash leading up to this event. She was surprised her dress had even fit when she'd zipped it up that night.

Princess began to squirm and whine desperately in her arms. Reluctantly, she set her down, but didn't let the leash out very far.

Melody tossed the butt aside and turned to Addison. Even in the poorly lit alley, she could see her assistant's red-rimmed eyes were swollen. Pale tear tracks ran down the blush on her cheeks.

"I'm so sorry." Melody's voice broke. "I only stepped outside for two minutes to have a smoke. I felt fine until one of the customers showed up and started screaming at me. Afterward my nerves were shot. I just needed to relax before the reveal. I gave all the dogs treats before I left. They were all happy, and healthy, and"—she stumbled over her words—"*there* when I left. I don't know what happened."

Addison felt bad for her. She'd obviously had a rough night too. "Are you sure the dogs didn't follow you when you went out the backstage door? Maybe they snuck out here when you weren't looking?" She glanced both ways down the dark alley, half hoping they were hanging around the Dumpsters. But there was only Princess relieving herself after Addison's long Q and A session with the cop.

"That's what the cops wondered too, because I stuck a storage container in the door to hold it open. So it wouldn't close and lock behind me, you know?" Melody began to tear up again, trying to control her wavering voice. "But I'm sure I would have seen them. I'm sure of it. I only planned to be a minute."

Tapping out another cigarette from the pack, she stuck it in her mouth and lit up. In the flare from the lighter, Addison could see fresh tears roll down her cheeks.

"I'm so sorry," she said again.

Addison shook her head, but she couldn't quite look her in the eye yet. "It's not your fault. We don't even know what happened. The police aren't exactly saying, but I can't see all those dogs running away. They're too well trained." She shook her head, unsure of what to think.

"You entrusted them to me. They were my responsibility. I let you down." She waved the cigarette around while she talked, the glowing end creating swirls in the dark before Addison's tired eyes.

"You didn't let me down. It wasn't like it was a normal setup. You're not to blame. Heck, if I'd been around—"

"Don't do that," Melody told her. "You deserved a break. I told you to go."

Addison had replayed the evening's events over and over a hundred times like she always rewatched *The Princess Bride*, her favorite movie. She'd considered all the if-onlys. If only she'd stuck around. If only she'd been watching the dogs and not dancing with Phillip Montgomery III. If only she hadn't bothered arguing with that nosy bartender, Felix. But dwelling on what might have been wasn't going to change what was. The dogs were gone.

She shook her head to snap herself out of the never-ending self-blame cycle. "Look, Melody. Why don't you just go home and get some rest. I know I have to go down to the police station tomorrow and answer more questions. Let's call it a night."

"Yeah, me too. You're right. Thanks." Melody sucked back the rest of her cigarette. "I'll talk to you tomorrow?"

"Sure thing."

As Melody passed the Dumpster, she tossed her near-full pack of smokes inside, along with her lighter, as though it was the cigarettes' fault the dogs disappeared. Addison thought it was likely she'd probably stop on the way home and pick up another pack. Heck, Addison already planned to stop for some Chunky Monkey ice cream herself.

Instead of taking her own advice to go home, Addison scooped Princess up and wandered back inside. She was hesitant to put her doxie down, as if the ballroom were some kind of Bermuda triangle. No one could explain what happened to the dogs. Although there were certainly enough theories that had been screamed at her before the police arrived to break things up. All of which blamed Addison.

Crossing the stage to the curtains, she peeked through a tiny gap. Most of the people had cleared out of the ballroom, except for a few stragglers. Slipping through to the other side, she went to the bar. Felix wasn't around, but she took a seat on one of the stools anyway, setting Princess down on the one next to her.

Addison banged her head on the bar's sticky countertop, hoping it might knock her senseless. If it did, at least she wouldn't have to answer any more of the cops' questions the next day. Questions that she wouldn't know the answers to.

Whether they ran away or they were stolen, how did seven purebred dogs get off the stage and waltz past hundreds of guests? The only other way had been out the back alley while Melody was out there smoking, but then surely she would have seen them. Unless, of course, she wasn't telling the truth. What else could explain their disappearing act?

It seemed the only explanation the missing dog owners were interested in involved pointing their fingers at Addison. No matter how it happened or why, it was *her* fault. Now what was she going to do about it?

Addison began to bang her head again, but a pair of hands held either side of it, gently raising it up. It was Felix.

He gave her a sympathetic smile. "You look like you could use that drink now."

"Then I must look better than I feel, because I feel like I could use the whole bottle." She sighed. "My career is over."

"It can't be that bad." He took his cloth and dabbed away the grenadine syrup stuck to her forehead.

"I lost my clients. Whole clients." She threw her arms

in the air. "These poor dogs might end up in some back-alley dog-fighting ring, getting torn to shreds, and it's all my fault." She imagined Kingy walking into the ring, dressed in the designer kimono.

"Look. I love dogs too, so I understand your concern for these little guys, but I think you need to consider the long run. Have you thought about lawyering up? Protecting yourself, just in case?"

Addison dropped her head into her hands. "I'm going to jail."

"You're not going to jail. Look, maybe they got loose and ran away," he said, trying to sound offhand about it. "They're dogs, after all." He shrugged. "They might turn up. No harm done."

"No harm?" Addison sputtered. "Except when it comes to my reputation." She knew he was only trying to cheer her up, but there was no cheer to be had. This was bad. Very bad. "Even if the dogs turn up perfectly unharmed, God willing, who is going to bring their dog to me for styling if they can't be sure they'll get them back?"

Addison grimaced in self-loathing. She hated throwing herself a pity party, hated thinking about anything but the dogs and how to get them back to their owners safely.

"There are other dog owners all over this city who will never even hear about this. This was just one event."

"A *big* event." She widened her eyes to show just how big.

"And it wasn't even your fault."

"It makes little difference to the owners," she said, refusing to be cheered. "The dogs were under *my* care."

"Correction: they were under your assistant's care."

"My assistant who works for *me*."

"Chin up," he said, setting a glass of orange liquid

down in front of her. When she eyeballed it, he said, "Don't worry. It's just orange juice. I'm not allowed to serve alcohol anymore tonight."

As she reached for the glass with a shaking hand, she realized she could use a bit of sugar. She downed it gratefully.

"Look," Felix said. "It's not over yet. They could still find the dogs. Besides, you don't strike me as the glass-half-empty type."

"Oh?" she said. "What type do you think I am?"

"Oh, I'm not going down that road again. I'm pleading the fifth." He raised his hands in the air and backed away. "I have the right to remain silent."

She eyeballed him. "Har-har."

"What? Too soon for the cop jokes?"

"Well considering I might be hearing those words repeated to me any time now, I'd say yes. And you're wrong. It *is* over. These next two weeks were my chance to make a name for myself, to build up interest for my fashion show. But the dog show community is very small. Talk will get around."

"Then it's a good thing dogs don't talk," he joked. "I'm just saying, so a few of these overpriced dog owners know. So what? It's not like these are the only people with dogs in town. San Francisco is a big city with lots of potential customers."

"Except it may not stop with local gossip. If it hits social media, we're talking national news. Global even."

Penny Peacock certainly had enough followers online to force Addison into hiding for the rest of her life. She wouldn't be able to start another business ever again. Maybe she wouldn't even be able to leave the house. She'd have to dye her hair and move to Canada.

"I guess I could always change my spa name," she said, making an effort at the glass-half-full thing. "Starting over from scratch might be easier than trying to repair the damage to my reputation."

"Exactly," he said. "Maybe you can even switch species."

"Species?"

"Yeah." He thought as he cleaned up for the day. "You could be a cat groomer."

"Maybe hamsters," she said. She spread her hands in front of her like she could see the billboard already. "San Francisco's premiere hamster hair stylist."

"That's the spirit. See? Your business will be fine. Besides, this was an isolated incident at a single event. Who really follows the dog shows? Chances are, no one will even hear about this." He poured another two glasses of orange juice and handed her one.

"You think?" she asked.

He clinked his glass against hers in cheers. "Absolutely."

They drank their juices in silence. Addison was already feeling a tiny bit better. Maybe things weren't so doom and gloom. But when the smile on Felix's face dropped and his thick eyebrows furrowed, that doomy feeling returned.

"Uh-oh," he said. His gaze was locked over her shoulder.

"What?" She turned around and wished she'd already left to look for the dogs.

The press had arrived in the form of a thin, platinum-blonde reporter clad in a bubble-gum pink pantsuit checking her hair in one of the silver serving platters near the cocktail tables. Behind her, the cameraman scrambled to set up his equipment. The reporter watched him, only lifting a finger to snap them while she snarled demands.

Felix was watching in fascination. "Is that *the* Holly Hart from Channel Five News?"

Addison groaned. "Yes. That's her."

"Do you know her?" He sounded awestruck, like she was an A-list actress.

"Yes. And I have a bad feeling about this."

"Why?"

"Because I know her."

Holly saw someone from across the ballroom and waved them over. Addison's orange juice turned sour in her stomach when she saw who it was: Penny Peacock and Alistair Yates. She was going to interview them on the news.

Holly spoke with them in hushed tones while the cameraman hoisted his burden onto his shoulder. Dread filled Addison as Holly took up her microphone and moved her mouth in some vocal exercises. She hoped they were simply making a plea to the community. The more people out there looking for the dogs, the better. If only they kept Addison's name out of it.

The cameraman counted down on his fingers. Three, two, one. Then Holly began.

"I'm standing in San Francisco's historic Regency Ballroom on Sutter Street, the location of the premiere event for this year's Western Dog Show, and boy have things gone to the dogs. I'm with Alistair Yates, longtime dog show enthusiast, and Penny Peacock, the top dog of the dog handling profession." She gestured to both of them in turn. "Mr. Yates, can you please explain to us what happened here tonight?" She turned the microphone on him.

He leaned on his cane and held his face close to the mic. "My precious Lilly is gone."

"Is Lilly your dog?" Holly asked.

"Yes, she's a tricolored beagle. She won the title of Best of Breed and Best in Show the last three years running. And she was stolen from me."

Holly gasped. "You think that she was dognapped? Why would someone want to take her?"

"Isn't it obvious?" he asked. "She's utterly perfect." He stared at the camera, a desperate look of plea on his face. "I'll do anything to get her back. I'm offering a fifty thousand dollar reward for anyone who returns my Lilly to me unharmed."

"I understand that more than just your dog went missing tonight," Holly said. "Is that correct?"

Penny leaned toward the microphone. "Yes. Six other dogs were stolen. Purebred dogs are often targeted by thieves because they're worth a lot of money when resold as pets or used to breed. Tonight, some of the best and brightest in the country were taken."

Holly sighed and tilted her head like the tragic heroine on the front cover of a cheesy romance novel. "I have an adorable Chinese crested, myself. I couldn't imagine what I would do if I ever lost her."

Addison rolled her eyes at the fake drama. She'd seen Holly's aversion to dogs, not to mention the reporter had severe allergies to them. The dog was probably made up to gain viewer sympathy. She wasn't concerned for the dogs, just her ratings.

"How could this tragic incident have possibly happened?" Holly turned the mic on Alistair.

"Oh no," Addison breathed. Her heart pounded beneath her dress. She felt sick to her stomach. "Don't say my name. Don't say my name. Don't say my name." She grabbed Princess and took a step closer to the group in order to hear what came next.

"I don't know, exactly. Lilly was in the care of a dog groomer at the time."

"Dog stylist," Addison said between clenched teeth.

Felix reached over the bar and grabbed her arm from behind, as though sensing she was teetering over the edge. "It's best to stay out of this right now," he told her. "Keep a low profile. Don't add fuel to the fire."

Penny grabbed the microphone right out of Holly's hand. "It was Addison Turner of Pampered Puppies. We'd entrusted Lilly to her care, under the pretense that Miss Turner was going to groom her."

"Pretense?" Addison inhaled sharply. She wrenched out of Felix's grip and before she knew it, she was grabbing the microphone from Holly's hand. She scowled at Penny. "I took great care of Lilly."

Holly tried to wrestle the microphone back. "But the beagle disappeared under your care, did she not, Miss Turner?"

"Well, yes, technically." Addison frowned. "But that doesn't mean I stole her or had anything to do with the dogs going missing."

Holly ripped the microphone away, gripping it possessively. "It's the perfect crime. Lure unsuspecting pups into your lair and snatch them up to make a quick buck."

Princess growled at Holly, defending Addison's reputation. If only everyone could translate dog—they'd probably have to bleep out a few words.

"My lair?" Addison cried. "Who am I? Cruella de Vil? And why would I want to give my business a bad name?"

Holly sneered, her bleached teeth flashing with the excitement of a hot story. "Make enough money from a few valuable show dogs, and you can move onto the next town and start the scam all over again."

Addison's mouth dropped open. Holly was making Addison enemy number one on television. Reaching out, she covered the microphone with her hand. "Whose side are you on, anyway?" she hissed at Holly. "Think about it. Why would I work my butt off for two years to build a reputation, just to steal a few dogs?"

Holly's shoulders raised in an indifferent shrug. "I can't play favorites, Addison. A good reporter is always impartial. I'm just looking for answers."

Addison flinched back, startled by Holly's carelessness. Addison had witnessed Holly target one of her best friends, Piper, from the rescue center the year before and knew just how dirty she could play, but now Holly's sights seemed to have homed in on Addison.

She glared at the hack reporter. "Why would you do this? After you helped me promote my business when I first launched? After you helped us gain community support for the rescue center last year?"

"Hey, You," Holly snapped at the cameraman, whose name Addison still hadn't heard to this day. "Cut that part. I don't want to remind the viewers that I have any association with this."

Addison gave a throaty noise of disgust. "Nice."

Holly smoothed out her blazer for take two. "I have a reputation to maintain, you know."

"Yeah, so do I," Addison shot back. "And you're ruining it."

"Maybe you should have thought about that before you dognapped six dogs."

"Seven," Penny said.

"Seven dogs," Holly corrected herself.

Addison stomped her heel on the hardwood floor. "I did not dognap them."

"Tell that to the cops." Holly waved a dismissive hand.

"I did," Addison growled. "And if you knew how to investigate, you'd know that there's no conclusive evidence that this was a theft." *Yet*, she added in her head.

At least she still hoped not, because that meant they might still be out there on the streets waiting to be found.

Holly clicked her fingers at Hey,You. "Cut that, too." She straightened her back with an air of trustworthy authority and stared into the camera.

"Well, there you have it, San Franciscans. It's dog show week, and there's a puppy pincher on the loose. Have they acquired their target among the missing or is this just the beginning? With such stiff competition, no one can be trusted in this dog-eat-dog event. This is Holly Hart for Channel Five News, signing out."

Hey, You gave a thumbs-up and Holly slouched in relief, but Addison was right in her face.

"What the hell was that?" Addison demanded. "You can't air that. It will destroy me."

"It's nothing personal. But when I got the call, I couldn't ignore it." She tossed her microphone to Hey, You, who was packing away all the equipment.

"The whole dog scene is kind of my thing now. My M.O. My calling card," she told Addison, all smiles now. "My ratings have gone through the roof since I started reporting on all this fluffy, happy dog crap. The viewers lap this stuff up, no pun intended. Oh wait"— she paused—"I think I'll write that one down for later." She drew out her phone and tapped the screen a few times.

"But you don't even have the full story," Addison argued. "This wasn't my fault."

Holly stopped her with a warning finger. "Don't even bother complaining to my producer. It's not like I said anything that wasn't true. Not exactly anyway. You're still the lead suspect."

"I am?" Addison hesitated. "The lead? Really?"

"Rumor has it."

"But—"

"Look, kid." Holly patted her on the head, even though she was probably less than three years older than Addison. "It's the kind of juicy story that the people want to hear. It's ripe with drama, drama, drama." She shuddered, like the word alone turned her on.

Princess snapped her jaws at Holly's hand, and she barely snatched it away in time.

Addison glared at Holly. "How is this drama supposed to help find the dogs? You didn't even make a plea to the community for help. And it's not exactly the publicity I wanted for my business or my new Fido Fashion line."

Holly smiled what she probably thought was supposed to be sympathetic. "Tough luck." She snapped her fingers. "Hey, You. Let's go, while the night is still young." Like nothing mattered but her ratings, she turned on her Manolo Blahniks and left.

Fuming, Addison held Princess close and stormed after her. She reached out for that over-bleached, platinum-blonde hair. But her fingers had barely brushed the over-processed locks before her feet left the ground and she was swept away. She kicked at the air, struggling against the strong hold around her waist.

"Let me go!" she yelled. "Let me go. I'm going to kill her."

When she finally stopped struggling—mostly because her nylons were starting to creep down her legs—she was released. She elbowed the person, shoving them away, and turned to find Felix grinning down at her.

"You're a feisty one, aren't you?"

"I'll show you feisty," she said, stomping past him. But it was pointless. With a sweep of his arm, she and Princess were right back in front of him again.

He shook his finger at her as if chastising a five-year-old. "Now don't do anything you're going to regret."

"Oh, I won't regret it," she said calmly.

"It will only add fuel to her story and you know it. Come on. Why don't we go find you a drink? My treat."

Addison frowned at the escaping news reporter. Because she couldn't take it out on her, she turned her glare on the bartender. "No one will know, huh?"

"Yeah, well," he pulled a sheepish expression. "I didn't exactly see that one coming."

"No. People don't generally get forewarned about the end of the world." She gripped her hair. "We're talking zombie apocalypse kind of stuff."

"It's not the end of the world. I bet if you just go home and get some rest, this will all blow over before you know it." He reached into his pocket and pulled out a business card. It flashed a metallic gold in the dim chandelier light. "Here. If you ever need anything, or you change your mind about that drink, give me a call."

Without looking at it, she shoved the card into the depths of her clutch, that special place reserved for old receipts, gum wrappers, and those bobby-pins she always seemed to lose.

There was only one number she'd wanted that night, and it wasn't Felix's. It was Phillip Montgomery III's digits. But after everything that happened that night, she'd be lucky if she even got to wash his dog.

Turning her back on Felix, Addison headed for her Caribbean Aqua Mini convertible to start scouring the city for the missing dogs.

5

Bone to Pick

Addison sat in her Mini convertible staring up at a canary yellow historic home, psyching herself up to get out. It was a bright and sunny Sunday morning, but the engraved sign out front seemed to loom over her with reproach: SAN FRANCISCO DACHSHUND RESCUE CENTER.

She glanced at the passenger seat where Princess sat with an entitled thrust to her barrel chest, waiting for her door to be opened. Her blonde head swung toward Addison impatiently. It was like driving Miss Daisy. But to Addison, she was worth the extra effort.

"Home sweet home," Addison said.

Princess barked and wagged her tail, the decorative pink ribbons Addison tied to it fluttering with each swipe. She pawed at the passenger door, eager to greet her subjects inside.

It had been Addison's home ever since she'd graduated from pet grooming school five years earlier. She'd been offering her pro bono services to different shelters around the city, both to hone her skills and to give a little TLC to those dogs in the most need. But the day she met Princess, she knew the Dachshund Rescue Center was her home for good. She fell in love with it and its inhabitants—both the two-legged and four-legged kind. She'd come back every week since then.

But it didn't feel like a second home to Addison this morning. Even with a pancake breakfast waiting inside. Today it was a reminder of her failed attempt at combining her two favorite things: dogs and beauty. Dogs were her passion. She volunteered her time rescuing them and finding them happy homes. She found lost dogs. She didn't lose them.

It was also a reminder of her broken promise to a friend, who happened to be a particularly powerful businessman, not to mention the boyfriend of Piper, one of her besties. The one and only Aiden Caldwell, prominent CEO of Caldwell and Son Investments and a key investor in her business.

How was she going to tell him that she'd lost seven dogs at the cocktail mixer? That her reputation was being slandered far and wide throughout the local Doggydom—if it hadn't gone national yet, that is. Most important, how would she explain that she'd taken the money he'd invested in her Fido Fashion line to help her get it off the ground and threw it all into one basket: the two weeks leading up to her fashion show.

Chances were, she wouldn't have to tell him. It was less than twelve hours after the horrible event, and the news had been posted on every social media site that Addison was on, and more than that she was sure. Aiden didn't take a day off work. Even on the weekends, he kept up with local news, and after Holly Hart's segment that morning, everyone in the city probably knew.

Addison's phone rang. Pulling it out of her purse, she checked the caller ID. It was her dad. She wasn't ready to tell him what had happened at the cocktail mixer the night before. It wasn't exactly like it was her fault, not really, but she was still embarrassed about the situation, regardless. She wanted him to be proud of her, and she wasn't feeling a lot of pride at the moment.

But it was her dad. They talked at least once a week. And right about now, she needed to hear his voice. Hitting the icon, she accepted the call. "Hi Dad."

"Hi sweetheart. How are you?" Just the sound of his voice was comforting, but it was tinted with concern. "I saw you on the news. What in the world happened?"

Great, even her dad who lived in Linda Mar had heard. "Oh that? Err, yeah, some dogs were stolen at the event I was working last night."

"Well, is everything okay? Have they found them yet? And why were those people blaming you for it?" He was asking questions faster than she could answer. Not that she had many answers for him, or for herself.

"The police are looking into it." Addison hesitated. She usually told her dad everything. But she'd already been to the cop shop that morning to answer more questions, and if they ended up finding the dogs then she didn't want to worry him for nothing. And if she was honest with herself, she didn't want to tell him how bad things were because she didn't want to disappoint him.

"It was all kind of a misunderstanding," she said, finally. "It's the dogs that I'm really worried about. They haven't found any trace of them yet."

"That's too bad," he said. "You're doing okay though, right?"

"Yeah, of course. You know me." She tried to muster some enthusiasm, but it sounded weak even to her.

"That's my girl. Nothing can get you down."

She rolled her eyes, mostly at herself. "You bet." She

hated lying to her dad, but she just needed a little time to figure out how bad things really were.

There was a moment's pause when her dad grew quiet on the other end. "I also called to give you some news."

"Oh? What is it?" She sat up straighter, glad the focus was shifting off her.

"Well, you know things haven't been going very well at the store," he began. "Dora and I have decided that it's time to sell. Or rather, the bank has decided for us. It's either sell fast or we'll be facing bankruptcy."

Addison blinked as she let the news wash over her. The corner store had practically been her second home growing up. "Dad. I had no idea things were that bad."

His laugh sounded strained over the line. "Me neither. I'd hoped we could turn things around."

Addison suddenly felt guilty. Her father was admitting his own dire situation to her while she was hiding her bad news. But at the same time, she knew it was the right decision. He had enough on his plate to worry about. She didn't need to add her own side dish.

"That's not good, Dad. I wish there was something I could do to help." And she really meant it. The timing was terrible. If only the police would hurry up and find the dogs. If only her fashion show would go well and her line would take off. If only she had the money to help them bail out their business. Or at least buy them a bit more time.

"Oh, don't worry about us. I just wanted to let you know what was going on." Now he sounded like the one trying and failing to muster some enthusiasm. "I'd better get going. Dora's keeping an eye on the store by herself. Lots to do. Anyway, I'll talk to you soon."

"Okay Dad. Love you."

"Love you too, muffin."

After she hung up, she stared at the phone, stunned and feeling utterly useless. Her dad was in trouble and there was nothing she could do about it. She knew that he would help her if he could—not that he could do anything about the poor missing pooches.

She was happy he'd told her, but also glad that she hadn't let on about her own problems, because he'd probably feel just as helpless as she did right now. With the dogs missing, and the future of her business on the line, she wasn't exactly in the best position to help him. If only there was a way to turn things around for herself, she might be able to do something for him.

A gentle breeze kicked up, and Addison caught the faint whiff of mouthwatering pancakes. Obviously so did Princess, because she began to whine and fidget on the seat. Addison sighed. She knew she couldn't hide in her car forever. It was Pancake Sunday, after all. And she could certainly use the comforting carbs after the lengthy little chat she'd had with the cops that morning.

"Well, Princess? Shall I go explain to Aiden how I lost his money?"

Princess didn't seem to care. She was too busy waving her nose in the air, searching for the source of that delicious smell wafting through the air.

Addison rounded her car to open the passenger door, as if she were Princess's chauffeur. The doxie dropped delicately to the pavement next to Addison's shoes and trotted up to the two-story 1910 farmhouse. The flagstone steps to the porch took a little extra effort as Princess limped awkwardly up each one.

Addison followed the doxie through the open French doors. She glanced around the sitting area near the fireplace and the reception desk. It was empty except for the exotic fish swimming around an aquarium that took up the entire back wall.

Addison heard laughter filter through the cozy home from the back, mingled with a few distant barks. Princess strutted toward the sounds, her Persian Pink toenails skittering along the recently upgraded, high quality laminate floor.

The back door was propped open. Addison was about to walk onto the wraparound porch when she heard footsteps shuffle on the floor behind her. She turned to find Marilyn, the center's manager, balancing a steaming plate of fresh pancakes. They sprung with delicious moistness.

"Would you be a dear and grab the syrup for me?" The clear dispenser dangled from her pinky finger and threatened to drop its gooey contents on the woman's heels. *Cheetah print*, Addison noted.

"Sure thing." Addison grabbed it. "Nice shoes, by the way. You dressed up for anyone in particular?" She gave Marilyn a sly wink.

"What? These old things?" She waved it away. "Just a silly way to make an old lady feel young."

"If you're old, then I'm a hundred and ten." The spry sixty-two-year-old British woman had more energy than Addison had at twenty-eight most days. The recent love glow that Marilyn wore only added to her youthful disposition.

Grinning to herself, Addison followed Marilyn out onto the wraparound porch where her dog Picasso was waiting patiently. He followed her everywhere, despite the fact that getting around was a bit harder for him than most dogs. Picasso was in a wheelchair.

Picasso was a blue dachshund that Marilyn rescued from a kill center. When she brought him back to the rescue center and had him checked over, it turned out that he'd already developed quite a severe case of intervertebral disc disease, which is not unheard of for doxies.

After the center had paid for Picasso's surgery, Marilyn cared for him at her home over the next several months of rehabilitation. Of course, once she had, she couldn't give him up to another home. She'd grown too attached, and so had he.

Unfortunately for Picasso, his spine worsened over time. Addison remembered a few months earlier when Marilyn had bought him a little doggy wheelchair to help him get around. It broke Addison's heart when she first saw him in it. But once he started rolling around the center on his own set of wheels rather than being carried, it seemed as though he'd become a puppy again. He could even frolic through the grassy field with the other dogs, travelling and playing fetch without pain.

However, remembering not to use stairs was something Picasso was still working on, so as Marilyn carried the pancakes to the gazebo where everyone gathered for their usual Sunday brunch, she took the wheelchair ramp. Picasso automatically followed her, as he always did. You never saw Marilyn without hearing the rolling of wheels on the floor.

Standing at the grill was Bob, Marilyn's sweetheart. He was brandishing a pair of barbecue tongs, flipping sausages. He'd become a recent addition to the group after he was assigned as the police detective to investigate a series of attacks against Piper and their old rescue center. Once the case had been closed, he kept finding excuse after excuse to come around the new center. Eventually, he stopped coming up with reasons, and no one bothered asking since it was obvious he was there to see Marilyn.

Seated at the picnic table were Addison's two besties in the whole world, Piper and Zoe, catching up on gossip, but Piper was slightly distracted. Her attention was fixed on the back of the property that was dominated by a fenced enclosure.

Addison followed her gaze and saw a handsome man in a pair of cargo pants and a polo shirt tossing a ball for some of the rescue dogs. Aiden. As though they were so in tune with each other, he glanced back to lock eyes with Piper. She waved him over, and he threw the ball one more time before joining them under the gazebo.

Addison's mouth went dry as she climbed the steps as if to the gallows. "Hey everyone. Sorry I'm late."

Bob waved his tongs at her. "Perfect timing. The sausages are just about done."

"Good, because here are the pancakes," Marilyn sang.

Addison dropped her purse under her chair and sat down across from Piper and Zoe. Or at least, they looked like her two besties, only they wore the strangest expressions. It was like a couple of aliens body-snatched her two best friends' bodies but put their faces on all wrong. Their smiles were strained, their expressions stiff.

"Hi," Piper said.

Zoe waved. "How are you?"

"Good," Addison hedged. Now that she really looked around, everyone was acting strangely except for Bob.

The detective placed a piping-hot plate of sausages in the middle of the table and took a seat next to Addison. "So how's business?" he asked her.

Zoe groaned, Piper cringed, and Marilyn swatted him with her napkin.

Addison suddenly realized what had everyone so on edge. They'd watched the news.

"What?" Bob asked. "What did I say?"

"Nothing," Addison said. "It's fine. Business is, err, swell." She studiously ignored glancing over at Aiden as he joined them at the table, afraid he'd be able to read the lie all over her face.

The truth was, she'd closed the spa for the day, since every last one of her customers had cancelled their appointments. She'd also given Melody the week off, because she didn't need anyone to watch the shop when no one was going to come in anyway. And as much as she didn't like to admit it, she still worried that maybe Melody had more to do with the missing dogs than she was letting on. Addison couldn't risk her being around any more of the show dogs until she was certain of her innocence.

"Swell?" Bob said. "Where's the usual enthusiasm? Don't you usually use words like 'fantabulous' or 'awesomeness'?"

"Maybe not 'swell,'" Addison said. "But it's good. It's okay. Fine, I suppose."

Zoe set her fork down. "Okay, let's not sugarcoat it. We all saw the news. Things are shit."

"Oh come on," Piper said. "It wasn't that bad. Besides, who really watches Holly Hart's Hounds anyway?" By the look on Piper's face, Addison could tell that she did.

Addison leveled her with a look. "Besides every dog lover in San Francisco? The segment's a hit. Holly's popularity has skyrocketed ever since she started it."

"All thanks to us," Zoe said. "If it hadn't been for our drama last year, Holly'd be back working at that cheap rag *The San Francisco Gate*."

"Yeah, and she couldn't wait to use my drama last night for another breaking story." Addison pushed her pancake around her plate.

"Do they have any leads?" Aiden asked.

Addison shrugged. "If they do, they're not saying."

Marilyn clicked her tongue. "All those dogs. They must be so scared. Right after I saw it on the news, I called all my contacts at the other shelters in town," she told Addison. "If you give me a list of the dogs that went missing, I'll call around on a regular basis to see if any of them get picked up."

"That's a great idea, Marilyn. Thank you."

"Bob, have you heard anything around the station?" Marilyn asked, pouring him some coffee.

"Sorry. It's not my case, nor my place to say anything," he said in his professional no-nonsense cop voice. As though realizing he wasn't on the record, his mouth softened beneath his salt-and-pepper moustache. "But what I can tell you is that a few missing dogs aren't exactly rating high on their radar, especially if they're not certain there was actually a crime committed. No one knows for sure that these dogs haven't run away on their own."

Addison frowned, once again doubting that it was possible for them to have snuck out, either past Melody while she was outside smoking or through an entire room full of guests entirely of their own volition.

She'd driven around until three in the morning through the hilly streets of San Francisco, working her way from the Regency Center out, down back alleys and through dark parking lots, shining her headlights into driveways. She didn't spot a stray. Not even so much as a cat.

Maybe it was a cop thing. They didn't want to say one way or the other until they had more evidence. But what would it take to make them see?

"The precinct has been strapped for staff lately," Bob said between bites. "On top of a few early retirements and the recent rash of murders in the city, let's just say we got caught with our pants down."

Zoe grinned. "I hate when that happens."

"Zoe," Piper chastised. "This is serious. Nobody wants to see Bob with his pants down." She cracked a smile and Zoe couldn't help but snicker.

Marilyn threw the girls a look as though they were a couple of silly teenagers. "So many murders lately. Those poor people." She shook her head. "I've been following it on the news for weeks."

"I hear they suspect it's a serial killer," Zoe said. "They've been calling him the San Fran Slayer."

Bob dabbed his napkin across his moustache, neither confirming nor denying it. "So you can see that with everything going on, a few missing dogs aren't going to justify pulling people off the murder cases."

Addison frowned, and she was obviously not the only one around the table doing so because Bob held up his hands in defense. "I'm not saying that these missing dogs aren't important, but the city is up in arms over these murders. The whole country is watching, demanding for the cases to be solved. Unless they can find evidence that it was dog theft, or unless it happens again, I don't think this case will be a top priority. The police force only has so many resources to go around."

"Well, at least there's one benefit to Holly sticking her big nose into the disappearances last night," Aiden said.

"What's that?" Piper asked.

"The case might get a little more public attention, meaning it will get solved faster."

Sure, Aiden had a point, and Addison's first concern was getting the dogs home safely. But she wished there was a better way. Aiden didn't know just what kind of money Addison had riding on the next two weeks. As in, all of it.

She turned to Bob. "So what you're saying, is my name won't be cleared any time soon, if at all?"

Bob frowned and took a moment too long to answer, worrying Addison. In his forty-plus years of service, he'd probably seen it all, the worst of it. Maybe Addison didn't want him to answer that.

Aiden cut in before the silence could continue for too long. "Things will die down," he said to her. "I remember the heat I faced last year when my company came under scrutiny over the old rescue center. As a business, you lay low, carry on as normal, and you'll weather the storm. Caldwell and Son Investments pulled through just fine. Heck, since the case has been put to rest, business has been better than ever."

Addison knew it wouldn't be that easy. She'd paid for the advertising and handed over free services and gift certificates to build new clientele in the dog show circles. The fashion show venue was booked and nonrefundable, and she'd ordered a surplus of her designs to have on hand for the big orders that were no longer going to roll in after the show. If she continued to lose customers, there would be no weathering the storm in that boat. It was going to sink like the *Titanic*.

But even as she opened her mouth to tell Aiden just how bad it was, she just couldn't face the music yet. She'd tell him. Eventually. *Maybe after pancakes*, she told herself. If only there was something she could do to fix it all. . . .

For the moment, she put on her best I-can-do-it face. "You're right. I'm sure it will all blow over soon. Maybe I'll just hold off on the marketing for a while. Maybe rebrand and make a comeback when things die down."

"That's the spirit. Smart business is not always about investing in a good product. It's about investing in people." Aiden gave her a sincere look. "And you, Addison, are a good investment."

Addison felt the heart-warming compliment like a blow to her gut. Her smile was frozen on her face. She imagined her makeup cracking as she tried her best not to let her smile waver. "Thanks."

Oh God. What was she going to say to him when it

all went horribly wrong? *Oops, sorry I blew all your money. But I thought you were investing in me, not my product.*

Everything Addison had worked so hard to build, all gone because of a bad rap. If she had no customers, she had no business, and no business meant no fashion show—not that anyone would volunteer their dogs to be models now.

Addison suddenly realized she'd been quiet for too long. Turning to Zoe, she tried to change the subject. "Hey, how is the planning for the dog show gala coming along?"

"Excellent." Zoe's eyes lit up. "I just have to confirm the band, meet with the caterer, send out the tickets, and pick out an outfit." Her gaze was focused on nothing in particular, as though she was consulting the to-do list in her mind. "Are you still coming?"

"Wouldn't miss it," Addison said. "Where is it being held again?"

"Actually, I've decided to change the venue, considering recent events. It will be held on the *San Francisco Belle.*"

"It's being held on a boat?" Bob asked.

"Well, I wanted to make sure the dog show guests were comfortable bringing their pets, since that's the whole theme. Once we've cast off, there will be no way on or off, for humans or dogs."

Addison winced slightly, as though the extra planning her friend had to do was somehow her fault too, but she smiled. "That's a fantabulous idea."

"There's our girl," Bob said.

Addison's phone buzzed in her purse beneath her. Pulling it out, she checked the new text message. It was another cancellation. This time for a fashion show model. The last one. A fashion show wasn't very effective with no dogs to wear her designs. It wasn't like she could wear them herself.

She'd been relying on the support of the dog show world to promote her line, as well as borrowing some of her furry friends from the rescue center. The core value she wanted to promote with her line was that every dog was beautiful, mixed breed and purebred alike. Her statement would lose its impact, not to mention a huge source of potential customers, without the latter.

And who could blame them? Those poor missing dogs.

Addison only wished she knew how to find them. If her life were a movie, she thought that now would be the time where the plot should twist, giving the main character hope. An invitation from Hogwarts, a fairy godmother's appearance, a yellow brick road maybe.

She sat staring at her plate and felt something nudge her leg. She glanced down to find Princess dragging her purse under her chair. She was licking the zippers and nosing her way through the pockets in search of the dog treats that Addison kept inside.

She snatched her purse back and was about to give the doxie heck when she saw something sticking out of the main compartment. A ray of sun hit it, like a sign from above, casting her in its golden reflection. It was Felix's business card.

Curiously, she pulled it out of her purse. She'd been running late for the cop shop that morning so she'd dumped the contents of her clutch from the cocktail mixer into her usual purse. Felix's card, which had been at the bottom, ended up on top.

She read the card. FELIX VAUGHN.

Addison remembered how well he knew the crowd at the mixer, how he could read his customers. Heck, he downright bragged about it. *I'm in the perfect position to people-watch, to observe the human species, to under-stand what makes them tick.*

If anyone would be able to help her save those dogs, it would be him. It might not be too late to help her father save his business, after all.

It wasn't a fairy godmother giving Addison an easy way out, but maybe it was the way to find her own way out.

6

Don't Have a Dog in This Fight

Addison stood on a gum-speckled sidewalk on the edges of the Mission District double-checking the address on her golden ticket one more time. She held Felix's card under a flickering streetlight to read the address. It was far from the glorious Chocolate Factory, but she was in the right place. When she crossed the street, she could read the faded sign at the top of the building that assured her she was at JOE'S DIVE.

She approached the heavy oak door and peered through the cracked stained-glass window next to it. It was only nine o'clock, but the lights inside the bar were so dim, she wondered if it had already closed and someone just forgot to turn off the flickering OPEN sign in the window. However, when she tried the grimy brass door handle and stepped inside, it was open, just sparsely populated with the Sunday-night faithfuls. And one quick scan of her surroundings told Addison that Joe couldn't have chosen a better name for the place.

Addison hesitated in the entrance to let her eyes adjust

to the weak glow of the filthy pendant lights dangling from the exposed ceiling. Dark leather booths hid the odd lone drinker and a young couple canoodling in the far corner.

The place could have passed for a chic industrial theme with very little effort, but Addison didn't think Joe'd had a particular décor in mind when he chose the mismatched wooden chairs and metal tables.

Addison's shifting eyes found the bar at the back of the room where a shelf lined with spirits stood behind it, along with Felix. His black button-up shirt collar gaped open to reveal a Rolling Stones T-shirt as he leaned across the bar to talk to a brunette in painted-on jeans. His thick black curls shone beneath the pendant lights and his white teeth flashed with a flirty smile.

The girl shifted beneath the light, and her cheap-looking red bra peeked out of her low-backed top. It was the server he'd been flirting with the night before at the cocktail mixer.

Felix hadn't seen Addison come in yet. She was tempted to stand there and watch him for a while, to observe him in his own element, to study the man who supposedly "sees all." To discover what made him tick. But as he laughed again at something Red Bra said, Addison found herself marching up to the bar.

She dropped her purse on the counter with a thud to catch his attention and instantly regretted it—the thick oak slab was sticky from a spilled drink.

Felix pulled away from Red Bra and sauntered over to Addison. He did a double take when he recognized her. Or maybe it was the low-cut hot-pink halter top she'd slipped on that night—and not by accident. She needed all the help she could get convincing Felix to join her cause. It was a graceless tactic, but Felix didn't strike her as the highbrow type. Besides, desperate times called for desperate measures.

He ran a hungry tongue across his bottom lip like an animal on the hunt. Halter top one, Felix zero. "Just couldn't resist me, could you?" he asked her.

I might be desperate, but not that desperate, she thought. "You're not as charming as you like to think, you know."

"You're here, aren't you?"

"Okay, you caught me." She batted her eyelashes, just in case the halter top wasn't enough. "Actually, there is something you've got that I want."

"There is? Well, I aim to please." He pushed his sleeves up and leaned his elbows on the bar. "Tell me. What is it that I can give you?" he said, lacing each word with meaning, or maybe a promise.

The deep hum of his voice washed over her, settling inside of her like a warmth, deep and low in her belly. She cleared her throat, ignoring the effect he had on her.

"I want information."

"Well I'm thirty-one, I like sports—the 49ers are my favorite team—I love music. The classics, mostly. You know, Rolling Stones, Zeppelin, Journey. Oh, and don't forget banana pancakes with caramel chocolate chips after a sleep-in on Sundays."

"Caramel chocolate chips?"

"I have a sweet tooth. Not that I'm not sweet enough already." He flashed that charming smile at her and Addison took it back; he *was* as charming as he thought he was—not that she'd ever tell him that.

She felt the surge rush over her again, this time very specifically beneath her miniskirt. His gaze drew her in, like a storewide sale on the last ticketed price. *Ahhh*.

Men like Felix were dangerous. Men who knew the

power they had over women. At the cocktail mixer he told her she was a target for men to take advantage of her. Well, if anyone knew how to read her and play her, it was going to be Felix. And when men knew how to use their power, it was usually because they exerted it often. Felix was bad news.

She shook her head, hoping to bring some of that blood flow back north of her waistline. "No. Not that kind of information."

"Well, we can get a little more personal, if you like. But you'll have to buy me dinner first."

Bad news, bad news, bad news, she repeated in her head. She crossed her legs, clamping them tight together. "No. I mean information about the other night at the cocktail mixer. You said you do the dog show circuit often."

The sudden change in direction put a furrow between his brows. "Every year for the last five," he said, after a moment.

"You know the contestants, the owners, the judges, the ins and outs of the competition."

"It's like having a backstage pass." He smiled, clearly happy she'd taken an interest in what he had to say the night before.

"So you know the owners of the missing dogs?"

"Sure. I know of them."

"And their dogs?"

"Sure." His eyes narrowed in suspicion. "Mostly."

Addison leaned in closer. "Even potential suspects?"

Understanding dawned on his face. "Now, hold on a minute." He held up a hand, pulling away from the bar, but she leaned even closer.

"You would know who was there last night, both contestants and the staff."

"Yes, but—"

"And anyone else with a vendetta against the past dog

show winners. Maybe someone with a grudge, or who runs an underground puppy mill. Or maybe someone who has a debt to the mob and their only way to pay it off is by selling show dogs. On the black dog market."

His expression screwed up with the tumult of ideas. "Black dog market? You've been watching too many mobster movies."

Addison ignored the jibe. She was onto something. She could feel it. "Or maybe it's someone who hates what dog shows stand for and they wanted to set them all free as a statement."

Felix reached across the sticky bar and shook Addison's shoulders to get her attention. "Whoa, Nancy Drew. You're getting a little ahead of yourself, aren't you?"

Her starry eyes focused again, and she returned to reality. "You're right. Sorry." She waved off the excitement. "You're the expert here. Where do you think we should begin?"

"How about with a cocktail?"

"Like as in the cocktail waitresses? You think it was one of the staff who took the dogs?" Her eyes shifted around the room. Secretly she hoped Red Bra was the criminal. At the very least, her fashion sense should have been considered a crime.

"No." Felix slammed a glass down in front of Addison, making her jump. "Cocktail. As in alcohol. This is a bar, sweetheart, and if you haven't noticed, I'm a bartender. Last time I checked that meant I serve drinks. I don't solve crimes."

He turned his back to her and picked out a few bottles of alcohol and mixers seemingly at random. As he began to slosh them into a battered old cocktail shaker, she reached into her purse and drew out his card.

She slapped it down on the bar, pointing at it like an accusation. "But you said if I ever needed anything—"

"Yeah, like a drink," he said, pouring the mystery contents into her glass. It came out in a shock of pink, like a glass of blended flamingos.

She narrowed her eyes at it. "What's this?"

"A consolation prize." He pushed it toward her.

"So you're not going to help me?"

"I am helping," he said. "I'm a very helpful guy. But I've got other customers I need to help right now." Reaching under the bar, he produced a pink umbrella and plunked it in her martini glass. "Enjoy."

Addison's shoulders slumped as Felix turned to a middle-aged man wearing a plaid shirt. However, Addison wasn't giving up that easily. It wasn't like he gave her a firm "no." Not exactly. There was still room for argument. Besides, without Felix and his Intel, her next best strategy was to hang posters around the city asking, HAVE YOU SEEN THIS DOG? Not exactly an investigation worthy of Sherlock Holmes.

Settling onto the bar stool, she eyed the drink in front of her suspiciously, wondering if he'd go so far as to poison her just to get rid of her. Not likely, she finally decided, then took a sip. Her taste buds sang with pleasure. It was like a liquefied tropical island, flamingos and all.

Addison took another sip as she waited for Felix to finish serving the lumberjack, but then another customer ordered a round of shots. Shots? Who drank shots on a Sunday night? But man, was her drink ever good. There couldn't be much alcohol in it, if any, she told herself. It practically tasted like juice.

After the minutes ticked by and more orders rolled in, she figured one more drink couldn't hurt, right? She'd had a rough week, after all.

At the cocktail mixer, Felix had looked smooth, polished, a man who could serve gentlemen with numbers at the end of their names—that is, until he'd opened his mouth. But he also seemed to fit in at this rough dive. The man was like Johnny Depp, a chameleon of roles. Here in the little hole in the wall, he was at ease. In fact, he seemed to thrive, a prince among thieves.

Finally, Felix finished serving an elderly woman a brandy and grabbed a cloth. He started to wipe down the counter, even though he'd barely let a drop hit the surface with his practiced hands.

Addison stared at those hands, wondering what else they were practiced at—not that she cared. She shook the thought right out of her head. She was still hoping to receive a call from Phillip Montgomery III. Okay, who was she kidding? After what happened at the cocktail mixer, she'd probably never see him again.

When Felix continued to ignore her, she switched bar stools to sit closer to where he was pretending to look busy. "Look, Felix. You said so yourself, you're in the perfect position to people-watch, to understand what makes them click."

"Tick," he corrected her with a smirk.

"Tick," she agreed, chasing her straw around with her tongue before catching it to take a sip.

"There's a reason people trust me," Felix said. "It's because I can keep my mouth shut. I certainly don't start investigations on them."

"No, no, no." She wagged her finger. "Not investigate. This is just a friendly chat. Between two professionals." She indicated him and herself, nearly knocking her drink over. "This is just business."

"And why would I want to talk to you?"

Addison flinched like he'd insulted her. *Why wouldn't he want to talk to me? And why do I want him to want to talk to me?* Now she wasn't even making sense to herself. She pushed the drink away, focusing her thoughts.

"Because it's about one professional helping another

professional. You know, helping? Caring? Because these poor dogs need our help? What have you got to lose?"

"My job," he said flatly.

"What do you mean?"

"I mean these rich snooty types live some interesting lives, lives they want to keep secret." He widened his eyes, and she wondered just what kind of secrets they kept. "If people suspect that I'm sneaking around and spying on them at functions, I won't get any more private gigs. Not to mention my boss, Joe, won't be too happy about the complaints. He's not exactly the forgiving type."

"Okay, fine. Mum's the word. I get it." She pretended to zip her lips. "How about I just talk and you listen. If I start to get close to guessing the truth, all you have to do is wink. Like this." She gave a slow wink, as though he needed a demonstration.

His stare remained even. "The answer is no."

"Good, good. Play along. That's good." She gave him a thumbs-up. "Okay, here we go. Do the missing dogs have something to do with the mob?"

She watched his eyes very carefully. His left eye moved, and for a second she thought it was a wink, but maybe it was more of an annoyed twitch.

"Okay, that's not it. Onto the next question."

He sighed and yelled out, "Last call!" making her jump.

Felix turned to move away from her. She opened her mouth to argue, but she was interrupted by the sharp clink of a glass on the counter in front of her. She looked down to find another tropical island sitting before her like a mirage.

Well, she figured, she wasn't leaving until she got the answers she was looking for, so one more couldn't hurt.

Imbibing the nectar of the gods, Addison watched Felix tidy up the bar. Every time he got a break between customers or cleaning, she tried once again to convince him. But every time she did, she found a fresh drink in front of her. Probably because she couldn't argue if her mouth was busy. *Little did he know*, she thought.

Addison was sticking another umbrella into her updo when the pendant lights above her shut off. She glanced around to discover she was the last customer in the bar. In fact, she and Felix were the last two people in the whole place.

There were noises coming from the adjacent room where she could see pool tables through the doorway. Sliding off the stool, she followed the sharp sounds of billiard balls cracking together and found Felix tidying up.

Startled, he glanced up to see her standing in the doorway.

"You're still here," he said.

"You can't get rid of me that easily," Addison said, leaning against one of the tables. "I haven't gotten what I wanted yet."

"You're a persistent little thing, aren't you?" He finished organizing the pool cues into their wall holders before shutting off the lights.

The bar was thrown into darkness, the only light filtering in through the dirty windows and cracked stained-glass accents. Streetlights glowed green and purple through images of grapes on vines, coloring Felix's tanned skin.

She followed his slow movements across the pool hall, slinking with that same animal allure that she'd seen in him earlier. A predator looking for the kill. No prey had ever been so eager to be caught.

Felix stopped in front of her and reached up. She thought he was going to touch her face, but then he plucked an umbrella out of her hair with a smirk. When a disappointed sigh escaped, she realized how badly she'd wanted him to touch her.

"What about me?" he asked. "If I'm putting my job on the line, what do I get out of this deal?"

"The satisfaction of knowing you helped save seven poor, defenseless dogs?"

"Not quite what I was thinking." She saw his bright teeth flash in the dark room, like a panther baring its fangs.

She couldn't help the pant that escaped her. Her body tensed, her senses heightened, as though waiting for him to pounce. Heat radiated off him, or maybe she imagined it. *When did he get so near*, she wondered.

"What did you have in mind?" she asked.

"I'll help you," he said. "I'll give you some leads . . . In exchange."

"Exchange for what?"

"A date with you."

Addison inhaled sharply, wondering if the drinks were making her foggy, or if it was Felix's nearness, the spice of his cologne, the way his eyes were holding hers.

"What makes you think I'd go on a date with you?"

"You're here aren't you?" he said, with a cocky tilt to his head.

"Only because I need your help."

"You know what I think?" he asked, closing the last few inches between them. "I think it's more than that. I think it's an excuse to come around and see me. I think you're interested and just won't admit it." The umbrella twirled between his fingers and he brushed the crepe paper against her neck, down the low neckline of her halter top.

She snorted, backing away, but her butt hit the pool table. "Delusional much?"

"Curious much?" he retorted, moving closer.

"What would I be curious about?"

"What it would be like to kiss me." His voice was filled with confidence, making Addison second-guess herself that he wasn't the Prince Charming she was looking for.

She scoffed, but her eyes automatically dropped to his lips.

He placed his hands on the pool table on either side of her, trapping his prey. "To feel my lips against yours."

"Ha." She turned her face away from him, but couldn't find the words to deny it as he brought his face to her neck. His wavy hair brushed her face, his breath tickled her skin, and his lips hovered over her, not yet touching, maybe waiting for her to give in.

"You're curious to feel what it's like to run your fingers through my hair, to press your body against mine." His lips finally grazed her neck, as light as a flicker of eyelashes. Her breath left her in a moan that startled her.

"Too close," she said. "Too close."

Felix froze, not coming any closer, but not pulling away. Although she couldn't see his face, she could sense him smile. "Then push me away."

Addison brought her hands up, but instead of shoving him away, those curious fingers of hers wove into his thick locks, dragging his face down to hers.

Like a panther pouncing, he finally made his move. He met her hungry need to taste him with his own animal hunger, his tongue finding hers over and over again.

His hot hands ran down her halter top and skirt, cupping her butt. As easily as he'd lifted the stools onto the bar, he set her on the edge of the pool table. Now they were at an even height so he could kiss behind her ears, along her neck, down her plunging neckline.

Felix settled there a moment, enjoying his face pressed against her breasts. He pushed his hips between her legs, parting her thighs, hiking up her skirt. It sat around her waist as he pressed himself against her pink lace booty shorts.

Addison's toes curled as his lips found that perfect spot beneath her ear. She couldn't take it anymore. Gripping his shirt, she yanked him closer. Felix didn't need any more encouragement. He hopped onto the pool table.

He laid her down against the green cloth and hard balls dug into her back. She quickly rolled them aside before gripping his shirt and dragging him down on top of her. Then he settled between her legs, and she could feel something else just as hard press against her. But it wasn't the pool balls.

Her moan was cut off as his mouth found hers again. This time their hands ran over each other with a new purpose, greedily, over clothes and under them, tugging impatiently at fabric.

Addison's head swam with a storm of sensations surging through her body. She'd never felt such a pull toward anyone. Maybe it was because she'd told herself she wasn't going to let herself have Felix, that he was a mistake. He was supposed to be off limits.

Addison had thought she was done choosing the wrong guy. She was supposed to be using her brain for once and ignoring her heart. The heart was unreliable. It was easily swayed. It couldn't tell the difference between an explanation and a lie. Couldn't tell deadbeat from dependable.

She was supposed to be choosing with her brain, choosing *the one*. The one who would be there for her through anything, for better or worse, not run out on her after three years when they found something that wasn't perfect about her. Who she could have adventures with or simply cuddle up on the couch and watch movies with. And that wasn't this guy.

Felix, with his faded band T-shirt and his constant five-o'clock shadow and his midnight bartending job that he probably used to hook up with the stragglers at the end of most nights. The girls who were desperate for attention and confused the bartender's glances and free drinks with affection. Girls who stayed after last call hoping there was something more. Girls, she realized belatedly, just like her.

Addison's arms that had been wrapped around Felix's sturdy body suddenly pressed against him, creating a wedge between their bodies. She shoved him as hard as she could, wriggling away from him on the stained cloth top.

"Get off. Get off."

Felix backed off, his hands in the air like he'd just burned himself on a stove. "What? What's wrong? Did I hurt you?"

"Not yet, you haven't. And you're never going to." She scrambled off the pool table, landing awkwardly. She gripped her head, suddenly feeling the full effects of those deadly pink drinks. Why did she have to be such a lightweight?

Felix flinched like she'd just slapped him. "What is that supposed to mean?"

"Look. I didn't come here for a make-out session. I came here for help." She jabbed a finger in the middle of his chest, unsure if she was angrier with him or herself. "Now are you going to help me or not?"

He glanced down at the finger poking him. "Not with that attitude I'm not."

"I'm not going to go on a date with you just because I'm desperate for information. It's coercion. It's extortion. It's—"

"Is it a deal?" He grabbed her finger, dragging her closer to him. But Addison wasn't playing, and as she pushed him away again, the look on his face showed that he finally got the hint.

"So you won't help me unless there's something in it for you?"

He shrugged, but the flirtatious smile had left his face. He was serious too. "A guy's got to try, right? Besides I have my own livelihood to look out for."

"And what about mine? What about the dogs?"

He pointed a thumb at his chest. "I've got to look out for number one."

"You're looking out for something, all right." Her eyes dipped down to the crotch of his well-worn jeans, which she couldn't help notice were a little tight at the moment. "You're exactly who I thought you were," she said. "Forget it. I'll figure it out on my own. Thanks for nothing."

"What about the free drinks, the company, and the hot make-out session? You call that nothing?"

Storming over to the bar, Addison reached into her purse and grabbed all the bills she had. She slammed the money down on the table. It definitely wouldn't cover the bill—not that he deserved a tip. It was only twenty-four dollars. But it would have to do.

"There. Now all I owe you is a bad memory."

"Keep your damned money," he said, thrusting it back at her.

"Is that how you get girls to go out with you? You liquor them up, find a way to take advantage of their situation because you have nothing else to offer? That doesn't surprise me!" she yelled, because if she didn't yell, she thought she might actually cry.

Why did she always fall for the wrong guy? Why was she so gullible? She wanted a good guy, like Phillip Montgomery III. She didn't want to want a guy like Felix. A guy that wouldn't inconvenience himself to help somebody unless something was in it for him.

But she wanted Felix. Oh, boy, she wanted him. Her damp booty shorts could attest to that, and she felt all the worse for it. She was hopeless.

"Excuse me?" Felix wasn't yelling, but his voice held a certain power, an authority. It was almost worse than if he did yell. She was so used to his cool, cocksure attitude that the little vein popping out on his forehead had her backing up. "I'm not trying to take advantage of you. And I'll have you know that I've got a lot going for me. I'm a catch. You came here looking for me tonight, remember?"

Addison didn't need the reminder. She scoffed. "A catch? Yeah, as in I might catch something from you."

He crossed his arms. "Why don't you tell me how you really feel?"

"Why bother?" she said, slinging her purse over her shoulder. "I don't want to waste my breath."

"You weren't able to catch your breath just a minute ago," he said. Addison turned on her heel, but he grabbed her arm. "Why the sudden change of heart?"

"I was faking." She flicked her hair in his face and marched toward the door.

"So that's a no to the date, I suppose?" Although by the sarcasm coating his voice, it didn't sound like he wanted one anymore.

Grasping the door handle, she glanced over her shoulder. "You've got about a dog's chance."

"That's good," he threw back at her, "because I hear you have bad luck keeping track of dogs anyway."

Addison's mouth dropped open and she stood there sputtering for a moment, caught between fury, humiliation, and outright insult. When all of the things she wanted to spit back at him, the insults and swearwords, balled into one, the only thing that came out was something between a grunt and a scream.

Wrenching on the heavy door, she flung it open and stormed out onto the sidewalk. The door slammed behind her and she heard the deadbolt snap home.

Addison was in no shape to drive, so she abandoned her car and stomped down the street in search of a cab. Her car would have to sit until she came back for it in the morning.

The walk did Addison good, the cool night air like a splash of water in her face. All the things she didn't say to Felix, the responses that wouldn't come to her, suddenly formed clearly in her head. Boy, were there some zingers. She was tempted to turn right around and throw them in his face, but at that moment a cab appeared. With a shaking hand, she hailed it and got in.

The taxi drove down the rolling San Francisco streets to her tiny Mission apartment. The eclectic mix of San Francisco row houses and colorful shops and bars passed outside her window. Looking for a distraction from her anger and her sudden self-loathing—because she was beginning to think she'd taken her anger out on the wrong person—she pulled out her phone to scroll through her contacts.

She didn't know many of the people at the cocktail mixer the other night. It's not like she'd been on the scene as long as Felix had. The only person she had connections with was Holly Hart, and she was the reason the entire incident escalated in the first place.

Addison just couldn't bring herself to suck it up and call her. Besides, Holly wouldn't help Addison prove her innocence. That would only take the wind out of Holly's own story, not to mention make her look like a sloppy reporter—which would be entirely true.

Addison was about to chuck her phone into her purse when a new text message caught her eye. It was from an unknown number. Dreading yet another appointment cancellation, she opened it.

Hello Addison. This is Phillip Montgomery III. I was able to track down your number from a client of yours. It was a pleasure meeting you at the cocktail mixer. I'm sorry events prevented us from getting to know one another better. I'd like to see you again. I'm still holding the fundraiser this week, if you're interested in attending. Regards, Phillip.

Addison clutched the phone, reading it over again. Phillip had tracked her number down. After losing seven dogs, her embarrassing debut on stage, the media blowup, and everyone blaming her, he had still tracked down her number.

She automatically touched her locks to see if there was a hair out of place—which, after her run-in with Felix, there were undoubtedly a lot. The giddiness she felt when she met Phillip at the cocktail mixer suddenly returned like a refreshing rain. It cleared her mind of any fog remaining from her heated pool table session.

Who cared if Felix saw her as a last-call girl when she was destined to be Mrs. Phillip Montgomery III?

7

Fight Like Cats and Dogs

Cinderella arrived at the prince's castle in her Mini convertible, only a little late. Unlike the real Cinderella, Addison didn't have a fairy godmother to magic her a gown and a classy hairstyle. But if she knew how to do anything, it was how to doll herself up. Besides, she preferred her Mini to a pumpkin anyway.

Her prince, on the other hand, really did have a castle. Well, it was close enough, she thought as she pulled up to a small circular drive in front of an Italian Renaissance mansion. The fact that he had a driveway at all in San Francisco was amazing enough, but the three-story home set atop a raised foundation of white stone was like something from a fairy tale.

Rearranging Princess's feather fascinator on her head, Addison got out of the car and handed the keys to the valet driver. The mansion's arched doorway was open and she could hear classical music drifting out from somewhere inside. Taking a deep breath, she suppressed a giddy squeal.

It may not have been the ball, but it was at least a date. Well, sort of. She was going to count it as one anyway, because if she didn't see it that way, it was going to be one awkward afternoon. An afternoon with her and Phillip, and about a hundred dog show hotshots, judges, and highbrow dog lovers. Most of whom still associated her with the missing show dogs, if they didn't outright accuse her of stealing them.

So instead, she raised her head high and climbed the stone stairs with Princess, who was dressed in a delicate lace sundress, by her side. She was Phillip's guest, after all. She deserved to be there. Besides, no amount of criticism was going to keep her from her dreams. No matter what anyone said, she knew what was in her own heart. She was just as worried about those dogs as everyone else and she planned to find out what happened . . . somehow.

Addison was just about to enter through the doors when two men in suits converged on her. By their dark sunglasses and the wires coiling into their ears, she assumed they were on security detail.

"Good afternoon, ma'am," one said. "We've been asked to greet all guests as they arrive today."

The other guard took out a tablet, jotting a few notes down. Addison kinked her neck to see what he was writing, but he frowned and tilted the screen away.

"Is this the only dog you have accompanying you today?" guard two asked.

"Yes," she said. "This is Princess."

He typed the name into his tablet while the first guard held up a small silver tag and a matching bracelet.

"Please attach the tag to your dog's collar, and we invite you to wear the bracelet. It is a gift from the host." Guard one held it up. "May I?"

Addison raised her wrist while he fastened it for her. The delicate bling glistened in the sunlight, and when she looked closer, she realized it wasn't just silver in color, it was actually white gold. Her eyes widened, thinking it was a bit much for a first date.

She noticed a little charm dangling from it and held it up to the sun to read it. There was a number engraved on it that matched the one on Princess's tag. Okay, so not exactly a gift specifically for her, she realized. Every guest would probably get one, or at least the ladies would. The men would receive something different.

Most of the guests would probably see it as a fun memento of the fundraiser, however the bracelet was of finer quality than most of the costume jewelry Addison had at home.

Guard one slipped the tag onto Princess's crystal collar. "Simply show the bracelet to the guard upon your exit from the property to ensure you have the correct pet."

"Thank you." Addison climbed the stairs to make her grand entrance, thinking that she was pretty sure she wouldn't forget Princess. Then it dawned on her that it wasn't to make sure the guests left with their own dog. It was to ensure they couldn't leave with anyone else's.

When she entered the double front doors, Phillip was waiting to greet her. He spotted her across the cavernous foyer, and his perfect smile spread across his face like a commercial for teeth-whitening strips.

Excusing himself from a conversation, he walked over to her and took her hands in his. "Addison. I'm so happy you came."

"Thank you for inviting us," she said.

He turned to his other guest and greeted her with a bow. "Hello Princess. It's a pleasure to see you again."

Princess sat down on the marble floor and stuck out her chest as if to say, *Of course it is.*

"Please, come in. Most of the guests are on the veranda," he said, gesturing.

He led Addison and Princess back, way back, toward a set of open doors leading outside. A stone veranda lay behind the house in front of a sizable backyard that stretched into the distance, a plot of grass so manicured it almost looked fake. It was the size of the small park that she often took Princess to. But she supposed that was what craploads of money got you in San Francisco.

Dotted around the backyard, guests leaned against pillars while nibbling on caviar and sipping champagne among marble statues. The furrier guests drank bottled water from gold-embossed bowls. The sun glinting off so many high-priced pieces of jewelry and watches almost blinded Addison.

She noticed a couple of faces turn her way, a frozen smile, a double take. They recognized her. Ignoring them, she kept a pleasant look on her face and followed her date.

Phillip didn't make it very far before he was stopped by a guest. When he spun to see who it was, Addison recognized the woman right away. It was Julia Edwards, one of her best customers. She looked about in her mid-forties wearing a sapphire blue dress. Her hair was pinned back to show off a pair of diamond earrings that probably cost more than Addison made in a year.

"Fabulous party, Phillip," she said. "Good turnout."

"Addison, I'd like you to meet Julia Edwards. Her cocker spaniel was the Best of Breed last year."

"Yes of course," Addison said. "We already know each other."

His eyebrows shot up. "You do?"

"Hello Addison. What a surprise to see you." Julia held her martini aloft while she leaned in to kiss the air next to Addison's cheek.

"Nice to see you, Julia," Addison said.

Phillip watched Julia's cocker spaniel and Princess

sniff each other with familiarity. "How do you two know each other?"

"Addison here is the reason Precious won his title last year," Julia told Phillip. "Wasn't she, Precious?" she asked the dog sitting at her feet.

The cocker spaniel's long fur fanned out on the stones like an elegant cream gown. He stared back passively, turning politely to each face now starting down at him.

Addison waved away the compliment. "Oh, I wouldn't go that far. Julia is a regular customer of mine," she told Phillip.

"Don't be so modest," Julia told Addison. "We wouldn't have won if I hadn't found you."

"Is that right?" Phillip said. "Well it's a lucky thing I found her then." He gave Addison a look that made her feel like *she* was the lucky one.

"She might be a whiz with a dog brush," a harsh nasally voice cut in, "but you run the risk of never seeing your pet again." Penny Peacock approached their group, swishing her appletini around her glass. She leaned down to whisper to Princess conspiratorially. "I'd be careful if I were you."

Princess growled in Addison's defense, causing her lace collar to ruffle up over her hackles.

Julia made a show of rolling her eyes. "Addison wasn't responsible for the missing dogs. She's not capable of something like that. Precious and I have been going to her faithfully every Saturday for two years now. Haven't we, Precious?" She bent down to her cocker spaniel and kissed him on the snout. "And that won't change now." She leveled Penny with an icy look. "Sensationalism. That's all that media nonsense was."

" 'Nonsense'?" Penny looked aghast. "Her carelessness while watching Lilly cost me this year's Best in Show title."

"You know *you're* not competing, right?" Julia asked her. "I know it's confusing when they refer to the *bitch* category, however they are referring to the dogs. Not you."

Penny's mouth dropped open with a squawk, reminding Addison of a parrot, and she had to smother a burst of laughter behind her hand. Even Phillip's cheeks were quivering with the effort to control himself.

"Ladies. Ladies," he said, trying to act the impartial host. "Let's not allow a little healthy competition ruin the afternoon."

"What competition?" Julia asked innocently. "Penny doesn't even have a dog to handle anymore. There is no competition."

Penny's grip on her martini glass tightened until Addison thought the neck would snap. "Maybe it was *you* who stole Lilly," she accused Julia. "You just couldn't stand to see me beat you again, could you?"

Julia yawned. "I'm not quite as obsessed with winning as you. I have a life." As though bored with the conversation, she turned to Phillip. "I'm going to go get some more of that quiche before it's gone."

"Of course. Enjoy yourself."

"See you on Saturday, Addison?" Julia gave her a wink.

"Four o'clock. As usual. See you then." Addison felt a little ray of hope burn inside. At least not everyone was willing to believe the rumors. When Addison turned back, Penny had already stormed off. Her day was getting better and better.

Phillip was shaking his head at Penny's retreating back. "Ignore her," he told Addison. "She's extremely competitive and is upset about what happened, and for good reason. But it wasn't your fault."

"Thank you for saying so," she said with an earnest smile.

It felt good to have his faith in her innocence. Of course, he wouldn't have invited her if he didn't believe her, but it was still nice to hear it while surrounded by so many people who would disagree with him.

"Besides," he said, lowering his voice, "Alistair couldn't have won for a fourth time in a row. Everyone knows that Lilly is past her prime. She was lucky to win last year. So don't let anyone here ruin your afternoon."

How could she be upset when she got to spend the afternoon with Phillip? Letting it roll off her back, she smiled up at him. "I don't intend to."

Phillip grinned down at her. At that moment, one of the security guards approached him and murmured something too low for Addison to hear.

Phillip nodded briefly and turned back to her. "I'm so sorry, Addison. This is Carson, my head of security. I'll have to go deal with this. Why don't you order a drink from the bar? I'll be right back."

"Of course," she said. "Take your time. You're the host."

He reached out and squeezed her hand. A pulse of energy coursed through her like he'd just transferred all his feelings into her with that one touch. He was totally into her. She just knew it.

With a grin on her face, she and Princess drifted over to the bar set up at the edge of the grass beneath a huge umbrella. Her doxie trotted next to her with the same tilt of her chin as Addison's, the one that said she belonged there. Even among the Best of Breeds and Best in Shows, Princess knew she was just as good as they were.

Addison looped Princess's leash onto the dog-minding hooks on the side of the counter and waited for the bartender to finish organizing his bottles. When he turned around, she scowled. "What are you doing here?"

Felix flashed a winning smile at her like he was actually happy to see her—unlike how she felt about him at the moment. "Well, hello to you too. Can I get you a drink, madam? Might I suggest a Dog's Lunch, or perhaps a Hair of the Dog? Or maybe you'd like a replay of the other night?" He waggled his dark eyebrows at her.

She made a repulsed, throaty sound. "No thank you. I'd rather forget about that."

"I meant the drink. What were you thinking about?" He clicked his tongue teasingly. "You should feel flattered. I've decided to name it after you. I've called it the Head *Turner*. It certainly seemed to turn *your* head."

Her scowl faded slightly. He'd named it after her? Not that it mattered. He probably did that kind of thing all the time to impress girls.

"You mean that pink drink you probably drugged?"

Felix was already grabbing bottles and mixing them into a cocktail shaker. "Drugged?"

"That's the only way I can explain why I lost all my marbles," she said with the most aloof air she could manage.

"Or maybe," he said, "it was because you'd been dying to kiss me ever since the cocktail mixer."

Some guys just can't take a hint. "Yeah right. I plead temporary insanity. Besides, I'm interested in someone else."

She glanced around the veranda, hoping Phillip would come back soon. More and more of the guests were beginning to throw her sharp glances. Addison could feel the daggers. Surely no one would cause a scene if he was there.

The clinking ice in Felix's cocktail mixer fell silent as he froze. "Who? Not Phillip Montgomery?"

"The third," she added airily.

He pulled a face. "Is he your Mr. Perfect?"

"Yes. We're practically dating now." *Kind of*, she

added in her head. They were sort of on a date now, so technically that meant they were almost dating, pretty much. Right?

He shook his head, pouring the familiar bright pink liquid into a glass. "Not that guy."

"Yes, that guy," she said. "He is perfect. He's a gentleman, he's got looks, manners, a good job—"

Felix glanced around, careful not to be overheard. "Being a rich man's son isn't a job. It's lucky genetics. It's not like he worked hard for it."

Addison frowned. Come to think of it, she didn't really know exactly what Phillip did for work, or much about him at all, really. But those were all just details. They would come in time. They had the rest of their lives together, after all.

"Well, he fundraises for good causes," she said. "Which is even more impressive. It means he's selfless."

"Well, I guess when you have nothing else to occupy your time, you have to do something." Felix set the drink in front of her.

She grinned over the bar. "Jealous much?"

"Desperate much?"

Her grin vanished. "What is that supposed to mean?"

"I called it the moment I met you. I knew you were desperate enough to jump at any guy who looked your way."

"Obviously not any guy. I didn't jump at you."

"I know a pool table that would disagree." The way his eyes roamed over her made her knees shake.

A flash of her visit to Joe's Dive and the memory of Felix's touch came to her. She could practically feel the billiard cloth rubbing against her skin.

While Felix set a gold bowl of Evian down for Princess, Addison slid onto one of the stools to hide her sudden weakness and took a gulp of her drink. She was just tired is all. Or nervous. Yes. She was nervous about seeing Phillip, not Felix. How could the two possibly compare? Felix was like the antagonist. The villain to Phillip's hero.

"He's not the one for you," Felix told Addison flatly. "You just want him to be."

Addison gaped at him like he'd just said he hadn't seen the movie *Lord of the Rings*. "What are you talking about? Phillip's utterly perfect. I'd be crazy not to want him."

"Are you trying to convince me or yourself?"

There was that cocky, all-knowing look again, like he saw right through her. It was an uncomfortable feeling. Something new. Like someone seeing her first thing in the morning with a rat's nest for hair, no makeup protecting her, and morning breath. It was unnerving.

She shifted uncomfortably and took another sip. "You don't even know me."

"You forget that I do. Remember?" He tapped the side of his head. "I hear all. I see all. And I saw you coming a mile away, sweetheart."

"I'm not your sweetheart," she snapped. "And you only think you know it all. But you won't bother to use your knowledge to help me find the show dogs."

Picking up his cloth, he began wiping down the counter. "That's *your* problem. Not mine."

She hopped to her feet, glaring across the counter. "You arrogant—"

"Addison." Phillip's voice brought her up short.

She quickly rearranged her expression into an innocent smile and turned around. "Phillip."

"Sorry about that," he said. "I'm all yours now. Would you like the grand tour of the house?"

"That would be lovely." She leaned to grab Princess's leash and whispered over the counter. "He's going to give me the grand tour." She threw Felix her best eyebrow waggle.

Phillip offered her his arm and Addison slid hers into place, feeling like a puzzle piece had just found its home. A subtle squeeze of his firm bicep told her it was a very nice home.

She gave Felix a dazzling smile over her shoulder, batting her eyelashes. "Thank you for the drink."

"You're welcome, madam," he said with a surprising amount of professionalism that made her feel more than a little childish.

The chatter of the guests died down as Phillip led her and Princess inside his mansion. Once she was hidden from all the piercing stares, she realized just how on edge she'd been. But now she was all alone with Phillip.

"Where's Baxter today?" she asked.

"Oh, probably sleeping somewhere. We went for a big run this morning before the fundraiser started."

"You like to run?"

"Yes. But not just run. I join at least one triathlon a year."

And it showed. She supposed that's how he occupied his time. When was the last time Felix entered a triathlon?

Although Phillip's home was well over a hundred years old, he had rather modern tastes in furniture and style. Addison's expression might have displayed a serene interest—at least, that's what she was going for—but her insides were doing cartwheels as they went from room to room, each more grand than the last.

Princess took it all in with an air of "been there, done that." Addison wondered if she was faking it too, since she was used to running around a tiny one-bedroom apartment.

Floral aromas tickled Addison's nose when they entered the sitting room. She inhaled deeply, recognizing the light scent in the air. She found a giant crystal vase of periwinkle hydrangeas on the table. She stopped a moment to smell them.

"Mmm. My favorite," she said.

When she turned back, she caught Phillip gazing at her. She blushed and looked away, feigning interest in a sculpture. They wandered through halls lined with gold-framed artwork, past rooms filled with high-end furniture and a grand pianoforte or two.

"Do you play?" she asked.

"No. I just enjoy the sound. Sometimes my guests play when they're here."

"Well, you have a beautiful home."

"Thank you." He seemed less interested in his surroundings than he was in her. "I'm happy to open it to people for such a good cause. Besides it's a good excuse to throw a party. I enjoy entertaining."

She noticed another security guard stationed at the end of the long hall, his posture rigid, as though he was tensed and ready to tackle someone. "Are your parties usually this"—she looked for the right word—"secure?"

"Oh, you mean the security? It's just a precaution." Phillip barely took note of the guard when they passed him, like he was a houseplant.

"Because of the missing dogs during the cocktail mixer?"

"Yes." He eyed her expression. "Don't pay any attention to the media and people like Penny Peacock. They just want someone to blame."

Addison laughed humorlessly. "So does the rest of the city, it seems." She sighed. "But it's good that you're taking precautions to protect the dogs here today. I just hope the missing show dogs are okay."

"The police are on the case, so it's only a matter of time before they turn up."

She didn't exactly want to explain that a serial killer was taking up all their time and resources. That life wasn't all pianofortes and crystal vases, and there was no reason to believe they'd simply "turn up." But the fact that Phillip was trying to comfort her made her cheeks flush again. She sighed, giving his bicep another squeeze.

"I'm sure you're right," she said. "It's not easy to keep a pack of dogs hidden without anyone noticing."

"I'm sure it will turn out all right and everyone will stop searching for a scapegoat. Your name will be cleared soon enough. Don't worry. And if there's anything I can do to help in the meantime, don't hesitate to ask."

"Thank you." She smiled gratefully, but she couldn't stop thinking about the poor missing dogs and worrying about their fate.

They came to a stop at the bottom of a staircase curving up to the second and third floors. "The third-story terrace has a great view of Pacific Heights. Shall we?"

"Of course."

He led the way up the marble staircase and through a drawing room. They had the terrace all to themselves. Princess found a spot in the sun and plopped down for a nap, sprawling out on her back like she was working on her tan.

The view really was amazing. The grounds sprawled out, the grass mowed in a perfect grid, like it was a chessboard and Phillip's guests the chess pieces. People walked their dogs while attendants followed behind ready to clean up after them. Manicured trees stood at attention down either side of the enclosed property, giving the opulent estate a sense of privacy, of distance from the busy city.

It was all so different from the life she grew up knowing. Her mother certainly wouldn't have left if her dad had all this. What would anyone have to complain about? To worry about?

Ever since her dad had told her that bankruptcy was a real possibility, she'd worried about his new wife Dora. Addison had been ecstatic for her father when they got married five years earlier. She was the sweetest woman, and her dad deserved no less. But as sweet as she was, Addison knew firsthand how finances could destroy a relationship. She watched it happen to her mom and dad.

Addison's father had been through enough the first time around. She just didn't want to see it happen to him again. Would this strain prove to be too much for him and Dora? What if he didn't sell the corner store in time and they went bankrupt? Would their marriage survive?

She considered her surroundings again with an appreciation of what it was like to go without. *What a life*, she thought. And the guy who owned all of it was interested in *her*. It really could be a rags-to-riches story. A dream come true. They'd certainly never have to worry about money. Heck, neither would her dad or Dora. Not when even a single pianoforte would bail them out.

"It's beautiful," Addison breathed.

"Not as beautiful as you."

She turned to Phillip to find him gazing into her eyes, as if all their surroundings, the opulence, the luxury was nothing compared to her. Reaching up, he held her chin as he dipped his face to hers for a kiss.

Now this, she thought, *I could definitely get used to.*

But just before their lips touched, there was a change in the atmosphere around them. A buzzing of agitated voices reached their ears.

The veranda was too far down for them to pick out

specific words, but a woman's shriek echoed across the yard. There was the soft rustle of quality fabric as though the entire party was moving as one, oxfords and heels clicking on the stone.

Phillip and Addison leaned over the bannister to look down on the party below. Addison was too short to see, but Phillip's square jaw clenched at whatever he saw.

"What's going on?" she asked.

"I'm not sure. I should go and check it out."

Addison tugged on Princess's leash but she resisted, enjoying her sunny nap. Bending down, Addison scooped her up and rushed to keep up with Phillip. They found the head of security at the base of the sweeping staircase to the foyer. Carson had removed his secret agent glasses, so things must have been serious.

"Carson, what's happening out there?" Phillip called down to him as he descended.

"It's the dogs, sir."

Phillip came to a stop at the bottom of the stairs, his chest moving evenly. Whereas Addison's rush through the house left her breathing a little heavier than usual, but then again, she was no triathlete.

"What about them?" Phillip asked.

"Some of them, well"—Carson hesitated—"they're gone."

8

Pack Mentality

"The dogs are gone?" Phillip repeated, cool and calm. But his stare was so intense, he might as well have been yelling at Carson. "As in 'disappeared from my property'? How many?"

The tone of voice and the way he held himself, chest puffed up, looking down his nose at Carson, spoke of a quiet fury. If it had been someone else, someone not used to stress and pressure like a security guard would be, Addison thought they might have melted beneath his steady gaze.

"Three, sir."

Phillip's nose rose an inch. "How could you let that happen?"

Without waiting for an answer, he pushed his way past Carson and headed through the house to the backyard. Addison held Princess close and rushed to keep up in her heels, which clicked on the marble floors, echoing around the absurdly cavernous hall. Princess grumbled as the jostling slowly dislodged the fascinator from her head.

Once Addison crossed the threshold to the veranda, exclaims and excited chatter accosted her ears like an angry hive of bees. The guests huddled around the tall wrought-iron fence at the edge of the property. The wall of bodies slowed Carson and Phillip down, and Addison was able to catch up, following in their wake as the guests made way.

She couldn't let herself fall behind. More dogs had gone missing. It had to be connected to the cocktail mixer somehow. Twice in one week couldn't be a coincidence. She held Princess tighter, like she might disappear right out of her arms.

Phillip pressed his way to the front of the crowd as Carson updated him. Addison strained to listen in.

"I'm not sure how it happened, sir. We're still looking into it. We have guards posted at every possible entrance. No one has left with any other dog but their own."

Phillip wheeled on the head of security, coming nose to nose with him. "Obviously someone did. Now what are you doing about it?"

"We have the place on lockdown. No one in or out. The police are on their way."

"Good," he said, turning away. "Keep me posted. And find my dog, Baxter."

Carson nodded and turned back around. He reached up to his earpiece and murmured something, but Addison missed what he said because the gathering crowd quickly swallowed him. She decided to stick with Phillip.

When she broke through the thick mass of people, she stumbled into a semicircle of open space. The commotion centered around three guests arguing with the security guards who had checked her in at the door.

"Just calm down sir. The police are on their way," guard one was saying.

A man in a toupee wagged a finger in his face. "The

police? The police? Then what are *you* here for? What were you doing when they disappeared?"

"Yeah, what are you doing to find them?" another man asked. He had his back to Addison, but she'd recognize that coiffed hair anywhere. Rex Harris.

A young woman with tears sparkling in her eyes ran over. "Phillip. Phillip." She grabbed the front of his sports jacket. "He's gone. Someone took my Lionel. You said it was safe here."

"Don't worry, Kayleigh." He patted her hands and gently dislodged them. "I'm taking care of it." He handed her his pocket square, and she dabbed at her eyes.

"You'll be lucky if I don't sue," said the man in the toupee, shaking his finger at Phillip.

"This is a disaster," Phillip muttered under his breath so only Addison could hear. "How could this have happened? I don't understand. I took precautions."

He looked distraught. In fact, she thought he looked the same way she probably had when the dogs had gone missing under her care. His body tensed like he wanted to take action, but it seemed there was nothing to do but wait for the police.

Addison laid a comforting hand on his arm. "It's not your fault. You did everything you could. Maybe they got out of the yard somehow? Found a gap in the fence, or dug a hole maybe."

Now she sounded like Felix. She recalled the way he'd comforted her at the cocktail party, tried to convince her it was going to be okay when all the facts pointed to the worst-case scenario. But now she understood why he did it, because she wanted to do the same for Phillip.

"My Rosie would never run away," Rex said to her. "She's too well behaved. She was stolen. I know it."

"My property was secure," Phillip said. "I took every precaution I could for this party."

"If it was secure, then how did the dogs get off the property without anyone noticing?" Rex practically shook with anger, his coiffed hair falling down in strands across his tall forehead.

Addison saw a finger rise from among the crowd to point straight at her. It was Penny's.

"It must have been Addison Turner," the famed handler called out. "It's the cocktail mixer all over again."

"What?" Addison sputtered, practically laughing at the absurdity of it. "Me?"

Phillip stepped forward. "Absolutely not. She was with me the entire time. She had nothing to do with it."

But Penny's comment sent a ripple of whispers and glances through the crowd. Those who hadn't recognized her now put a face to the name they'd all heard circulating the dog show circuit and from the media.

"Funny that she was present during both incidents," Penny noted coolly.

"So were you," Phillip said. "So were all of us."

"You can't blame me for this one," Addison told her. "I'm just a guest here."

"Maybe you had help," she said. "A partner in crime."

There were noises of affirmation scattered among the guests. Addison saw heads nod up and down.

Addison threw up her hands. "Like who?"

A honking horn interrupted her. Through the vines covering the wrought-iron fence, Addison could see a vehicle pull through the private drive to the mansion's back access.

The crowd surged forward, eager to see what the commotion was about. Addison was bulldozed closer to a set of gates in the fence separating the yard from the driveway. She cradled Princess close to protect her from bumps and elbows, afraid for a moment that they'd be trampled.

The van crawled up to the iron gates that blocked its

path. The driver honked the horn impatiently, but the security guards kept it firmly shut.

Guards one and two rushed ahead of everyone. They waved their hands in the air to signal the van to stop. Guard two moved a hand across his throat in a kill-the-engine motion.

The van door popped open and the impatient driver jumped down onto the flagstone driveway. It was Red Bra girl.

She took in the gathered crowd from the other side of the iron bars. "What's going on?"

Carson pushed his way through the mob with Baxter on a leash. Phillip rushed over and grabbed the leash, bending down to his English mastiff, like he had to touch him to believe he was safe.

Carson stalked up to the gate, nose to nose with Red Bra. "Where have you been?" he asked.

"The bar. Making a supply run." She was eyeing the crowd, clearly confused.

Guard one turned to his boss. "This was the only vehicle to leave the premises."

"Did anyone search this van when it left?" Phillip demanded.

The security guards glanced at each other. Eventually one said, "Yeah, but it was just full of empty barrels and boxes."

"How do you know they were empty?" Carson asked them. "Did you look inside of them?"

They silently conferred with each other again before shaking their heads.

Carson swore. "Who was in charge of this vehicle!?" he called out, as though it was the guests' job to know and not his.

"I'm the manager." A deep voice carried across the crowd from behind Addison.

She turned, along with everyone else, to see Felix walking down the drive. He came to a stop next to her and crossed his arms.

"How can I help you?" he asked. But with the scowl on his face and his head cocked like he was ready for a fight, he didn't come off as very helpful at the moment.

Carson faced him, calling his tough guy bluff. "Were you aware that your employee left the premises?"

"Of course. I'm the one who sent her. We ran out of supplies. She went to the bar to stock up on a few items." Felix was close enough to Addison that she heard him mutter to her, "The Head Turner was more popular than I expected."

Out of the corner of her eye, she saw Penny take note of the exchange. The look on her pinched face made Addison's toes curl in her pink heels with annoyance.

Red Bra grabbed the iron bars and stared helplessly through them at Felix and Carson, as if she'd already been condemned. "What have I done wrong?"

"How long ago did you leave?" Carson asked her.

Felix stepped in and answered before she could, keeping the focus on him. "About an hour ago."

"That was when I last saw Gumball," the man with the toupee said.

"This guy was at the cocktail mixer last weekend too," Rex said, indicating Felix as "this guy." "Maybe *he* stole those dogs."

Penny Peacock turned to Addison, almost gleefully. "Looks like we've found your partner in crime," she said, eliciting a sudden uproar from those around her. It sounded like calls for blood to Addison's ears.

"She had nothing to do with this," Phillip yelled over them all. "She's my guest here."

"I saw them talking together earlier at the bar," Kayleigh said between shuddering sobs.

"Probably conspiring," Rex added.

Addison shot daggers across the stone driveway at Rex, sorry she'd considered him attractive for even a second. "I was ordering a drink."

"They must be working together," toupee agreed.

Penny never said another word. She didn't have to— her nasty theory had taken root and was growing all on its own.

Addison threw her hands up, ready to argue, but Felix sidled close to her and muttered under his breath. "You're dealing with a mob mentality here. You're going to lose. Stop before they pull out their torches and pitchforks and you have a real problem on your hands."

She glared at him like this was somehow his fault. Heck, maybe it was. Maybe he did steal the dogs. After all, she thought, he was so determined not to help her find the guilty party. Maybe that was because *he* was the guilty party. But by the looks on everyone's faces, he was probably right about keeping quiet, so she took his advice.

She held Princess close to her chest protectively, like someone might want to get revenge through her own dog, an eye for an eye. "Yeah, well it looks like it's not just my problem anymore," she informed Felix coolly. "Now it's yours too."

9

End of the Tether

Whispers seemed to follow Addison wherever she went in Phillip's mansion. Whispers, gossip, secrets, and lies.

The estate had seemed so large a couple of hours before, but now that no one was allowed to leave, the place felt stifling. It was stuffed with shifting eyes, pointing fingers, subtle head nods, and the whispers. Whispers that seemed to follow Addison no matter where she tried to hide from all those suspicious looks.

She thought that would have stopped now that there was a new suspect: Felix. But it hadn't. The speculations had merely changed.

Addison could hear them murmuring with their backs turned in their exclusive clusters in the foyer, in the halls, on the terrace. Their voices grew louder as the police statements were taken and the alcohol had time to sink in: Addison and Felix were in league with each other in black market dog trading. No, an illegal dog fighting business. No, they were criminal dog breeders out for a monopoly on the best dog litters in the country.

Some of the guests eyed Princess, as though Addison should feel guilty that she still had her dog. Or maybe it was because they were considering stealing the doxie out of revenge. Addison rarely let Princess down except to drink water or stretch her legs on the grass in the back-yard. Even then she was always on a leash that was wrapped securely around Addison's wrist.

Whispers, gossip, secrets, lies. Addison circulated through the property, attempting to overhear them all without being too obvious about it. The last thing she wanted was to draw more attention to herself, but even more dogs were at stake now. She needed to start look-ing for clues. To figure out how to find the dogs and get them home safe—and hopefully to clear her name. With or without Felix's help.

As she passed the drawing room, she overheard Phil-lip talking to the head of security, or rather, *at* him, as he paced back and forth across the marble flooring.

"How could you let this happen?" he demanded.

"Well, sir. We—"

"What am I paying you for?" he interrupted. "I thought you were supposed to have this place secure."

"We did everything—"

"Your company was supposed to be the best in town."

Addison didn't blame Phillip for being upset. Those three dogs disappeared right from under his nose, in his own home. She imagined he felt like she did the night of the cocktail mixer.

Pretending to appreciate a painting in the hallway, she peeked into the drawing room to see Phillip rubbing a hand over his clean-shaven jaw. The sight of him so fraz-zled filled her with guilt. He was the last person she wanted to spy on.

Besides, she already knew Phillip couldn't be guilty. She just knew it. Someone whose eyes sparkled like diamonds couldn't be evil. Phillip practically glowed with angelic innocence.

Addison tiptoed past the doors to sneak away, but then she heard him call out, "Addison!"

Totally busted. She waited in the hallway, trying to think of some excuse. However, when he caught up to her, he was the one who looked guilty.

"I'm so sorry," he said. "I know I've been a bit distracted. I haven't been ignoring you, I promise."

"Of course," she said. "I completely understand. There's so much that you have to deal with."

He sighed. "Not exactly the fundraising event I had planned."

"It seems someone else had their own plans for your party."

"I'm sorry that you got caught up in all this." And he did look remorseful.

He was so sweet.

"It's not your fault. They just need someone to blame." *I just wish it wasn't me.*

The tension around his eyes and perfectly sculpted lips relaxed. He slowly reached out to her, and she thought he might try to kiss her again. But then frantic barking and yelling carried down the hall, echoing throughout the expansive home.

Phillip's hand froze in midair and he gave a small, frustrated groan. "I'd better go check that out."

The tension was getting to humans and canines alike. After being cooped up for so long, it wasn't the first dogfight that had broken out. It was only a matter of time before the humans started to snap and the first punch was thrown. She just hoped she wasn't on the receiving end.

Addison sighed in disappointment as he walked away. But that disappointment quickly turned to annoyance.

Annoyance at the situation, the unknown surrounding the poor lost dogs, at her own vulnerability and public disgrace.

Not only had the new round of missing dogs seemed to convince people that Addison was somehow involved, but her date with Phillip had been ruined. And for some reason, the only person she could think of to blame was Felix. Not that it was his fault, exactly. It wasn't like he took the dogs himself. Or had he?

Felix was the one in charge of that van and had sent it back to the bar, after all. Maybe he and Red Bra were in on it together. If that was the case then Addison needed to find him.

Spinning on her heel, she stormed outside to find Felix so she could . . . well she didn't know what yet. Rub it in his face now that he was the one accused? To spy on him, maybe even interrogate him until he snapped like a brittle nail?

The first place Addison looked for him was at the temporary bar near the lawn, but when she didn't find him there she wandered around to the private drive where the van had been parked. Felix was nowhere to be seen, but his van was still there. For now. A tow truck was currently backing up to it. She watched the truck driver jump out to speak with the police.

Making her way around the other side of the house, she froze when she heard Felix's voice nearby.

"I'm sorry," he said. "It's not like I planned for this to happen. I was bartending the whole time."

Addison and Princess peered around the corner of the old mansion. Felix had his back to her. The muscles under his shirt looked tense as he talked on his phone.

He kicked a stone in frustration. "I know this is a big deal, but there's got to be a way to fix it."

It sounded like he was talking about the missing dogs.

She wondered who was on the other end. There was only one way to find out.

Glancing over her shoulder, she checked to see if anyone was watching. Once she was sure the coast was clear, she snuck behind him and into a gap in the pruned hedges he was pacing in front of.

"Who cares what a bunch of uptight customers say?" he growled into the phone.

Uptight? Who was he calling uptight? Well, okay, some of them she could see, but that didn't include her, did it?

She crept closer, but thick tree branches blocked her view of him. Setting Princess down on the ground, she shuffled even closer and swept a branch out of the way to see him better.

He was pacing back and forth, his posture stiff. He was actually a little scary-looking when he was mad. He might have cleaned up as well as some of the gentlemen at the party, but looks could be deceiving. Felix was definitely no gentleman. Addison was pretty sure he could hold his own in a fight.

"I had nothing to do with it," Felix said. "Come on, you've known me for four years." He ran a rough hand through his hair, gripping it in frustration as he listened. "But this is *my* livelihood too."

Livelihood? Addison wondered if he was talking to his boss. Maybe he was getting fired.

"But I've been banking on the extra side work. I've got bills to pay. . . . Yeah. Fine. I understand. . . . Good-bye."

Felix hung up and jammed the phone into his pocket. He closed his eyes and exhaled slowly.

Addison shrank back from her viewpoint. Felix might have deserved a taste of his own medicine, to be the one accused after he refused to help her. But that didn't mean he deserved to get fired.

Guilt tickled at her insides for listening in. Some spy *she* made.

She began to sneak away before he discovered her hiding in the bushes, prying into his personal affairs. But that's what private eyes like Dick Tracy did, right? Surely they never felt guilty while on a stakeout or squeezing information out of informants.

Addison took another step backward. Her foot came down, and there was a loud snap as a twig broke under her weight. She froze.

"Who's there?" Felix said.

"Crap," she hissed. Now it was definitely time to scram.

Addison spun around, intending to bolt before Felix discovered her, but when she turned, she came face to face with a half-naked woman. A yelp escaped from her lungs before she realized it was only a moss-covered statue. She clamped a hand over her mouth, but it was too late. She'd outed herself.

The grass swished outside her shelter as Felix approached. "All right. Come on out."

Addison searched for an escape route, but she'd trapped herself in an alcove of sorts. Like a romantic little nook, nestled into a horseshoe of vegetation long since overgrown and forgotten.

She glanced at Princess for help, but the doxie was too busy sniffing the ground. Giving up, Addison tried to act natural. She slung an arm around the statue like she was just hanging out there by complete coincidence.

When Felix brushed the hedge aside and his eyes landed on her, his scowl eased slightly. "Oh, it's you."

She gave him a look like *Fancy meeting you here*. "Oh, hello."

"Eavesdropping much?"

She wrinkled her nose at him. "Paranoid much? The

world doesn't revolve around you, you know. Princess had to pee." She waved at her dog in evidence. Thankfully, Princess decided to corroborate her story and squatted near the base of the statue.

He narrowed an eye suspiciously. "In here?"

"Princess has a shy bladder," Addison said. "She's a lady."

He shrugged it off, either believing her weak story or because he didn't really care. "Well in case you didn't catch every word, I've been laid off."

"I'm sorry."

His head snapped to her like he thought maybe she was being sarcastic.

"No, really. That sucks," she said, giving him a small, earnest frown. "Trust me. I know what you're going through. I'm facing losing my own income." Not just her income, but her business, her passion, her dream.

"Well, it's not indefinitely," he said. "It's just until things calm down with this damn dognapping business. Joe doesn't want to lose me, but he also has to appease the customers who are calling for blood. He does a lot of private gigs for these rich types." He waved a tired hand in the general direction of the house. "As long as I'm working for him, people are threatening to cancel their private bookings through his bar."

He took a seat on the curved marble bench in the center of the alcove.

She sat down next to him. "That's not fair."

"I'm associated with this whole dognapping crime, fair or not." He shrugged. "Isn't that exactly what happened to you? Was it fair then?"

She was surprised by his sincerity, at this temporary truce that seemed to form between them. When he was the one who admitted it, it took the satisfying "Aha! In your face" feeling out of it. Now Addison just kind of felt bad for him. Maybe for both of them.

"No. You're right," she said. "So, are you going to look for a new job now?"

"A new job? No way." He shook his head. "This gig pays great. Besides that will take too long. I'm on a tight deadline."

She smirked. "Loan shark got a hit out on you?"

He gave her a withering look. "Ha-ha. Very funny."

"So then what are you going to do?"

He sat up straight and seemed to consider the question for a moment. "I'm going to clear my name. Prove that I had nothing to do with the stolen dogs."

"What?" She laughed, for what seemed like the first time in days. "Sure. *Now* you're interested in helping me find the real dog snatcher?"

"I didn't say anything about helping *you*." He flashed a wolfish smile. "I just have to prove it wasn't *me*."

She groaned. So much for the truce. "You're a real prince, you know that? Ever hear of a damsel in distress?"

"It's the twenty-first century, sweetheart. Damsels help themselves now. Gender equality and all that."

Addison stood up. "Well good luck then. Things don't look good for you either, you know. After today, the evidence is stacked against you." She grabbed Princess's leash, marching out of the hidden alcove.

"Okay, okay." Felix tugged on Addison's arm and pulled her back inside. "You're right. Things don't look good for me. But how are we going to fix this?"

She snorted. "So now you want my help? Why should I help you? You weren't exactly leaping to my rescue." She remembered his own ultimatum. Shoving her fists on her hips, she stared him down. "What's in it for me?"

"One"—he held up a finger—"we're their two lead

suspects. Or at least as far as the public is concerned we are, and sometimes rumors are all that matters in the service industry. Even if they can't send us to jail, we'll *both* be searching the help wanted ads within a few weeks."

He took a step closer to her until his cologne overpowered the smell of the foliage around them, but she stood her ground. He held up a second finger.

"Two, I'm far too pretty to go to jail. I'll be someone's bitch for sure. And three"—he closed the gap between them until she was staring straight at the lips she was sucking on just a few days before—"they're saying we're in cahoots, that we've somehow set this all up like we're a pair of criminal canine masterminds." Felix reached up and held her chin. "So like it or not, damsel, we're in this together."

She groaned, swatting his hand away. "Fine. I guess two heads are better than one, anyway."

"Great." He rubbed his hands together. "And I'll do it for only ninety percent of Lilly's reward money Alistair Yates offered on the news at the cocktail mixer."

"What?" She balked. "How do you figure that?"

He crossed his arms with a giant grin on his face. "Well, it's my expertise and knowledge that's going to solve the case."

"I don't think so," she said. "Fifty-fifty."

"Sixty-forty and that's my final offer."

Addison gritted her teeth. "Fine. I was going to be nice and offer you a ride, but I'm sure with all your expertise and knowledge you can find your own way home."

"What makes you think I'd need a ride in your girl-mobile?"

"Because your ride is being towed as we speak," she informed him with a satisfied grin. "Probably for evidence."

"What?" Felix's snide grin faltered. He shoved past her, out of the alcove, and circled around to the private driveway.

Addison followed behind smugly. Even Princess seemed a little self-satisfied. When the empty driveway came into view, Felix slowed his steps. He ran a hand through his thick waves, gripping them like he wanted to pull them right out.

He swore under his breath. "My car is in the shop. Joe was letting me use the company van for the week."

"Then I guess you'll need my girl-mobile to solve the crime." Addison patted him on the back, giving him her sweetest smile. "Don't worry. I'll let you have forty percent."

10

Bone of Contention

Addison hit the brakes as she and Felix approached Joe's Dive, which was even divier in the light of day. She whipped into a free space along the street like they were shooting a scene from *Tokyo Drift*.

It took a moment for Felix to release his death grip on the seat. He gave her a look, but said nothing. It's not like he had a choice in transportation. His company van was still being dusted for prints after it was towed at the fundraiser the day before.

Addison tipped her fedora up and studied the joint, watching her mirrors to make sure she hadn't been followed. She felt like a regular gumshoe, ready to crack the canine case. She'd even worn quiet shoes—or gumshoes, if you will—in case she needed to do some sneaking around. The fedora was just a fun accessory, though she decided to skip the trench coat. She was wearing her sexy fifties-style dress, and it would have been a shame to cover it up.

Addison grabbed a notebook from her purse and ran

down a list that already included Kitty Carlisle, Melody, Julia Edwards, and—at Felix's insistence—Phillip Montgomery III.

At least it gave her a reason to see Phillip again, to remind him of what he's missing out on, since she'd probably never hear from him again after what had happened at his fundraiser. Not with all of his guests still blaming her for the missing dogs.

But the first one on her list was Red Bra, which is why they'd come to the bar. She clicked her pen on, holding it at the ready. "So do you think we've missed anyone on our list?" she asked Felix.

"Oh probably about a hundred names."

She glared at him. "I'm serious."

"So am I. But we can only do so much. We're assuming that the dogs were stolen for one of two reasons. Money or competition."

"So who else can we list with competition as their motive?"

"Well, anyone who's had their dog stolen is automatically off the list. They can't exactly show a dog that's supposed to be missing. No competition there."

Addison tapped her pen on the steering wheel. "That still leaves a lot of dogs that have the potential for Best in Show, and the potential for thieving owners. The Western Dog Show is a big competition."

"We have to start somewhere. That's why we've got your customer Julia Edwards."

Addison was reluctant to put Julia on the list, but she recalled how Ms. Edwards had baited Penny Peacock at Phillip's party. There was more than a healthy dose of competition between them.

Felix pointed to the list. "Why Kitty Carlisle? She hasn't competed in years. I thought her dog was too old."

"Yeah, but she got major creep-factor points."

"Creep factor?" He raised a skeptical eyebrow. "So we're basing our investigation off of your heebeegeebees now?"

"No. If that was the case, *you'd* still be on there." She smiled sweetly. "But Kitty was the only one hanging around the stage area when her dog was getting groomed. She could have been casing the joint."

Addison ran through the list of names under the "financial gain" category. "The breeders and owners wouldn't likely steal a dog to sell it for gain," she said. "They compete because they love animals. They wouldn't want anything bad to happen to them. It would have to be someone outside of the competition. One of the staff at the parties."

"Right. Or someone on the outside using them as an inside man. Someone who overlapped both the cocktail mixer and Phillip's fundraiser. That leaves our list of staff to investigate pretty small since there weren't many who worked both."

"Except for you," she said, with a suggestive tone to her voice.

"And you," he shot back.

She stuck out her tongue at him. "Don't forget Red Bra. She was at both events too."

His forehead wrinkled. "Who's Red Bra?"

"The server with the red bra. The one you were flirting with at the cocktail mixer and at Joe's Dive."

"You mean Charlotte?" He laughed. "Jealous much?"

She felt her cheeks warm. "You wish."

Gripping the wheel, she psyched herself up for her first interrogation. She could sense Felix eyeing her from the passenger seat.

"Are you okay?" he asked her.

"Yeah. You know, just going over the plan in my head. So how are we going to do this? Are we going to drill her? Good cop, bad cop kind of thing?" She punched the palm of her hand in case it wasn't clear who the bad cop was.

"No. We're going to sit down with Charlotte and have a chat thing. Maybe a snack, if you're good."

"And if she doesn't spill?" Addison punched her palm again.

"Stop with the gumshoe talk. And what's with the fedora?" Plucking it off her head, he tossed it in the backseat of her convertible. "Charlotte is a friend."

"But she was the one who drove the van away from Phillip's house. And that's the only way those dogs could have been taken off the property."

"We don't know that for sure yet. The police are still searching the van for clues. Besides, I know Charlotte wouldn't do something like that."

"How do you know?"

"Because I trust her," he said, in an end-of-story kind of way.

But Addison wasn't about to take his word for it. She'd be the judge of that.

"We're just going to see if she knows anything," Felix said. "Maybe she's heard something from the other staff. She hangs out with some of them outside of work."

"And you don't?"

"No. I go home after work. I tend to keep my work life and personal life separate." He reached for the door handle. "Come on. I've already texted her. She's expecting us."

Addison looked at him in surprise. She thought he'd be more the party type. But she kept this thought to herself as they got out of the car and headed across the street to Joe's Dive.

The afternoon sun hit the dirt on the bar's windows, making them look like they hadn't been cleaned in years.

Addison skirted around a suspicious stain on the sidewalk that she thought could use a good hosing off. Beneath the grime and the neglect, she imagined the bar could be a pretty cute place if Joe took a little pride in it.

Felix held the door open for her and they stepped into the dim interior. The dirt caking the windows didn't allow much light to filter in, but she figured those already drinking at one in the afternoon probably wanted to hide in dark corners.

Addison scanned the room and spotted Red Bra, or Charlotte, right away. She was picking up an order of drinks at the bar.

Felix waved and she smiled back, nodding her head to the side of the room. Heading for the corner, Felix slid into a booth. Addison sat across from him. She watched as Charlotte finished serving a table their sandwiches and beer.

"So when are we going to go talk to your assistant?" Felix punched his own palm, making fun of her earlier good cop, bad cop routine.

"Not yet," she said. "I can't just roll up and ask her, 'So, steal any dogs lately?' We've got to be crafty about it. If she's hiding something, then she's hiding it well. Otherwise the police would have arrested her by now."

Besides, Addison really liked Melody. She didn't like even suspecting her, but facts were facts. However, if it turned out she really was innocent, she didn't want to lose Melody as an assistant because she'd wrongly accused her.

Charlotte finished up with her table and went to talk to an older guy with a shaved head behind the bar. The guy nodded and held up a hand showing five fingers. Charlotte nodded and took off her apron, crossing over to join their booth.

"Hey Felix," she said, with a smile Addison thought too cheerful and friendly to be real.

"Hey," he said. "Thanks for talking to us."

"No problem. Joe says I've only got five minutes. We're working short staffed today. Jayden never showed up for his shift. Apparently he came down with food poisoning or something." She dropped her voice. "Between you and me, I think he helped himself to some of that leftover quiche after it had been out in the sun too long."

Addison took her pen and pad out of her purse and wrote down JAYDEN.

When she looked up, both Felix and Charlotte were staring at her.

"Don't worry about her," Felix told his friend. "How have you been?"

"Okay. It could have been worse. I didn't get much backlash from the Montgomery event. I just got pulled from the high-profile events for the week. But what about you?" She laid her hand on Felix's arm. "Joe said you're done."

Felix shrugged. "I'm only laid off for the time being. I'll be fine. I have some savings set aside."

"But what about your down payment?" Charlotte asked. "You won't save up enough by the deadline."

Addison frowned. *Down payment?* She resisted the urge to start jotting down questions she needed to ask Felix too.

"That's exactly why we need your help, Charlotte."

"Of course, anything for you." She beamed at him. "What did you have in mind?"

It was like Addison wasn't even in the room. Okay, well, she hadn't really said anything, so that might be why. She pretended to jot a note down on the pad just to feel useful.

Felix lowered his voice, as though he might be overheard. "If we can figure out whodunit, then I can clear my name."

"Our names," Addison cut in.

"Our names," Felix corrected. "And I can pick up extra gigs to make up for lost pay. I can still make the deadline."

DEADLINE? Addison wrote down.

"Oh sure," Charlotte said. "I'll help if I can. What did you need to know?" She sat up straighter, finally pulling away from Felix. Not that Addison noticed or anything.

"When you were at the Montgomery event getting ready to head back to the bar, did you see anyone hanging around? One of the guests, maybe? Did anyone help you load up the empty kegs or crates?"

"Not that I can remember." She glanced back at the bald man behind the bar, who Addison assumed was Joe.

Joe gave her a pointed look, tapping his watch.

"I can't say for sure," she added quickly. "It was a pretty busy event. I was in and out making kitchen runs around that time."

"How about any of the other staff from either that event or the cocktail mixer? Have you heard any talk going around?"

"No. Nothing much just—"

"Charlotte!" Joe barked from behind the bar. "Orders are backing up. Break's over."

"Coming!" she called, slipping out of the stall.

Addison leaned forward, not ready to let her go. " 'Just' what? What were you going to say?"

Charlotte raised a red bra–strapped shoulder. "Just the usual gossip, but nothing that would be of any help to you."

Addison wanted to ask her more, but Joe dinged the bell sitting on the counter and threw her a sour look.

Charlotte rolled her eyes.

"Thanks for talking to us," Felix said.

"Yeah, no problem. Sorry I can't be of more help." She gave him an apologetic wave over her shoulder as she ran back for her apron. "Good luck!"

The moment they were out of the bar, Addison returned to her bubbly self. "Okay, where to next?"

Felix gave her a weird look.

"What?" she asked.

"What was that?"

"What was what?" She unconsciously reached for her hair to check that every curl was perfectly in place.

"You could have been a little nicer."

She began walking back to the car, not meeting his gaze. "There's something off about her. I just don't trust Red Bra."

He opened his mouth to speak, but she held up a hand. "It's not jealousy."

"What's the big deal about wearing a red bra, anyway? Is it a fashion faux pas?"

"Nothing's wrong with it. I have plenty of colored bras. Red ones, pink ones, blue ones, animal print ones . . ." She tapered off as his eyes drifted down to her dress's neckline, as though he was wondering what color she was wearing today. "But I don't show everyone. That's reserved for VIP eyes only."

"Really? How does one get on this VIP list?" His lips curled into that hungry wolfish smile she recalled from the night at the bar.

As they passed a bespoke tailors shop, she glanced into the window. "Sorry," she said. "It's a black tie event."

Addison paused to gaze at the storefront display. Three mannequins lined up in the window were dressed in quality suits, handmade from the finest fabrics.

"There's just something about a man in a suit, you know?"

"Can't say I do," he said.

"A well-tailored suit is to a woman what lingerie is to a man."

"I can assure you that's not true," he said, eyeing up her neckline again like he had Superman's X-ray vision.

"Oh but it is," she argued. "It's romantic. It's mysterious. It takes a man's game to a whole new level. Heck, it might even clean *you* up a little."

Addison eyed up the tux in the middle, practically drooling as she imagined Felix filling it out to perfection. "*Men in Black* wouldn't be the same if Will Smith ran around in sweatpants. James Bond would otherwise be just a ruffian, but the suit transforms him into a gentleman. A tuxedo on Bruce Wayne is as powerful as the Batsuit on Batman."

When she finally turned away from the window, Felix was staring at her. "What's your obsession with movies, anyway?"

The abrupt question caught her off guard, and it took her a moment to recover. She blinked, wondering why he cared. "My parents ran a corner store that rented videos. I watched a lot of movies growing up."

Addison headed back for the car, weaving in and out of people window-shopping, mostly so she wouldn't have to talk about it anymore. She didn't have the worst of childhoods, but there were aspects she didn't exactly reflect fondly upon.

He trailed behind her, not dropping the subject. "I bet you had the perfect life growing up. Let me guess. Cheerleader? Homecoming queen?" he teased. "Life must have been so easy for you. Like one of your fairy tale movies."

Addison snorted. It was far from a fairy tale. Maybe that's why she escaped into movies growing up. So she could imagine herself in a different life, with a mom around, and a dad who didn't have to work all the time. Instead, she was raised by the Addams Family, Willy Wonka, and good old Walt Disney.

"My mom left when I was seven. My dad had to raise me on his own while trying to keep the corner store he owned afloat. It kept him pretty busy so I had to entertain myself." She shrugged. "So I watched movies. It was like a free babysitter."

"Sounds rough," he said. "I'm sorry. A kid needs both parents."

Addison glanced at him, wondering if he spoke from experience. By the furrow between his brow she thought he might, but she didn't want to pry.

Addison could still remember the night she'd woken up from a bad dream and stumbled into her parents' bedroom to find her mother loading her belongings into a suitcase. When she'd asked her mother why she was leaving, she'd said it was because they didn't have enough money for all three of them to survive on. Like she was being selfless.

For years Addison wondered about that. How could one less income earner in the household make things any better? But what her mother had really meant was that there wasn't enough money for *her*.

The almighty dollar had ripped their family apart, had left her father working sixteen-hour days to keep the convenience store they owned afloat. Had left Addison in her cousin's hand-me-downs. Had left her without a mother.

But she was an adult now. Her life could be whatever she wanted it to be. A choose-your-own-story adventure. She wasn't going to settle for anything less than her happily ever after, something she'd been imagining since she was a kid watching those movies in the back room of the store.

So she waved the heavy mood away. "I don't have any regrets. If my mom didn't want to be a part of my life, then no big loss. My dad did the best he could. He worked very hard to take care of me and keep a roof over our heads. And I hope to return the favor one day. As in *soon*, since he's about to lose his roof. And his wife."

"His wife?"

"Well, not really," she said. "But money problems can tear relationships apart, you know?"

"Not if your relationship is strong enough." Felix spoke with such certainty, that again, she wondered about his past.

She made a noncommittal noise. It wasn't like she'd been old enough to really understand the dynamics between her parents. "I just worry. Dad's been through a lot. He deserves to be happy, and Dora makes him happy. I just don't want to see them struggle."

Felix gave her an amused look. "So you're going to save them."

"Well, I can help. But first things first." She gave a peppy go-get-'em fist pump as she rounded the car. "We have a mystery to solve."

Felix stood on the other side of the car regarding her with a curious look. Not giving him the opportunity to throw her a pity party, she gave him a wink and hopped behind the wheel.

The moment Felix slid into the passenger seat, she whipped out her notepad. "Okay, so who's this Jayden character that Charlotte mentioned?"

"He's a new kid," he said. "I don't know him too well. We'll put him on the list to check out."

Addison flipped back a couple of pages in her notebook and added Jayden's name to the list, then returned to her questions. "Charlotte mentioned a down payment, that you had a deadline. What was she talking about?"

"Is that part of your investigation?"

"Maybe," she said vaguely. "I have to consider all angles."

He sighed, but his mouth quirked into a smile. "I am going to buy a bar. Or at least I'm hoping to."

"Really? A bar?" she practically blurted. "You want to start your own business?"

"Well, you don't have to say it like that." He actually looked affronted.

"No. That's great. It . . . it just surprised me, is all. I had no idea."

Felix stared at her for a moment, and she felt the weight of his next words. "There's a lot you don't know about me."

Addison was certainly beginning to think so.

"I've got goals," he said. "What do you think? I want to be a minimum-wage wonder for the rest of my life?"

Addison shrugged. In fact, that was exactly what she'd assumed. "No. Of course not."

"A buddy of mine is going to sell his Irish pub in the South of Market area. He knew I was interested so he's letting me have first crack at it before putting it on the market. But I have to come up with the down payment by the end of this month. I've been working my ass off." His hand clenched into a fist on his knee. "I almost had it too."

Addison could see how much this meant to him. It looked like they both had dreams to protect.

"And you still will. It's not over yet," she said with conviction. "Let's see, who's next on our list today? Ah, yes. William Jackson. Do you have an address for him?"

"You bet I do."

"Great. I just want to make a quick stop at the Regency Center first."

Felix was reading the list over her shoulder curiously. He reached over and pointed at RED BRA written on the notepad. "You can cross Charlotte's name off the list."

Her pen hovered over the page uncertainly. "Did you notice how cagey she got when we started asking her questions?"

"She wasn't cagey." Felix leaned back and put his seatbelt on. "Joe was rushing her. He can be a total dick sometimes."

Addison pretended to scratch her name off the list, but closed it before Felix could see that she actually put a star next to it.

11

Play Fetch

Felix and Addison stared up at the imposing white facade of the Regency Center as they waited to cross the street. Addison didn't ever want to show her face there again, but it was the best way to wrap her head around the events of the cocktail mixer. That night had left her too rattled to even begin to ask the important questions at the time. Right now, she wanted to know *how* the dogs disappeared. If they could figure out the how, maybe it would lead to the who.

"What are we doing here?" Felix asked. "Want to relive your big moment on stage?"

She glared at him over her sunglasses. "So not funny." Hitting the crosswalk button, she waited for the light to change. "We're here to do a little crime scene investigation. It might give us more insight before we start pointing fingers."

"What do you expect to find that the police didn't?"

"Nothing," she said. "I just hope to figure out whatever they did. They probably uncovered everything they could find, but it's not like they're going to tell us about it, are they?"

"So you just hope to find something to help our own investigation." Felix nodded while giving her an astonished look, like he'd just seen a miracle performed. "That's pretty clever."

Addison swatted him on the arm. "You don't have to say it like that."

The light turned and their pedestrian symbol lit up. They crossed the street and headed up the stairs to the Regency Center entrance. Felix held the door open for her, but she paused just outside to remove one of her crystal earrings.

"What are you doing?" he asked. "The earrings don't match your shoes?"

Addison gave him a smug look. "You'll see."

Placing the earring in her dress pocket, she slipped inside. The doors closed behind them, muffling the traffic noises. It was like stepping back in time to 1909 when the center was built and the loudest things out on the street were the clip-clop of horse and buggies or the odd trolley car rolling by.

Men and women lingered in the lobby dressed in suits and sensible pencil skirts. A few heads turned their way, but after they gave them the once-over and realized Addison and Felix weren't part of their event, they returned to their conversations.

Addison scanned the room, searching for someone in charge. It didn't take long before the center's event organizer from the night of the cocktail mixer approached them.

Darcy's warm customer-service smile faltered when he spotted Addison. "Good afternoon," he said, with a dubious squint to his eye. "How can I help you?"

Felix turned expectantly to Addison for a cue, but she was already prepared.

"Hi. I'm so sorry to bother you. I'm not sure if you remember me, but—"

"Oh, I remember you." His face tightened as he battled to keep the smile in place. She wondered if he'd ever had an event go so wrong.

"Well, I think I lost an earring while working on the stage that night," she told him. "I was wondering if I could have a look for it." It was a simple enough fib. Which was a good thing, since Addison was a terrible liar.

Darcy hesitated, glancing back at the guests in the lobby. They were filtering through a set of doors, and he looked ready to follow.

"Please," Addison begged. "It will only take a few minutes. They were my grandmother's earrings, and she was very special to me." She tilted her head to the side to show the one lone earring left in her lobe.

Darcy considered the now-empty lobby one more time before giving her a brief nod. "Okay. But it will have to be quick. They are about to start a presentation that I need to introduce." He curled an impatient finger. "This way, please."

He led Addison and Felix through the lobby and into the ballroom. It was less romantic than she remembered without the candles, dimmed lights, and, of course, Phillip. However, with the lights turned up and the room cleared of guests and furniture, she could appreciate just how rich and detailed a setting it truly was, from the intricate ceiling moldings to the pattern in the hardwood floor.

"I'm sure our cleaning staff would have found it," Darcy said, as he climbed the stage stairs. "Or else it might have gotten thrown out with the trash."

Addison gasped, as though afraid her heirloom was lost forever and couldn't possibly be replaced at any cheap jewelry store. Which was exactly where she'd bought it.

He may not have been pleased with her but he at least looked abashed at his comment. "Don't worry," he added quickly. "I'm sure we'll find it."

Felix assessed her with a shrewd look. Either he judged her for being such a schemer, or he was impressed. She suspected it was the latter.

Strolling to the center of the stage, Darcy spun on his oxford heel. "Here we are," he said, as if Addison might have missed it.

"Thank you so much," she said.

Darcy nodded, but remained fixed to the spot, as though waiting for her to begin her search. She suddenly realized he wasn't going to leave them alone.

Crap. That was about as far as her plan went.

Awkwardly, she bent over and began scouring the stage. She hemmed and hawed. "I remember being over here."

Felix began looking for the nonexistent earring too while Darcy scrutinized them. He didn't help them look, of course, but stood there watching like he didn't trust them. For good reason, she thought, but it still annoyed her. It wasn't like they could take a good look around the place with him standing right there.

Addison continued to mumble things while throwing covert looks around the stage, however she was too nervous with him around. After a few minutes of fake searching and Darcy clicking his tongue impatiently every so often, a young redhead interrupted them.

"Excuse me, Darcy." She hovered at the base of the stage. "The Covington party says they can't get the projector to work."

"What?" Darcy practically leapt to attention. He descended the steps two at a time, waving over his shoulder as he walk-sprinted. "I'll be right back." It almost sounded like a threat to Addison's ears.

Once the redhead was gone. Addison began to look in earnest. But for what, she wasn't sure.

Felix crossed over to her. "Nicely done on the earring story. So what are we looking for?"

"I don't know," she said.

"What do you mean? This was your idea."

Addison positioned herself in the middle of the stage, staring out to an invisible audience. But when the cocktail mixer came rushing back to her, and an image of the angry crowd flashed through her mind, it didn't feel so invisible.

The room seemed to swell around her, the floor beneath her feet shaking—or maybe that was her legs. She closed her eyes and took a deep breath, clearing the memory. After a moment, she opened them again to find Felix staring at her curiously.

She ignored the look. "Well, we know the dogs couldn't have left the stage through the curtains. There were hundreds of people here that night. Someone would have seen them." Turning, she faced the glowing EXIT sign off to the side of the stage, hanging above the door to the back alley. "And we know they didn't leave through the alley because Melody would have seen them."

"That's if she wasn't the one who took them," he said.

"Well, let's just say she didn't. How else could they have gotten out of here?"

Felix grew quiet as he considered this. He rubbed the scruff of his five-o'clock shadow, and it scraped beneath his hands. It brought back memories of the night at Joe's Dive and she could almost feel the rough hair brushing against the skin of her neck again.

She shivered, in a good way—which was bad, very

bad—and mentally slapped herself. Phillip was going to call any time now to ask her out again. She was sure of it.

Addison tried to put herself in the shoes of a criminal mastermind. She tilted her head back to glance at the rafters above, the spotlights, and the curtain tracks. Could the dogs have been hoisted up in a cage somehow? Which was maybe slid out of a window using a complicated system of pulleys and cables, and then deposited in a garbage truck making a late-night run? Then she remembered this wasn't *Ocean's Eleven* and continued to brainstorm.

Felix was skirting the open area, running his hands over walls, flipping back curtains, and opening and closing the alley door.

The backstage was simplistic, bare bones. No place to hide, no mysterious doors, no windows, no props or equipment. Addison could feel the clock ticking. Darcy would be back any minute, and they were no further ahead. She wanted to prove Melody's innocence. Or at least have a reason not to suspect her anymore.

"Ugh. I'd hoped there'd be something here." She stomped her foot like a five-year-old.

Felix spun to face her, giving her the strangest look. She blushed at her childishness. "Sorry."

Then he stomped his foot.

For a second, Addison thought he was making fun of her. But then he did it again, and she heard the difference. She could hear the wood beneath his feet, but there was a hollow sound to it. Like an echo of an empty room. A room beneath them.

Their eyes dropped to the floor at the same time, searching for something, anything that stood out among the black paint. Addison spotted something. A notch cut out between the wooden floor panels, just large enough to slip her fingers into.

Checking over her shoulder to make sure Darcy wasn't coming, she reached down and pulled on the panel. The entire thing lifted right up, revealing a trap room below. She set the panel aside and squatted by the hole in the floor. Squinting down into the darkness, Addison had a fleeting vision of all the things lurking down there.

Felix took out his phone and shone the light inside. He moved it around, highlighting the framework beneath. It was a five-foot drop into the black pit.

Addison bit her lip. "I suppose one of us should go down."

"I'll go." Felix held his phone out to her. "Here, hold this."

Addison fought her instincts that told her there were all sorts of scary things down there, or maybe that was all the horror movies talking.

"No. I'll go. I'm smaller and lighter, so you can help me back up."

She sat down and dangled her legs over the edge. The cold floor made her bare legs tighten with goose bumps beneath her fifties-style dress. She wiggled her way forward, wondering what the best way to land was when Felix grabbed her hands and extended her arms above her head.

"Hold on," he told her. Bracing himself on either side of her, he lowered her into the black pit beneath the stage.

Even when her feet were firmly on the ground, she didn't want to let go of Felix. But as his hands slipped from hers, she felt the darkness envelop her and could sense all the zombies and vampires lurking around her.

She took a step back and brushed against something. She spun around. A scream built inside her lungs just as Felix's phone shone down on her and her mysterious attacker.

It wasn't Freddy Krueger. It was just a wooden post. Addison grunted, clutching her chest in relief.

"See anything?" Felix asked, passing her his phone so she could see better.

"Not yet." She couldn't mask the shake in her voice.

Addison knew she didn't have much time. She needed to do this. For the sake of the missing dogs, for her dad, for her passion, and maybe a little for Felix, she supposed. So swallowing her fear, she took the phone and shone it around the space.

The stage was held up with a series of crisscrossed beams and posts with enough space left between them for performers to move freely. She assumed it was so they could pass things up through the trap doors or pop up during a certain moment in a play or concert.

Shining the light at her feet, she weaved in and out of the wooden framework beneath the stage. All she could see was a thick layer of dust coating the floor. Overhead, cracks of light shone down on her face from more trap doors. Felix's footsteps shifted above her head, echoing through the hollow space around her.

Addison took another hesitant step forward and felt a crunch beneath her shoe. She pulled her foot back and held the phone over the spot, half-expecting to see human bones. It glistened as the light hit it, sparkling bright among the thick, gray dust. Whatever it was, it obviously hadn't been there long.

Her fear momentarily forgotten, she bent down and picked it up. She recognized it right away—the hand-crafted details, the careful color choices. It was a tiara that she'd outfitted a Chow Chow with at the cocktail mixer.

She glanced up. The accessory wouldn't have fallen through the cracks around the hidden trap doors. They were too small. So small that she hadn't even noticed the doors were there in the first place. And by the lack of footprints in the settled dust, neither had the cops. Paw prints, however, were a different story.

Addison hadn't noticed the prints before, but now she saw them everywhere. Big ones, little ones, scattered haphazardly around the floor. Or at least they appeared that way until she followed them with the light and saw that they all headed in the same general direction. She was tempted to follow them, but if the cops hadn't been down there to investigate, then they'd want to see all the evidence intact.

She put the tiara back on the ground where she found it and carefully retraced her steps. She didn't want to disrupt the crime scene any more than she already had.

As she made her way back, her fears began to creep up again, tickling her scalp like a thousand bugs crawling over her skin. By the time she stood beneath the opening in the stage floor and Felix's face hovered above her, she'd never thought she could be so happy to see him.

Darcy's face appeared next to Felix's. He on the other hand, didn't look particularly happy to see her. However, she didn't exactly care at the moment. The monsters were converging again, the dusty floor pulling her under. With shaking hands, she reached up to Felix.

His strong hands gripped hers. Grunting, he hoisted her out of the pit of doom. She stumbled against him and her fingers curled automatically around his shirt, allowing his solid presence to soothe her frantic heartbeat, grounding her from the inexplicable terror that had consumed her down below.

"Are you all right?" Felix asked, his eyes scanning her face.

She wasn't sure what expression she wore, but it made that crease form between his brows.

She nodded, but still hadn't let go of his shirt. "Yeah. I found it."

Felix inhaled sharply, indicating that he understood more than she was saying. Handing him back his phone, she reached into her pocket and pulled out the "missing" earring.

"Good. You found it." Darcy clapped his hands. "So you'll be on your way now." He waved toward the stage stairs, in a polite "get the heck out" way.

Addison stayed put, her hand still gripping Felix's shirt. "Is there any way out from under that stage? Does it go anywhere?"

Darcy frowned, clearly anxious to be rid of them. "Yes. It leads to a side entrance. Why?"

Addison let out the breath she was holding. "Bingo." When Felix gave her a strange look, she made a mental note to come up with a better "aha" word. "Call the police. They'll want to see what's down there."

"I've had just about enough police for one week," Darcy said. "They've already completed their investigation."

Felix ignored him. "What's going on?"

"That's how the dogs got out of the building. From underneath the stage. I found evidence down there."

Without any more explanation, Felix pulled out his phone again and dialed. Addison managed to pry her hand free of him to replace her "found" earring.

Darcy's face had turned red since she last looked at him. He glanced at his watch. "I have an event booked in this room in four hours. This was the last thing I needed today."

Addison scowled. "I'm sure losing their beloved pets was the last thing the cocktail mixer guests needed too, but this might help them get the dogs back. So suck it up."

Felix was half-listening to their conversation. His eyebrows rose at her lecture. She shrugged at him and he stifled a chuckle.

Darcy shut his trap, thankfully. But now that the subject had been broached and he was a bit sheepish, Addison decided to take advantage.

"Are there any cameras in this room?" she asked, scanning the corners.

"Only at the exits," he said. "And before you ask, there isn't one at the exit for beneath the stage. Only ones that guests would normally use."

But Addison wasn't thinking only about the dogs. She was thinking about her assistant. "Do you have access to the video footage from the cocktail mixer? Of the back alley exit?"

"Yes. But the police have that now." He stiffened a little with self-importance. "Not that I would be able to show anyone if we did have them."

Addison figured he'd say something like that.

"I can tell you that if it hadn't been for your assistant neglecting the dogs for a cigarette, this wouldn't have happened."

"She didn't neglect the dogs. She took a break." She crossed her arms. "Maybe your facilities are to blame." Then it dawned on her what he'd said. She paused. "How did you know she went out for a smoke?"

"Because the camera caught her heading outside holding a lighter and a pack of cigarettes. Doesn't take a genius to figure out what she was doing."

Felix covered the mouthpiece on the phone. "The police are on their way."

Addison nodded in response. She was surprised at how well their investigation was going already, considering the only experience she had solving crimes was watching *Sherlock Holmes*. Even then, the context was a bit outdated.

The new evidence was good and bad. She was happy it supported Melody's innocence. It didn't completely absolve her, though, since she could have had a smoke while helping load up the dogs into a truck or something, but it certainly looked a whole lot better for her. However, with the discovery of the real escape route for the dogs, it opened up all new possibilities. Now the dognapper could have been almost anyone at the party.

Addison suddenly realized how much work they had ahead of them.

12

Sniff Out

Addison sped through the streets of San Francisco until they arrived at Laurel Heights for another undercover operation. This time, they planned to engage a suspect. She took the next corner without slowing down, and Felix white knuckled the doorframe.

"Where did you learn to drive?"

Addison thought for a moment. "*The Fast and the Furious, Days of Thunder, The Love Bug.*"

"That explains it," he said.

"I'm making up for lost time, okay? Talking to the police really set us back." She pulled up to a stop sign. "Do you think they believed my earring story?"

Felix gave her a *Seriously?* look from the passenger seat. "I don't think you're as good of an actress as you think you are."

"But I don't think I'm a very good actress at all."

"Exactly."

She stuck her tongue out at him and whipped into traffic. "Just for that, you can talk to William Jackson. I think I remember this guy from the cocktail mixer. Kind of balding on the top, right?"

Felix ran a hand through his hair. "Not everyone can have ridiculously luscious locks like mine."

Addison snorted, but had to admit it was true. His hair was so full and wavy, it was unfair. He probably just rolled out of bed that way too. She couldn't see Felix waking up a few minutes early to style it—although, it could help with the messy look. But she didn't know many guys who could pull off hair that was any longer than your usual man-clip. With hair as awesome as Felix's, it would have been a crime against humanity to cut it.

"I think he had a Maltese, right?" she asked. "What do you know about him?"

"Just that he's been competing in dog shows for years and has never won," Felix said. "Last year his dog actually made it to the podium. Just as the judge went to congratulate them, the dog shook his coat out like it was a living powder puff, covering the judge in talcum."

"I remember reading something about that in *Doggy Digest*," Addison said. "He was disqualified for using unnatural products to enhance his dog. Serves the selfish jerk right. Powder can be terrible for a dog's respiratory system." She made a mental note to jot that down in her notebook when they pulled over.

Addison would never have thought of a suspect like William Jackson without Felix, not that she'd admit she actually needed him. "So I take it he falls under the revenge category of motives?"

Felix pulled a face, like *Oh yeah*. "I served him at the bar last year after he'd been disqualified, and he spilled his guts to me. Let's just say I wouldn't put it past him to go to extremes."

She thought back to the cocktail mixer. "I think he's the one who ordered the pawdicure. I remember he liked the Rainbow Frenzy nail polish. I brought a sample of it with me."

Felix glanced back at the multitude of pink gift bags in the backseat. "You hand out a lot of free stuff. You know you'll never get anywhere if you keep giving it away."

Addison snorted. "You're one to talk."

He glowered at her from the passenger seat. "What does that mean?"

"Oh please." She rolled her eyes. "You and Red Bra seem close."

"Yes," he replied evenly. "Charlotte and I are close."

Addison frowned at the response. She'd expected a smart comeback, but now she just kept recalling the image of them sitting next to each other in Joe's Dive. Not that she was jealous or anything.

"Besides, you gave me free drinks at the bar," she said. "Think of it like promotional services. You give someone free drinks and that person will tell their friends about your bar, which in turn will generate more business. I'm doing the same thing."

"That's the kind of marketing help I need when I open my own bar. But I didn't give you those drinks as freebies. I was just testing out a new concoction on you."

"You used me as a guinea pig?" she teased.

"I didn't see you complaining." His eyebrow quirked up. "I certainly wasn't."

"You liquored me up just to get a kiss, didn't you?" She pretended to be outraged, but looking back, she knew it wasn't the liquor that had her fired up over him.

"Excuse me. You kissed me, remember? Besides"— he grinned—"if I wanted to get in your pants, I would have gotten in them."

"Yeah right." She batted her eyelashes. "I'm a lady, I'll have you know."

"Right."

Her mouth dropped open in real offense. "Excuse me? You think I'm not? Who do you think—"

"No, *right*. Turn right." He pointed at the intersection they were driving through. "Right!"

"Hang on." She cranked her wheel. The tires screeched around the next corner as a couple of angry honks sounded behind them.

Felix gripped the door, holding on for dear life. When they'd made the turn and were still alive, he said, "Maybe a little less flirting while we're driving. I don't think you need any distractions."

"Who's flirting?" she asked innocently, but she knew very well that she was.

He was fun to flirt with. It was impossible for her not to. He had a personality that double-dog-dared you to just try and ignore him, which only made you think of him that much more. But she promised herself she wouldn't go down that path with guys like Felix anymore. Guys just out to use her.

She recalled her sort-of date with the far more appropriate Phillip, smiling at how well things had gone. Now *there* was a guy she could bring home to meet her dad. Not a guy who wanted to take her home after the bar closed. Then her smile disappeared just as quickly. Well, the date had gone well before all the dog stealing, and police interrogations, and accusations. That was probably why she hadn't heard from him yet. They must be keeping him very busy. He'd probably text her any moment.

She glared at her phone in its holder, willing it to ring.

Felix pointed up the road to a peach-colored home with white trim. "Number thirty-four. I think that's Jackson's house over there, but park here across the street. We don't want to be seen together."

"I'll agree with that," she said, eliciting a glare out of Felix.

Addison pulled over and parked behind a van to block her Mini from sight. She decided to leave the top down just in case Felix needed to make a quick getaway.

He got out of the car, stretching as he did so. "Why am I the one doing this again?"

"Because it was your idea to do a fake survey of our suspects experience with Pampered Puppies, remember? You said people love talking about themselves. So get them to talk about the dog grooming services they received while at the cocktail mixer. Then just go from there." She smiled extra sweetly. "You're good at reading people. I'm sure you'll think of something." She reached behind the seat, producing a frilly pink bag. "Don't forget the samples and the coupons." She shook it playfully.

"Anything else?" he asked sarcastically.

"Remember, you're a representative of my company." She bared her sparkling white teeth and pointed to them. "So smile."

With an exaggerated eye roll, he reached over and grabbed the bag of samples. Waving it with a sour enthusiasm, he crossed the street.

Addison spun in her seat to watch him climb Jackson's front steps and ring the doorbell. She couldn't help but note how nicely those faded jeans hung on his hips. They might not have been an expensive label—heck, they looked so old that the label had probably fallen off by now—however, that butt could have made any pants look like a million bucks.

While Felix waited for someone to answer the door, a white Audi drove up and parked on the street in front of the house. Addison ducked down. The last thing she wanted was for anyone to realize they were sneaking around asking questions. It wasn't like her car was exactly covert with its Caribbean Aqua paint job.

William Jackson stepped out of the Audi. She recognized him by the cul-de-sac hairstyle he unwillingly sported. He moved around to the back of the car and popped the trunk. Reaching inside, he drew out armloads of shopping bags.

Felix noticed him and descended the long stairs. By the gestures he was making, it looked like he was offering to help carry some bags. William waved his arms, almost shooing Felix away.

Felix just gave him a smile and took several of the bags up the steps anyway. Jackson rushed to unlock the front door. The moment it swung open, he practically flung the shopping bags into the house. Squeezing in after them, he smiled and waved at Felix, while simultaneously closing the door in his face.

Felix was left standing on the porch with the frilly pink bag still in his hands. After a few seconds, he shrugged and returned to the car.

"What was that about?" Addison asked.

"I'm not sure," he said. "He was pretty edgy, though. He didn't even want the samples."

"Maybe you made him nervous," she said. "I know you scare me."

He threw her a sour look. "Ha-ha."

"What was in the bags?"

"I didn't get to see."

She sighed, turning over the engine and pulling away from the curb. "Well that was a bust."

Felix drew out a long, crumpled slip of paper from his pocket. "Not necessarily."

She glanced at it while driving. "What's that?"

"Jackson's shopping receipt," Felix said, scanning it.

Addison's mouth dropped open. "You can't just take

that. What if he needs to return something? You know a lot of stores won't do returns or exchanges without a receipt."

"Did you want us to turn around and give it back?"

"No," she said. "I guess not."

Felix went quiet for a few moments as he read each item. "How many dogs did you say this guy had?"

"Just the one. Why?" She pulled up to a stop sign and looked over to see him frowning over the paper.

"Why would a man with one dog need twelve leather dog collars and leashes?"

"What? Let me see that." She snatched the paper away and read it herself.

She scanned the itemized list. Not only were there twelve collars and leashes, but there were bones, food dishes, brushes, and chew toys.

"That's a lot of pet supplies," she finally said. "Seems like he owns more than one dog."

Felix took the receipt and waved it in the air like it was the winning lottery ticket. "Or we've just found our dognapper."

13

Horndogs

Addison crouched down low to peer through the gap in William Jackson's fence, feeling the cool night air blow up her short dress. Shivering as it caressed her bare legs, she wished she'd worn something a little more practical for their clandestine operation. When she'd planned her outfit that morning, she'd never imagined she'd be crawling through creepy spaces beneath stages or breaking into people's property. At least her cute fifties-style dress was black so she could blend into the night.

Unable to see anything, she got on her hands and knees to look through a hole in the wood picket. There wasn't a single light on in William Jackson's backyard. Since his house was in the middle of the block, they'd been lucky it wasn't a row house or they wouldn't have had access to the backyard.

"Can you see anything?" she whispered to Felix.

"Oh yeah," he said from behind her "I've got a great view from here."

She glanced over her shoulder to find him standing back and enjoying the "view" of her backside.

Addison tugged her skirt down and returned to her peephole. "Stop screwing around and get over here. What if something happens and we miss it?"

"Oh, I think something's going to happen." She felt his hands slide up the back of her leg, pushing her skirt up. "I feel it."

"I'm serious," she hissed, slapping him away.

Felix sighed, letting her skirt fall back down. "All we can do is wait and watch. If the dogs are here, eventually Jackson will have to bring them outside to do their business."

He settled down on his side in the grass next to her, head resting on his fist. "We have to assume he's taking reasonable care of them if he bought all those supplies today. Leashes for walking them, dishes for feeding them, even toys for playing with them."

After Felix had swiped Jackson's receipt that afternoon, they had to kill several hours before returning after dark. While Felix was just full of suggestions that involved her backseat—no matter how small it was—they'd settled on dinner at a nearby Mexican restaurant.

When they returned after nightfall, they'd sat outside his home to case the place, picking away at leftovers as they watched car after car roll up and park on William's street. So far they'd counted at least eight people who knocked on his door.

"Why do you think there are so many people here?" Addison asked Felix. "Do you think they're all involved in the dognapping?"

"I don't know. Maybe he's selling them off or something. An auction to the highest bidder?"

Addison kept her eyes on the hole in the fence, but she sensed Felix's eyes on her while they continued to wait.

"So why dogs?" he asked. "Why not groom and dress people? Why the tutus, and the nails, and piercings, and dyed hair? It's torturous enough on humans. It borders on animal cruelty," he joked.

"Figures you'd say that. Looks like it's been a while since you've even had a haircut."

He snorted, but didn't deny it.

"First of all," she said, "I don't condone piercing dogs' ears. That's a cruel practice just for fashion's sake. And I guess it's because everyone needs to feel beautiful, even dogs."

"Because dogs care if they're up to date on the latest fashion?"

"Maybe not, but they enjoy the pampering, the sense that they're important. And in turn, it gets them positive attention, which makes them happy and feel even more loved."

"So is that why you do it?"

"Do what?" she asked distractedly, focused on the hole again.

"The hair, the makeup, the carefully calculated outfits." He tugged on her dress. "Because it gets you attention?"

Addison finally tore her attention away from William Jackson's backyard. "No. I don't do it for anyone else. I happen to enjoy fashion."

"That kind of beauty is only skin deep," he said with a sneer. Not at her, but maybe at the general idea of it. "It means nothing."

"Why the face?" Addison asked. "You have something against a little hygiene and self-care? Oh wait"—she fingered a hole near the neckline of his Metallica T-shirt— "look who I'm asking."

He frowned. "Hey, this is vintage, I'll have you know. I guess I believe there's more to a person than what they look like on the outside."

"You think that I'm superficial just because I like to dress nice and spend time on my hair?" she asked. "I don't think there's anything wrong with wrapping the gift in paper that matches the quality of the present inside. I mean you wouldn't buy a ring from Tiffany's and stick it in a shoebox, would you?"

In the light from the street, she saw his eyes brighten. "And you're the Tiffany ring?" She liked that his tone wasn't his usual sarcasm. It was full of excitement. Maybe anticipation at the idea of opening that gift.

"Honey, I'm the whole store." She gave him a wink. "I like to bring the internal beauty to the outside. There's beauty in everything and everyone. Even you, Felix Vaughn. It's somewhere in there." She gave him a playful shove. "Deep down in there." She poked his chest. "Deep, deep, deep, deep . . ."

He smiled, grabbing her finger playfully.

Addison really did try to see the good in Felix, but he made it hard sometimes. There would be a ray of hope, a glimmer of a deeper man beneath the wolfish smile and the cocky attitude. But then he would go and say something stupid and ruin the moment.

"The hair and makeup are just the finishing touches," Addison said. "A way to reflect the beauty a person has within. Not to mask a defective personality."

His finger trailed down her arm, causing goose bumps. "Well, if your wrapping is any indication of what's hidden beneath, then you must be perfect inside." His teeth flashed in the darkness, matching the white hibiscus growing next to him.

The smile dropped from Addison's face. She knew he was just being his flirtatious self, but the words made her wonder. Maybe she was subconsciously hiding something. Finding ways to make herself perfect on the outside, using makeup and clothes to cover up the defect on the inside.

"Did I say something wrong?" he asked.

He hadn't meant anything by it. Of course not. It's not like he knew it was actually true.

"I . . . I think I heard something," she lied. But as they grew silent to listen, she did hear a noise coming from inside Jackson's house.

"Bark, bark, bark."

"Is that . . . ?" Felix began.

"Woof, woof."

Addison held her ear closer to the fence. "Someone barking like a dog?"

The answer came in the form of a long, drawn-out howl. Not canine but . . . human.

"Come on," Addison said. "Let's get a better look."

Unfortunately, there was no gate on that side of the house, but there was a garbage can. She lined it up where the fence met the house.

She waved Felix over. "Come and help me up."

Felix steadied her as she balanced on the trash can, his hand gripping her thigh—maybe a little higher than he needed to.

"Now that's what I call getting a better look," he said.

She could hear the amusement in his voice, and she turned to see him staring up her dress. If she'd had a free hand she would have swatted him.

Addison swung a leg over the fence. She moved her foot around until she found the horizontal rail on the other side to place it on, then climbed over. The wood scraped her legs as she lowered herself to the ground.

Darkness enveloped her and she felt cornered in the yard, fearing that at any moment the exterior lights could flick on and Jackson would discover her and set the entire pack of stolen dogs on her. The possibility that she could go to jail for breaking and entering became very real in that moment. However, if she didn't do something to find the missing dogs, she might go to jail anyway. Talk about being caught between a tight budget and a flash sale.

It didn't take very long before Felix was standing next to Addison in the dark yard, making her feel safer, less alone. At least if she was going down, he'd be going down with her.

They made their way through the yard behind the house, and Addison felt her chest shake with each powerful beat of her frightened heart. Every step brought them closer to being discovered. It was unsettling, yet thrilling. For better or for worse, she was glad Felix was by her side.

Most of the curtains had been drawn closed. No light escaped the house except from the sliding glass doors facing the backyard. The long drapes had caught on the carpet, allowing a small glimpse into the home.

Together, Addison and Felix crept up to the doors and got down on their hands and knees to peer inside. They pressed their heads together so they could both see the view. And what a view they saw.

The leather collars were being put to good use, only they weren't around furry necks. They were around the necks of William Jackson and several of his male friends. At the other end, women in various stages of undress held the leashes.

Addison's eyes widened. She clamped a hand over her mouth to keep from laughing—or screaming, she wasn't sure which. "Oh my God."

Meanwhile, Felix was snickering next to her. "Why wasn't I invited to this party?"

"Something tells me they don't want anyone to see this. Even a bartender."

He gave her a wolfish smile. "I meant as a guest."

She hit him on the arm, but she was laughing herself. Then she heard a muffled gasp from inside the house. The music stopped.

"Did anyone hear that?" a female voice asked. "I think someone's out there."

Addison and Felix froze, ready to make a run for the fence. Felix cupped a hand over his mouth like a megaphone. "Woof, woof," he barked.

He barely got through it before he lost control, his body convulsing as his stomach seized with rich laughs. Addison succumbed to her own giggles, making it difficult to move even as footsteps thudded toward the sliding glass door from inside.

Felix clamped a hand around her wrist and dragged her back to the fence. He interlaced his fingers and held them low so that she could step on them. Lifting herself up, Addison straddled the wooden pickets as she searched for the trash can on the other side with her foot. She found the metal lid just as she heard the sliding glass door hiss open.

Worried shouts and questions carried into the yard. Addison leapt off the garbage can. Within seconds Felix was next to her, running by her side down the street and to the car.

"Do you think they'll call the cops?" she panted as she reached for the door handle.

"And tell them what?" Felix rounded the car and hopped in. "Their freaky sex party was interrupted? Time to go," he said, buckling up. "Use some of those *Fast and Furious* skills to get us out of here. And hurry."

Addison didn't need to be told twice. She started the

engine and pumped the gas a couple of times before peeling away.

They sped by William Jackson's house in a blur just as she saw the shine of his balding head beneath the front porch lights. He squinted through the dark, probably trying to read her license plate, but then he was yanked back inside by a tug on his leash.

By the time the Mini reached the end of the street, Addison and Felix had dissolved into laughter.

14

Dog Eat Dog

The high-gloss red door swung open to Addison's ridiculously enthusiastic smile.

"Hello. I don't know if you remember me. My name is Addison Turner. I've come to do a brief survey on your experience with Pampered Puppies. Would you be interested in participating?"

Kitty Carlisle stood inside her classic San Francisco painted-lady home with its adorable olive scalloped siding and yellow trim, staring out with a blank expression on her pinched face.

"It will only take five minutes of your time," Addison added. "And you'll receive this complementary bag of free samples." She held the frilly pink bag out, practically forcing Kitty to take it.

Once it was in her hands, Addison cheerfully barged her way through the front door and into the foyer. Even though the old lady creeped her out, she had to get a closer look. Felix wasn't able to get into William Jackson's house the day before—which might have been for the best—but she knew this time around she needed to get closer, much closer if she was going to investigate. After all, there wasn't a lot she could uncover from the front stoop.

Kitty peered at the street behind Addison with her bulgy eyes, as though looking for other people. Or maybe witnesses, Addison thought with a shiver, remembering the lady's crazed looks at the cocktail mixer.

"Oh, all right," she relented. "Come in."

But Addison was already inside, scoping out the place. Her gaze darted around the room. The entrance was full of fake flowers and framed pictures of what she assumed were the woman's kids and grandkids. Then her eyes fell on Kitty's bichon frisé sitting by the door. He'd been so well behaved that she hadn't noticed him.

Squatting down, she reached out to pet him, but still he didn't move. When her hand touched his white fur, it felt cold and hard. She snatched her hand back in surprise. It was a carved statue.

Kitty giggled. "So lifelike, isn't it? I had that commissioned at the height of Elvis's competitive career. I wanted him to have a reminder of the glory days."

"It's"—Addison hesitated—"beautiful." She suppressed a shudder, but couldn't stop from wiping her hand subtly on her leggings.

Kitty led Addison into the sitting room and invited her to take a seat on a green floral sofa covered in a layer of protective plastic. It squeaked under Addison's butt as she sat.

For a moment she felt a flutter of panic beneath her chest and the urge to run screaming out of there before she was axe-murdered. But as she took in the rest of the room and saw the plastic sticker still stuck on the television screen, and the dog show trophies displayed in separate display cases, she realized the couch cover wasn't to hide evidence. The woman was just fastidious.

Kitty sat quietly in her armchair waiting for Addison to begin, pug eyes watching her carefully. "What was it that you wanted to ask me?"

"Umm," Addison referred to her clipboard—which she thought made her look very official. "How many dogs do you currently have?"

"Just the one. Elvis!" she called out. "Come here, Elvis!" There was a light jingling and padding of paws before Kitty's dog twin floated into the room like a little white cloud on a sunny day.

"There's my boy," Kitty said, picking him up and placing him on her lap.

"He's a beautiful bichon frisé," Addison said.

"Thank you. Elvis here had a good run, but he's retired now." She indicated the row of trophies on the mantel.

That's when Addison spotted the detailed painting hanging above the fireplace. What she'd mistook before as a portrait of Kitty with her white beehive, was actually a commissioned painting of Elvis. He sat nobly with his chin resting on his paw, replete in a green paisley vest, a cravat, a monocle over one eye, and a pocket watch to top the outfit off.

Addison almost laughed, but then she thought it was likely not meant to be cute and whimsical, but rather a serious rendition of Elvis, which made it even odder. She shifted uncomfortably on the sofa. Her butt squeaked on the plastic again.

Kitty nuzzled the dog's halo of white fur. "We had a good run, didn't we pookie?"

Addison cleared her throat and focused on her clipboard. "Do you think you'll compete in dog shows again in the future?"

"Not anytime soon. It just wouldn't be the same without Elvis," she said a little sadly. "But I still attend the events each year and enjoy being part of the association. I've been on the judging panel for a few years now."

"Oh, I didn't realize that. That's exciting." Addison made a note of that, even though she wasn't exactly sure what it meant for her investigation. If Kitty was a judge, surely she wouldn't want to steal the dogs entering the competition.

"Upholding the standards are important to me," Kitty told Addison. "And if you ask me, they've been slipping under Judge Walter Boyd's watch."

She remembered the large man Phillip had introduced her to at the cocktail mixer. "How have they been slipping?"

Kitty huffed. "Oh please. His Best in Show choice last year? Alistair's beagle?" She scoffed at the ridiculousness of it. "Who was Walter kidding? Everyone could see there was favoritism there. Judge Walter's own dogs are hounds, you see. Lilly's rein should have ended the year before last."

The plastic squeaked as Kitty leaned in close like someone might overhear them in her own sitting room. "Between you and me, Alistair was beginning to look a little ridiculous continuing to show Lilly. She was past her prime. He needed to move on. It was becoming a little embarrassing."

"Oh." Addison considered this for a second. It didn't exactly make Kitty suspect number one, because she'd heard Phillip say something similar at his fundraiser. She mentally tucked it away, though, to scribble it down in her notebook later. It would be too obvious to do it right in front of Kitty.

For now she moved down the list of questions on her clipboard. "In your experience with Pampered Puppies,

on a scale from one to ten, what was your level of satisfaction with the results?"

"Oh, ten. Elvis's fur hasn't been this soft in years."

Addison beamed. "Oh, that's the jojoba and coconut
oil cleanser. It prevents tangles while increasing luster
and flexibility. It's our most popular product," she ram-
bled off, excited to talk about business. "On a scale from
one to ten, how safe did you feel leaving Elvis with Pampered Puppies?"

"Oh, well," Kitty's eyes dropped, considering Elvis
cuddled in her arms. "You're always nervous leaving your
pet. Elvis is like my child."

"I feel the same way about my Princess. I understand."
Addison understood more than the woman was outright
saying. She could see the apprehension in her eyes. Kitty
was an anxious woman to begin with, but the dognapping probably had her on edge. It had everyone on edge.

Kitty's eyes flicked to Addison. "Is it true?" she asked.
"Did all those dogs really get stolen?"

"It seems that way."

"How?" She held Elvis closer, like maybe Addison
would snatch him from her arms in broad daylight and
make a run for it.

Of course she suspected Addison. Kitty had been
there the night of the cocktail mixer; she'd heard the rumors. Who hadn't? That was what made their little undercover investigation so difficult. No one trusted her or
Felix.

"They weren't certain until it happened again this
weekend at Phillip Montgomery's fundraiser. The police
suspect it was an inside job. One of the staff or a guest at
the party." Addison observed the woman for a sign, a
twitch, a tell. Maybe just as closely as Kitty was watching her.

"Well, thankfully I don't need to worry about that." She kissed Elvis on the head. "He's twelve years old now. Not coming out of retirement. He's no threat to anyone."

Addison stared at the woman. "So you think it's someone who wants to win the contest taking out the competition?"

Kitty's painted-on eyebrows rose. "Certainly. It's not like we haven't all thought about it." She laughed like it was an obvious conclusion, and the titters sent shivers down Addison's spine. She didn't want to think what Kitty might have done for all those trophies lining the mantel.

Kitty tilted onto one buttock to lean in close. The plastic on her chair groaned, sounding like a fart. "You want to know the truth about conformation? It's rife with jealousy and bitter competition. Prohibited plastic surgeries, opponents snipping out patches of fur on other dogs or scratching the pads of paws so they can't walk properly. Opponents will try to oust the competition in any way." She covered Elvis's ears so he wouldn't hear. "Even by nobbling."

Addison twitched, the word rubbing her the wrong way. "Nobbling?"

"Disabling the competition by drugging or poisoning. Food tainted with laxatives, sleeping pills, or even chocolate. It leaves a nasty film around the mouth, you see."

Addison had completely forgotten about her list of questions. She stared at the woman in disbelief. "But you're talking about dog lovers. How could they do something to harm another animal?"

"They say these tactics exist only in the minds of disgruntled owners that have lost a competition, that there's no truth to them. Only rumors. But I've seen enough in my day to know it exists. But *this*," she said. "These dognappings are bold. This reeks of desperation. Of insanity." Her pug eyes bulged out of her head.

Addison suddenly felt cold, her fingertips tingling from lack of circulation. If Kitty Carlisle deemed it "insanity," then Addison was afraid of what she and Felix might uncover.

Elvis had been very still on Kitty's lap for some time, as though he'd been replaced with the statue in her entranceway. The only way she could tell he was alive was by the occasional blink of his dark eyes. His constant stare was beginning to freak her out.

Kitty sat upright in her chair again, her air of aloofness settling back over her. "I hope they find whoever is doing this. It makes a mockery of what the association and the shows stand for. At the heart of it, it's about discovering and preserving the best genetics of any particular breed. And because," she said simply, "we truly love our dogs."

That much was apparent. Maybe a little too much in Kitty's case.

As though Elvis could understand her, he leaned back and gave her a kiss on the chin to let her know he felt the same way.

It was interesting to see the other side of the coin. The local animal activist group that her friend Piper used to volunteer for demonstrated against the dog shows because they loved animals. Meanwhile breeders continued to support dog shows for the same reason. Addison didn't know which side she stood on yet. All she knew was she loved every dog. Perfect genetics or not.

There was a click from the wall as the cuckoo clock struck four. Instead of a bird to signal the time, a dog leapt out of a miniature doghouse. Addison jumped at the mechanical barks. Elvis continued to stare at her with those bottomless black eyes.

"Was there anything else?" Kitty asked, drawing her attention back.

Addison mentally shook herself, but she stiffened, anxious to leave. "Oh, yes." She glanced at her clipboard. "On a scale from one to ten. How likely are you to use Pampered Puppies' services again or recommend it to a friend?"

Kitty reached out to touch Elvis, as though weighing the risk of someone stealing him versus the featherlike caress of his jojoba-infused fur. Now that Addison knew what people in her world were willing to do to win, she didn't blame her.

"I think I'll stick to my regular girl for now."

Addison nodded and held back a disappointed sigh. The fact that Kitty had even considered meant she was interested in the services, but the speculation surrounding the dog disappearances had everyone on edge. And if the roles were reversed, Addison wouldn't want to risk anything happening to Princess either.

But the "for now" gave her hope. It meant that maybe once Addison's name was cleared, Kitty would reconsider. And others might follow. That was, if her business survived that long.

Addison was shown to the door. Elvis took a seat next to his younger clay rendition where they both watching her steadily as she walked through the door and turned back.

"Well, if you reconsider," Addison said, "here's a ten-dollar-off coupon, along with some free samples of my homemade jojoba coconut cleanser."

Kitty's pug eyes widened as she peeked into the bag. "Oh, thank you." She bent down and picked Elvis up to wave his little paw at Addison. "Good luck with your survey."

Addison returned to her Mini parked on the street, a smile on her face. Maybe things weren't so bleak. Maybe she could repair her reputation, one customer at a time. Ground up sort of thing. It would be hard work, but she could do it.

When she climbed into the convertible, Felix eyed her expression from the passenger seat. "So? How did it go?"

"Okay. Kitty doesn't want my services. But I'm hopeful. If I can just clear my name—"

"No, I meant is she our dognapper?"

"Oh, that. It's tough to say." She took out her notebook and mulled it over. "Her passion for dog shows borders on obsession. But she seems to truly love dogs, so I'm not sure if she's capable."

Addison reviewed everything that was discussed during her shakedown. As crazy as Kitty seemed, Addison thought her an unlikely culprit, but she wasn't ready to scratch her off the list quite yet.

"But she did mention one name," Addison said.

"Who's that?"

"Judge Walter Boyd. She complained that he's letting the judging standards slip. I don't know if it means anything, but it isn't the first time I've heard that."

"Well, then I guess we know who to talk to next."

15

Hot Diggety Dog!

The dense woods at the edge of the Presidio seemed to drive the sun away as Addison and Felix pulled onto the dead end street. Situated at the end of the block, Judge Walter Boyd's Spanish-style home backed onto the dense woods that lined Lobos Creek. It made for a great view, but gave it an uber-creepy feeling after the last light drained from the sky.

Addison stared out the front window of her car at the white columns and arches along the first- and second-floor balconies. They looked like the bared teeth of a guard dog, warning them away. A cool breeze blew through the open top. Her curls tickled her neck and made her shiver. Reaching for the controls, she closed the roof.

Felix was texting on his phone in the passenger seat. Addison couldn't help but glance at the name at the top of the screen. It was a girl's name. Celia. She wondered if she was his sister or something, but she thought he would accuse her of being jealous again if she asked. And she was so not jealous.

"I've got a bad feeling about this guy," she told Felix. "Like creep factor ten."

He glanced up from his text. "Why?"

"Just a feeling, I guess." She shrugged. "He called Princess the b-word."

Felix's mouth twitched. "A bitch?"

She scowled and held a finger to her lips. "Shhh."

"That's because Princess *is* one."

"I know," she said. "But I didn't like the way he said it."

They sat back and watched the place for a while, waiting for—well, Addison wasn't quite sure what. Maybe for a pack of dogs to come rushing out of the gate or a chorus of howls at the moon. But that would be too easy.

Her phone chimed. It was a text from her dad. *A potential buyer came to view the store today. They seemed very interested. Keep your fingers crossed.*

Addison frowned. She was running out of time to help her dad. Things with the sale were moving a lot faster than she'd hoped. Or rather, their investigation was going a lot slower.

That's great news Dad, she texted. *Is that what you want? Are you happy?*

A moment later, her phone chimed again. *It's not ideal. But it's the best scenario for our situation.*

No, she thought. The best scenario would be for her to find the dogs, return them to their worried owners, win back her customers, launch a successful fashion line, and save her dad's business. Then everyone could live happily ever after.

But it wasn't like she could make any promises, so she texted, *Then I'm happy for you. Fingers and toes are crossed for you.*

I'll keep you updated. Love you.

Love you too. Say hi to Dora for me. X

After twenty minutes, a car's headlights appeared in Addison's rearview mirror.

"Car," she said.

They ducked down as it passed by, then watched its progress until it pulled up to Walter Boyd's house and parked outside the property's stone wall. The driver got out, ducking their head as they headed for the house. Before they went through the gate, the person glanced nervously around the street, and Addison caught sight of the person's profile and the telltale hooked nose.

Her mouth dropped open. "No way. That's Penny Peacock. What do you think she's doing here?"

Felix sat forward in his seat. "A handler fraternizing with a judge? It's got to be against the show rules."

"Come on," she said. "Let's get a closer look."

They got out of the car and snuck up to the judge's yard. The driveway was barricaded by a steel gate, but they were able to hop over the low stone wall. Addison was happy she'd chosen a more spy-appropriate ensemble tonight: black leggings, a loose tank top in case more acrobatics were required, and a black leather jacket for nighttime camouflage. Not to mention a badass flare.

Felix wore his usual attire, which she'd dubbed ruggedly-sexy-in-a-completely-careless-way-style. While he claimed not to care about fashion, she knew he was a liar. She'd caught him checking her tush out more than once that night. It wouldn't have been quite the same if she were wearing baggy sweats.

Sticking to the hedges lining the drive, she and Felix crept around the side of the house. When they passed the kitchen window, Addison could see Walter and

Penny's silhouettes, one round and the other skinny, through the sheer curtains. It looked like a comical shadow puppet show.

"Come on," Felix said. "We're too exposed here. A neighbor might spot us."

Addison nodded and followed him around to the back. The main part of the yard was fenced off. Felix unlatched the gate, but as it swung open, it creaked, sounding like a siren in the night.

Felix grimaced. They both froze, straining their ears for a hint that someone had heard them, but after a few painful heartbeats, no one came.

Felix made a silent show of blowing out a sigh of relief and slipped into the back. Addison followed him, but at the last second she searched around for something to prop the gate open with so it wouldn't squeak when they wanted to leave. She spotted a garden gnome hiding beneath an azalea bush. Snatching it up, she placed it in front of the gate.

The backyard was pitch black. The moon hung low in the night sky, blanketed by the thick cover of trees hugging the property line. She made her way forward more by feel than sight.

She shuffled her feet through the grass, bumping into Felix whenever he stopped to listen. After the third time that she face-planted into his muscular back, he reached around and grabbed her hand.

Addison tried to snatch it away, but he held it firmly, tugging her along. As they crept farther onto the heart of the property and into the open where they could be spotted from a back window, she found she was holding his hand in earnest.

A scent crawled its way up Addison's nose, stinging her nostrils. The smell was caustic and hinted at chemicals, but was so out of place that she struggled to find a name for it. She wrinkled her nose, fighting the urge to sneeze.

Just as they began to creep toward the back porch, a light flicked on in one of the windows.

Addison winced, momentarily blinded. Felix's body tensed next to her. She squeezed his hand as though she could silently communicate, *Oh crap, oh crap, oh crap, oh crap.*

Then the porch light turned on. It lit up the two of them like a spotlight. Addison caught a glance of Felix's clenched jaw before the back door cracked open. Voices drifted out.

Felix hesitated and glanced back the way they came, probably wondering if they should make a run for it. In that frozen moment, Addison whipped her head around, ignoring the sweat forming down her spine. Her darting eyes landed on a small shed on the other side of the yard. Maybe ten feet away, she calculated.

Gripping Felix's hand, she made a dash for it, silently tugged him along. She didn't dare look behind her, in case she stumbled.

By the time they reached it, her lungs were aching with a suppressed scream. She fumbled for the handle. Her shaking fingers finally wrapped around it. Wrenching the door open, she ducked inside, Felix right behind her.

A wave of heat hit her, nearly knocking her over, but she was in too much of a rush to care. The strong scent of cedar overpowered her senses. They'd barely shut the door behind them before the voices became clearer.

Addison held her breath, listening for signs that they'd been seen or heard. When no one had called "Release the hounds!" and there were no footsteps drawing closer to their hiding spot, she dared a peek out of the small window at the top of the shed door.

Walter and Penny were stepping out onto the back porch with a pair of basset hounds at their heels. And they were in their bathing suits.

Addison's hair shifted as Felix came up behind her. His stubbled jaw brushed against her hair as he came close enough to try and see out the window. She flushed at how close he was. Was it just her, or was it really hot?

"What's going on?" Felix asked.

She shivered as his breath tickled her neck. "They're in their bathing suits," she said. His nearness was preventing her heart from slowing down after their mad dash.

Felix inhaled sharply.

"I know, right?" she said. "You don't want to see Judge Boyd in his speedo. Once you see it, you can't unsee it. It doesn't get worse than that."

"Oh yes it does." There was a tinge of panic in his voice. "That means they might come in here."

"What?" She spun to take in her surroundings clearly for the first time.

She glanced around, taking in the dark panels of wood that made up their hiding spot. The entire structure was made of cedar, which was why the air was so heavy with its musk. She stepped away from the window to allow the light to flow into the shed. But it wasn't a shed. They'd found their refuge in a sauna. And the reason it was so unbearably warm in there was because it was heating up to be used.

Addison backed away from the door, staring at it like it could open at any moment. "What do we do?"

Felix gripped her like he was ready to throw her over his shoulder and carry her out if it came to that. Or else throw her aside and leave her behind to take the fall. "If they come in here, we'll just barrel past them. They'll be taken by surprise if we're quick enough."

"Okay, but we can't let them see our faces."

Addison dared another look out the window to see if Penny and Walter were headed that way, but they were still on the porch, climbing a set of stairs to a platform. No. Not a platform, she realized as Penny threw a leg over it. It was a hot tub.

"That's what that smell was," she breathed. "Chlorine. They're going in a hot tub."

Felix ducked down to look out the window. "So, we're okay for now. But eventually they'll come in here or he wouldn't be warming it up."

Addison tugged the collar of her leather jacket away from her neck. "You mean it's going to get hotter in here?"

"We'll have to make a run for it at some point," he said. "Maybe they'll have a quick soak and head inside for a bit."

Penny's moan drifted over from the porch. "Oh, yes. Yes! Mmmm. Right there."

Addison tensed. "Ummm, did you hear that?"

"You like that, baby?" Walter asked Penny.

"Mmmm. Don't stop."

Addison's eyes widened. "Or maybe they'll be a little longer."

She couldn't believe her ears. Her gaze automatically returned to the window and she instantly regretted it. Penny had removed her bikini top and was straddling Judge Boyd in the hot tub.

Thank God for jet bubbles, she thought, averting her eyes. But the image was already seared into her retinas.

"I wouldn't look out there if I were you."

Felix blew out a breath. "It's kind of hot."

"Eww. Whatever floats your boat, I suppose." Addison tried to wave herself with her hand, but it was just wafting hot air around. She turned back to Felix who was

now standing there half-naked. He'd peeled off his shirt
to reveal a tight six-pack.

"Oh, you mean in here. Yeah. Hot." She swallowed,
but her mouth had already gone dry. "Very hot."

Now that she was thinking about it, it was hot. Stifling.
Following Felix's lead, she pulled off her jacket, but it
didn't help much. She was already sweating. And the
walls felt so close. The sauna was just big enough for two
people—and in Judge Boyd's case, one.

She sank down to the cedar floor where it was cooler
and rested her head against the bench seat. She tried not
to think about the walls closing in like when Luke Sky-
walker and the others were in the Death Star garbage
compactor. Felix sat across from her, making it impossible not to stare at his muscular chest.

The stove in the corner clicked and clacked as it heated
up the pile of stones on top of it. Addison closed her eyes,
trying to imagine she was on vacation, lying on a hot
beach somewhere in the Caribbean. It wasn't hard, what
with a half-naked man across from her. She pictured a
big, wide, open beach. Not a tiny, cramped, suffocating
hotbox.

"How long do you think they'll be?" she asked Felix.

He snorted. "Are you really asking me about Judge
Boyd's stamina right now?"

"It's just hot. Like really, really hot." The dry heat
made it impossible to breathe. Her next breath came in a
gasp. "Aren't you hot?"

He bit his lip, eyeing the neckline of her tank top. "I
know a way to take your mind off things."

She didn't answer. Instead, she focused on inhal-
ing slowly, counting in her mind as she did so. *One Mississippi, Two Mississippi* . . . But it wasn't long before
the famous river lost a few syllables and she was panting,

clawing at her chest. It was similar to the feeling she got when she was under the stage floor, only this time, there was no way out—unless she wanted to go to jail.

Felix had been talking, although she hadn't really been paying attention. Suddenly he went quiet.

"Addison, are you okay?" He eyed her warily. "You're not claustrophobic, are you?"

"I—I don't think so. It's just," she breathed, "so hot." Addison lifted her hair off her neck, hoping that would help.

After a moment, Felix shifted to kneel next to her. Reaching out, he grabbed a handful of her hair. "Turn around."

Lacking the energy or witty comeback to argue, she did as he asked. He settled in behind her and after a moment she felt soft tugs on her hair. Felix Vaughn was French braiding her hair. Addison couldn't believe it.

His fingers slid gently along her scalp, combing through her waves. As he expertly wove each lock together, Addison closed her eyes, focusing on each sensation.

Her body was on alert, feeling each tug on her hair as though it were a limb. It was different than any way he'd touched her so far, like they'd suddenly leapt to an entirely new level of intimacy. Felix's usual behavior was rough and brusque. This new tenderness was so unexpected that Addison found herself entirely focused on each subtle movement rather than on her panic.

Curiosity nagged at her about this astonishing skill of his. Felix was the last person on Earth she would have thought could braid hair, far less French braid it. "How do you know how to do this?" she asked.

"I'm a man of many talents, Addy," was all he said. She could hear the teasing smile in his voice.

His own labored breaths caressed the back of her neck. It hit the sweat forming on her skin, sending goose bumps trickling down the length of her arms and back. Finally, he got to the end and tucked the tail in at the nape of her neck to prevent it from unraveling.

However, despite the rush of air against the damp skin of her neck and shoulders, her relief was only temporary. The heat continued to rise, and Addison could feel herself slipping back into panic mode. She rested her back against the cedar wall. If Felix hadn't been with her, she would have started stripping right there and then.

She took a deep breath through her nose and out her mouth. "Felix, say something. Talk about something. Distract me."

She closed her eyes again, waiting for his usual nonsense to spill out of his mouth. But a heartbeat later, she felt his soft lips against hers.

She inhaled sharply, but he didn't pull away. His lips remained pressed against her. He held them there, still as a statue. When she made no move to push him away, he began to kiss her softly.

His mouth tasted of peppermint breath mints, his lips as soft as melting ice cream, and just as satisfying. Automatically, her tongue darted out to taste them. The slow, methodical movements of his mouth against hers were reassuring.

Felix kept the tempo even, never allowing it to heat up. His breathing flowed rhythmically, hypnotizing her, and she soon found that her own chest rose and fell in time with his.

Felix's body didn't touch hers, not an ab or a pec, not even his hands. He hovered as far away as he could, careful not to add to her own body heat or the sensation that the walls were closing in. But she could feel his comforting presence.

Their last kiss at the bar had overwhelmed her, excited her to the point that she wanted to lose control. But now she let him control her, losing herself in the sweetness of his kisses, sweeter than she'd expected from the barbarian.

Addison's eyes fluttered open. Felix had his own eyes closed as he kissed her gently. His body shook with the strain of physically supporting himself in the awkward position. Or was it because he was holding back when he wanted more? Addison couldn't tell.

It wasn't like before where she wanted him to ravage her on a pool table—wham, bam, thank you, ma'am. She thought that if they weren't under the serious medical threat of dehydration or heat stroke, she'd quite like to stay there with him, just like that. It felt, well, nice.

Now *that* was an effective distraction, she realized, closing her eyes again.

After what could have been a few minutes or twenty, the sound of deep barking echoed outside their hiding place. Felix's mouth froze. Addison was the first to pull away.

"Do you think his hounds sniffed us out?" she whispered.

Felix pushed himself to his feet and staggered slightly as he moved to the window. Addison had been too busy panicking to consider how much the heat had been affecting him.

Felix braced himself against the doorframe. Wiping away the condensation on the window, he stared out. "They're getting out of the hot tub."

Addison grabbed her leather jacket and Felix's T-shirt. "Are they coming this way?"

"No. They're running through the yard. And you're right." He chuckled. "That's not something I can unsee."

Over the hum of the stove in the corner heating the

rocks, Addison could hear the barking fade into the distance while Walter and Penny yelled and whistled after it.

"Come back Mr. Vandermutton!" Walter called. "Come back!"

Addison snickered, feeling a little delirious. "Mr. Vandermutton?"

"Did you leave the gate open?" Felix asked.

Addison paused and forced her foggy brain to think back. "Yeah, I did."

"I think one of the dogs got out of the yard. Penny and Walter are heading toward the tree line." He shifted his position to try and see farther. "I think we should make our break for it."

Reaching down, he helped Addison to her feet. The tiny sauna spun, and her vision faded to black around the edges. She swooned slightly, stumbling against him, but he held her up. Wrapping an arm around her, he supported her as he reached for the door handle.

She grinned up at him, a little dopily. "What happened to not helping a damsel in distress?"

"It's in my genetic code. Besides, most damsels aren't as cute as you." He squeezed his arm tighter around her. "Ready?"

She nodded.

Felix burst through the door. The cold night air shocked her damp skin like a Brazilian wax. Together they stumbled across the grassy lot and out through the open gate.

Addison could hear Penny and Judge Boyd yelling into the trees, huffing and shrieking at the chill of the night on their hot tub--warmed bodies. But Addison's own overheated body basked in the relief.

She let the cool air wash over her, and felt the life flow

back into her legs. Energized but still slightly shaky, she let Felix guide them back to the safety of her car. Once she'd regained her focus, they drove to the nearest gas station for two bottles of Gatorade each.

16

Chase Tail

Addison stood back, sizing up the erect form before her. The length, the thickness, the subtle curve. A fine specimen, but still, she frowned at it. It didn't look quite right.

"Maybe I should give it a few more strokes," she said to Melody.

Her assistant hovered next to her for a closer look. "Do you think that will make it look bigger?"

"If I rough it up a bit, maybe." Addison shrugged. "It might make it look thicker. Every inch counts."

She dove in, teasing, stroking, tugging furiously until its owner began to wriggle and squirm under her skilled touch. When her wrist began to ache from the effort, she stood back to examine the results.

"I think that's the best I can do," she said.

"We're not quite done yet. Let me finish him off." Melody drew a length of ribbon out of her supplies and wrapped it snug around the shaft, arranging it into an artful bow. When she was finished, it began to wag back and forth in front of their faces.

Addison nodded in approval. As long as her customers were happy, she thought. And boy, was this one happy.

He jumped up, planting a wet kiss on her cheek in appreciation.

Now if only I could get that kind of affection from a man and not Julia Edwards's cocker spaniel, Precious, she thought.

Ever since her visit to Judge Boyd's sauna the night before, she'd been craving the affections of one man in particular: Felix Vaughn. She just couldn't seem to get him off her mind. Everything had suddenly become an innuendo to her sex-deprived mind.

But a few good days spent with Felix couldn't erase years of bad choices with men, men just like Felix. Her brain was still telling her that Phillip was the right choice. So then why hadn't she texted him yet?

"Idiot," she told herself.

Precious grumbled in offense. "Not you, Precious. Don't worry."

Addison gave the dog a treat as an apology. She couldn't afford to offend Precious. It seemed he was her last remaining loyal customer. At least Julia hadn't been persuaded by all the gossip and conjecture.

She hoped all the bonus treatments she gave him that day would be an added incentive to keep them coming back. She'd scraped, polished, buffed, combed, shined, and moisturized every square inch of the pooch, and he was wagging his tail like he was a new dog. He was going to be a major contender in the show the next weekend.

"Well, I think that's it for today," Addison said to Melody. "We don't have any bookings for the rest of the day, so why don't you take off early?"

"Are you sure? I could tidy up the back."

Addison sighed. "The back has been tidied and retidied

a dozen times in the last week. I've had nothing else to do. I'm sure it's okay."

"Okay. Well if you're sure." Melody hung her apron in the cupboard and grabbed her purse. "I'll see you later?"

"You bet. Enjoy your afternoon."

Addison watched her leave, happy to have her company back. After the cocktail mixer, she'd given Melody a few days off to recuperate emotionally. However, since she'd been playing spies with Felix, her shop had to be closed with no one to watch it. With the evidence they found at the Regency Center, she'd felt confident enough in Melody's innocence to let her come back. However, there still wasn't enough business to keep them both busy, even with the odd walk-in.

Addison finished cleaning up and took Precious into the back where he could relax in the lounge. Being the only customer, he had free rein of the various play areas: the toy box, the puppy palace, the lapdog lounge, the pillow pit.

Once she'd settled him in the back, bribing his patronage with another treat, she was left with nothing to do but think, and wonder, and worry, and pace.

Princess's curious brown eyes roved back and forth across the spa from her miniature velvet settee, following Addison's anxious path. Addison was wearing a trail into the black-and-white checkered flooring with her ballet flats. She gnawed on a sunset pink gel nail while eyeing up her phone on the counter.

"It's already been like twenty minutes. I can look again, right?" she asked Princess.

The doxie made a throaty, exasperated growl and laid her head back down on her paws.

"Okay maybe only twelve." She glared at her phone, her annoyingly silent phone, like it had personally insulted her.

The date of her fashion show was drawing near, and the RSVP list still amounted to a big fat zero. Not to mention, there'd been no calls, no emails, no texts, or tweets, or chimes of any sort. Not from customers, not from Phillip, not even from Felix. Not that she cared about the last. At least, that's what she was trying to convince herself. But he said he was following up on a couple of leads that afternoon. Shouldn't he be giving her moment by-moment updates? They were supposed to be in this together, whatever that meant.

Her phone rang. *Finally.*

Addison practically sprinted across the spa and flung herself over the hot pink shabby chic desk.

She hit the accept button. "Hello? Hello?" she panted into the phone.

"Congratulations," a recorded voice said. "You've been selected to—"

Groaning, she hung up. But she clung to the bedazzled phone like it was a discounted angora sweater.

"It couldn't hurt to check," she told Princess. "Someone might have RSVP'd by now. It is the weekend. People are off work, catching up on emails," she reasoned.

She opened an app to view the reservations for her fashion show. Determined that this time there would be good news, that by the sheer strength of her positivity she could change the numbers on the screen, she held her breath and hit the icon.

And frowned.

There must have been something wrong with her positive mojo. The RSVP list hadn't changed. It was still that big, lonely, empty-looking zero. Slumping across the desk, she tossed her phone aside just as another chime rang out. This time from the front door.

She looked up at the newcomer walking through the front door. "It's you," she said. "Thank God."

Felix beamed down at her. "Couldn't stand being without me. I totally understand."

She felt herself blush a little at the comment, unable to meet his eyes. "You wish."

Ever since the night before, she'd found herself imagining Felix in different ways. Not as the single-minded, womanizing bartender she first thought he was, but a guy who maybe she'd misjudged. A guy who could actually be pretty sweet once you got to know him.

"Why haven't you called?" she asked. "What did you find out today? Have you got a lead? Do we need another stakeout?"

"Eager for a repeat of last night?"

"I'm eager to end it."

He leaned on the desk, batting his eyelashes at her. "Not all of it, I hope."

She gave him a coy smile, trying not to give anything away. "I'm talking about solving the crime."

"You know what's a crime? That we're all alone and you're still fully dressed." His hair was messier than usual, windblown like he'd walked all the way there from the pub. She found her fingers itching to reach up and pat it down.

"I'm serious." She pushed him away playfully. "What did you discover from your leads?"

"Nothing."

She pouted. "Nothing?"

"Zilch, nada, zero. I checked in on Jayden, our new hire at the pub. He really did have food poisoning. No way was he busy stealing a bunch of dogs while he was making sweet love to a toilet bowl." He pulled a face.

"Well, we still have to look into Julia Edwards. Her dog is here right now, actually." Addison nodded her head toward the general area of the back room. "She told me earlier that she's going to be leaving for the rest of the weekend. We could always case her house tonight."

He rubbed a hand over the back of his neck. "Sorry. I've actually got plans tonight."

"Okay." His reaction seemed strangely apologetic.

She was tempted to ask what those plans entailed, but she told herself it was none of her business.

He held up a finger, interrupting her jealous train of thought. "But I have a problem you can help me solve."

"Like I need any more problems."

"Wait here. I'll be right back."

Felix ducked out of the spa, and when the door chimed again, Addison turned to see a mangy furball on four legs. The dog was so mixed breed, she couldn't begin to guess its family heritage. His gray wiry fur stuck up in tangled tufts, his ears pressed back against his head as if ashamed of his appearance.

Big brown eyes turned to look up at her, as though asking her, *Help me.*

"This is Oliver," Felix said. "He's not exactly at his best today. I tried a few DIY tricks at home to groom him, but they didn't work."

Princess padded over from her settee, the little bells on her ballerina dress tinkling. She gave Oliver the once-over, sniffing in distaste at his mangy state.

"I didn't know you had a dog," Addison said. "Why didn't you tell me?"

"There's a lot you don't know about me. All you have to do is ask." Felix hopped onto one of the bright pink Queen Anne chairs, kicking his feet up on the coffee table.

Addison rounded her desk and knelt down in front of the dog. "Well hello, Oliver. It's nice to meet you." She held out a hand, and he automatically raised his paw for her to shake.

"He's quite the gentleman," she said.

"So am I." Felix locked his hands behind his head like it was a relaxing Saturday afternoon on the beach. "When I want to be."

"So, that would be never?" She gave him her brightest smile and he returned it.

"So what seems to be the problem?" Addison reached out to pet Oliver, assessing him at the same time with her practiced eye, looking for matted hair or dry skin patches. She quickly discovered the problem on his wagging tail. The long fur had been painfully matted with what could only be described as pink goo.

"What happened here?"

"There was a bubble-gum incident," Felix said.

"How did it get so matted in there?"

"Oh, that was my attempt to fix it." He rubbed the back of his neck sheepishly.

She stood up and headed over to her cabinet full of various oils, tinctures, potions, and lotions. The bottles clinked as she rummaged through them to find the right antidote.

"I wouldn't have taken you for a bubble-gum guy," she called back.

"What kind of guy do you take me for?" She heard him come up behind her.

Now there was a loaded question. "Spearmint, maybe. Spicy cinnamon?"

He ran a slow finger down her back where her floral dress dipped low. "Sounds hot."

Addison shivered, but slapped his hand away and continued to search the cupboard for the cure. "I'm going to have to use the big guns."

"Big guns?"

"Peanut butter. Works like a charm," she said. "And makes a great snack."

"Mmmm." He brought his lips down to her exposed neck, and moaned against it. "I know I could use a bite." His teeth grazed her as he playfully began nibbling her skin.

"Hey!" She laughed. "I'm a professional here. I have a job to do. Maybe we should take care of your little problem first."

"Seems you've created a whole new problem." His eyes dropped down as a hint. She followed his gaze to his jeans, which had a curious bulge she didn't think belonged to his phone.

"You can go take care of that," she said. "In the meantime, I'll be taking a look at this tail." She bent down to assess Oliver's mess again.

Felix bit his lip and ran his eyes down her body. "And in the meantime, I'll be checking out yours."

"I have ways of dealing with bad dogs like you," she warned with a hint of a smile. "Sit," she ordered.

Felix returned to his position in the waiting area with a smirk.

"Good boy."

Addison could feel his eyes on her as she began, first meticulously working out the cherry pink bubble-gum, one glob at a time.

"So how long have you been in business?" Felix asked her.

"About two years now," she said. "Princess was actually my inspiration for finally taking the chance."

"How so? She loan you the money?"

Addison snorted. "Because show dog or not, I believe every dog deserves the same care and attention. They're all beautiful in their own way. I just like to help them look as beautiful on the outside as they are on the inside. And Princess is just as beautiful as any other show dog."

"Did Princess ever compete?"

"She was bred to be a show dog, but it just wasn't in the cards for her. She was born with one leg shorter than the others."

Felix was quiet for a moment, and when she looked over at him, his mouth was pursed thoughtfully, different from his usual sly smirk. "She hides the defect well. You'd hardly know unless you looked closely."

His scrutiny made her uncomfortable. She got that feeling again, like he could see through her makeup, past the perfectly liquid-lined eyes, through the sun-kissed bronzer, and under the pouty pink lips to the real her.

Addison ducked her head, focusing intently on Oliver's tail. "Just because a dog has a so-called defect, doesn't mean they're any less perfect or lovable than the next one. Everyone deserves to be happy."

"Dog," he said.

"What?"

"Every dog. You said every*one*." The serious expression remained on his face.

"Oh." She laughed it off. "Whatever. You understood what I meant."

His lips pursed again and he nodded. "I think I do. For the first time, I think I finally understand you."

Addison doubled her vigorous scrubbing, ready to finish the conversation. When she'd combed the last glob of it out, she patted the side of her leg and called Oliver over to the shower stalls.

He lopped after her, toenails clicking on the tiles. She made a mental note to cut them after a quick hair trim.

Once Oliver was in the pink mosaic shower stall, Addison turned on the rain shower. Water drizzled down from above like a warm tropical storm. For a minute, the dog tensed and danced skittishly. Once she began to work the seaweed and jasmine cleanser into his matted fur, he relaxed under her massaging hands. His leg began vibrating with pleasure at each scratch of her nails under his chin, a little to the left, in that "Oh yeah, right there" spot.

The last of the suds finally washed down the drain. Addison reached over to turn off the water. When she straightened up, she felt something press against her from behind.

She yelped in surprise and spun around. Out of instinct she clenched her fist, realizing too late that the spray nozzle was still in her hand.

The trigger activated. Water shot out. Felix yelped, jumping back, but not before his plaid shirt was soaked through.

Addison dropped the nozzle and held a hand to her mouth, mostly to hide her giggles. "I'm so sorry. I didn't even hear you sneak up."

Felix gave her a sour look. He spread his arms out helplessly. To add salt to the wound, Oliver hopped out of the shower and shook his coat, spraying Felix from head to toe before going to curl up next to Princess.

Pressing her lips together to hide her smile, Addison shrugged innocently. "At least I didn't ruin a nice shirt."

Now his expression darkened. That predatory look was back. Addison was already shuffling back as he took his first step toward her.

"Now look," she said, in a totally calm and reasonable manner, "it was just an accident."

He took another step, forcing her back. Reaching into his pocket, he drew out his phone and laid it on the table outside of the shower stalls. She didn't know what that meant, but it couldn't be good.

"Let me get you a towel," she offered, trying to go around him.

But Felix cut her off. His lowered gaze was fixed on

hers. His fan of thick black lashes made his eyes look darker as he glowered menacingly. There was the smallest hint of a smile, but it had a devilish tinge to it.

His shoes squelched on the wet tiles until he'd backed her all the way to the shower at the end of the row.

Addison hesitated at the edge of the stall. "I just reacted. I didn't mean to spray you."

He was nose to nose with her, or rather forehead to chin, since he was that much taller. Without a word, he took a final step and forced her back into the stall. Reaching out, he grasped the shower handle.

Addison gasped. "Don't you d—"

She squealed as water shot down from above, feeling not so much like a soothing tropical rainforest sprinkle as it did a chilly Dublin mist.

Gasping and grunting between short breaths, she scrambled to push past him and out of the stall. But Felix planted a hand on either side of her, his thick arms caging her in.

"Not so fast," he said.

Felix was in the shower with her now, water drenching his hair, plastering the dark curls to his face and neck. His T-shirt molded to his body like Superman's spandex, revealing the contours and swells of a figure not unlike the Man of Steel's.

As though her hands had a mind of their own, they reached up, crawling their way over his six-pack that she'd gotten a sneak preview of the night before.

He ducked his head, bringing his face closer to hers. Water ran in a stream down the bridge of his nose and hit her cheek, connecting their bodies. She imagined she could feel the connection. Could sense the heat from his body warming the water before it ran across her own skin, down her neck, her chest, past her neckline to caress her breasts. It was like an extension of his own body exploring hers, a finger running lightly down her stomach, soaking into the lace of her underwear.

Addison closed the space between them. She pressed her lips against his, water sprinkling into her mouth. It mixed with the taste of his kiss as she sucked the water from his lips, as though she could drink him in.

The shower rained down on her bare arms and shoulders, tickling, energizing. Her skin felt electrically charged, sensitive to every touch.

While his tongue played with hers in a teasing game, rivulets of water ran from the hem of her drenched dress, down the curves of her legs, snaking along her thighs. Her nipples hardened under the cool water, skin tightened, breath hitched.

Felix backed her up to the tiles and pressed himself against her. His hot hands moved like refreshing fire over the swells of her breasts and up her neck. His lips moved faster against her own, harder and harder, his tongue filling her mouth with his hungry desire.

Addison felt the drizzle of water rushing over them as though it were the salty spray of seawater on a pirate ship in the Caribbean. She closed her eyes. Yes, they were on the *Black Pearl*. Felix was her Jack Sparrow and she was his naughty wench. Even caught in a raging storm, they couldn't keep their hands off each other, their lust keeping them warm.

Through her thin dress she felt the heat of his hands. His grip tightened over the swell of her ample hips and pulled them closer to his, grinding them against his own until it was no longer just water soaking her underwear.

Eager hands searched her body, gripped her butt, assessing the size, the weight, the feel of it through the fabric. Fingers explored the hemline of her dress, pushing it up her thigh until those exploring fingers traced the edge of her panties. They tugged at them but went no further, as though knocking at her door, waiting for an invitation.

She answered the gentle knock by reaching down to his belt and with a flick of leather, a jingle of metal, there came the satisfying *zip* as she pulled out Jack Sparrow's mighty cutlass sword.

Then there was a *ding*, like someone had forgotten to turn off their cell phone during a movie.

The sound snapped Addison back to reality like a cold shower—aided by the fact that they were actually in a cold shower. It was the front door. Someone had entered the spa.

Breaking away from Felix, Addison pushed against his chest. Why did this keep happening? Why did she keep letting it? Not letting it, encouraging it. Jack Sparrow was the bad boy. *Bad*, she repeated in her head.

Felix was like a scary movie that she knew she should shut off, but she kept watching through her fingers despite herself. Yet, as he leaned against the tiled wall across from her catching his breath, his fly splayed open, dripping wet, the only thing scary was just how bad she wanted him.

And maybe that wasn't the worst thing. Maybe for once her instincts were right, her heart's as well as her primal instincts. Maybe she'd made so many mistakes that she was lumping him in with all the rest. When in reality, she'd found her prince beneath those pauper's clothes. She'd found her Aladdin.

Addison turned off the shower, and that's when she heard the high-pitched "Hello-o-o?"

"Oh no," Addison hissed. "It's Julia. I wasn't expecting her for another couple of hours." She glanced down at her sopping dress. How was she going to explain this? Some professional she was.

"Coming!" she called, wringing out some of the water

dripping from her sodden outfit. But it was futile. Unsure of how she was going to explain her appearance, she sighed and reluctantly headed up front.

When Julia spotted Addison, she pushed her Prada sunglasses on top of her head. Her eyes bulged as she took Addison in from her tangled hair to the puddle forming under her.

"What on Earth happened to you?"

"I, umm . . ." Addison heard shuffling feet behind her and cringed. She should have told Felix to stay put. The situation was bad enough already. Gritting her teeth, she turned to glare at him.

Felix was holding the wrench she usually kept under the sink. "A line burst," he told Julia, waving the wrench like it was cold hard evidence. "Water everywhere. It's best you stay clear."

Julia looked as surprised as Addison felt. "Oh dear. Your poor dress, Addison."

Addison's expression froze in what she hoped was angelic innocence. Cheeks burning, she clapped her hands and changed the subject. "You must be missing Precious."

"Yes." Julia set down her Coach purse. "How is my boy?"

"He's just hanging out in the lounge. Right this way, please."

Addison did her best to block the woman's view of the shower stalls and the pooling water on the floor.

As she passed Felix, she crossed her eyes in relief and mouthed "Thank you."

He responded with a silent salute with the wrench.

Julia followed Addison past Princess and a damp Oliver to the playroom. "Where's my Precious?" she called out as they walked down the hall. "Where's my special little boy?"

"He's waiting for you right back here. . . ." Addison tapered off as she opened the door.

With a shaking hand, she turned the dimmer switch up until every light in the room was blazing. Her body was suddenly crippled with fear. She'd been wrong before: *this* was the horror movie.

Addison leaned against the wall, her breaths coming in gulps, like she was drowning. Her frantic eyes scanned the space, from the toy box to the puppy palace to the lapdog lounge to the pillow pit.

But Precious was gone.

17

Give a Dog a Bad Name

"No. No. No." Addison leaned against the doorframe, feeling like the lounge room was spinning. "This can't be happening. Not again."

Running past Julia and over to the pillow pit, she began tossing pillows aside. She rammed her head into the plastic halls of the puppy palace. But she couldn't find head nor tail of her last remaining customer.

"Where is he?" Julia's voice shook as she collapsed among the pillows. "Where's my Precious? Precious!"

"Addison!" Felix called. "Back here!"

She followed the sound of Felix's voice to the hall. He was headed for the door to the back alley still gripping the wrench. It had been left ajar, daylight streaming through.

She ran after him, Julia close on her heels, hissing "Precious! My Precious!" like a distraught Gollum from *The Lord of the Rings*.

Felix threw his weight against the metal door and burst into the alley. It swung open and Addison caught a glimpse of a dark van parked outside.

"Hey!" Felix yelled.

The door swung shut again, blocking Addison's view. By the time she caught up and opened it again, Felix was struggling with the van's back doors, heaving on the handles, one foot on the bumper for leverage.

Taking the wrench, he smashed in the back window, but there was metal mesh on the inside, preventing him from reaching in.

Addison ran to the passenger door where she could see a person sitting behind the wheel. She tried the handle but it was locked. Bringing a fist up, she banged on the window. When the person turned to her, their face was hidden beneath a black balaclava.

The driver fumbled with the keys before the engine started and revved. Addison was banging and kicking the door when she was grabbed from behind.

Her feet left the ground and she was whirled away just as the tires squeaked, skidding over where she'd been standing a second before. The van took off, leaving them in a cloud of dust.

Felix released Addison and took off after it on foot.

Coughing, Addison blinked her vision clear and stumbled after him. The van struggled to pick its way down the narrow alley. The garbage and parked cars created an obstacle course, forcing it to slow down.

Addison chased after Felix, but hindered by shorter legs, a wet dress clinging to her thighs, and flimsy ballet flats, she quickly fell behind. She didn't think Dick Tracy had to deal with problems like this.

She watched Felix forge on, sprinting down the alley after the van, proving those muscles weren't just for looks.

"Get 'em, Felix!" she cheered with more blood lust than she thought she had in her.

At the end of the alley the van cranked it, lilting to one side as it turned and peeled onto the main street.

Fists pumping, legs surging him forward, Felix ran out into the street after it. There was a screech of tires and a horn honk as a car narrowly missed him. Another skidded to a stop, inches from his body. Addison gasped, flinching from the sight.

But Felix leapt over the car's hood and continued down the street after the van. Then he was gone from Addison's sight.

There were distant sounds of horn honks and disrupted traffic. Addison's heart skipped a beat with each noise. Her legs tensed, ready to run after him, to see that he was okay. But she hesitated, knowing she'd be of no help to him that way.

Going against her instincts, she dashed back into the spa. Julia hovered on the other side of the door tugging nervously on her pearl necklace.

"But, but, my Precious." Her eyes bulged as she gripped Addison's arms, frantic gel nails digging into her soft skin. "My Precious."

Addison's heart clenched for Julia's sudden loss, but the sooner she called the police, the better. Addison wrenched away from her grip, and Julia's blubbering faded away as she ran for the showers where Felix's phone still lay on the counter. The moment she entered the room, Oliver and Princess got to their feet, ready for action.

Addison's fingers shook as she dialed 9-1-1, in fact, her whole body was shaking. Partly from her cold, wet dress, but mostly from anger. No, fury. She'd never felt so furious in all her life, forget the positivity, forget the good cop, bad cop routine. She wanted blood. Someone was taking advantage of her, and she wasn't going to stand for it. Now it was personal.

When the police picked up, she said, "Hello? Yes. I own a spa and someone just stole my customer."

"You're reporting a kidnapping?" the female voice on the other end asked.

"Yes. They took him in a van and drove off with him. We tried to run after them but they got away." Addison tried to rearrange her scattered thoughts to give as much detail as possible. Anything to help get Precious back.

"It's important for your safety that you no longer follow them," the operator advised. "Is anyone still in pursuit?"

"Yes. I think so, but I can't contact him." She frowned, wondering what would happen to Felix if he succeeded in catching up to the dognappers.

"Did you get a license plate number from the van?"

"No license plate," Addison said. "But it was a dark van. Black, I think, with dark windows. It looked new." She rattled off her spa's address, just in case they wanted to send all units in the area ASAP.

"Did you see your customer when they were taken? Were they still conscious?"

The answer caught in Addison's throat. She thought back and couldn't recall hearing Precious bark or growl. There were no sounds of a fight. Surely she would have heard it. What if they'd done something to Precious, drugged or hurt him to keep him quiet?

"No I didn't," she said, finally. "But if he was conscious, I'm sure he would have been biting and scratching."

The operator hesitated. "Biting?"

"Yes, he gives me a good nip, now and then."

"Is he combative?"

"Only when I trim his nails," Addison said, distracted. She was peeking out the storefront, hoping she would see Felix strolling up at any moment.

Julia hovered nearby, following Addison's nervous pacing around the room like a shadow.

"What is his name?" the operator asked.

"Emerald Hill's Sir Precious Vandersnout Edwards. But he goes by Precious."

"Precious? Okay . . . ."

Addison could hear typing on the other end of the line.

"Can you describe Mr. Edwards for me?" the operator asked.

"He's about fifteen inches tall, brown eyes, long blond hair."

"Buff," Julia said between sobs. "Buff hair."

"Right. Buff," Addison repeated.

"Fifteen inches?" The operator's calm and collected voice suddenly increased in volume. "Is the victim an infant?"

"No. He's fully grown."

"Is he disabled in any way?"

"Oh no," Addison assured her. "He's the perfect specimen."

There was a pause on the other side of the line. "Specimen of what?"

"Of a cocker spaniel."

"The victim *is a dog*, ma'am?"

"Yes, of course," Addison said, like it was completely obvious. "I run a dog spa." She must have said that already, hadn't she? She glanced out the window again, but there was still no sign of Felix.

"Are you sure you meant to call the police and not animal control?"

"No. This is serious. Precious has been stolen. He is a major contender in this year's Western Dog Show. There have been other dogs stolen before this. It's part of an ongoing police investigation." At least Addison hoped it was, because she wasn't doing a very good job cracking it herself.

She saw Julia nodding along with her statement, but her red eyes had glazed over as she stared at the checkered floor tiles.

"We've dispatched a unit." The operator's voice, which had always been calm, now lacked urgency too. "They should arrive there shortly."

"But I've described the van." Addison gripped the phone, as if she could keep her on the line that way. "They might still be in the neighborhood. Maybe they can head them off."

"The officers will decide the best course of action after they speak with you," she said with no emotion. "They will be there soon. Is there anything else? Would you like me to wait on the line with you until they arrive?"

"No. I guess not. Thank you." Addison hung up the phone and frowned at it.

It wasn't like she expected them to send out the SWAT team or anything, but she'd expected a little more get-up-and-go. Maybe just a helicopter or two? Especially since it was related to the previous dognappings.

Didn't they care? Didn't they understand? These dogs were like family to their owners. Not to mention the genetic protectors of their purebred line.

"What now?" Julia asked quietly.

"I suppose we wait for the police to come."

Julia sank onto the hot pink sofa, staring at her hands. Addison sat down next to her. Princess seemed to sense the seriousness of the situation and came over to stare at her. Addison picked her up and held her for comfort.

The dognappers were picking off the show dogs one at a time. And now Precious had joined their numbers, like some sick list was being checked off somewhere.

The longer the police took to search for the dogs, the less chance they had of ever finding them, of ever reuniting them with their owners. Their unknown fate was beginning to feel more certain as each day passed, but Addison didn't like to consider what that could mean. It made her insides churn with dread.

Julia sniffed, dabbing at her tears with a tissue. *Poor Julia*, Addison thought. *Poor Precious.*

Details of the afternoon, the van, the driver, swam through her mind as she scoured for information that could possibly help the police track down the bad guys. When she began to make a mental list of facts to mention, she suddenly realized that maybe she should be a little more concerned about her own predicament. If she hadn't been suspect number one before, she would be now.

This was the worst thing that could have happened. At least during the other two nappings, people speculated and gossiped, but no one could point their finger directly at her. This time, she'd have a tough time convincing customers, maybe even the cops, that she was innocent. She suddenly had an image of getting dragged away in handcuffs. Feeling anxious, she began to pace.

At least she had Felix as a witness—they definitely had an alibi. But maybe that was worse. They'd already been accused of being in cahoots, and now they were alone together when another show dog disappeared.

How was she going to deny it now? And where was Felix anyway? Was he okay? Her emotions were flip-flopping sporadically and she had to sit down before her shaky legs gave way.

Felix should have been back. She tried to think positively, that he might have caught up to the van, grabbed the bad guys, and saved the day. But then again, what if they'd fought back or run him over?

Just days ago she wouldn't have shed a tear if Felix had been hit by a van. Well, that was a bit extreme. Maybe just clipped by the mirror or something. Oh, how things had changed in such a short period of time. Now she found herself pacing the spa, dreading the worst-case scenario.

Now that she was facing all the dreadful outcomes rushing through her scattered brain at once, she knew these changes had nothing to do with her undeniable physical attraction to him. There was more between them.

Felix couldn't be the selfish womanizer she'd first thought he was. He was helping her find the dognapper, and while he said it was because he was under the heat too, she knew it wasn't that simple. She recalled the way he looked after her in the sauna, how he took care of her when she was freaking out. Felix had genuinely been there for her when she needed him. And he had a dog too, so he must have cared about those missing animals as much as she did.

It was like he was hiding the good man he really was under that gruff exterior. Beneath it all was an attentive man, a man who did care about the damsel in distress. His indifferent attitude was all an act. It had to be.

Addison jumped to her feet, setting Princess down. "Julia, I'm going to go search for Felix."

"But I thought the police told us to wait."

"I know, but I'm worried that something has happened to him," she said over her shoulder, already headed for the back door.

The worst-case scenarios continued to play over and over again in Addison's head. Her heart rate increased with each outcome she imagined. And with each quickening beat of her heart, her ballet flats slapped the floor to match it until she was sprinting down the hall.

Addison burst through the back door, staggering into the alley. The phone in her hand buzzed. She didn't even realize she'd still been gripping it.

She automatically glanced at the screen, and what she saw brought her to a halt. Surrounded by a multitude of kissy-face emoticons and hearts was a message.

I miss you. Come home soon. Can't wait to see you tonight. XOXO

Addison read the woman's name at the top of the conversation: Celia. It was the same woman he'd been texting the night before. Another message popped up, consisting of emoji burgers, sushi rolls, and various other foods.

Felix had said he had plans. Addison just hadn't imagined they were with another woman. Not while he had a hard-on for her. And not just any woman, she thought. Clearly someone he's been seeing for a while. Someone important, if the all those hearts were any indication.

Out of some sick need, or maybe a hope that this wasn't what she thought it was, that it was all just a misunderstanding, she scrolled up to view the previous text from Felix.

How's my girl?

Addison clenched the phone in her hand and looked away. All the energy that had filled her moments before drained away into the alley gutter.

Felix suddenly appeared at the end of the alley, his tired steps scuffing the pavement. When he saw her standing there, his pace quickened.

"They got away!" he yelled, scowling. "I never got a license plate either."

He got closer and took in the expression on Addison's face. She wasn't sure what it looked like at that moment. Shocked. Hurt, maybe. Filled with embarrassment? To think that even for a moment, she reconsidered that he could be anything but the arrogant jerk she first thought he was. He was only out to use her, after all.

Whatever her expression looked like, he'd misread, because his scowl softened and his arms opened wide for her. For a split second it called to Addison, invited her in, so warm and comforting, so genuine. But then his phone vibrated in her hand and when she looked at it, the message was from Celia.

I love you.

And she knew it was all just an act.

Before he could touch her, she chucked the phone at him. He grunted as it connected with his chest, and he lunged to catch it before it hit the ground.

Turning her back on him, she marched inside to wait for the police, slamming the door in his bewildered face.

18

Sick as a Dog

Bang. Bang. Bang.

The army of bare-chested men used their bulging muscles to swing their mighty battering ram against the heavy gates.

Bang. Bang. Bang.

They were led by none other than her Prince Charming, Phillip. He was there to save her and Princess. They'd been locked away, high in a tower by a dragon. Princess barked to let them know where they were. Addison had felt so trapped, so scared, so helpless. But it was okay because Phillip was there.

Bang. Bang. Bang. Bang.

The banging was louder this time, startling Addison right out of her sleep. She lurched up in bed and then instantly grabbed her head.

"Oh God," she groaned.

Princess barked, causing her brain to split in two. Suddenly those burly men were using that battering ram to break their way out of her skull.

"Princess. Shhh." But shushing a dachshund was as useless as wishing ice cream had fewer calories.

Addison blinked, wondering why the room was spinning, and why she felt like a zombie from *Dawn of the Dead*. Her eyes landed on the bottle of Shiraz on her nightstand. *That would explain it.*

She flopped back onto her pillow, closing her scratchy eyes. She couldn't move. She couldn't think. That is, until Princess licked her face and her mind began to spark with connecting memories: the stolen dogs, her ruined business, dashed hopes and dreams, the shower, Felix, his hands, his mouth, his mmm . . .

She began to drift off when the banging came once again.

Bang. Bang. Bang.

This time she realized it wasn't the throbbing in her head. Just the thing making it worse. It was someone at the door.

"Coming!" Addison called out, feeling the word reverberate inside her head. She clambered out of bed. In the process, she knocked over the remainder of her red wine, splattering her lace curtain.

"Crap." She picked Princess up and set her on the ground so she wouldn't jump and hurt herself. "Who bangs on someone's door at"—she glanced at her alarm clock—"ten thirty in the morning?"

She supposed the second empty wine bottle sitting on the hallway table explained the late start. After everything that had happened with Precious at the spa the day before, she'd gone into meltdown mode. A state that could only be remedied with ice cream, red wine, and a chick-flick marathon.

On her way past her tiny bathroom, she grabbed her fluffy housecoat from behind the door, banging her elbow on the doorframe. She swore under her breath, adding the injury to the list of things she'd like to yell at the unexpected visitor for. Along with her worsening headache.

She stumbled bleary-eyed across her apartment, stubbing her toe on the coffee table leg. By the time she wrenched open the door, she was already feeling like the Hulk, but when she saw who was on the other side, she saw green.

"What are you doing here?" she demanded.

"Good morning to you too." Felix pulled his most charming smile out.

Groaning, she tried to slam the door closed, but Felix stuck his foot out before it could shut in his face.

Determined that it would be a Felix-free day, no, make that week—hopefully life—she leaned against the door with her entire body weight. But since she was no Hulk, he managed to slip his hand inside.

It was grasping a Starbucks cup.

"Peace offering?" he said, jiggling it temptingly.

She glared at the green mermaid. She was taunting Addison with her steamy, delicious caffeineness, like a siren calling to her. Unable to resist, she swiped the cup from the hand and pulled away from the door.

She took a sip to calm her nerves before turning around. "What do you want?"

"You know you're going to have to talk to me at some point." He hovered in the doorway. "We still have a mystery to solve."

Princess sniffed at his feet, pawing at his leg as though asking where her treat was. When all he did was pet her and scratch her neck, she huffed and went in search of her own treat.

"What's the point?" Addison asked. "We still don't

know where those poor dogs are. We've run out of lead suspects and I've lost the last customer that actually still believed in me."

"Chin up. Don't get so down. There's still hope yet." He was acting supernice. Too nice. Maybe he knew that she saw the texts and he was there to suck up. Well, she wasn't about to fall for it.

"What is this?" she mumbled into her cup. "Role reversal?"

"You're usually so positive. What happened to that Addison?"

He took a few steps into her apartment, leaving the door cracked open. Maybe he sensed that her inner Hulk was ready to come out and play and he might need a quick getaway.

"I'm sorry. I guess it's the wine." *Why am I apologizing to him?* "Did you want something? I'd like to nurse my hangover here."

Felix wandered into her kitchen and began rummaging through her cupboards like he owned the place. Finally, he found what he was looking for and pulled out a bottle. He gave it a shake and it sounded like music to her sensitive ears.

"Nothing a couple of aspirin can't cure," he said.

Felix shook out a couple of pills and poured her a glass of water. "And as far as the investigation goes, we still have plenty of suspects. It's always the last one you check out." He handed her the glass and medication. "So get better so we can carry on."

Addison studied the pills in her hand dubiously before downing them. For a moment, she considered the possibility of resuming where they left off—the investigation, not the shower.

There were only a few days left before they were both screwed. The dog show started on Saturday, less than a week away. If she didn't clear her name soon, her fashion show and the launch of Fido Fashion would be a flop. Besides, didn't Felix have his own deadline to keep? If his own name wasn't cleared so he could start getting gigs soon, he wouldn't have the money for his down payment in time. Good-bye bar.

"How about tonight?" she asked.

Felix pulled a face. "I can't tonight. I work late. And I have, err, plans the next day."

"Plans?" Her eyebrows drew together. She remembered his "plans" with Celia.

"But maybe tomorrow night." He said it like a promise, maybe a mischievous warning as he stepped toward her. Running a finger along the collar of her housecoat, he spread it until he could see the swell of her breasts beneath her lacy tank top. "And then . . ." His voice trailed off suggestively. "Who knows?"

Princess hopped up on the couch as though getting comfy to watch the show unfold.

Felix's behavior only erased what little patience the coffee had bestowed upon Addison. She slapped his hand away. "And then nothing. You should be ashamed of yourself."

"What?" He held his hands up like she was wielding a gun. Her anger certainly felt as dangerous.

"I don't know what kind of girl you think I am." Heck, she didn't even know what kind of girl she was. She thought she knew what she wanted, and that was Phillip. So then why couldn't she seem to resist Felix? Why had she been so upset to discover he'd been playing the field? It wasn't even like they were dating.

Old habits die hard, she told herself. But she was determined to be done with that kind of guy. Hadn't she learned her lesson by now?

It was a good thing they were interrupted in the

shower. She had Phillip, after all. Phillip, Phillip, Phillip. He was the far superior choice. Her blockbuster hit, all the critics would agree. Felix, on the other hand, was the straight-to-DVD guy.

Phillip had a good job, he volunteered, he had manners, education, style, and breeding. Felix was a bar rat looking for a casual hook-up.

Well that wasn't going to be her. Sure, there was the pool table, and the sauna, and now the shower. But that was it. No take two, no additional after credit scene, no sequel. The end.

Felix laughed incredulously. "What are you talking about? Are those aspirin or crazy pills?" He picked up the bottle and pretended to scan the label.

"Oh, so now I'm crazy?" she said, maybe just a little crazily.

"You're acting crazy."

"Maybe because men like you have driven me crazy."

"Men like me," he repeated.

"With your lies, and your 'I'm one of the good ones,' 'I'd never do anything to hurt you,' and all your empty promises."

"What promises? I've never said anything like that."

Okay, she thought, *maybe that wasn't him exactly, but all the guys before him that were just like him.*

Princess's eyes flicked back and forth between them, amused by the human drama.

Addison stomped toward Felix. "It's like a game to you, isn't it? To test your skills, see how good you are at pulling the wool over a girl's eyes."

"I have no wool." He laughed at the ridiculousness of it, spreading his hands to show his complete lack of wool.

But he wasn't getting off that easily. The way he was mocking her only made her anger feel completely justified. Not unreasonable or hangover-fueled at all.

She jabbed a finger in his chest. "You're a bamboo-zler."

"A bamboozler?"

"You, you bamboozle." Her voice cracked with emotion. And here she thought she'd done such a good job smothering her feelings with the wine.

"You think I've bamboozled you?" he asked seriously, clearly trying not to piss her off any more.

"Oh no, sir. Not me. I'm onto you, mister. But what about your girlfriend? She probably thinks you're working late or taking your dog in for grooming. Meanwhile, you're out dry-humping girls on pool tables and feeling their naughty bits in the shower."

She could feel the tears start to form, stinging her eyes. She blinked them away, using her anger to keep them at bay.

"Girl." He held up a finger. "As in singular. Just you. I just did that with *you*."

"Oh great. So I guess that makes me the other woman." She crossed her arms. "Well I'm not that kind of girl."

Felix threw his hands up in frustration. "What other woman?" He half-laughed, half-yelled.

"How about Celia?"

"Celia." This seemed to catch him off guard. "How do you know about her?"

"When I used your phone to call the cops yesterday, she texted you." She rolled her eyes. " 'I miss you. Come home soon.' " She scowled, and he backed up as she advanced on him, forcing him to the door so she could kick him out. Out of her life forever. "The hearts? The kissy faces?"

Felix covered his face with his hands, like he was embarrassed he'd been caught. *Good,* Addison thought. He *should* feel embarrassed.

"So what is she? A girlfriend? Or just some poor girl

you're stringing along like me?" What was she saying? She wasn't being strung along. She didn't care. Nope, not at all.

Beneath his hands, his face had turned red. His shoulders began to shake, and Addison hesitated. Was he crying? But the noises that came out of his mouth next weren't sobs, they were pure, gut-aching, uncontrollable laughter.

Addison stared at him, stupefied. Her fists clenched and she could feel her own face grow hot with fury. Felix was actually laughing at her. "This is funny to you?"

He leaned against the wall for support, like he was struggling to compose himself, his whole body rigid with laughter. "Yes. It's hilarious," he finally managed between gasps.

"You have no scruples, do you?" Addison's nostrils flared with anger. "I've had enough. You can leave right now."

Felix wiped a tear from his eye. "I'm not dating anyone." He took a calming breath. "Yes, the text was from Celia's phone, but she was texting on behalf of someone else."

"Who?"

"My girl."

Not wanting to hear another word, Addison reached for the half-open door and flung it open. She hadn't been expecting anyone on the other side, so when she found a little girl standing at her door like something out of *The Shining*, she screamed and jumped back.

Princess seemed to sense the newcomer and began to bark furiously, but was just too lazy to leave her perch on the sofa to investigate.

Addison clenched her fuzzy housecoat together. *What now?* She didn't think any of her neighbors had a kid, and she would have recognized this one since she was pretty cute. Two cinnamon braids ran down either side of the little girl's head, a stuffed rabbit dangling from one hand, its feet dragging on the hardwood floor.

Princess was still barking, making Addison's head throb again.

"Princess. Shhh."

Addison rubbed her temples. Not the best start to nursing a hangover. She'd had quite enough of this morning already. All she wanted to do was climb back into bed.

"Hello," the little girl said. She couldn't have been more than five years old.

"Are you lost, sweetheart?" Addison asked the girl. It didn't look like she was there to sell Girl Scout cookies—although Addison could have really used some chocolate right then.

"Have you seen my dad?" the girl asked.

"Your dad?" Addison leaned outside the door and looked both ways down the hall, but she didn't see anyone around.

"Addison," Felix said, dragging the door open farther. He gestured to the little girl. "Meet *my girl*."

The moment the girl saw Felix, she ran into Addison's apartment and into his arms. He picked her up like she was as light as her ragged stuffed bunny. "Addison, this is my daughter. Naia."

Addison gawked at the girl cradled in his arms as if she were an alien. "You have a daughter?"

"I do." Felix was watching her reaction very carefully. He wasn't laughing anymore. In fact, he looked nervous.

"I had no idea," she said, unsure of what reaction she was supposed to have. What had he expected? "I never would have thought."

"There's a lot you don't know about me." It was his usual sarcastic response, but his expression was more serious than she'd ever seen.

The battering ram inside her head finally broke through and her head throbbed. She collapsed onto the couch.

Felix sat next to her, an awkward distance away. Or maybe it just seemed that way to Addison. Naia shifted in his lap to peer at Addison from the crook of his neck.

Princess crawled over Addison's lap to greet the little girl. Naia's eyes widened and she held out her hand for Princess to lick. Forgetting her shyness, she slid off her dad's lap to pet the doxie, who Addison had never seen act so submissive. Normally she was the queen bee. Instead, she flopped on her side, exposing her belly for a rub.

"Look," Felix said. "I know you're still mad at me about, well, come to think of it, I'm not sure what you're mad about anymore."

Addison half-laughed, half-sighed. "You and me both."

"But I'm kind of in a bind. Joe was desperate for someone to cover a split shift today at the bar. He said he'd allow me back for the day, but my babysitter's come down with the flu."

Addison stared at him blankly, the rusty cogs in her brain struggling to turn. She needed more aspirin. Or chocolate. Suddenly she remembered her coffee and took a regenerating sip, trying to make sense of where Felix was going with all this.

"All my usual backup babysitters aren't available," he said.

She continued to stare at him, uncomprehending.

"So I was hoping, if you weren't busy, that you might be able to look after Naia for a few hours."

"What?" Addison sat up, spilling coffee on herself. "Me?"

"I know it's a lot to ask, but I wouldn't unless I was desperate. With everything that's going on, I feel like Joe is just one excuse away from firing me. As it is, I'm lucky he's giving me this shift. I can't lose this job, Addison." He reached over and grabbed her hand, squeezing it. "Please."

His forehead creased with worry, and she supposed with his job on the line, she didn't blame him. And with a daughter to provide for . . . God, a daughter. Her thoughts were still reeling from the news, especially after she thought it was a girlfriend he was hiding from her. And why did he hide it from her in the first place?

"I don't want you to lose your job," she said. "But me? I've never really taken care of a kid. I'm not sure I'd even know what to do."

"It's not like she's in diapers or anything. She's five years old. Just play with her, hang out. She'll let you know if she needs anything."

Addison considered the little girl for a moment. She supposed he was right. It wasn't rocket science. It might even be fun. You know, compared to the full day of wallowing she had scheduled. But she had to wonder why he'd trust her with his daughter. Or was it just out of complete desperation that he was asking?

"Please," he said again.

She smiled. "Sure. We can hang out," she said, more to Naia than Felix. "What do you say?"

Naia nodded shyly.

"Awesome. Let me grab her stuff." Felix practically shot out the front door. In less than ten seconds he returned with an armload of stuff. "Here's her car seat, her favorite book, and a list of emergency numbers in case you need them." He handed her an overstuffed bag that weighed a ton. "And I've packed the two of you a picnic so you don't have to worry about cooking."

Addison stared at all the stuff that he'd obviously stashed out in the hall. "What if I'd said no?"

"I knew you'd say yes. You're too sweet." Before she could react, Felix leaned over and kissed her on the cheek.

Her skin warmed where his lips had touched, and for some reason her brain finally caught up. Just in time to remind her that Felix was beaming at her like he always did, but this time she had no makeup on, her hair was a mess, her breath tasted like stale wine, and her unshaven leg hair prickled beneath her frumpy housecoat.

He waved as he headed for the door. "You're the best. I owe you one. Just name it."

Addison watched Felix leave with a dazed expression. She plunked down next to Naia on the couch. Naia looked at her expectantly, and all Addison could think of was that she wanted another aspirin.

19

Hair of the Dog That Dumped You

Naia released a blood-curdling scream, running for her life across the field, a pack of wild doxies hot on her tail. Her two little legs were no match for their four stumpy ones. They surrounded her, jumping up and attacking her with vicious licks and the odd slap of a happy tail wag.

Naia's scream morphed into giggles until she just couldn't take it anymore. Whipping her arm back, she tossed the ball as far away from her as she could which was only about ten feet. The wild pack took off after it, droopy ears flapping in the wind. She let them fight over it before stealing it back and starting the process all over again.

Addison watched on from the gazebo while she ate her Sunday pancakes. Apparently it didn't take long to fill up a five-year-old tummy, but it looked like Naia had found plenty to keep her occupied around the rescue center.

Piper had abandoned her seat at the picnic table for Aiden's lap, where he lounged on the grass. Princess was sprawled out next to him, her pink belly exposed. He rubbed it absently while his own dog, Sophie, was part of the pack wrestling with Naia.

Piper watched the little girl play with a distant look in her eye. Addison recognized that face. It was the baby face. She'd had that look once herself.

Addison wondered if her friend was feeling the pressure of the ticking clock yet. She was twenty-seven. Had she and Aiden discussed it? She figured it wouldn't be long before they were married and popping out ridiculously beautiful babies.

It had been a long time since Addison last thought about having kids. *Could* think about having kids. That was one fantasy she didn't allow herself to dream about. Because it was one dream that would never come true.

"She's a cute little girl," Marilyn said, observing Addison over her teacup. She'd taken Picasso out of his tiny wheelchair, and he sat on her lap while she spoiled him with little bits of pancake.

"She sure is," Addison said.

Bob placed another plate of sausages in the center of the picnic table and helped himself to one before sitting back down next to Marilyn. "You're good with her, you know."

"Maybe I've found my backup career," she said. "Professional babysitter."

Addison hadn't planned on showing up for their traditional rescue center pancake breakfast, considering her hangover and plans to wallow all day. But it quickly became apparent that there was little to interest a five-year-old in her apartment besides, of course, a ton of Disney movies.

So Addison put *Frozen* on and grabbed a quick shower before heading to the center for some help entertaining Naia. But it turned out Naia was pretty good at entertaining herself. Well, the rescue dogs were entertaining her, and she seemed pretty thrilled by so many playmates.

When Addison shifted her attention from Naia back to her group of friends, she found Marilyn giving her a strange look again. Addison wondered if maybe she had something on her face and wiped a napkin over her mouth. But when the look didn't disappear, Addison stuck her fork in another pancake. Not because she was hungry, but because she just wanted to avoid Marilyn's probing eyes.

"So Addison," Piper called from Aiden's lap. "Still no news from the police, huh?"

Addison had been trying to avoid the topic around Aiden. She still hadn't told him just how bad business was, and if she didn't figure out who was stealing the dogs, it was only going to get worse. But there was still a chance that she could turn things around. She didn't want to tell him if it wasn't necessary. Or rather, she was too embarrassed to.

"No," Addison said. "But Felix has been helping me look for information about the dognappings. He knows a lot of people who were working both parties when the dogs went missing."

She stuffed another mouthful of pancake into her face. She didn't want to explain exactly how they were looking, since it would probably worry her friends. Not to mention, some of it hadn't exactly been legal, and what with Bob being a cop and all, she didn't think he would approve.

"So you two have been working closely," Piper said, hopping off Aiden's lap and sliding onto the picnic table bench next to Zoe. "Spending a lot of time together."

Her two best friends were watching her from across the table, watching her, she noted eerily, as closely as

Marilyn. She fidgeted under their scrutiny and shoveled more pancake into her mouth.

"You and Felix, huh?" Zoe asked.

Addison cleared her throat, pretending not to notice the thick layer of suggestiveness in her voice. "Yeah, he's got his ear to the ground. He knows a lot of people in his line of work. He's got his hands in everything."

"Everything, huh?" Zoe bit her lip. "And how are those hands?"

Addison shot her friend a look, but could feel heat crawling up her neck beneath her polka dot scarf. "It's not like that. We're only working together to figure out what's going on. We have a mutual interest in finding the dognapper. That's all." She jabbed another piece of syrupy pancake to show there was nothing more to say.

Zoe grinned back, clearly with plenty more to say. "Oh. I'm sure there's loads of mutual interest."

"We're just coworkers. Associates."

"An associate who babysits?" Piper asked.

"He was just desperate," Addison said. "He needed someone to watch Naia or he might have lost his job."

"He wouldn't have trusted you with his kid if he didn't feel comfortable with you."

"I suppose," she said, wondering if she should grab another pancake so they'd leave her alone, but she was already stuffed. "But it's no big deal. We've just gotten to know each other well, that's all."

Then again, Addison thought, she obviously had a lot to learn about him yet. But he'd gotten to know her. If he already trusted her with his daughter, maybe it was kind of a big deal, after all. But what did that even mean?

Addison grabbed another pancake, ignoring that line of thought, because it didn't go anywhere, right? He wasn't that kind of guy. The one-woman, settle-down guy, and that was what she wanted. Although, she also wouldn't have pegged him as a dad guy, either. And yet, here Naia was.

What exactly did a guy like Felix want?

"Phillip on the other hand," Addison said. "Now there's potential."

Zoe leaned on her fist. "Oh, do tell."

"Well, he's cultured, and a humanitarian for animals, and a gentleman. Of course the good looks don't hurt." She was counting all the amazing things about him off on her fingers. "We'd never have to worry about money. If any big expenses came up, it wouldn't be a big deal." The thought of her dad's business suddenly popped into her head. She wouldn't be the only one who wouldn't have to worry about her livelihood or her marriage surviving financial hardships.

It wasn't the first time she'd dreamed about it. Heck, over the years she'd imagined a million different scenarios of how she could save her dad and herself from bills, and budgets, and bank loans. She felt a little guilty for spending Phillip's money, even if it was only in her head, but what if . . . ? And what was the point of money if you didn't use it to help the ones you loved?

Phillip was a great catch who just so happened to be rich. It's not like she'd planned to meet a man with a large trust fund, but she wasn't about to complain either. Ending up with a guy like him would be like having that Prada dress and wearing it too.

"Sounds exciting," Marilyn said. "Not to mention you could spend your weekends flying to Paris or Milan or London."

Addison sighed wistfully. "It does sound exciting, doesn't it?"

"Will we get to meet this Phillip at the gala on Friday?" Zoe asked.

"I hope so."

Marilyn poured herself another cup of Yorkshire tea. "So after Paris and London, then what?"

"Well. . . ." Addison hesitated.

As she thought about the answer, Marilyn added sugar to her teacup. Her spoon clinked loudly in the silence. Everyone had stopped whatever it was they were doing, waiting for her answer.

She spread her hands. "The sky's the limit."

"Come on," Piper said. "We know you better than that. I'm sure you've daydreamed your way through every romance flick ever made."

"Yeah, like when Bridget Jones finally notices Mark Darcy," Zoe said.

"Or the one where you're Audrey Hepburn and he's Humphrey Bogart."

"Have you imagined him as a sparkly vampire yet?" Zoe asked. "Or better yet, *Fifty Shades of Grey*." Her eyes practically rolled back into her head.

"Audrey Hepburn? Vampires?" Marilyn shook her head. "It's all well and good to daydream about this man, but are you thinking about him? About what life would be like together? That's the real test. Have you thought about what it would be like to live with him? Does he pick up after himself? What about waking up next to him when he's got drool stuck in his moustache?"

Zoe was fighting a grin. "Speaking from experience, Marilyn?" She glanced meaningfully at Bob's thick moustache.

Bob subconsciously dabbed at it with his napkin. Marilyn turned a shade of red that Addison had never seen on the woman before. And she'd known her for five years.

Raising her chin, the proper British woman focused studiously on stirring her already-stirred tea. "I'm just saying that it's important to be realistic. Imagine your man the way he really is. Not how you want him to be."

"Does he leave the toilet seat up?" Piper asked.

Zoe rolled her eyes. "Does he get crabby when he doesn't get his way?"

Addison remembered how Phillip treated his head of security after the dogs disappeared at his fundraiser. She didn't blame him for being upset, but she also thought he'd been a bit harsh. Maybe even a little condescending. At the time she tried to blow it off, but she realized that it bothered her even now.

Piper's eyes drifted over to where Aiden sat on the grass. "Do you dream about holding hands with him when you're wrinkly and old?"

Addison pushed her half-eaten pancake around her plate, feeling suddenly deflated. Drool and toilet seats weren't quite as romantic as sparkly vampires and dreams of Paris in the spring.

She supposed she was getting a little ahead of herself. It was something she always did when she started to date someone new. Even when she gave out her number. Okay, she'd even done it when a guy gave her a wink while serving her a latte the other week—and she was pretty sure he was gay.

But the stories in her head always went so much better than real life. They were places where anything could happen. She could have any life she wanted. It could be perfect.

As Addison helped clean up after breakfast, she recalled the last time she'd truly dreamed about the real things with a man. Not just dreamed. She'd been living it. Buying matching comforter and sheet sets, comparing paint swatches for the nursery, and making a home in the Sunset area with her then-boyfriend where she could imagine their children playing in the yard.

At the time, it felt like a fairy tale, like she'd found her happily ever after. But it must have been a fairy tale told by Brothers Grimm, because the baby was never born.

It was a cervical pregnancy. One that led to severe hemorrhaging that threatened Addison's life. The emergency room surgeon had no choice but to perform a hysterectomy.

Addison recovered, physically anyway. Eventually she came to terms with her loss, both of her pregnancy and any potential to have a child. However, her boyfriend never did.

He wanted a family, and apparently she alone wasn't family enough for him. When she'd suggested they adopt, he said he wanted a family of "his own."

Soon the sheet sets were divided in half and the home rented out to a new family. No more happily ever after for Addison. Or at least she'd thought so.

Addison was walking back from inside the house for more dirty dishes when she paused on the wraparound porch to watch Naia play with the dogs again. She wasn't sure how long her focus had been on the little girl, but when Marilyn laid a hand on her shoulder, she jumped in surprise like she'd forgotten where she was.

Marilyn gave her a look, one that made Addison feel like she could read her mind. Of course Marilyn knew all about her past. She'd known her since Addison had first graduated from pet grooming school five years earlier. The volunteers at the rescue center had become like family to her, and Marilyn like a mother. Although she was sure Marilyn wouldn't appreciate being thought of like that.

Marilyn wrapped an arm around Addison and watched Naia with her. She chuckled as Colin, Piper's black and tan doxie, grabbed the ball right out of her little hand, like *Mine. All mine!*

Addison sighed. "I guess I haven't really thought about the real things with Phillip. It's still pretty new."

Since the moment she met Phillip, heck, even in the moments leading up to it, she imagined life could be perfect with him. She supposed she didn't really know what to expect yet. She'd formulated ideas about him before she'd really gotten to know him. The same way she did about Felix. And look at how wrong those were turning out to be.

"Well, think about it," Marilyn said in her no-nonsense tone. "Really think about it. You might think you know what you want. But sometimes life doesn't always give us what we want. If you're lucky, it gives us what we truly need."

Addison nodded, taking the advice to heart. So what was it that she really needed?

20

Dogfaced

Dearest Addison,
I'm sorry I have been so busy since my fundraiser
flop earlier in the week. The best thing about my
week was seeing you. I would really enjoy spend-
ing time with you again soon. Would you like to
have dinner at my place this Wednesday night?
　　　　　　　　　　　　　　　　Phillip

Addison clutched her phone to her chest and sighed. Naia looked up from her bubble-gum ice cream dripping its way down her wrists and chin.

"What's wrong?" the little girl asked between licks.

Addison smiled back and had another taste of her liquorice ice cream. "Absolutely nothing. Everything is perfect."

She'd been right. Phillip was still interested in her. A sense of victory pulsed through her muscles until she wanted to do a cartwheel. He'd probably been too busy dealing with police and outraged dog owners to text her. But her fantasy romance was back on track.

With a little squeal of delight, she hit the reply button. Her finger hovered over the keyboard, hesitating with all the things she wanted to say, like @#$% *Yes!* But she struggled to find the right response, the not-too-eager, just-the-right-amount-of-interest, with-a-dash-of-flirtatiousness response.

After a few seconds, she scowled and gave up. She'd think of something eloquent to text Phillip later. Besides, it wasn't a good idea to text back right away; she needed to make him sweat a little.

She tucked her phone away and they carried on down the park path in Alamo Square, enjoying their after-lunch treats. Princess trotted ahead, greeting each dog that happened by—and there were plenty. The off-leash dog park attracted many a local and tourist, especially with all the colorful painted-lady homes facing the green space.

Her day with Naia was actually a lot easier than Addison had expected. She wasn't sure what she'd been so worried about. Naia was easy. Great, in fact. Addison was having fun.

The picnic that Felix had packed for them had been delicious. The man could cook. Who would have thought? All along she had imagined he was some bachelor probably living off takeout—one of the many things she'd assumed about him. But Naia's appearance had flipped all her presumptions about him upside down. Now she didn't know what to think.

It was like getting to know him, the real him, all over again. Addison was able to look back over the last couple of weeks with new eyes. Each interaction seemed completely different now. Like how he said he didn't hang out and party after work. It was because he was rushing to get back to Naia.

It was as though Addison had created an alternate version of Felix in her mind. In reality, there was so much more to see, like a movie she'd rather buy than rent so she could watch the rest of the story: the director's cut, some extra features, and definitely the bloopers. And part of that story was right there in front of her, licking bubble-gum ice cream.

"So it's just you and your daddy, huh?" Addison asked, hoping to discover a little more.

Lick. "Yup."

"What about your mom?"

"She lives in Urup." Lick. Lick. A pink trickle ran down her forearm.

"Do you mean Europe?"

Naia tilted the cone to lick the drip on her hand, spilling more down the other side. "Yeah. That's it."

Addison's eyes widened in shock, but she kept her voice neutral. "Europe is really far away. Do you see her much?"

"No. Daddy says it's too far for her to come to America."

"Oh," was all Addison could say. She watched the little girl closely, but there seemed to be no sadness there. It was like she was just stating a fact. Maybe she didn't know her mother at all.

"My daddy raised me all by himself too," Addison said.

"Really? Oh, but Celia takes care of me when Daddy's at work," Naia offered.

"Does anyone else take care of you? Other girls Daddy's age?"

"No, not really."

The news made Addison strangely relieved. It was like

she'd received an exclusive club card at her favorite store. Still, she couldn't help but wonder why, out of all the people he could invite into Naia's life, he chose her. The girl he'd made out with a few times.

"Celia has lots of toys," Naia told her. "Sometimes we watch movies."

"That sounds fun," Addison said. "I love movies. What kind do you like to watch?"

"Make-believe stuff. I like *Cinderella*, and *Alice in Wonderland*, and *Beauty and the Beast*."

"Really? Me too. I love those." Now this she could do. Common ground, some way she could relate to a five-year-old. Although, if a twenty-eight-year old could relate to a child, maybe that wasn't such a good thing.

"Dad likes superhero movies," Naia said. "We've seen *Iron Man* like a million times."

"Really? I never would have guessed." Addison tried to imagine this other Felix, watching Disney movies on the couch with his daughter. She wanted to know more, and found herself plying Naia for information. Then she wondered at what point she started to care so much.

"So what else does your dad like, other than movies?"

"I guess dad stuff. Like making me school lunches, and taking me to preschool, and having tea parties with me." Naia listed each one off as she went along, spreading the ice cream on her hands even more.

Addison snorted when an image of Felix in a bonnet and pearls popped into her head. "Tea parties?"

"Yeah, Dad likes peppermint tea."

"Peppermint tea? Is that so?" She swallowed her laughter. She knew these were the things he had to do, but she was certain he enjoyed it because it was for his daughter.

All this time, she'd figured he was trying to get into

the pants of last-call girls and hooking up with red-bra'd waitresses. But instead of working the late shift to party, he did it so he could be there to make Naia breakfast. When Addison had imagined him tucking a girl with a teddy into bed, it hadn't been the stuffed kind.

"How's your ice cream?" Addison asked.

"Good. Bubble-gum's my favorite," Naia told her between licks.

"Is it?" Addison remembered Oliver's visit to her spa and thought it made sense now.

Naia tried to lick the pink streams before they dripped off her elbows, but the hot afternoon sun was making faster work of her ice cream than she was. She held her arms out like she'd been contaminated. "I think I'm done now."

"Okay, me too." Addison took the soggy cone and threw hers out with it.

Naia was a pink mess. Addison dug through her purse to look for an emergency ice cream cleaner. All she managed to find were her makeup remover wipes and hand sanitizer. Between the two, it did the job and Naia was clean again, albeit smelling of bubble gum.

"Princess, let's play hide-and-seek," she squealed, taking off up the grassy knoll.

Addison held Princess back by her shiny pink collar, giving Naia a head start. Once she was hidden behind a thick cedar tree, Addison could hear soft giggles and she knew Naia was ready.

"Princess, where's Naia?" Addison asked. "Where is she?"

Princess sprang into action, but since she didn't know exactly what she was supposed to be doing, she ran in excited circles, barking at Addison's feet.

"Go get her. Where's Naia?" Addison encouraged. Slowly, she led Princess to where Naia's jean dress peeked out from behind the tree trunk.

When Princess came across her, Naia scream-giggled like she was on a roller coaster and ran for her next hiding spot.

"Good girl, Princess." Addison gave the doxie a treat from her purse, distracting her while Naia settled in behind a cypress.

This time, Princess found her with little coaxing. By the fourth round of the game, Princess beelined it straight for Naia, reveling in the congratulations and treats she received each time she found her.

Addison suspected Princess was just following the soft giggling around the park, but when Naia chose a hiding spot near the playground, it tested the dachshund's sniffer and big, sensitive ears.

Princess circled the enclosed playground a couple of times, past screaming kids, ignoring a golden lab that tried to talk to her. Focused on her mission, she bypassed them all, hot on an invisible trail.

Addison followed her weaving path like a drunk person until Princess came to a bench. Naia was lying flat on the seat. Princess barked and stood on her hind legs, pawing at her find.

Naia leapt to her feet on the bench, screaming and laughing at the same time. Addison handed her the dog treat. Once the girl fed it to Princess, she jumped into Addison's arms.

"You must be part badger," Addison told her.

"What's a badger?"

"It's an animal." Addison set her down and brought up a photo of it on her phone to show her. "Dachshunds are really good at hunting them."

Before they moved on, Addison pulled out a Pampered Puppies coupon from her purse and approached the golden lab's owners. They were splayed out on a blanket, enjoying a picnic of their own.

"If you happen to be looking for a dog groomer, I have a spa nearby," she told them. "If you bring in that coupon, I'll give you twenty percent off any services that day."

They thanked her, and she and Naia headed down the path.

"What did you give those people?" Naia peered into Addison's purse curiously, as though hoping it had been bubble gum.

"It was a coupon for my business. I'm looking for more customers to come get their dogs cleaned at my spa." *Or any customers really.* Instead of focusing her marketing efforts, she was tossing out promotional material to just about anyone now. She thought it wouldn't be long until she began begging every dog owner in the city.

"Customers?" Naia's big brown eyes studied the park. They landed on a bench beneath a shady cypress near the path.

Addison followed her gaze to a man with a panama hat throwing a ball for his dog.

"There's someone." Naia pointed at him like it was an accusation. "He has a dog. Is he a customer?"

"He might be. Good eye." Addison smiled. "I need you on my marketing team. What do you say? Did you want to give him a coupon for me?"

Addison held out the pink piece of paper, and Naia's eyes grew wide with excitement and nerves.

"Yeah." She took the coupon reverently with both hands and carried it over to the man as if she were carrying the crown jewels. She plopped down next to him on the bench and thrust out the coupon. "Excuse me. Do you want your dog cleaned?"

All that time spent studying marketing tactics and honing sales pitches, and the simplest offer from a five-year-old was more effective than an entire marketing-and-promotions team. Addison made a mental note to add Naia to the payroll.

The man in the tan hat turned his attention away from his English foxhound and jumped in surprise to find the little girl beside him. "Oh. Thank you."

Taking the coupon, he held it up to the light, tilting his head back like he needed glasses. His hat brim rose, and the sun hit his face. That's when Addison recognized him.

"Alistair Yates."

He angled himself on the bench to look at her. His expression transformed, from one of pleasant surprise to consternation. Yet when Addison approached, he grabbed his cane to stand and removed his hat, perhaps out of polite habit.

"Miss Turner." He frowned. "Good day."

The English foxhound lopped to Alistair's side and placed the ball next to his shoe. When it began to roll away, the dog nudged it back into place and sat patiently, waiting for him to throw it again.

The dog acknowledged Princess, but was probably too well trained to start sniffing. Princess on the other hand could hardly bother herself to take notice. She puffed out her chest, demonstrating her clear superiority.

"Is that your dog?" Addison blurted.

"Of course it's my dog," Alistair said. "Do I look like a dog walker to you?"

Addison blinked, still staring open-mouthed at the foxhound. She supposed it was a stupid question, but she just hadn't expected Alistair to move on so quickly.

"She's beautiful," she said honestly.

His deep lines relaxed a little and his loose wrinkles fell back into place like a heavy curtain.

"Yes, she is. Not the natural show dog Lilly was." A flit of emotion crossed his aged face, his frown lines twitching. "*Is*," he corrected himself. "The natural Lilly *is*. Fancy here is lacking some of the natural abilities for the show, but has potential if she works with Penny."

"How long have you had her?"

"Since she was a pup."

So Alistair had a second dog waiting in the wings all along. "Are you going to show her this weekend?"

"What other dog do I have to show?" Alistair retorted.

Addison felt a twinge of pity for the man, despite everything that had passed between them. The accusations, the interview with Holly that sent her customers running. It wasn't even like she could blame Alistair. He'd lost his beloved dog.

She'd worked with enough owners to know that, for some, the lines blurred between their dog and a human. It wasn't just time and money they poured into their pets. It was love, sometimes bordering on obsession as in Kitty Carlisle's case. Their four-legged friends ate at their supper table, slept in their same bed, and dressed in the same outfits—something Addison knew about herself— as though they were truly family. Like the dog was their child. And Alistair Yates had lost his.

Fancy finally lost her patience and nudged Alistair's hand, greedy for more play. Leaning on his cane, Alistair bent down to pick up the ball and tossed it out into the field.

"Mr. Yates," Addison began, "I'm so sorry you lost

Lilly. If there was something I could do." She paused, swallowing hard.

Well there was something she could do; find those responsible. How many people had lost their dogs? Their best friends? Not to mention, the future of her business was sinking like the *Titanic*. Then there was Felix. He wasn't just losing out on a dream of owning a bar, it was a way to support his daughter as well.

"There is something you can do," Alistair said.

"Of course," Addison answered. "Anything."

He clenched his cane, his knuckles turning white. "You can stay away from this dog."

Turning to Naia, Alistair handed her back the pink coupon. "Thank you, my dear. But I won't be needing this."

Naia took it back with a pouty lip, but he patted her on the head kindly. He whistled through his teeth, such a loud and startling noise from the quiet, mild-mannered man. Addison flinched at the sound.

"Come on, Fancy." Placing his hat back on his head, he dipped it briefly at Addison in a farewell that looked like an involuntary twitch.

As he walked away, Addison couldn't take her eyes off of the English foxhound. She was no dog show judge, but she'd seen a lot of dogs come through her spa, and even a layman could see that Fancy was utterly perfect. So how could he think she wasn't ready? Maybe he was blinded by his love for Lilly.

Naia stared at the unwanted coupon in her hands. "He didn't want a clean dog?"

Alistair might have had a backup dog already waiting to replace the old one, but Addison knew he couldn't be a suspect. He had the most to lose out of everyone. By stealing his own dog, he'd never be able to show Lilly in public anywhere, certainly not at a conformation show, ever again. While Felix was the one who knew people in general, Addison knew dog owners. And Alistair was one sad pup.

"No," she said, watching Alistair leave. "I think that dog is clean."

21

A Dog's Life

Princess Addison lay slumbering on her bed of flowers, trapped in a deep sleep, awaiting her prince to wake her with a kiss. She sensed him draw near. For even though she was unable to open her eyes, she knew it was him. She felt it resound deep in her bones like the promise of destiny.

He dipped down to lay a kiss on her full lips, and she felt his heat warm her, his sweet breath on her face, and finally that magical kiss. The one that trumps all others, a kiss so honest and true. *The one.*

Startled, Addison's eyes flicked open and she let out a yelp. Her arms flew out. The palm of her hand connected with flesh in a loud *thwack.*

"Ouch!" the prince cried.

Heart racing, Addison blinked her dream away and focused on the reality around her. She wasn't lying on a bed of flowers but on a threadbare floral couch in a living room not her own. And that was most certainly not her one true love. It was Felix.

He rubbed the bright pink spot on his cheek where her stinging palm told her she'd slapped him.

Addison struggled to sit up and look around her. It was strange not to find Princess curled up next to her. She suddenly remembered she was at Felix's house, and she'd dropped Princess off at home, but her foggy brain was still dwelling on the feel of his lips on hers.

"Morning, Sleeping Beauty," he said, with a scowl.

Her eyes bulged. Had she been talking in her sleep or had he just read her mind? "What did you say?" She squinted through one eye, blinded by the light from the TV screen saver.

"Although right about now, I'd like to take back the beauty part."

She touched her lips. "You kissed me."

"It's not like it was the first time." He looked away and shrugged. "You looked kind of cute lying there. You know when your mouth was closed and you weren't annoying me."

"Annoying?" She was staring at him, bewildered by the change in the usual cocky bartender. Like he was almost embarrassed or shy.

"Where's Naia?" he asked.

She yawned. "Who?"

"My daughter? About yay tall." He held his hand up to his hip. "Big brown eyes, a hell of a sharp attitude. Kind of like yours, actually."

"Naia." Addison's blurry focus flicked to the heap of blankets and pillows at the other end of the couch. They'd constructed them into a fort to watch movies from. But Naia wasn't there.

"Naia?" Addison tore apart the mini-fort like maybe the little girl was smaller than she remembered. "I swear she was sleeping right here. I don't know. I just closed my eyes for a second."

"She's not in her room," he said. "I checked."

Felix sounded a lot calmer than she felt. He'd left his daughter with her for less than a day and she'd lost her. First show dogs and now a child. Maybe she should go to jail.

Addison began searching the room. Naia couldn't have gotten far, right? Could you put leashes on kids? *No*—she shook her head—*she wasn't a dog.*

Felix watched her quietly from the middle of the living room. When she turned around, her eyes wide with fear, he laughed. When she realized he was laughing at her, she scowled.

"Don't worry." He held his hands up, trying to rein in his amusement, although she didn't find it very funny. "I think I might know where she is."

Felix ducked into the kitchen and headed for the back entrance where Oliver's kennel sat in the corner. As Felix got closer, Addison noticed a furry tail twitch back and forth, but the dog didn't leave the safety of his kennel to greet his master. Once she got closer, she saw why: two tiny feet were dangling out of the opening.

Addison peered inside. Naia had crawled into the kennel to curl up against Oliver's warm flank. Her head nestled against him, her small hand curled over a clump of his belly fur. It looked rather painful for Oliver, really, but he didn't seem to mind.

The dog held still while Felix reached in and drew his daughter out. The jostling roused her but only enough for her to clamp two little arms around Felix's neck.

Addison followed them back into the living room and waited at the base of the stairs while he carried Naia up to tuck her in. Before he came back down, she checked herself in the mirror on the wall and fixed her couch hair.

She quickly tidied up the fort, folding blankets and

rearranging pillows. When she turned around to switch off the TV, Felix was at the door watching her.

Addison hit the power button on the remote. "So, you have a daughter," she said, like it was just small talk.

"You've noticed," he said, just as casually.

"Why didn't you tell me?"

"Some women get kind of freaked out when you mention you're a single dad." He shrugged but then pulled a guilty face, or maybe it was a little more dejected. Clearly he'd had more than one girl run out on him because of it.

Addison nodded. She couldn't blame him for keeping it a secret.

"She's my angel," he said. "My everything. She's the reason I want to buy my buddy's bar so badly."

"Owning your own business is tough," she said. "It has its perks, but it's tough."

"Well, it's the perks I'm doing it for." He crossed the living room and flopped onto the couch. "Like being able to schedule my own hours so I can spend more time with her, be here to put her to bed every night, send her off to school every day next year. I don't want to pay a babysitter to raise my own kid." He stared at his hands, and it was clear to Addison that he'd thought long and hard about his goals.

"You're a good dad," she said. "You want to be there for her. Not just for the big things like putting a roof over her head and dinner on the table. You really want to be there." It brought to mind her own dad and how hard he'd worked to raise her and provide for her.

"Shouldn't I?" he asked, like it was the most obvious thing in the world.

"Not all parents do. My mom never did." She shrugged at the tenderness that flickered in his eyes at the comment. "She's a lucky girl to have you in her life. I hope you get your bar."

"I know it won't be easy, but it will be worth it," he said. "Or at least it would have been. Every day that I lose another gig is less money I have for the down payment."

He rubbed a hand over his face and let it rest there until she thought he'd fallen asleep. She supposed the double shift that day might have something to do with that.

"Don't talk like that," she said. "It's going to happen. There's still time. For both of us." She sat down next to him, catching a whiff of sweet alcohol on his skin and clothes.

"We'll clear our names, and you'll get all the work you could want this weekend," she said with certainty. "People will feel so bad that they wrongly accused you, they will shower you with tips. And I'll have a full house for the fashion show and everyone will want to order my fabulous designs."

When he still hadn't looked at her, she laid a hand on his hunched back. "Everything will work out for both of us. You'll see."

His tired head finally swiveled to take in her upbeat smile. "Okay Miss Positivity, Sunshine, and Rainbows. How are we going to accomplish this feat?"

"We're going to keep looking. We won't give up." She brought a determined fist down against her palm. "Okay, let's review. What do we know so far?"

"Well, we're still on the fence about Kitty Carlisle. And we can scratch Julia Edwards off the list since Precious was stolen."

"Oh," Addison interrupted. "I ran into Alistair Yates at the dog park today."

"The dog park?" Felix cringed. "That's depressing."

"No he had a dog with him."

"A new dog? He moved on quick."

"Turns out he's always had this one. He just didn't

think she was ready to compete. He still seems so shaken up over Lilly." She sighed, recalling his depressed demeanor in the park. "So who do we have left?"

"Well, if the motive is to simply steal the dogs for financial gain, whether it's for breeding or reselling them, then we have less to go on."

"Have you heard anything about your coworkers?" Addison asked hopefully. "Any of the servers?"

"Well, the servers certainly had access, but I was the manager. If they weren't pulling their weight or disappeared to steal dogs, I would have known. Besides, on their own, they don't exactly have the resources to pull it off."

"They could have had help."

"I know." He rubbed a hand over his face. "And if that's the case, then the possibilities are endless."

"Well, during the first two events, the dogs were taken as a group. Gathered together, they were an easy target. But Precious was the only one taken from my spa. Someone had to go out of their way for just one dog."

Felix grew quiet as he considered this. "What if they didn't have to go that far out of their way?"

"What do you mean?"

"You told me that Melody was there just before I showed up. What if she came back?"

Addison wanted to deny it, to stick up for Melody. But she knew it was a possibility, and lying to herself wouldn't help them figure things out.

"It's possible," she relented. "But it wouldn't explain the missing dogs from Phillip's fundraiser. Maybe we should be assuming the thief is someone who either has a vendetta against the show or is desperate to win it themselves."

"You mean someone who wants to make sure they win Best of Breed."

"Or maybe even Best in Show."

Felix picked at a loose thread on the couch cushion. "It would definitely shorten up our list. It may be our best bet."

"So whoever wins is probably the culprit because if they've gone this far, they'll have ensured that they've taken out their major competitors."

"But the winner won't be decided until Sunday," he said. "It will be too late then. I won't get my money and you'll have no models or audience for your fashion show."

"Not to mention the dog owners won't have their competitors back for the show." She ran her fingers through her hair and gripped it like that would help her think. "Well, we can at least keep going with some of the other names on the list that still have dogs. I know it's scraping the bottom of the kennel, but we've got to try something."

"I'm free on Wednesday," he said. "My babysitter's available that day."

"Okay. It's a date." She felt a flutter of excitement in her chest, and she hesitated. "Well, not a date."

His eyelids lowered seductively. "If you want a date, Addy, all you have to do is ask."

It always surprised her how he could go from all business to fun and games—oh, lots of fun—in a blink of her jet-black waterproof eyelashes. Not to mention how quickly her body reacted.

"Well," he said. "On second thought, maybe a little begging couldn't hurt."

She answered him with a sour look. Only the slight smirk gave away her excitement.

"Okay, no begging," he said, backtracking. "You just have to ask." When she didn't reply, he said. "Suggest? Allude to? Hint? Okay, okay, just wink right now if you want a date." He was nearly begging her, wearing down her resolve. It was actually pretty cute, making him seem like a big softie.

Suddenly, he reached out and drew her close to him on the couch. She accidentally rubbed against his jeans and retracted the idea that he was soft. He was definitely not soft.

"Hey," she said, holding a hand up between them.

"But you winked," he said innocently.

She laughed. "No. I blinked. It's what eyes do sometimes."

"I like to think of it as two winks at the exact same time. Even better."

He dove for her neck, but she pushed him away. "You have a daughter sleeping right upstairs, and all you can think about is getting some action?"

"She's asleep. And I'm not looking to *get some action*." His tone tainted the words like they were the sticky film of alcohol coating his bar top.

"Then what are you looking for?" It just flew out of her mouth. It seemed like the most natural thing to say. The thing she'd wondered for days now.

Felix's scowl slipped away. He was staring at her with that same apprehension he wore that morning when he revealed he had a daughter. He looked so rejected.

"Something . . . more."

"Daddy?" Naia's voice drifted down the stairs.

"Coming sweetheart!" Felix called back.

He seemed to snap out of it, his confidence settling back in place as he stood up. The confidence of a parent that had his crap together and was sure of his one true job in life.

"So we'll continue our search on Wednesday?"

"Fine," she said, feeling ripped out of some kind of moment. "I'll have another look at our suspect list tonight. Maybe I can come up with a few more."

She bit her lip for a moment. They were running out of suspects, and one name kept nagging at her. There was no time left to skirt around it. "What about your friend Red Bra?"

Felix was already headed for the stairs, but he froze at the bottom. "Charlotte? I told you she didn't do it."

Addison crossed her arms. "Why? Because you say so?"

"Because I know her. I know she wouldn't do this to a bunch of pets. To *me*."

She didn't like the way he said it, with such familiarity. She felt a flare of possessiveness. She wasn't about to give in. "I just want to be thorough."

Turning back, he moved toward her. "Are you"—a slow smiled crept across his lips—"jealous?"

"Jealous? Of her? Ha!" Addison tried to laugh for real, but she couldn't make it sound that way because the words stung. He was right. She was jealous.

He crossed his own arms, mirroring her determination. "Well, if you want to be thorough, then the next name on our list should be Phillip Montgomery the third. He was at both events. Hell, the second event was at his house. And he could have easily found out the time of Julia's appointment at your spa."

Addison twitched at that, remembering her conversation with Julia at Phillip's fundraiser. They had discussed the exact time and date of her appointment right in front of him. She shook her head. "No. It's not possible."

"Not to mention," Felix continued, "he's one of the last key competitors who still has a dog to compete in the show."

Addison laughed as if it were a joke. "He's not going on the list."

But that little line between his brows deepened. "Why? Because you say so?" He threw the words back at her.

"Because I know him."

"You don't know him. You only know what you've created in here." He tapped the side of her blonde head.

She swiped his hand away. "That is not true." Then she remembered her conversation with her friends just that morning over breakfast. But as good as Felix was at reading people, he couldn't read her mind. It ticked her off that he thought he could. And even more so because he was right.

"Just because you have the hots for Phillip doesn't mean he's innocent," he said. "Maybe he's just getting close to you in order to set you up. To use you as a scapegoat. You ever think of that?"

"That's ridiculous." Addison stormed over to the kitchen table and grabbed her purse to leave.

Felix gripped her arm to stop her from taking off. "Think about it. The dogs disappeared the night of the mixer while you were dancing with him."

"So he couldn't have done it because he was too busy gazing longingly into my eyes." She batted her eyelashes facetiously.

"He might have had an accomplice. Phillip was distracting you."

Addison yanked her arm away, but Felix was too strong. "Phillip got major heat over the dogs getting stolen from his house."

"Which is exactly why he invited you," he reasoned. "To take some of the focus off him."

"So I guess that's the only way a guy like him would be interested in me?" She was glad she'd turned off the TV or the light would be sparkling off the tears building in her eyes.

"He's just using you." Felix's grip tightened. "There's nothing there between you. Can't you see?"

She narrowed her eyes, her nose an inch away from his. "You're just jealous."

"Jealous? Of that pompous asshole? Ha!" But his laugh didn't sound real either.

"Daddy!" Naia called again.

"Coming!" he yelled back. "Don't go anywhere." He pointed a finger at Addison, like he could be talking to anyone else. "We're not done talking about this."

"Oh, we're done," she said, throwing her purse over her shoulder. But Addison stayed behind because the more she thought about it, the more perfect comebacks she came up with.

Who does Felix think he is? She wasn't some smitten little girl who'd lost her head just because some guy was interested in her. It wasn't like she didn't have anything riding on this mystery. But Phillip was innocent. She was sure of it. He'd even offered to help in any way he could. Now that was a supportive man.

Felix on the other hand had to be backed into a corner before he'd agreed to help her. Something had to be in it for him. He clearly thought that "something" might be *her*.

As if, she thought. *Felix wished. What kind of fairy-tale ending would that be for me?*

The longer she stood there and thought, the more incensed she grew. She began pacing back and forth in the living room.

Felix was cocky and arrogant, and it's not like he even had a good job. He was a struggling bartender, well, struggling under the circumstances. As was she, but still.

Besides, he had a kid. Children just weren't in the cards for her anymore. She hadn't considered it in years. Not that she'd had much choice in that matter. The hysterectomy had made that decision for her.

But that might have been for the best, she told herself, just like she'd convinced herself a million times before. She was twenty-eight and unattached. She could do anything, go anywhere, nothing to tie her down or hold her back. She could fulfill any one of her fantasies.

Phillip would be a great life partner to share that with. Yes, she could see her life with him now. More or less.

Whipping out her phone, Addison brought up Phillip's earlier text, the one she'd completely forgotten about for some reason, and hit the reply button.

I would love to come over for dinner Wednesday night.

Tapping the send button with a flourish, she grinned triumphantly to herself. *"Just using her," my ass,* she thought. *That* would show Felix.

She wanted to see the look on his face when she told him about her date with Phillip. She'd tell him as soon as he came back down. Then she'd leave.

Just where was Felix, anyway? What was taking him so long?

Addison glanced at the time. It had been nearly twenty minutes already. Well, she certainly wasn't going to wait around for him all night. She would tell him he's on his own for the investigation on Wednesday, and then she was out of there.

Trudging up the stairs, she headed for the room at the end of the hall with a picture of a crown on the door and *Naia* written beneath it. Addison gripped the phone in her hand, ready to shove it in Felix's face.

"Ha!" she would say. "How about that for 'he's just using you'?" Or something slightly more clever.

Maybe she wouldn't say anything at all. Yes, let the message speak for itself. Much more refined. Like Phillip.

Addison poked her head through the cracked door, but Felix didn't exactly look like he was ready to continue their discussion. Or even cared about Phillip anymore.

He was curled up on My Little Pony bed sheets next to Naia, drooling on a heart pillow.

The sight brought Addison up short. She hovered uncertainly in the doorway. There'd been a time when she'd wanted that life. Had dreamed of a family, before the chance had literally been ripped out of her, and she'd been tossed aside like damaged goods.

Addison hadn't thought about it much since then. She figured she'd end up with someone who didn't want any kids with her, who maybe even saw it as a bonus that they couldn't accidentally knock her up. That this life wasn't destined for her. Or maybe, just maybe that they loved her so much that she was enough for them, unlike her ex.

But as she stood there watching Felix and Naia, she could see it like a movie playing out in her head, the scenes flicking by like a montage to a Sarah McLachlan song. Evenings with the three of them making dinner while dancing to music in the kitchen. Felix casually kissing her as he stirred the spaghetti sauce. The look on Naia's face on Christmas morning when she saw Santa had come. Nights spent tucking Naia into bed and reading her a fairy tale. And of course there was tucking Felix into bed after.

It gave Addison a flutter of excitement to imagine it. Not just her and Felix together, but all of it. Was that what he'd meant when he said he wanted something more? Not just for last-call hook-ups on pool tables, but for all of it.

But he was a dad. *A dad*. He was responsible for a little life. Cared for her full time, provided for her, fed her, clothed her.

All along, Addison had imagined him as a guy who rolled out of bed in the morning and grabbed any old scruffy T-shirt because he was too lazy to find a half-decent one. But it was because he was too busy getting someone else ready, too busy being a full-time dad, a full-time bartender, to care. That, and he probably had poor fashion taste as well.

Suddenly, the whole argument Addison had built up in her head seemed trivial now. She put away her phone. For a few minutes, she watched them and considered the little Sleeping Beauty breathing quietly next to her dad. Considered both of them, the life they lived. The life Addison could have if she chose him.

It certainly wasn't the perfect setup she imagined. Felix wasn't her white knight in shining armor. It wasn't a fairy tale. It was . . . real.

Marilyn's words from earlier that day came back to Addison.

Sometimes life doesn't always give us what we want. If you're lucky, it gives us what we truly need.

Addison knew what she wanted, or at least she'd thought she did. But what did she *need*?

Shutting the door softly, she turned and headed back downstairs. She tried to imagine her life with a man like Phillip. She could think of a million things she wanted from him. But what would she need from him? And could he provide those things?

Addison was going to go to his place for dinner on Wednesday, he'd probably wine and dine her over the weeks to come, romance her, and then if things went well, whisk her away to all sorts of places. And then what?

Addison climbed into her Mini and glanced back at the shabby row house, considering the life she could have with the sleeping pair inside. It was no fairy tale, that was true. It was real.

But was it too real for her?

22

Barking Up the Wrong Tree

The date was perfect. The wine glasses sparkled in the moonlight, a gentle breeze blew the fragrant scent of roses from the garden below, the roasted lamb fell apart delectably in Addison's mouth. Phillip looked perfect. The way he was staring at her in her strapless dress let her know she looked perfect too. Just perfect, perfect, perfect.

"This is wonderful." Addison indicated the balcony, the candles, and the soft music in the background. "Thank you."

"You're welcome." Phillip took a sip of his wine. "A special meal for a special lady."

Addison's cheeks warmed. She *was* special. Well, at least *he* must have thought so, since he went through all the trouble of making their wonderful dinner.

"This dish is delicious," Addison said.

"It's Raphael's, my chef's, specialty."

Addison slapped herself mentally. Of course he didn't make the food himself, but that didn't mean she wasn't worth the effort. He probably never cooked. However, he obviously had requested his chef's specialty for their date, so at least he'd put thought into it that way.

"He makes it every Wednesday night," Phillip added.

Or not, she thought.

Oh, well. Who cared if Phillip didn't make it when it tasted that good? Although, Felix had made the picnic for her and Naia a few days earlier, and that turned out to be surprisingly tasty. And it had obviously taken a lot of time and effort, which was very thoughtful.

Never mind about Felix, Addison told herself. She was with Phillip in his beautiful house, on his terrace, for an evening spent under the stars. It was such a romantic idea for Phillip to come up with.

"The balcony was a wonderful idea," she said. "It's such a nice night."

"Yes, my butler saw how mild the weather was going to be this evening and suggested it."

"Oh, that was thoughtful of him." Okay, well, he may not have had anything to do with dinner or the idea for the terrace, but his touch could be seen in the details. The moment she'd sat down at the table, she'd noticed a vase of periwinkle hydrangeas arranged as the centerpiece.

"You remembered my favorite flowers."

Phillip seemed pleased she liked them. "How could I forget when you're all I can think about?"

Addison's eyes dropped to her plate, embarrassed by the dazzling smile he gave her. "Thank you."

"So I had my maid pick them up from the flower shop this afternoon, especially for our evening."

"That's so"—she hesitated a beat—"thoughtful." *Of his maid*, she added in her head.

Addison struggled not to roll her eyes. But at least he'd thought about the flowers, and it was the thought that counted, right? Unable to find anything else to say, she took another bite of Raphael's lamb.

Silence settled over them except for the tinkling of silver on plates. She paused to take a sip of wine. The rich flavor burst in her mouth and she almost moaned with delight. Oh! The wine. Addison had never tasted one so complex. Phillip must have picked it out himself. Such good taste he had. Such refinement. "This wine is amazing."

"Yes, it is," Phillip agreed. "I enjoy a good wine. Although, my wine cellar isn't quite as grand as Alistair Yates's is claimed to be."

Addison shifted uncomfortably at the mention of Alistair. She was still bothered by her run-in with him at the park.

Phillip turned and called over his shoulder. "Hugh, could you please grab us another bottle from the cellar?"

His butler seemed to appear from the shadows. "We're all out of that particular Cabernet, sir."

"No problem," Phillip said. "Just choose whatever you think is best. You did a fine job with this one."

So the wine wasn't exactly his idea either. At least he'd thought to invite her to dinner, she told herself. Unless, of course, he outsourced his text messages too.

When they'd finished their meal, Phillip invited her to sit on a marble bench on the other side of the terrace. He sat close enough that she could smell his cologne. Her nose wrinkled at the citrus tang of it, reminding her a little of a toilet bowl cleaner. She made a mental note to jot cologne down as a potential Christmas gift and instead tried to focus on the scent of the flowering vine that draped over the bannister behind them and fell all the way down to the garden.

"You look lovely tonight," he told her.

"Thank you."

"I'm so glad you said yes to dinner tonight. I know it's been a difficult couple of weeks for you. You probably have a lot keeping you busy right now."

"It's been a little crazy." To say the least, she thought, but it wasn't like she could babble about that on a date, about undercover ops, and weird dog-themed sex parties, and dog show intrigue, and Felix.

The only person who would understand her crazy life at the moment and what she was going through was Felix himself. But she wasn't exactly talking to him at the moment. Not after how they'd left things at his house on Sunday. But Addison's life had been so consumed by all of their crazy adventures that she didn't have much else to talk about.

"But I'm sure it will all turn around soon," she said, giving her best peppy cheerleader smile.

"That's the spirit," Phillip said, clearly oblivious to the strain in her voice.

"I just feel so bad for all those owners who lost their dogs," she said. "I hope they find them."

"I couldn't imagine losing Baxter." He shook his head. "I'm even hesitant to bring him to the gala on Friday evening, but they assure us it's completely secure. Are you going?" he asked her, with a hopeful expression.

"Yes, I was planning to. My friend Zoe is the event coordinator, and I can assure you it will be very secure."

Phillip slid closer to her on the bench until their legs were brushing against each other. "Well, if you're going. And I'm going," he said suggestively. He laid a hand on her bare leg where the slit in her skirt had parted. His fingers felt stiff and clammy, making her shiver. "Perhaps we should go together?"

"I'd love that," she said, when she'd recovered, hoping he thought it was a judder of excitement.

Felix had originally been booked to work the gala. Although, if they didn't solve the case before then, he wouldn't be.

Annoyed with herself for thinking about Felix when she was on a date with Philip, Addison looked deep into those perfect blue eyes in front of her. Not muddy brown like Felix's. Well, not muddy exactly. Felix's eyes were a bit warmer, like a rich polished mahogany wood. Very much like Naia's. And Naia's sparkled when she smiled, she supposed a little like her dad's.

But she wasn't going to think about Felix. She was focused entirely on Phillip's perfect hair and perfect teeth. She noticed his perfect eyes studying her mouth, and his perfect lips as he brought them closer to hers. His perfect hands reached for her face and he ran his fingers though her wavy blonde locks.

"Ouch." She winced as his watch caught in her hair. "I think I'm stuck."

"Oh, I'm so sorry." He tried to pull away but froze as she flinched again.

"That's okay," she said. "It's just pulling a little."

"Here, let me help." He fiddled with his watch, tugging on her hair for a few seconds until she was free. "There. That's better."

"Thanks."

He gave her a sheepish look. "Were you ready for some dessert?"

Now that the moment between them had been totally blown, Addison didn't know what else to do but nod. "Yes, thank you."

Addison needed something sweet to calm her nerves. Her heart was pounding in her chest. Her hands had turned cold and clammy while anxiety buzzed through her whole body until she just couldn't sit still. Something wasn't right.

I'm just overly excited, Addison told herself. *A hot date with Phillip Montgomery III? What girl wouldn't be thrown off her game?*

Phillip got to his feet and headed for the French doors leading into the drawing room. "I'll go see what's keeping Hugh."

"Sure thing." Addison watched Phillip go back into the house, noticing that his butt was perfect too.

The moment he disappeared from sight, she frantically smoothed her locks back into place. She rearranged herself on the bench into a come-hither position to await Phillip's return. *No,* she thought, *maybe sultry's better.* She crossed one leg over the other. The slit in her dress gaped open to reveal just enough thigh to be seductive but not slutty. Yes, seductive was definitely best. She decided to nudge the slit open an inch wider and waited in that frozen position.

In the silence that could only be found in an oasis like Phillip's property, there was a faint rustle. Breaking her pose, Addison glanced behind her, half-expecting a wild animal. But she saw nothing in the creeping vines along the bannister.

Addison returned to her seductive pose, only to be startled by another noise a moment later. This time the rustling was closer. The green leaves along the bannister vibrated like there was something caught in the ivy, too big to be a bug or a bird. Maybe it *was* some kind of animal. Faint grunts and heavy breathing reached her ears. A very big animal.

Leaping to her feet, she backed away from the bench. She was about to scream out when a hand reached over the bannister, gripping the vines for dear life. A head of dark curls surfaced over the edge, followed by a pair of mahogany eyes.

"Felix?" Addison hissed.

He gave her a strained, lopsided grin. There was a snap. The vine he was gripping broke away. He grunted, disappearing from sight.

Addison gasped and ran to the edge of the terrace. Fearing the worst, she peered over the bannister on her tiptoes. She saw Felix's hand clamped desperately around a flimsy vine just on the other side. It groaned ominously under his weight.

"Oh my God." Addison lunged forward and gripped his wrist.

She tugged and heaved as Felix grunted his way up the wall of ivy. She probably wasn't helping much, but by the time he'd thrown his leg over the bannister and landed safely on the stone terrace, she was panting from the effort.

"What are you doing here?" she whispered between gasps for air.

Felix flopped down on the bench, face red, arms bright with pink and red welts from climbing the vines. He glanced up at her. "What am *I* doing here? What are *you* doing here?"

"What do you think I'm doing here?"

His eyes widened as he took in her dress. He started to nod with understanding. "You're spying on him, aren't you? Deep undercover stuff. That's good. That's good. You really went all out." He ran a finger down the front of her dress, and she felt it like hot candle wax running from her breast to her belly where his touch lingered.

"You look"—Felix's eyes darkened—"seductive."

His words were like honey, thick and sweet. She glanced at his lips and felt the urge to suck more of those words right out of his mouth.

Addison shook her head, trying to clear her mind. "Is that what you're doing here?" she demanded. "You're here to spy on Phillip?"

"Of course, we still haven't crossed him off the list yet." He clapped his hands and rubbed them together. "So what have you found out so far?"

"Nothing." Addison tried to drag Felix to his feet, but it was like trying to move a mule. "You can't be here right now."

"Why not?" A devilish smile curled his lips, and his fingers found their way to the slit in her dress. He laid his palm against the inside of her thigh, caressing her smooth skin. As it rose higher and higher, her legs automatically parted ever so slightly, enough for him to run a finger along the silk between her thighs.

From his position on the bench, he was at the perfect height to press his face against her, teasing her with kisses over her thin dress. She could feel the heat of his breath and his lips working against the fabric like they were searching.

For a moment, Addison forgot where she was and the risk of them being discovered together. Or maybe she reveled in it.

The gamble, the excitement, the rush. It heightened her need for Felix, made her want to rip off his clothes right there and see if she could have him before their time was up. Like a race against the clock, only there was no way to know when the alarm was set to go off.

It seemed to be a common occurrence with the two of them. Maybe it was their thing, or maybe Addison just wanted Felix anywhere, any way.

"No," she panted. "Phillip will be back soon. He'll catch you here," she said, even as she ran her fingers through his hair. She felt like Juliet urging her Romeo away to safety. The forbidden feeling of their meeting at war with their undeniable attraction.

But that wasn't the only thing to consider. She needed

to make the smart decision, to use her head. Wasn't that what she'd set out to do with Phillip in the first place? To choose the right guy?

However, that was when she'd written Felix off as just another bad choice. Then she actually got to know him. And Naia. It didn't feel so cut and dry anymore. But standing with Felix on Phillip's terrace while on a date wasn't exactly the best place to weigh her options.

"Wait. Stop." Addison pushed Felix away. "You have to go."

"Why?" He stared up at her in surprise, like what could possibly be so wrong about the situation? "I haven't had time to look around."

She glanced back through the French doors into the mansion, afraid she'd see Phillip returning any second. "Because this is a date."

Felix's shoulders dropped. He leaned back so he could really look at her. "You're not serious."

The ironic look on his face ignited something inside of her. She recalled his words from the last time they spoke. How he thought Phillip was just using her, like she wouldn't actually be able to get a guy like him interested in her otherwise. Suddenly she was as angry as the night they fought at his house.

"I'm perfectly serious. Why wouldn't I be on a date?" She crossed her arms. "And it's not like it's any of your business anyway."

But she wasn't sure that was true anymore. She rubbed her temples. She had so much to think about. For now, she had to get him out of there.

Addison hovered over him, ready to throw Felix back over the bannister if Phillip returned.

Felix's face screwed up. "A date? At his house? Isn't it a little early for a sleepover?"

But Addison didn't think that was any of his business either, and her irritation spiked. "Well, when it's right, it's right," she said vaguely.

"What makes him right?" He stood up, towering over her.

Despite their whispers, she could hear the anger behind his words. But she didn't think he was angry with her. Frustrated maybe.

"Is it because he's rich? Because every year *The Gate* lists him as one of San Francisco's most eligible bachelors?" That little vein in his forehead pulsed. His eyes narrowed. "Because you're so desperate you'll fall for any man?"

She inhaled sharply, clenching her fists at her sides. "I'm not desperate enough to fall for you."

The moment it flew out of her mouth, she regretted it. Both because his face flinched like she'd shoved a hot curling iron against his stomach and because she felt that same pain, in answer to his own. Because she knew it wasn't true.

The anger faded from Felix's face and his breathing slowed like the fight was leaving him. "Fine," he said flatly. "Enjoy your date. But I'm not relying on your fantasy obsession to tell if he's innocent or not. I'm scoping the place out myself."

"Felix." Her voice wavered with building tears. "I—"

Footsteps thumped in the hall, echoing down the cavernous expanse. Addison's apology caught in her throat. She began shoving Felix back toward the bannister.

"Someone's coming. Go back down the wall," she hissed.

Felix's eyes went wide. "I can't. The chef and butler were down there. They heard me earlier and searched the grounds. I was backed into a corner. That's why I came up here."

"Then hide," she urged. "Quick."

Felix's head whipped back and forth, looking for a place to hide. Racing through the French doors, he dove for the thick, floor-length curtains draped on either side. Once he was hidden behind them, Addison rearranged them to look natural again.

"I'll distract him," she told the curtains. "You can sneak out."

Felix peeked his head out. "How are you going to—"

"I hope you like crème brûlée," Phillip called out as he swept into the room with two small dishes on a silver tray.

Felix whipped the curtain back into place just as Phillip entered the room.

Addison jumped away from Felix. "Sounds delicious," she said, her voice a little too high-pitched. She cleared her throat.

"Sorry I took so long," he said. "Apparently the maid thought she saw someone sneaking around on the grounds, so Hugh went to check into it."

"You're kidding?" Addison opened her mouth in what she hoped looked like shock. She might have loved movies, but she'd never be nominated for an Emmy, that was for sure. "Should we call the cops?"

The curtain twitched, and Addison could practically feel the agitation building behind them.

"No. No." Phillip was busy arranging the dishes and dessert forks on the coffee table, clearly not used to serving himself. "I'm sure it's just a stray animal or something. Nothing to worry about. I wouldn't want to ruin our night together."

Addison's body felt stiff and unnatural. All she could think about was trying not to look at the curtain, so of course that was all she wanted to do. She was paranoid, certain Phillip would somehow see Felix or hear him breathing behind the drapes.

"Shall we go back out on the balcony for a while?" she asked. If she could just get Phillip out of the room, Felix could make a run for it.

But Phillip sat down on the leather sofa. "I was thinking we would be more comfortable in here. I wouldn't want you to get too cold."

His usual polite and mild demeanor shifted, and his voice became throaty with lust. Addison could see it in his half-lidded eyes, taking in the sight of her standing in the doorway. She suddenly felt self-conscious. Was she still flushed from Felix's touch?

Phillip patted the seat next to him. "I'm sure I could keep you warm in here."

There was a soft snort from behind the curtain—too soft for Phillip to hear across the room, Addison hoped.

"That sounds even better." Addison smiled coyly, but cursed in her head. It would appear strange if she argued, so she had no choice but to sashay across the room and cozy up next to him. By the way Phillip watched her hips move beneath her dress, she doubted it would be very hard to distract him.

Addison took a seat, close enough to Phillip that her body rubbed against his. She crossed her legs, and the slit in her skirt fell open, revealing a whole lot of thigh.

Phillip slipped an arm around the backrest behind her. She caught his gaze drinking in the view down her neckline.

"See?" he said. "Isn't that better?"

"Much warmer," she agreed.

He caressed her exposed knee with a shy fingertip, sliding it slowly up her thigh. "I'm feeling a little warm myself."

There was another snort, this time loud enough for the

both of them to hear. Addison froze. When Phillip pulled away, she knew he'd heard it too.

His focus shifted across the room, and he moved to stand. She couldn't let him near those curtains.

Addison practically lunged at Phillip. Grabbing his chiseled jaw in her hands, she planted her lips on his, desperate to keep him there.

His kiss wasn't exactly how she imagined, not warm and luscious, not falling into step with hers like two professional flamingo dancers. In fact, his lips were a little cold and thin, slipping over hers like wet hands trying to grasp a slimy bar of soap in a bathtub.

Phillip grabbed her bare shoulders and gently pushed her away, but she resisted.

"Did you hear something a second ago?" he asked against her mouth.

"Nu-uh," she mumbled.

She shoved her tongue in his mouth, effectively shutting him up. Her leg swung around until she straddled him on the couch, pinning him there. Now all he could focus on was her and her tongue caressing his, her hips grinding his lap. What strange man behind the curtain?

Phillip's hands were no longer pushing her away, they were groping, tugging her skirt out of the way, exploring. He gyrated beneath her, inviting her swirling tongue into his mouth with his own. He gripped her thighs, pulling her against his moving hips, and grinded against her.

Soon Addison began to feel him stiffen beneath her, digging hard between her legs. His breaths came harder, faster. He let out an eager grunt in her mouth. Cupping her butt, he flipped her onto her back. She yelped in surprise as her back hit the sofa.

The desserts lay forgotten on the table. Phillip practically dove on top of her, nestling between her legs. His cool lips slithered their way across her cheek and down to her neck, over her collarbone.

Addison moaned and squirmed beneath him, encouraging him to keep going, but her focus was on the curtain across the room. She shifted her head to the side to see over Phillip's hunched back. He obviously took this as a sign to begin nuzzling her neck.

It tickled a little. In fact, it felt gross as his tongue ran and flicked in annoying circles over her skin. She cringed, but continued to encourage him.

"Yes," she purred. "Oh yeah."

His awkward hand slid up the slit in her dress, crawling against her bare skin until he reached her panties. He ran a finger over the smooth material.

The curtain shifted a fraction, and Felix's head poked out. When his searching eyes fell on the sofa, he froze. He didn't look angry. His jaw didn't so much as clench, and his eyelash didn't even bat.

Finally Addison waved him on, as in *Go,* while faking another,"Yes. Oooh, right there."

Phillip rubbed a finger over the silk between her legs, where Felix had been exploring not long before. He groaned as he did so, rubbing with a new fervor.

Addison realized with embarrassment that it was because she felt wet. He must have thought he excited her.

But it had been Felix's doing on the balcony. It had been him that her body reacted to. While her brain had been telling her Phillip was the one from the start, her body couldn't lie.

Perhaps, she thought, it was time to let her heart speak up.

Felix took his chance. Darting out from behind the curtain, he dashed across the room, stepping light as a burglar. When he made it to the door, Addison's body relaxed in relief. That is, until Felix caught her eye.

They locked gazes and just stared at each other as her so-called Prince Charming grinded on top of her. Suddenly, she snapped out of the fantasy she was trying to hold on to, the stars, the candles, the wine, and fell back to reality.

It was like when someone munched on popcorn in the theater behind you, pulling you from the trance of the big screen. No matter how hard you tried to ignore it, you just couldn't return to that place of ignorant bliss. The mindset that you escaped to during a movie, allowing yourself to believe that anything was possible.

When Felix turned away for the last time, she saw a grimace contort his handsome face. She felt her heart contract painfully. Her eyes began to sting and a single sob escaped her.

Phillip must have interpreted this as frustrated pleasure, like she just couldn't wait any longer, because his fumbling fingers tugged her panties aside. Her body automatically recoiled. It suddenly felt so wrong.

Clamping her legs shut, she pushed him away. Phillip stared down at her in shock as she struggled to find something to say.

"What about dessert?" she asked, as airily as she could.

"I've got dessert right here." He descended on her again, but she forced him back, unable to stand another second of his kisses and touch.

Phillip drew away, kneeling on the sofa between her parted legs, staring down in confusion.

She shook her head as though waking from a really long dream and sat up. "I'm sorry." She tugged her skirt back down. "It's getting a bit late. I should go."

She couldn't look him in the eye. Heck, she didn't even know how she'd look at her own reflection in the eye when she got home.

"Of course," he said, clearly abashed. "I'm sorry."

"No. Don't be sorry." She smiled warmly at him. It wasn't him; it was *her.* "I had a wonderful time tonight, but I should get going."

"I'll show you out." But Phillip still looked confused. Maybe as confused as she felt. "Will you still be going to the gala?" he asked as they headed down his sweeping staircase to the foyer.

"I will." She smiled again, but couldn't seem to make it reach her eyes. "I'll see you there."

He looked disappointed but tried to hide it with a gracious smile as he opened the front door for her. "Great. I'll see you there."

She'd agreed to be his date, but she was so flustered at the moment. It wasn't a yes, but it wasn't a no. She needed time to think.

"Thank you for a nice evening." To make sure he knew she meant it, she stood on her tiptoes and kissed him goodnight on the cheek. "I look forward to seeing you again." Because she did. She just didn't know in what capacity any more.

Outside, the night felt colder. She wrapped her arms around herself and headed for her Mini. Once inside, she sighed and checked her phone. There was a text from Felix.

Checked the house. Your boyfriend, Prince Charming, appears to be clean. Enjoy your fantasy.

23

A Dog's Chance

The princess was supposed to run *to* the prince and his castle, not *away* from it. But that's exactly what Addison was doing, speeding away in her Mini. No. Not away from Phillip, well, not permanently, anyway. Or maybe she was. She didn't know what to think anymore.

Seeing Felix there threw her off, and it wasn't just because three's a crowd. She couldn't deny it anymore. She had feelings for Felix. Strong ones, and that wasn't just her hormones talking. They were real feelings that she'd been pushing away from the start. And why? Because he wasn't the Prince Charming she'd always imagined she'd end up with?

Although Felix was certainly charming, he wasn't rich, or well spoken, not ivy league, or poised, or fashionable like a Ralph Lauren poster boy. Not a knight in shining armor who came to her rescue from the start. He was a different kind of hero. One that battled the nine-to-five workweek, vanquished utility bills, and conquered the home-cooked meal.

Of course, when Felix had told Addison that he wouldn't help her find the dognapper, it was because he had to look out for "number one." At the time she thought he'd been referring to himself, but he was talking about Naia. He was afraid of losing his job, his ability to support Naia and take care of her. Addison couldn't blame him for that. If anything, she admired him for it.

Addison gripped the steering wheel until it hurt. How wrong she'd had it. Right from the moment she met him. She'd pegged Felix as the court jester, but maybe he'd been the prince all along. Well, in his own way.

Each new thing she'd learned about him opened her eyes to a different man, so different from her usual fantasy. But this wasn't a fantasy. This was reality, and Felix, as rough around the edges as he was, was a real man. One who hadn't been looking to use her as a one-night stand at the bar. He was looking for "something more."

But what did that mean? Maybe he wanted a girlfriend, someone to share that "number one" status with Naia.

Addison paused at the next stop sign and considered what it would feel like to hold that title in his life, to share that crown. It would mean picnics in the park with Felix and Naia, nights spent watching Disney movies in pillow forts, eating bubble-gum ice cream, and more showers with Felix. Addison hadn't noticed the smile spreading across her face until her cheeks began to hurt, but it wouldn't go away.

She didn't know yet if it was right for her. This could be life's way of offering her what she really needed, something she'd been denying herself because she thought it impossible. She just had to stop being so obstinate and reach out and grab it.

Addison needed time to think. Her emotions were in turmoil, chaotic like an apocalypse movie. The dust in her mind had to settle before she could rebuild her thoughts.

However, those big decisions would have to wait. For now, there was work to do. She'd spent the night on what she thought would be a magical date with Phillip when she should have been helping Felix solve the mystery of the disappearing dogs.

Addison drove blindly through the rolling streets of San Francisco, considering what her next move should be. All signs led to more dogs being taken at the gala on Friday night. She knew Zoe had pulled out all the stops for security measures or no one would have even thought about attending her bash. But what if someone managed to crash the party and get to the rest of the show dogs?

If that was the culprit's true motive, then they would have accomplished what they set out to do and Addison's leads would go cold. Then their chance of catching the criminal would be gone, and Addison and Felix would forever be dog show pariahs.

Ever since their meeting with Felix's friend Charlotte, something had been eating away at Addison. Okay, some of that she could now admit had been jealousy, but that wasn't the only reason. Charlotte had been edgy when they'd questioned her. She'd been hiding something; Addison was sure of it. Felix was just too close to truly see.

Pulling into a 7-Eleven, Addison parked to check her trusty notebook. She still had Charlotte's address from her previous research. She punched it into her phone and found it on the map. It was on the way home.

There was no harm driving by the place, maybe peeking in a window or two. Right?

On a new mission, Addison raced to the Sunset address. When she pulled onto the street, it was like driving between two colorful walls. Solid row houses lined both sides of the street, not a breath between them. Even in the dark, she could see siding roted away, paint chipping, and windows cracking.

Most of the street parking had been taken, but she found a free spot farther down the street, far enough away that she wouldn't be seen. The streetlight above her car had burnt out, casting her in shadow as she watched the house for signs of life.

The lights inside Charlotte's plain Marina-style home were off, but the sporadic flashing through the angled bay windows on the second story told Addison that the TV was on in the living room. Someone was home.

Addison shut off the engine and killed the lights. Waiting for signs of movement, she sat back and watched the flickering windows. Only a few minutes went by before she saw a female-esque figure pass in front of a window, blocking the TV's light for a second as she sat down in front of it.

Addison held off a while longer to see if Charlotte was alone or if there was anyone else in the house. To pass the time, she checked her website for any online reservations for the spa. When her calendar popped up on the screen, she grimaced. No bookings.

Pampered Puppies was still getting the odd walk-in from random passersby who hadn't heard of the place, but business had practically trickled to a stop. If her business had been a movie, she would have sent it out of theaters and onto Netflix a week ago.

How things had changed for her. Only a few months earlier she'd presented her business plan to Aiden as an investor. She'd shown him numbers, pie charts, customer surveys, and market comparisons. Her Fido Fashion line was going to be a huge success. There was a demand for it, a hole in the market that her designs were perfect to fill.

It was supposed to be a blockbuster hit. Instead it was

turning into a straight-to-DVD, right-to-the-bargain-bin idea. She'd never be able to help her dad out now. Maybe his love life was about to become as messy as hers was.

Keeping her eye on Charlotte's house, she checked the RSVPs for her fashion show. She held her breath as the screen refreshed. Then it whooshed out in a disappointed sigh as the message popped up.

Zero guests.

Her grip tightened around her phone, breaking off a pink rhinestone. She wasn't giving up that easily. Tucking the phone into her jacket pocket, she slipped out of her Mini and onto the sidewalk. The street was poorly lit, helping to hide her approach, but she was still cautious.

Her head swiveled, on the lookout for witnesses. Thankfully it was late enough that most of the neighbors had turned in for the night. When the coast looked clear, she approached Charlotte's home.

Since the Marina-style house sat above the garage, most of the windows were on the second story. That night's recon mission was going to take some acrobatics.

So far she'd been lucky enough to spy on suspects living in wealthy homes, but the rundown row house was crammed between two identical houses on either side in typical San Francisco fashion. She studied the stucco facade, searching for a way up to the second story, but it seemed her best bet was to climb up the front of the home.

The only part of the structure that stuck out enough to get a handhold on was a drainpipe that ran down one corner of the house. She shook it to check for sturdiness, and then tested her weight on the bracket holding the pipe in place, bouncing on it a couple of times.

Headlights flashed against the white stucco facade. It glowed all around her, warning her of an approaching car.

She dropped to the ground and crept along the side of the house. The only thing to hide behind was an oversized bush bursting with trumpet-shaped flowers. Squeezing between it and the house's rough siding, she waited for the vehicle to pass.

The rumbling sound of the engine drew near. She waited for it to fade off into the distance, but instead the noise slowed to a chug. Gravel crunched as the car pulled up to the curb, the engine puttering just outside her hiding spot.

The driver shut off the engine and it clicked as it cooled down, like a hammer banging in the night, so loud on the quiet street. Or maybe that was Addison's heart.

Keys jingled, a door slammed, heavy footsteps approached.

Addison pressed herself harder against the house, kicking herself for not learning to say no to the occasional second helping of Mad Mousse and Orange Peel ice cream. She wished the person wouldn't come too close, wouldn't glance her way and spot her. She wished it so hard that she made a silent promise to herself that the diet would start tomorrow.

Addison held as still as she could in case a mere twitch sent the leaves rustling, giving her away. A tickle on her arm had her squirming, imagining it to be the worst kind of shrub spider there was. But she gritted her teeth and waited as the person passed her by.

The footsteps changed rhythm, and she realized they were climbing Charlotte's stairs. Of all the houses on the street, why that one?

With the stress of that night, Addison definitely needed a pint of Peppermint Marshmallow ice cream when she got home. *Make that fat-free sherbet*, she added in her head, remembering her promise.

The doorbell rang inside Charlotte's home. There was shuffling from within as she came to answer the door.

It's a bit late for a visit, Addison thought. Charlotte must have known the person. Either it was a booty call or a meeting she didn't want anyone to know about—sometimes those things were synonymous.

But only two days remained until the dog show began. Something told her chances were slim that it was just an average house call. Everyone knew secret bad guy dealings only happened at night. Every blockbuster thriller couldn't be wrong. If that was the case, she'd be ready with her phone to record the two evildoers explaining their dognapping plans in full detail, which is what bad guys always did.

She inched her way along the house, careful not to rustle the leaves. She peered around the corner and up the stairs to Charlotte's door. The man's face was turned away from her, but she'd recognize those hot buns in those faded jeans any day. Felix.

Her eyes widened, and she scrambled back before he could see her. Through the gaps in the bush she could see the van parked next to the sidewalk with JOE'S DIVE written on the side.

Addison was shaking worse than ever now. Maybe because Felix would be pissed if he knew she was there spying on Charlotte. Maybe because of what had passed between them at Phillip's house earlier that night. Or maybe it was jealousy that suddenly flared inside of her at the sight of him standing at Charlotte's door.

Addison's breaths left her in panicked pants until she worried that he might hear. There was a squeak as the front door opened.

"Felix," Charlotte said. "I'm so glad you came."

There was so much longing in her voice, almost

desperate with emotion—like she would have burst into tears if he'd taken any longer to arrive.

"Of course I came. I'll always come when you call." His response was thick with sincerity.

Addison closed her eyes. She'd thought this was an evil rendezvous, but she realized a long time ago that Felix couldn't be involved. He had too much on the line. So did that mean his visit was for the other reason? Was he there for a booty call? Felix said he and Charlotte were just friends. It couldn't be.

Her hands balled at her sides, her gel nails digging into her soft skin until she wanted to cry out. Their voices faded as Felix went inside. The door closed, and Addison was alone again.

Scrambling out of her hiding spot, she returned to the drainpipe and crammed her designer shoe onto the bracket. Thankfully her toes were pointed and fit nicely into the space.

Using the drainpipe and the electrical pipe running next to it, she shimmied her way up the front of the house. She broke two nails along the way, and quickly realized her fashionable shoes weren't exactly made for breaking and entering. They slipped and scraped over the metal, probably rubbing the leather raw—at least she'd bought them on a wicked online sale.

Finally, she reached the windowsill on the second floor. The wood felt rotted and weak beneath her fingers, but she leaned against it to peer into the living room. The split in her dress allowed her to sprawl against the facade of the house like Spider-Man. She knew that if anyone drove by at that moment, she'd be totally busted, but she just couldn't resist.

Charlotte had flicked a couple of warm lights on in the living room. Addison scanned the old home just in time to see them climb to the top of the stairs. Felix pulled off his leather jacket, looking at ease in the surroundings. He'd barely hung it on the coat rack before Charlotte threw herself into his arms.

Addison gasped. Her foot slipped and she gripped the windowsill for dear life. But instead of climbing back down to safety, she leaned in closer.

Her breath fogging up the window, she waited for Felix to shove Charlotte away, to hold up a hand and say, "Sorry, but there's only one girl for me." And of course that one girl would be Addison.

But he didn't. Because she'd insulted him, she'd dismissed him time and time again. Just a couple of hours before, she'd told him she didn't want him and then made him watch her make out with another man.

Felix didn't hesitate. His arms encircled Charlotte, drawing her close to him as he rubbed her back slowly. She slumped against him in relief.

Addison couldn't see what happened after that because everything was suddenly blurry. She reached up to the window to wipe away the fog until she realized it was her tears obscuring the view.

Climbing back down to ground level, Addison headed back to her car. All she wanted now was to go home to Princess, eat a whole gallon of Triple Chocolate ice cream, and watch a marathon of chick flicks because there was nothing left for her there. That happily ever after was now a happily *never* after.

24

Wienerella

High heels and wingtips clicked and clacked on weathered wooden planks over the dark waters of the bay. Rocking gently on the waves that lapped the dock posts, the *San Francisco Belle* stood like a grand river castle. Only instead of turrets and throne rooms, it had three enclosed decks topped with a sundeck to enjoy the clear night. Its captain was its king, and its loyal subjects were a mix of show dogs and their entourages.

Addison stood at the bottom of the gangway admiring the paddleboat. Strings of lights wrapped around every railing and post to create a magical effect, lighting up the turn-of-the-last-century riverboat like a floating lantern in the night.

Cinderella had made it to the ball. And Addison certainly felt like Cinderella in her pink and black tulle ball gown. Even Princess had pulled out all the stops in her morganite collar necklace and matching tiara.

In other words, they looked fabulous, and they were ready to attend the ball. Only it wasn't to meet Addison's prince. Her prince turned out to be, well, someone else's prince. And Phillip? She supposed it was still a possibility. That was why she'd agreed to meet him at the gala. To give it a chance.

Phillip was still all those things she'd first thought him to be: handsome, magnanimous, polite. But somehow all those things had lost their appeal. Each time she tried to conjure up an image of Mr. Perfect, an image of Felix's face would pop into her fantasy or she would recall his belly laugh or how he looked tucked up next to his daughter in her My Little Pony bed. That would open the floodgates to all sorts of funny feelings, like she imagined Oscar nominees got when the drums rolled and the winner's name was announced—and it wasn't them.

Addison drew herself up and mentally focused on the night ahead. She wasn't there for the prince anyway. Sure, Phillip would be there and she'd talk to him, dance with him, give him a chance, because maybe even Cinderella had doubts. But first and foremost, she was there to protect the remaining dogs and hopefully catch the criminal in the act if they were stupid enough to try anything.

It was her last chance to rescue the dogs of people like Alistair, and Julia, and even Rex Harris, to salvage her business, and to save Felix's job.

So grasping her oversized skirts, Addison hoisted them up and squeezed her way across the narrow gangway with Princess in tow on her jeweled leash. The doxie's glittering open-pawed shoes sparkled beneath the multitude of string lights as they approached the deck.

There to greet them at the other end was someone that, if the dog-doo hit the hair dryer that night, Addison knew would have her back.

"Zoe!"

Her friend looked up from her tablet. She held out her

arms and hugged Addison in a way reserved for when girls are all dolled up and don't want to smudge makeup or mess up hair.

"Addy. I'm so glad you came."

"I wouldn't miss it for the world." Addison remained in her friend's arms a few seconds longer than normal, soaking up the love. She'd texted Piper and Zoe late the night before for some moral support, so they were up to speed, but Addison was in definite need of some girl time.

"You look great."

"Thanks for not crossing me off the guest list," Addison said. "I'm sure there will be more than one guest not thrilled to see me tonight."

"If they've got a problem with my guest list, they can deal with me." Zoe flicked her jet-black hair, like *Bring it on*. "Besides, it's not a party if my best friends aren't here."

Addison pitied any soul who decided to take Zoe on. "Are Piper and Aiden already here?"

"Yeah, I think they're at the bar on the second deck."

An older couple crossed the gangway behind Addison, holding their pugs in their arms. Since Addison's massive dress was blocking the entrance, she moved to leave as Zoe brought up the guest list on her tablet again.

"Go enjoy yourself," Zoe told Addison. "You can leave Princess on the sundeck. She'll be safe there."

"Thanks."

"Oh," she called out after her. "I should warn you. Holly Hart's here. Sorry." She pulled a face. "It couldn't be helped. She's someone's plus-one."

"Great." Addison rolled her eyes. Just what she needed. "Good luck tonight." She waved as she headed toward the double doors and into the enclosed lower deck.

The moment she stepped inside, Addison felt wrapped in luxury. It certainly didn't look like a normal boat in-

terior to her. Rich carpet softened her steps as she made
her way to the central lobby staircase that doubled back
on itself overhead. The chandelier dangling from the very
top shed warm light on the gold bannisters and swirling
rail designs. She followed them to the very top and then
found a secondary staircase that took her to the open sundeck.

As she stepped out into the open air, her heels sank
into soft grass. The entire sundeck had been laid with sod
for the dogs to play and roll around on. A white picket
fence wrapped around the deck rail, a cute continuation
of the yardlike theme. It also prevented the curious tea-
cups and minis from squeezing through the rail gaps and
doing a somersault dive into the water far below.

Enough kennels to house each and every dog in atten-
dance lined one side. Bright red fire hydrants, where the
dogs marked their territory, were placed at intervals between them.

A dog minder approached Addison, dressed in his
postal worker's uniform. She snickered, but didn't think
the minder would find it funny, so she stifled it before she
handed Princess over. The minder took her name and
asked for ID. She gave her doxie a kiss good-bye before
Princess trotted over for a drink of water from an oversized dish that looked like a toilet bowl.

She watched Princess for a few moments, hesitant to
leave her behind. As she eyed up the other guests out on
the deck, they seemed just as nervous. They weren't the
ones she needed to be concerned about.

As though sensing her reluctance, the minder said,
"Don't worry. They're perfectly safe up here. There are
only two entrances onto this deck." He pointed them out
on each side of the grassy area. "We know everyone who
comes and goes from here. No one is taking anyone's
dogs tonight."

She knew he was right. They were three stories high. Besides, she couldn't very well keep Princess with her while she was trying to investigate.

"Thanks," she told him.

"If it's an evacuation you're worried about, the kennels on board are all designed to float on water." He gestured to the kennels.

Addison noticed for the first time that they had plastic, waterproof doors instead of open wire ones. The top was punctured with several breathing holes and the bases were oversized, probably heavy enough to stay upright but buoyant enough to keep even a mastiff afloat.

Addison wondered if she should remind him that dogs actually swam, but then she remembered how far they'd be from shore and how small and delicate some of the show dogs aboard would be. It was actually a pretty good idea. Even if it was just for the owners' peace of mind.

With one more glance at Princess—who'd found a stuffed cat toy to chew on—she went to look around the deck. Although there were dog minders to pick up after the guests, Addison hiked up her dress, careful not to drag it as she made her way to the rail. She peered over the white picket fence at the view of the docks below.

Zoe couldn't have picked a more perfect venue. The paddleboat must have been forty or fifty feet tall, which meant that once they'd cast off, no one—two legged or four legged—was going to sneak on or off the boat. The dogs would be completely protected.

Maybe Addison really had nothing to worry about, after all. But if it was impossible to steal more dogs, she realized that she might lose her last opportunity to uncover the dognapper.

Deckhands scrambled below, their movements practiced and swift as they prepared to cast off. Addison studied them with suspicion, watching for any odd behaviors or clues—like grappling hooks or suction cups stuffed into their pockets revealing them as some kind of *Mission: Impossible* agents or something.

Just as they were unraveling the thick rope fastening the *Belle* to the dock, she noticed a few latecomers scurry toward the boat, their shoes clacking musically on the dock, echoing across the water. The deckhands waved them on, waiting for them to board. It wasn't until the twinkling string lights sparkled down on their heads that Addison recognized them.

She only saw a flash of their faces before they'd boarded, but she recognized them instantly, like an image carved painfully onto her heart. It was Felix with Naia and Oliver. And he'd brought Charlotte as his date.

Addison drew back from the rail like she'd been burned. Well, she supposed she had been. But wasn't she the one who had rejected him? Scorned him? Insulted him? Sent him running into Charlotte's arms?

So why did it hurt to breathe, like those two pints of Raspberry Lemon ice cream that she'd cried into the night before had tightened the bodice on her dress. And it certainly wasn't the cool night breeze that was making her eyes sting so badly.

A *thunk* shook the floor beneath her feet. A thunderous whistle released from somewhere above. Addison jumped, and her high heel stuck in the grass. The ship lurched and she faltered.

Slowly the *Belle* began to pull away from the dock. The dogs were in a tizzy, barking because of the horn, and then barking because of the barking. That's why she didn't hear anyone approach until a sharp finger jabbed her on a bare shoulder.

Addison spun around. Her eyes narrowed when she saw who it was. "Penny."

"Haven't stolen enough dogs for your collection yet?"

Addison's teeth clenched. "I didn't take the dogs." She tried to go around the famed handler, but Penny blocked her path.

Out of the corner of her eye, Addison noticed Holly Hart lurking nearby. Of course her cameraman, Hey, You, wouldn't be there, but the reporter clung awkwardly to her phone, like she was ready to start recording Addison and Penny if a cat fight, or rather dog fight, broke out.

Penny leered at Addison. "Even if you didn't steal Lilly, your carelessness makes you just as guilty as if you did."

"Lilly wasn't even your dog."

"A handler loves their dog as much, if not more, than the owner. We train it, we shape it, mold it into the pinnacle of excellence. We become one with it. And you tore all that time, effort, and love away from me."

Over Penny's shoulder, Addison could see Kitty Carlisle. When Kitty's shifting eyes landed on Addison, she flinched. Picking Elvis up, she moved to the other side of the deck, as if afraid that Addison could make her bichon frisé disappear with a simple look.

Groaning, she pushed past Penny. "I need a drink," she muttered to herself.

The last couple of weeks had taken their toll on Addison's patience. She was tired of the stares, the nervous glances, the whispered accusations behind her back—and sometimes to her face.

Addison descended the stairs and marched through the double doors to the second deck. The clinking of glasses told her there was a bar nearby. *Thank God,* she thought. When she glanced over, she spotted Piper and Aiden standing next to the rich mahogany and marble bar.

As usual, they were unable to see anyone but each other. Even their two lovesick doxies had wound their leashes around their owners' legs to get as close as they could. Addison smiled. It wouldn't be long before they were engaged.

Thankfully, Aiden's attention was too focused on Piper to notice Addison. She wasn't ready to face him. Not yet. Not tonight. She still had hope, however small, that she could uncover the dognapper. She just had to keep her eyes peeled and be ready for anything.

A waiter carrying crystal dog bowls filled with amber liquid passed by. By the smell, Addison guessed it could only be Hound Hooch, liquefied chicken made to look like beer. Addison ducked behind him and kept pace as he swept to the other side of the room in order to hide herself from the lovey-dovey couple.

The waiter suddenly turned away, exposing her. Addison spun, hoping to find cover among eager dancers already heating up the dance floor to a waltz before dinner. However, she took one too many turns. An elbow from a server, a stray hip from a dancer, and Addison was sent stumbling.

Her heel caught on a flowing piece of her tulle gown. She skidded on the parquet floor and her foot slipped out from under her. Her hands flew out, automatically reaching for the nearest thing.

She grazed a cashmere jacket as she fell against a man. Arms wrapped around her to brace her fall. When she opened her eyes, she found herself staring up at Phillip.

"We've got to stop meeting like this," he said. There was that smile that had so enamored her right from the start. He was still that smart, charming, polite man. He *was* a catch.

And because she'd made a promise to herself that she'd give him a chance, when he held out his hand and asked her, "May I have this dance?" she replied, "Of course."

She placed her hand in his. His other hand trailed down her low-backed dress and pressed her closer to his tennis-toned body. And then he spun her around the dance floor.

Addison's rhinestones glittered beneath the chandeliers, and the tulle of her dress trailed delicately behind her as they spun over and over again. The waltz was so romantic and the historic boat took her back to another time, another world. She became so lost in the moment, the beauty, the fantasy, forgetting her doubts and her worries until she felt like a princess.

He dipped her low and she let her head tilt back, enjoying the magic of it all. Then she saw him enter the room: Felix.

Phillip set Addison on her feet, grinning mischievously over his suave move, but she barely noticed.

On their next spin around a nearby couple, Addison glanced at the front doors again. Charlotte had her arm linked through Felix's, holding him tight—maybe a little possessively, she thought.

Felix's dark eyes scanned the room. Addison's head moved around to keep him in sight. When his gaze fell on her, she faltered and stepped on Phillip's toe.

"Ouch," he hissed.

"Sorry," she mumbled, but she was too busy weaving and bobbing her head to get a better view.

Felix had shaved. Not only that but he'd trimmed his ebony waves and combed them neatly back from his face. And was that . . . ? Yes. He wore one of the bespoke suits they'd admired in the shop across from Joe's Dive.

He looked even better than Addison thought he would. This new Felix was deceptive. This cleaned-up version looked civilized and blended in with the lavish surroundings. The way he carried himself, however, that certain swagger and that piercing look, belied the capable, cunning man beneath. The promise that he was so much more than everyone else in that room could know. Addison had only begun to learn how much more. She supposed it would be Charlotte who would now find out how much.

She lost the rhythm again and did a sort of half-turn instead of a quarter turn.

"Ouch." Phillip winced.

"Sorry."

Phillip led her around the dance floor again, and Felix was swallowed by the crowd. Addison tugged, and dragged, and redirected their steps to get back on the other side again, until she was practically leading. She moved her head this way and that to see over Phillip's broad shoulders.

"Ouch," Phillip said again.

Phillip's next few steps were more like limps. That's when Addison decided to ignore Felix entirely. He was there with someone else, after all. Not her. It obviously didn't take him long to move on, so he couldn't have liked Addison very much. No big loss, right?

Images flashed through Addison's mind, of Charlotte in Felix's arms. He had clearly made his decision. Addison was here with Phillip, anyway. *P-H-I-L-L-I-P*, she reminded herself sternly.

She turned her gaze upward and batted her eyelashes at him. He gave her a flirtatious wink, or maybe it was another wince of pain as she stomped his foot yet again.

By the time they rounded the dance floor once more, Addison saw Felix and Charlotte cozied up in a dark, secluded corner. Charlotte leaned her face up toward Felix. He ducked his head so she could whisper sweet nothings in his ear.

Their faces were so close together, her lips almost brushing his cheek to be heard over the big band on the stage. He turned his face toward Charlotte, as though about to kiss her.

Addison's eyes widened, pressure building in her chest as she forgot to breathe.

"Ooof." Phillip lurched forward.

"Ouch!" Addison cried as he bumped into her.

"Sorry," they said simultaneously.

Addison belatedly realized that she'd stopped dancing altogether and had caused a traffic jam behind them on the dance floor. At that moment, the song thankfully came to an end.

Addison gave a brief boblike curtsy. "Thank you for the dance. Sorry. Must be the waves throwing me off-balance or something."

"No problem," he said, gracious enough not to point out that it wasn't really a wavy ride.

Near the edge of the parquet floor, Addison spotted Holly Hart holding her phone out. She was staring down at the screen as though checking her messages. However, as Addison continued to stare at the reporter, a naughty smile creased the corners of her eyes.

Was she following Addison around to record her? Maybe Holly thought she was conducting her own investigation that night.

It was suddenly very warm in there. Too many people crowded that deck, too many people who hated Addison, who were waiting to see if she'd do something wrong. She needed to get out of there. But there was no way out, no way off that moving vessel beyond diving into the cold bay, which she tucked away as a good backup plan.

"Save another dance for me later?" she asked Phillip.

"Maybe I'll buy you a drink instead," he said, wiping her footprint off his wingtip shoe.

She smiled sheepishly, but was already backing away from the dance floor. "I'm going to go get some fresh air. Excuse me."

"Certainly."

She bumped Holly's shoulder as she passed, causing her to drop her phone. Addison "accidentally" kicked it across the floor. She ignored Holly's shouts at her back, just as she tried to ignore the suspicious looks from the other guests as she weaved through them.

They whispered behind their hands as she walked by. She could feel the blame in their postures and gazes. There were so many against her, rooting for her to fail. Even Felix's cool gaze swept over her blankly as she passed by the lovebirds in the corner.

Addison's pace picked up as she headed for the exit. The room was suddenly too small, and was that three-hundred-foot boat really big enough for all of them? What's worse, hidden among them all could be the real bad guy, waiting for the right moment to strike again.

If Addison didn't catch them before the night was over, if they got away with it all again, those missing dogs would stay missing forever. Not to mention, her life would be ruined, and this time for good. She was already doing a fine job of accomplishing that all on her own.

25

Wagging the Dog

Addison burst through the doors and onto the outer deck of the *Belle*. She leaned against the rail, almost tempted to dive right overboard to escape the suffocating feeling of being trapped on the paddleboat with so many people. People who didn't want her there.

The crisp night air was like a splash of cold water on her bare shoulders and neck. She reached back and swept her hair off her neck, but it only reminded her of when Felix had braided her hair in the sauna, the last time she felt claustrophobic, so she let it drop again.

The dark bay water sparkled all around the boat with the reflection of thousands of string lights. They'd left the Embarcadero behind with its busy streets and the ships coming and going from the piers. A haze had settled over San Francisco, emphasizing the bright cityscape as though it were one solid band of light. From a distance, the financial district looked so magical and foreign.

The bay was dark and lonely except for the occasional boat floating by. The *Belle* chugged away leisurely, the paddle wheel churning at the back of the boat, urging them beneath the Bay Bridge. Underneath the heavy sky, the bridge stood out like a thick black strip over Addison's head.

Her clutch suddenly vibrated in her hand. She popped the clasp and pulled out her phone. The display said DAD.

At the very thought of him, the tensed muscles in her back relaxed and she answered. "Dad?"

"Hi muffin. I thought you had your dog party tonight. I didn't expect you to answer. I was just going to leave a message."

"I'm just taking a break." *Sort of.* "What's up?"

"I just called to let you know that we got some good news tonight," he said, cheerily. "We sold the corner store."

Addison's heart clenched and she felt her breath whoosh out of her in defeat. She gripped the rail in front of her. "You did?"

There was silence on the other end before he said, "You don't sound quite as happy as I thought you would. Is everything okay?"

Addison's memories rushed back to her as she recalled all the movies she'd watched in that little corner store, how she'd do her homework behind the counter, how she'd wash people's windshields for a bit of pocket change to buy candy. She'd whiled away many happy hours there growing up. It had been like a second home to her. And then she considered all the years of hard work her dad put into it, and for what? To sell it at a loss out of desperation?

Shaking off the sudden emotions eating at her, Addison closed her eyes and tried to put aside her own selfish disappointment at the news. Her dad seemed genuinely relieved.

"No. No. It's good news," she said, trying to put a

smile on her face as though he could see it. But it fell flat. "I just . . . I guess I was hoping that I might be able to help you somehow. That if my fashion line did well enough, I could pay you back for sending me to pet grooming school, for all you've done to help me get myself set up here in the city."

"Sweetheart—"

"I know it wouldn't have been much," she said, realizing how silly she was being. "But it might have helped hold off the banks until, I don't know, maybe business got better." Saying it out loud suddenly made her feel childish. Like she was holding onto an unrealistic fantasy—not for the first time, it seemed.

Her dad chuckled, but she could hear the kindness behind it. "I appreciate the thought. It's very sweet. But you need to worry about yourself. Dora and I can take care of ourselves."

Addison sighed. "I guess I just worry about the two of you. I know that things can get tough when money is tight."

"Dora and I will be just fine. We'll get through this. It's an opportunity to do something new, have new experiences together."

He really sounded excited, and she knew that was probably Dora's doing. The corner store was the only thing her dad had ever known, while Dora was more the adventurer. Whatever was about to come next would need a sense of adventure, and Addison was glad that Dora was going to be the one beside him for it.

"So"—she hesitated—"you two are fine then? I mean, you and Dora are going to work through it together?"

"Of course." He laughed again, maybe in surprise. "Dora and I are partners. We'll get through anything that life throws at us. We love each other."

"But you and Mom—"

"Your mother and I had a lot of things, but we didn't have what it took to get through the bad times. We didn't have enough love. Dora and I have that."

Addison went quiet on her end. She wondered if it would be enough.

As though he read her mind, he said, "With enough love, you can make it through anything. There's more to life than money."

Addison knew that. Of course she did. But at the same time, hearing it come from her father meant so much more than reading the old adage off a bumper sticker or coffee mug. After he'd lost so much because of money and had to work so hard for it, if he could still say that, then it must be true.

Here she'd been worrying about ending up in a relationship where money would never be an issue, like with Phillip. But while money was an issue for Dora and her father, they didn't let it come between them.

"That's good. I'm happy for the two of you." This time the smile on her face felt real.

"So don't worry about us," he said. "Who's the parent here, anyway? Shouldn't I be the one worrying about you?"

"I just wanted to make you proud, to show you that your sacrifices for me haven't been for nothing." And ever since the dogs had gone missing, she'd been feeling just that.

"Of course I'm proud of you. I'd be proud of you no matter what."

"No matter what?" she asked.

"Absolutely. Dora and I are looking forward to your fashion show on Sunday. We'll be the ones cheering from the front."

Addison swallowed hard, wondering if there would even be a fashion show at this rate. However, there was still a chance. If she could uncover the dognappers, the fashion show could still be a success. It reminded her of why she'd come to the gala that night. It wasn't to dance with Phillip or cry over Felix. It was her last chance to solve this mystery once and for all. Saying good-bye to her dad, she ended the call.

As she was tucking her phone away in her clutch, the doors to the covered deck opened behind her. A bubble of laughter and the sounds of mingling drifted out.

"There's the prettiest girl at the ball."

Addison recognized Piper's voice. She turned to find Piper and Zoe coming out to join her.

"I'm sure Aiden would disagree with that statement," Addison told Piper.

"But Phillip would agree," Piper said, with a hint of cheekiness. "I saw you two dancing. So I take it the two of you are picking up where you left off on Wednesday night?"

"Maybe." Addison hesitated. "I mean, he's a great guy."

"Really?" Zoe asked with a skeptical tilt to her head. "Is that why you were busy eyeing up that guy across the room?"

Addison scowled, mostly because she was annoyed at getting caught. "I wasn't eyeing Felix."

"That was Felix?" Zoe's eyebrows shot up. Clearly the suit was doing it for her too. "I thought I recognized Naia when they came aboard. He told me he couldn't find a babysitter. A few other guests brought older kids, so it wasn't a big deal."

Piper leaned on the rail next to Addison. "From how you talked about him, he's not quite what I expected."

Addison laughed, but it sounded weak. "Yeah, me neither."

Piper and Zoe exchanged looks over Addison's head, but it was Zoe, always so direct, who asked, "Want to talk about it?"

"I'm not sure." Addison stared down at the water rippling below them. "Have you ever wanted something so bad for so long that when you finally get it you realize that it was only a nice dream? Because now that it's right in front of me, I'm not sure it's what I want anymore."

"Like a dog chasing its tail." Piper nodded. "When it finally catches it, it doesn't know what to do with it and lets it go."

"Something like that," she said. "Maybe Phillip's my tail."

"So if not Phillip, then what do you want?" Zoe asked.

Addison had been thinking about it so much lately, but it was scarier to admit it out loud, especially to the two people who knew her best. "Something I didn't even realize I wanted. Something I thought I could never have."

"A tattoo?" Zoe asked.

"Zero-calorie ice cream," Piper suggested.

Zoe smirked. "A penis?"

Addison laughed, happy she still knew how to do that. "A family."

Piper slung an arm around her. "We're your family, Addy. We always will be. You know that, right?"

"Thanks. I feel the same way." She rested her head on Piper's shoulder. "But you know what I mean. One to go home to at the end of the day."

"So are we just speaking hypothetically?" Zoe asked. "Or do you have a particular family in mind?"

"Well, I . . ." Addison thought she had, maybe, possibly. But after watching Felix and Charlotte board the

Belle that night, she realized that boat had sailed. "I don't think so. Not anymore."

Zoe's tablet began to jingle. "Shit. It's almost time for dinner to begin."

"That's okay," Addison said. "Go ahead. You've got a busy night. We'll talk later."

Piper squeezed Addison a little tighter. "Are you going to be okay?"

"Yeah. I will be." Maybe she'd lost her chance with Felix, but at least she was on track to figuring out what she really wanted. It was time to wake up and find her happiness. Not just dream about it.

"We are long overdue for a sleepover," Zoe said. "How about later this weekend, after all your fashion show craziness is over."

Addison winced. That was if the fashion show was even going to happen. She smiled, putting on a brave face for her friends. "For sure. We'll catch up."

Zoe gave her a wink before fitting an earpiece into her ear—very official looking—and heading up the stairs. A few minutes later, her sensual voice carried over the *Belle*'s intercom system.

"Attention please. Dinner is about to be served. Will everyone kindly make their way to the lower deck? We will begin in fifteen minutes."

"Are you coming?" Piper asked Addison.

"Yeah, I'll be right there."

Once Piper waved good-bye and headed back inside, Addison resumed her contemplative position at the deck rail, but this time she wasn't contemplating the view of the shore. She was watching the guests filter downstairs.

Her eyes were peeled for clues. But no one was wearing ski masks or creeping along with big sacks of puppies slung across their backs. In fact, almost no one had a dog with them at all. The few people who had brought their furry friends had left them on the sundeck where they could be monitored by the dog minders.

Once the coast was clear, Addison hurried back inside. The parquet dance floor clicked under her heels as she scoped out the nearly empty room. It was the size of a traditional ballroom, broken up only by the ornate support columns. She weaved in and out of them, trying to act casual while she searched for potential evildoers.

Her eyes flitted to the people still in the room, mostly workers. On the small stage, band members were tuning their instruments. The bartender was placing fresh glasses behind the bar and restocking the liquor. Servers cleaned up empty cocktail glasses. The only shifty-looking one seemed to be her.

Addison skirted around the side of the bar to head for the back staircase. As she passed by, she noticed a clipboard on the counter with a list of all the guests' names. She glanced over at the bartender. He had his back to her while he restocked the cupboard.

Tucking her clutch under her arm, Addison swiped the clipboard and kept on moving before he noticed. She climbed the stairs to the third enclosed deck, holding the list aloft, very official-like. But the deck, which had been set up for cocktails and socializing after dinner, was deserted.

Tired of taking the stairs in high heels, Addison headed for the elevator inside. Once she managed to squeeze into it, her poofy dress took up half of the enclosed space. It was like shoving an open umbrella into a car.

She hit the button for the first deck and held her dress aside until the door slid closed. At the last second an arm shot out, stopping it from shutting. When the metal door slid open, Felix was standing on the other side.

"Oh, hi," Addison said.

"Hi," he answered, hesitating at the door. "What are you doing here? Shouldn't you be down at dinner?"

"I'm casing the joint." She figured some vernacular would help her seem far more qualified to do it on her own than she felt.

He seemed to take her in from top to bottom, his gaze finally landing on the clipboard in her hand. "Are you helping your friend with the event?"

"Oh. No. I just thought the guest list might come in handy."

He nodded. "Good thinking."

He was still holding the door open, but when it began to alarm, he shuffled inside the elevator somewhat reluctantly. Addison tried to hold her marshmallow dress aside to create room, but the space was so tight he still had to press up against her.

A few moments of awkward elevator silence passed where neither of them knew where to look. There wasn't even cheesy music to help ease it. The ride seemed longer than it should have been for only two floors.

"You look pretty," he finally said.

When she looked at him, he was staring at her in earnest. Of course, he was there with Charlotte, so he just meant to be nice. But when he kept staring at her, she fidgeted uncomfortably and looked away.

"Thank you," she said. "You look good in that suit."

"I had a good fashion advisor."

Addison smiled at that, but didn't know what else to say. The elevator dinged as they reached their destination. The doors slid open. "Well, I'll let you get back to your date," she said.

Felix made no move to leave. "Charlotte knows I need to check the place out for clues, so she's watching Naia for me on the sundeck."

Addison's eyebrows automatically furrowed at the

mention of the server's name. "So I suppose she's helping you track down the dognappers now?"

"She is actually." He said it so casually, but she could see he was hiding some emotion. Whatever it was, it was pretty raw because the vein started to stand out on his forehead. "Where's Phillip?" He scowled as he said the name.

"He's waiting for me at dinner," she lied. She hoisted her skirt up as though about to step out of the elevator, but couldn't seem to make her legs go forward. "He's probably wondering where I am."

As the door started to close, Felix stopped it and gestured for her to go first. "You wouldn't want to keep Mr. Perfect waiting. If you're late, he might think you're not so perfect yourself."

"That's not possible since we both know I am."

He snorted derisively.

Heat crawled beneath Addison's skin, but she maintained her aloof attitude. "You know, I'm so happy Charlotte could find a dress to hide those red bra straps of hers." Her eyelashes batted innocently.

Felix laughed, but managed to scowl at the same time. "Jealous much?"

"Yes." Her answer came out as a light breath, so quiet she hadn't realized it came out of her own mouth until his head whipped toward her. By the expression on his face, he was wondering if he'd imagined it too.

The truth had slipped out before she'd even had the chance to think of a scathing response. The honesty and earnestness in that one word surprised even her. It hung in the air between them, filling the silent elevator.

Felix opened his mouth to speak, but whatever he was about to say was cut off by a loud blast from the boat's horn.

Startled, Addison jumped. A high-pitched hum from

the engine vibrated the floor beneath their feet. There was a sudden change in speed, like the boat had slammed on its brakes—if it even had brakes.

The lurch shook Felix and Addison in the small space, and she fell against him. Automatically, his arms came up and wrapped around her. Being held by him, his touch, his hands—unlike Phillip's—felt warm and right . . . like home.

The elevator door shut automatically. Addison wanted to stay there forever, but she was dimly aware of hollering outside their little space. Dishes clattered on the dining deck and footsteps shuffled through the lobby.

After a moment, Felix pressed the *door open* button. By the time the doors slid open, the lobby was filled to capacity. Most of the dinner guests had pressed their way to the bow of the boat. Those who couldn't fit outside on the outer deck weaved their heads back and forth, rubbernecking for a view of whatever was going on outside.

Their awkwardness forgotten, Felix and Addison shared a look. The foreboding in the air made her shiver.

He stepped out and Addison squeezed her puffy dress through of the elevator after him. They didn't get any farther since the lobby was too packed. Chatter drifted back through the crowd like a game of telephone.

"We hit something," someone said.

"Did we hit the shore?" Addison asked the woman next to her.

"I don't know," she answered.

"Who's driving this thing?" a random voice demanded.

"Oh my God!" someone cried out. "Are we sinking?"

"I think we hit another boat," another voice called out.

"I wonder if my pooky is okay," the woman next to Addison said. "They probably got quite a fright up there."

Addison tuned into the sounds outside of the chaotic lobby. She could hear the captain arguing with someone, presumably the other boat's operator, from his wheelhouse on the very top deck.

"Felix!" a female voice called out from across the lobby.

Addison recognized Charlotte's voice. She turned to find the server pushing her way through the crowd. Along the way, Charlotte got a few nasty looks and a "Hey, watch it!" but she didn't seem to care.

She was huffing by the time she reached Addison and Felix, her cheeks flushed pink. "Felix. Here you are. I've been looking everywhere for you."

"Charlotte. What's wrong?" Felix glanced behind her and all around her. "Where's Naia?"

She shook her head, her chin quivering slightly. "I'm so sorry. I've looked everywhere for her. I thought maybe she'd found you somehow."

"You mean you don't know where she is?" His voice was loud even among the excited chatter all around them. He took a deep breath through his nose before continuing. "All right, when did you last see her?"

"Fifteen minutes ago, maybe. I-I don't know what happened. She was with me the whole time. I only turned my back for like a second, I swear. When I turned around, she was gone."

Felix laid a hand on her arm and spoke calmly to her. "Don't worry. I'm sure she's still up there hiding somewhere. We'll go up and take a look."

But when he turned back to the elevator, his actions were anything but calm. He jabbed the elevator button repeatedly until Addison thought it might break. Finally, the door slid open.

As he got in, he looked over his shoulder. "Addison?"

Felix didn't have to say any more. The question was already there in his voice, along with the pleading and the worry.

Addison nodded, squeezing her oversized dress inside with Charlotte and Felix. "I'll help you find her."

Felix's hand shook slightly as he reached out and hit the button for the third deck.

"Oh, Felix." Charlotte suddenly sobbed. "I'm so sorry. I swear I only looked away for a second."

"I know," he said. "We'll find her."

"But I've looked everywhere, and they had the door closed and the gates in front of the stairs to keep the dogs from escaping. I don't think she could have gotten out that way. I just don't know where else she could be. And there are all those railings and she's so little. And what, if"—she hiccuped—"what if . . ." Charlotte broke down into full sobs, unable to say the words.

The color left Felix's face and he didn't look like he wanted to hear any more.

"The fence is too tall," Addison cut in. "She couldn't have climbed over or gotten through any of the gaps. They secured the entire deck for teacup dogs," she assured Felix. "Naia would have been fine."

Felix nodded, looking slightly relieved by the news. Charlotte was still crying. He reached out and rubbed her back as she cried into his chest.

"Oh God. I'm so sorry Felix," she said, between gasps for air. "You trusted me with her and . . . I'm going to make such a terrible mother."

Addison's head whipped to Charlotte, her mouth dropping open, but neither she nor Felix seemed to notice. They were too lost in their worried thoughts. Addison glanced from the server to Felix and back again.

Mother? Charlotte didn't mean . . . Isn't it a little too

soon to be talking like that? Addison wondered. *After they'd only just started dating?*

But she couldn't ignore the ache in her chest reminding her that Felix and Charlotte were close. They'd worked together for years. He always defended her, protected her, and, after what Addison had witnessed in Charlotte's home, there could be no doubt. Heck, it wasn't even like she knew a lot about Felix's past. Maybe they'd dated before.

Charlotte and Felix were obviously serious. Maybe it was just meant to be. Isn't that what Addison told Felix when he asked about Phillip? *When it's right, it's right.*

Addison stared down at the clutch in her hands, unable to look at the two of them together anymore. She wondered if they were on the longest elevator ride in history. At least Addison had never lost Naia. Well, maybe she did, but only for a second, and she wasn't really lost. She was in Oliver's kennel the whole time.

Addison gasped. "That's it!"

Charlotte pulled away and tried to wipe her face with the back of her hand. "What's it?"

"Naia must be in Oliver's kennel."

Felix seemed to exhale a thousand held breaths. "Of course. She was scared of coming on the boat. That's why she wanted to stay with Oliver on the sundeck, because she felt safer up there with him."

Charlotte just blinked. "I didn't even think to look. It makes sense. I knew she couldn't have gotten off that floor."

The moment the doors opened, Felix ran for the stairs to the sundeck, taking two at a time. Charlotte followed close behind, but Addison struggled to keep up with them in her high heels.

On her way to the stairs, she passed the captain and a

few of the other staff heading to deal with whatever was going on below. They nodded their heads but otherwise took no note of her.

She leaned over the side rail to see what the holdup was. The *Belle* had, in fact, collided with another smaller recreational vessel. The boater was busy arguing with the staff on the first deck, even though it was clear he was the one who ran into them.

Squeezing into the stairwell, Addison followed Charlotte and Felix to the top, hoping that she was right and Naia was safe in Oliver's kennel. But before she even got to the last steps, she felt something wasn't right.

She would have expected with all of the commotion down below that the dogs would be barking, sensing something was wrong. But the only yapping and barking were coming from the human guests down on the first deck.

The bodice on Addison's dress seemed tighter than ever. She strained to hear any doglike noises coming from the top deck, but it was eerily silent. When she shot out the top of the staircase, she saw why.

The entire sundeck was deserted. All the dogs, all the kennels, were gone. Including Princess. And Oliver. And Naia.

In the middle of the grass, Charlotte had sunk to her knees. Her shoulders shook with silent tears. Felix stood off to the side, staring blankly into his hands. The clipboard dropped from Addison's hand, clattering to the floor, her legs moving toward him without even thinking about it.

As she got closer, she realized Felix was holding something: Naia's stuffed bunny.

Addison's footsteps faltered at the sight of the stuffed animal in his hand, limp and bereft without its owner. Felix's fist was clenched around the toy, his fingers white. He turned to face her.

"She's gone," he told her. "Naia's gone."

The deck swam before Addison's eyes and her stomach felt like it had flipped inside out. The dognapper had struck again. Only now, they were also a kidnapper.

26

Sea Dogs

Felix stood in the middle of the sundeck's makeshift lawn, running one hand over his head, gripping his hair like he wanted to rip it out. The other was still clenched around Naia's stuffed bunny. His mouth opened in a wordless scream before his chin dropped to his chest and he closed his eyes.

Addison was afraid to touch him because he looked about ready to explode, or maybe to curl up into the fetal position and cry. She didn't know which one would be worse. All she knew was she wanted to hold him and tell him it would be all right.

But Charlotte was with him, murmuring that it would be okay, that his daughter was still on the ship somewhere. Addison turned away to give them privacy, but she doubted very much that that was the case, and by the look on Felix's face, so did he.

Addison wanted to search the sundeck, search the whole ship and the surrounding waters. But all the show dogs disappearing at once could only mean one thing. The dognappers had gotten what they finally wanted, and then some. Along with it, they had taken both Naia and Princess.

Princess. A tear rolled down her cheek before she even knew she was crying. Addison felt both distraught and selfish at the same time. Felix was missing his daughter, his baby, and she was crying over her dog. But in a way, Princess was Addison's baby. If she wasn't, then why did it feel like someone had taken one of the silver spoons from the dining deck and hollowed out her insides?

She wished she had a DeLorean like in *Back to the Future,* to go back in time. She would tell her past self not to bring Princess that night, to leave her at home. She'd tell Felix not to bring Naia. Hell, while she was at it, she'd kiss Felix on Phillip's balcony rather than push him away.

Her head spun, caught in a useless cycle of regrets and random thoughts—fear for her precious Princess, guilt for worrying about Princess when Naia was missing too, pity for Felix. She glanced at Felix, but he was hugging Charlotte now so she turned away, adding self-loathing to the mix of emotions circulating through her.

Hugging herself, Addison shuffled to the back of the boat, heels sinking into the fresh sod. She leaned against the white picket fence and stared out into the night.

There was quiet splashing in the water below. Addison thought it had come from the bow, where the deckhands were probably attempting to dislodge the small boat that had crashed into the *Belle*. But then there was another splash behind her. It was soft and rhythmic, coming from the stern.

She peered into the night. More fog had rolled in since she was last outside with Zoe and Piper. Maybe that was why the recreational boat hadn't seen the *Belle*. Although she couldn't see how, since it was a three-hundred-foot-long floating torch made up of string lights.

The bay water was so dark beyond the boat, reflecting their own halo of light immediately around them. She searched for the source of the splashing and saw a dark shape drifting inside the halo's sparkling ripples. It was a boat, big enough for about ten people.

Oars dipped in and out of the water as it rowed away. In the light, gold letters flashed along the side of its hull. *San Francisco Belle*. It was one of the *Belle*'s lifeboats. Inside the hull was a stack of boxes.

Addison's frantic brain finally caught up with the scene playing out before her. They weren't boxes. They were dog kennels. The kennels. The dogs. Naia. Princess. Her knees buckled and she gripped the railing for support.

The dognappers were right there, still so close. She should have been able to hear the dogs' barking and whining echo across the water, but they were silent. Her mouth went dry as she considered why.

"Felix." Her voice was barely a whisper. She licked her lips and tried again. "Felix, look!"

It felt like a bad dream. Surely this wasn't happening. She couldn't be the only one to see this happening. But then again, at that very moment, all the guests and crew were distracted by the head-on collision up front.

She suddenly realized the "accident" had been intended as a distraction. The smaller boat had intentionally run into them. But surely all the dog minders hired to watch over the show dogs hadn't run to gawk at the accident. Where were they?

Addison heard Felix's footsteps swishing across the grass, but she didn't want to take her eyes away from the shape in case she blinked and lost it. She pointed straight out into the darkness, and Felix's eyes followed her finger. She knew he saw it when his grip tightened around one of the fake fence posts and it busted off in his hand.

The lifeboat disappeared from the *Belle*'s aura of light, blending into the foggy night. She yelled, "Stop!" But her voice was downed out by the long blast of the horn.

The *Belle*'s engine whirred somewhere in its depths. The dark waters below churned around the stern of the boat until it looked like boiling water. The paddle wheel slowly began to turn and the *Belle* inched forward, away from all of the dogs floating away.

Felix threw the piece of wood aside. "We have to go after them."

Charlotte gripped Felix's jacket and shook her head. "They'll be long gone by the time we dock. Besides, Naia might still be on the boat. We'll go talk to the captain."

Addison barely heard Charlotte. Her eyes were moving over the crime scene.

"Maybe we don't have to wait," Addison told Felix, pointing to the other side of the ship. "Look. There's another lifeboat. They haven't gotten very far. We can follow them."

Felix was already tucking Naia's bunny into his inside jacket pocket, charging toward the spare lifeboat. Addison hurried after him, her heels digging into the grass like lawn darts, slowing her down. By the time she reached the boat, Felix had already climbed inside and was grabbing the power controls to lower it into the water.

"Wait. Where are you going?" Charlotte asked him.

"To get my daughter back."

"We haven't even called nine-one-one yet," she said. "Why don't you wait for the police?"

"That will take too long. We haven't been able to catch this guy yet. If we let him go now, we might not be able to find Nai—" He couldn't finish the thought. He blinked, long and slow. "This could be my only chance."

Addison threw a leg into the boat. "You mean *our* only chance."

Felix held a hand up to stop her. "Where do you think you're going?"

"With you."

"No you're not. It might be dangerous."

He tried to push her out, but she swatted his hand away.

"I'm going and you can't stop me. I want to help you get Naia and Princess back. The longer we argue about it, the more we risk them getting away." She fixed him with a steady stare. "We're in this together, remember?"

Felix seemed to consider this a moment before reaching out and helping Addison to climb inside the hull. Her poofy dress took up nearly the entire width of the boat. The moment her butt hit the bench across from him, he hit the down button on the control switch.

The lifeboat jerked to life. Addison gripped the bench beneath her. With a whir of gears and pulleys, they descended the three decks to the water below.

"Charlotte!" Addison called up. "Go find Zoe, the event coordinator of this party, and tell her everything that's happened!"

She saw Charlotte nod just before they hit the water. Addison squealed and shivered as the spray from the paddle wheel reached them. Felix took off his jacket and tossed it to her.

"Thanks," she said, wrapping it around herself. She felt the bulge of Naia's stuffed bunny inside the jacket and swallowed hard.

"I can't move in the monkey suit, anyway," he said.

Felix reached down to pick up the oars resting next to

their feet. He placed them in the eyelets on either side and started rowing in the general direction the dognapper had gone.

Addison knew they needed to make up for lost time, so she spun around, her back to Felix. Setting her clutch down next to her so it didn't fall in the water, she grabbed another pair of oars and began to row. As they floated farther and farther away, the bay fog swallowed the *San Francisco Belle*.

Addison tried to keep the same pace as Felix, but she felt the powerful surge of their little boat with each one of his strokes, and she knew she wasn't helping much. Her oversized ball gown getting in the way of the oars didn't exactly help either. And since there were two more sets of oarlocks, it was definitely not meant to be a two-person rowboat. But every inch counted, every inch brought them closer to Naia, to Princess, to all the stolen dogs. To saving the day.

This is what Addison tried to remind herself of when her back began to ache, when her muscles screamed as though the flesh was being torn from her bones, when her arms felt like hardening cement. But still she rowed. For Naia, for Princess, for all the dogs and their worried owners—and to keep her dad feeling proud of her.

Felix's grunts grew louder with each stroke, but he never slowed for a second. Addison bit hard on her lip to keep from crying out each time she dipped the oars into the water and heaved back as hard as she could. She didn't want to be the reason they lost the other boat.

The fog weighed down on them, much thicker than before. Addison glanced behind her every couple of minutes, worried they could be ten feet from the other boat and never see it. But they kept making their way toward the bright glow breaking through the fog: the Financial District.

Soon, over Addison's own heavy breathing, Felix's grunting, and the splashing of their oars on the water, she heard another set of rhythmic splashes. Muffled as it was by the haze, Addison knew they were gaining on the dognapper. There was no doubt it was him because who else would be crazy enough to row a boat out on the bay in the dark and the fog?

Biting down so hard on her lip that she tasted blood, Addison worked through the pain. She knew Felix could hear the sound too, because their boat's momentum suddenly increased with his sudden burst of power. A last desperate effort.

The distant splashing suddenly stopped. Addison and Felix kept rowing. With each stroke, Addison's heart quickened. What was going to happen when they caught up to the thief?

Someone yelled out. "Throw me the rope!"

Addison heard answering calls. Her eyes grew wide as she realized there were more than one dognapper. But of course there were. In order to steal this many dogs, there'd have to be.

The hidden voice reached their ears again. "Come on, hurry!"

Moments later, a loud roar echoed across the water, followed by the quiet purr of an engine.

Felix grunted. "They're going to get away."

He groaned, and Addison imagined him trying to go faster, but they'd been going so long.

"Okay, go, go, go!" that mystery voice yelled over the engine.

The purr turned into a growl as the engine revved. Then it quickly faded into the distance, until all that was left was the splashing of Felix's and Addison's oars.

Felix stopped rowing. "Shhhh."

Addison turned around to see him holding up his hand, tilting his head to listen. But there was only silence.

In mere seconds their lifeboat floated over white foam, churned up by a motor. They'd been so close, but the boat, the dogs, and Naia were gone.

27

Up the Creek without a Doggy Paddle

"Shit!" Felix threw down an oar, spraying Addison in the process. "We lost them. Goddammit."

He grabbed the other oar and flung it, sending it flying into the bay. It landed with an unsatisfyingly quiet splash.

It looked like he wanted to rage, to punch something, but they were stuck on the little lifeboat, so he pressed his face into his hands and yelled into them until he turned red.

Addison spun on her bench to face him, her heart breaking to see his pain. This time she couldn't help but reach out to him and hold his hand. He grabbed it readily and squeezed.

"We might still catch up to them," she said. "They still have to unload the kennels. That will take time. We're not too far from shore." The glow had in fact brightened, the angular outlines of the skyscrapers poking out of the fog above them.

"They wouldn't be headed back to the Embarcadero,"

he said bitterly. "Too many witnesses. They could be headed anywhere." He kicked the hull of the boat, causing it to rock.

"Maybe Zoe's contacted the Coast Guard by now. Maybe they're already searching." Addison opened her clutch and dug through it to find her phone. "I'll just call her."

"Why bother? It's not like the police have been able to find any of them since they first started to disappear." Felix's voice hitched and Addison's heart lurched at the sound of it.

"But we can just call and see if—"

"What good are they going to do, Addison!?"

Addison flinched, startled by his anger. "Don't yell at me!" she yelled back. "I'm trying to help!"

"I'm sorry." He rubbed his face. "I'm sorry. I'm a little on edge. I've just lost my daughter, if you haven't noticed."

"I know, but yelling at me isn't going to help get her back. I lost my baby too, you know."

He laughed humorlessly. "Princess isn't your baby."

Addison scowled. "She is to me."

"It's a dog, for God's sake. Not a child," he said, sounding tired. "If you want a baby then go have a real one." He stopped and his hands clenched, like he was fighting himself. "I'm sorry. I didn't mean that. I'm just—"

"Scared," she said, reining in her anger. "I know. I can't imagine how awful this is for you right now, but don't pretend like I haven't lost anything."

"You're right. I'm sorry."

She knew he was only lashing out because he was worried about Naia, but he'd accidentally hit a sore spot. She swallowed her indignation, but hated it when her next words wavered. "And I can't."

He lifted his gaze from his feet to look at her in question, but she couldn't meet his eyes.

"I can't have kids," she told him. "I had a hysterectomy when I was twenty-two. Princess is as close as I'm ever going to get to having one." She raised her eyes to meet his. "So just don't pretend like I haven't lost anything today, okay? Because Princess is all I've got."

"I'm sorry," he repeated softly.

But now she was looking at her own feet, wishing she'd worn closed-toed shoes because the cold bay water was making them ache.

When she didn't respond, she felt the boat shift as Felix came to sit next to her. He shoved her plentiful skirts aside in order to get close.

"I mean it," he said. "I'm sorry. Both for what I said, and for what happened to you. I guess there are a lot of things that I don't know about you either."

Addison felt the sincerity behind those words and she sank against him. Now that they'd stopped moving, she started to shiver even with Felix's jacket on. He wrapped an arm around her and pulled her close to keep her warm.

It was a nice place to be, in his arms, so warm and comforting. Again she felt the loss of something potentially amazing, that she'd missed the boat. Literally and figuratively.

They fell into an anxious silence. Felix fidgeted next to her, ready for action, but there was nothing they could do without knowing where the kidnappers went.

Waves lapped against the side of the boat, rocking them as they listened to the distant sounds of the city. As cold as it was getting in their damp formal wear, neither of them moved or suggested they head for shore, as though that would mean they gave up. If they continued to float for eternity, then maybe they wouldn't have to admit they were up the river without a paddle, so to speak. If they never went to shore, they wouldn't have to face the truth or what came next.

They'd been so desperate to not only save the dogs, but also their jobs, their reputations. Those things seemed so menial now that a human life was on the line. And not just any human. The most precious little angel Addison had ever met.

She began to wonder if the thieves even knew she was in Oliver's kennel. What would they do when they discovered her?

Addison stopped that line of thinking, closing her mind off to any possibility that meant they didn't succeed, that they didn't find Naia. Because Addison Turner didn't give up. She didn't give up when her business faced total ruin. And it was a hundred times more important that she not give up now.

"There has to be something we can do." Addison sat straight up in her seat. "Maybe we can call Channel Five and have them fire up the chopper."

Felix snorted, despite the situation, or maybe because he looked like if he didn't laugh he might throw himself overboard. "Except that you forget, Holly Hart isn't exactly on your team right now."

"For the promise of a good story she might help," she said doubtfully.

"I shouldn't have brought Naia," Felix said. "I should have stayed home. I should have just given up on the reward money and the bar. It's all meaningless without her."

"This isn't your fault," she told him. "This party was supposed to be safe. Who knew they would go to such lengths to get to the dogs?"

"But I suspected they were going to try something, or else I wouldn't have come. Charlotte was going to identify who's been stealing all the dogs."

Addison shifted on her seat as much as her dress would allow in order to look at him. "Hold on. What? How does Charlotte know who's behind it?"

He hesitated, his eyes flickering with a wince. "Well, she might have had something to do with it." He spoke slowly, as though gauging her expression with each word.

"Charlotte stole the dogs?" she asked, but it was barely a whisper.

"She didn't steal them," he said. "She just helped. Sort of." He frowned and pulled a face like even he couldn't talk his way out of this one.

Addison's teeth clenched. "What do you mean, 'sort of'?"

"Well, she didn't have anything to do with the cock-tail mixer. But she might have, kind of, helped hide the dogs in the back of the van at Phillip's fundraiser."

She gripped the oar next to her, ready to smash it over his head. "Then *you* sent her on her merry way out the front gates with them."

"It's not like I knew they were in there, did I?"

Addison could no longer feel the cold. All she could feel was hot anger flowing through her. "But you vouched for her. You promised that she had nothing to do with this. And the whole time she knew who it was. She lied straight to our faces when we asked her about it."

She got to her feet, unable to stand being near him any longer. The boat began to rock beneath her, and she nearly lost her balance. Felix pulled her back down.

"How long have you known?" she demanded.

He held up his hands. "I swear I had no idea until she told me Wednesday night."

"You mean when you went to her place?"

He did a double take. "How do you know about that?"

Addison's eyebrow rose stubbornly. "You have your secrets. I have mine. And you kept this from me." She didn't know if she was more angry or hurt.

He seemed to tuck that piece of information away for

later. "Look, you don't know the whole story. Charlotte had no choice."

"Of course you're still defending her." Addison moved across the boat to the other bench because that was as far as she could get from him at the moment. When really, she wanted nothing more than to storm away, or rather swim away, from Felix and never see him again.

He opened his mouth to speak, but she held up a hand to stop him. "You know what? I don't care anymore. It doesn't matter."

"You're right. What matters is finding Naia." He rubbed a hand through his hair, removing the last of the hair product until his hair flopped around his face as usual.

Addison found she preferred this Felix to the fashionable one. It was more natural, more him. It annoyed her all the more that she even noticed.

"Maybe I should have put a leash on her," he said. "Strapped her to my back and not let her out of my sight. Or at least surgically implanted a homing beacon on her like any reasonable parent would have done."

The words nudged something in the back of Addison's brain. Her heart skipped a beat or maybe it had stopped altogether. "What did you just say?"

Felix saw the shock on her face. "I was just kidding. Well"—he shrugged—"sort of."

"A homing beacon," she murmured quietly, lost in thought. "A tracking device."

"Well, they don't work very well after the fact. You kind of have to attach it before they disappear."

But Addison wasn't listening, her mind was racing. "I dressed Princess in her morganite necklace tonight."

Felix sighed. "Look, I know you're worried about Princess. Maybe you're right. Maybe the Coast Guard has already intercepted them." Felix reached across the gap to place a hand over hers comfortingly.

But she wasn't upset. She was smiling.

His face filled with concern. He was staring at her like she'd lost her mind. "Are you feeling okay?" He held a hand to her forehead and let it linger there as though he was really afraid she was coming down with something.

"Why didn't I think about it before now? I've wasted so much time." She dug through her clutch again, looking for her phone.

Felix reached down and picked up her oars. "We should get into shore. You'll catch a cold."

"Yes. Back to shore." She was practically vibrating in her seat. "We might be able to catch up to them before they get away."

He began to row, much slower and stiffer than before. "I think you've had too much excitement for one night."

"No. Listen to me. The necklace that Princess is wearing is my own design. In every high-end outfit of the Fido Fashion line, I've inserted a GPS tracking device to help find runaway pets."

His expression turned blank as his arms froze, oars sticking out to the sides. "Princess is wearing one of them?"

"Yes."

"Does it work?"

Addison pulled out her phone. "The software designers developed an experimental app that I can track her with. It's still in the trial phase, but so far it's been pretty reliable."

Felix didn't wait for her to say any more. He dipped both oars back into the water and headed for the glowing skyscrapers lighting up the night.

Addison's hands shook with cold and excitement as she tried to unlock her screen. She used both hands to hold it steady while Felix raced them to shore. It only took a moment for the app to open and a flashing pink dot to appear on a map of San Francisco.

"That's her." She pointed at the screen. "It's tracking Princess."

"Where are they?" he asked between strokes.

Addison zoomed in on the pink dot. She frowned. "They've already left the docks. But it's okay. The signal will remain strong in the city. As long as they don't remove the necklace, we can track them."

"Then we'll get to her before that." His expression was hard with grim determination. "And if we find Princess—"

"We find Naia."

28

Sold a Pup

A half-mile row to shore, a ten-dollar taxi back to Addison's Mini, and a thirty-minute drive across the city on the trail of a flashing pink dot led Felix and Addison straight to the old-money neighborhood of Seacliff.

Felix studied Addison's phone as she came close to the end of the street with the best views in the city, not to mention the highest views. Staring at Addison's phone, Felix tapped the dash excitedly.

"This is it. This is the place," he said. "Pull up there out of sight."

Addison swerved to the side of the road and slammed on the breaks in front of a sign that said LAND'S END. Felix lurched forward in his seat, bracing himself against the dash, but he didn't even seem to notice, far less comment, on her Mad Max driving techniques.

The mansions had given way to trees, as they'd parked at what appeared to be the head of the walking trail that skirted the cliffside.

"Looks like this is the end of the line," Addison said.

She just hoped it wasn't the end for them. She shivered despite her car's heater being set on overdrive.

She'd swapped her puffy Cinderella ball gown and heels for a hoodie, jeans, and Converse sneakers that she kept in her trunk for fashion emergencies. She'd originally anticipated a ripped seam or an accidental stain, but freezing to death after a boat ride in a tulle dress definitely constituted an emergency.

"Let's see the map," she said. "Can we tell which house it is?"

"Don't need it," Felix said. "I already know where we are. I've served for a couple of house parties here before."

Addison's eyes grew wide. "For who?"

Felix frowned. "Alistair Yates."

"No," she breathed. "I don't believe it. I could have sworn he was innocent. Alistair seemed so devastated to lose Lilly. Why would he steal his own dog that he meant to enter into the dog show?"

"I don't know. But now that we know he has a backup, maybe he never meant to show Lilly in the first place." His forehead creased. He seemed as confused as she felt by the turn of events. "But why the head game? Did he want to lower everyone else's guard? Take them by surprise?"

"Phillip mentioned something about it before." Addison didn't miss Felix's flinch when she mentioned Phillip's name. "He said it was well known that Lilly wasn't the favorite to win. That she was past her prime."

Felix shrugged. "Maybe Alistair knew it too. But why go to such extremes to remove your dog from the show? Why not just withdraw?"

"Pride?" Addison suggested. "For some of these owners, when their dogs lose, they lose too. They take it personally." She hesitated. "I just never expected that from Alistair."

Felix grabbed his suit jacket from the backseat. Reaching into the inside pocket, he pulled out Naia's bunny and held it in his hands. "Yeah, well it got a little too personal for me."

Addison laid a hand on his shoulder. "Don't worry. You'll get Naia back."

He covered her hand with his, squeezing it slightly. Picking up his jacket again, he slipped it on.

"What are you doing?" she asked.

"Covering up my shirt. It's too light. It'll be too easy to spot me."

"Spot you?"

He handed Addison her phone. "Call the cops. Wait for them here. I'm going to find a way around the back. There are probably cameras at the front entrance." Felix got out of her car, shutting the door quietly behind him.

Addison sat there for a moment in silence, her mouth hanging open. What they hell was he going to do? Rambo his way in?

She grabbed her keys and scrambled out of the car. She took a moment to text Zoe their location to give to the cops before running after him. When she caught up, Felix was already marching toward the trailhead, eyeing the thick pine trees and shrubs clinging to the sloping cliffside between them and Alistair's backyard. The dirt trail skirted along the steep slope that dropped down into darkness, into steep ravines, and beyond that, the cold waters of the bay.

Felix swung a leg over the low fence next to the trail and tested his footing. Addison grabbed him by the jacket collar, dragging him back.

"Felix, you can't go in alone."

"I'm not waiting out here when my daughter's in there." He pointed to the seaside mansion a few houses in.

"I'm not letting you go. Stay and wait for the cops with me." She pulled Felix back onto the trail like she could overpower him and force him to stay. "It's too dangerous. Something could happen to you." As the words spilled out, she realized how true it was and just how much she couldn't let that happen. "You don't know what's waiting in there."

He reached out and squeezed her shoulders comfortingly. "You're safe out here. There are neighbors close by if you need to run somewhere and hide. Just lay low. You'll be okay."

His expression was so reassuring and soothing, so full of concern. And it pissed her off. He couldn't just charge in there like some macho superhero and leave her behind like a useless token damsel in distress.

She whacked him on the arm. "I'm not worried about me. I'm worried about you, you idiot."

Felix might not have been her man, but he was still a good one, and a good father who only wanted what was best for Naia. The thought of Naia being rescued, only to have something happen to Felix tore at Addison's already-raw insides.

"Stop being a hothead." Her grip on him tightened. "Please. For Naia's sake. Stay here. Wait for the police with me."

"It's for Naia's sake that I have to go in there." He jabbed a finger at the home. His eyes closed for a second and he took a calming breath. He wrapped his big hands around hers and gently dislodged them from his jacket collar. She squeezed his hands, if only to hold him there longer.

"If it was a person you loved in there," he said, "I know you'd do the same thing. Because you're a beautiful person."

The comment startled a snort from her and out of habit

she brought a hand up to fix her hair, which was damp and matted with seawater.

Felix smiled and chuckled lightly, but he was too worried for it to crease his eyes. "I don't mean on the outside. That part is obvious."

Self-consciously, she tried to tuck in a stray lock. He reached up and pulled her fidgeting hand away. His bottom lip twitched like he wanted to say more, and he paused a moment to run a tender knuckle down her cheek.

"I mean, you're a beautiful person on the inside. Phillip is a lucky man."

Before she could move, or blink, or tell him she wasn't even interested in Phillip, he bent down and kissed her. It was only a quick peck on the lips, but it was firm with passion and meaning, and maybe because he worried it might be his last.

Addison reached up to keep him there but he broke free of her arms and disappeared over the fence and into the night. She stumbled slightly, feeling unbalanced without him there beside her.

She stood there listening to the rustling of the bushes as he forged a path through the thick underbrush to Alistair's home. It took only the briefest of moments for her to realize that Felix was right; she would do the same for the person she loved, because she was already chasing after him.

It wasn't just for Felix. Addison may not have known Naia for more than a few days, but how could anyone not love that little girl? Not want to protect her? Then there was her own baby, Princess.

So it was for Felix's sake, and Naia's, and Princess's, and all the other lost pups that Addison maneuvered her way along the steep slope, finding her footholds in the roots of trees that clung to the soil and grasping wads of grass that tickled her arms like insects—or maybe they were insects. Swallowing her desire to scream each time, she moved along the land's mysterious terrain by touch since she was too busy holding on for dear life to use her phone up to light her surroundings.

Finally, she reached Alistair's property. A tall stone wall rose up out of the steep cliffs. The stones were smooth, and there was no way to gain leverage for a hand or foot. Inching her way around the wall, she searched for a way up, a handhold on the wall, a magical ladder that would descend when she pressed on the right rock.

She was always one slippery misstep from a one-way ticket to the bottom of the ravine. Or worse, the bottom of the cliffs, to the rocky waters below. She could hear the crashing waves hissing in the distance, mocking her.

Addison's next footstep landed on the dewy grass clinging to the rough rock beneath. Her foot slipped. She fell on her stomach, her breath leaving in a grunt. Twigs poked, rocks scraped as she slid down the damp slope.

Her flailing hands scrambled for purchase, and her fingers brushed against an exposed root. She clamped onto it, crying out as her arm stretched back.

Gritting her teeth, she pulled, and tugged, and wormed her way back up until she was safe on firm ground again. Heart thumping in her throat, Addison laid her head against the ground, breathing in the scent of wild flowers and soil until she found the courage to move again.

When she neared the base of the house, the ground tapered off. She flopped down on the grass to catch her breath, not caring if the dew was soaking through her pants.

She pulled out her phone and checked Princess's GPS location once again, but this time, when the app opened, it told her the signal could not be acquired. If something had happened to the tracking chip, then did that mean something had happened to Princess?

But she didn't have time to dwell on that thought, to give into tears or pain. Who knew how much farther ahead Felix was. Not wasting any more time, Addison hit the flashlight icon on her phone and lit up the path ahead. She scurried around the wall, searching for a way onto the forbidding property. She found no hidden ladders or steps, but there was an old gnarly tree. Its thick branches reached out beyond the walls high above her and into the backyard.

Grateful once again for her emergency clothes, Addison assessed the gnarled branches and rough bark, imagining her progress up the tree. In her mind, she visualized her body contorting and twisting, flinging from branch to branch before she swung out over the property and somersaulted into the backyard like a ninja.

No problem at all.

Instead, when she began to climb, she hugged the tree for dear life, clinging to the bark with her gel nails, snapping one or two in the process. She hissed and stifled cries as multiple slivers pierced her, digging into her skin.

When she was high enough, she clamped her eyes shut, ignoring the drop below as she inched like a worm to the end of the longest limb. It shook and swayed beneath her weight until she fell like a rock into Alistair's backyard, very un-ninja-like.

Addison hit the ground hard, knocking the wind from her lungs and smacking the back of her head on the turf. A burst of light shot across her vision. She gasped and sputtered for air, staring up at the tree branch shaking above her in the wind like it was laughing at her. She glared at it, remaining very still until her chest began to rise and fall normally and the stars finally disappeared.

Addison picked herself up as soon as she could and found cover behind a rose bush. While she was hidden from sight, she took stock of her injuries. Her back ached, her chest throbbed, and it hurt to breathe. Her legs and arms stung with countless scratches, and she was pretty sure she'd have a goose egg on the back of her head tomorrow. But she'd live.

Lights shone down from the windows of the imposing home, casting dark shadows over the landscaped yard. The land rose and fell in a multileveled fashion, swelling and twisting with the natural contours of the grassy cliffside.

She searched for signs of Felix. Her eyes followed the winding stone staircase that hugged the curves and swells of the yard all the way up to the house. When she saw no sign of him, she knew she'd have to sneak closer to the back door. Unfortunately, it seemed to offer the least amount of concealment.

Crouching low, Addison kept to the thick garden plants, hiding behind shrubs and trees that reminded her of swirling ice cream cones. To prevent being out in the open too long and risk being spotted from a window, she moved as quickly and stealthily as she could—which mostly meant she tripped and stumbled her way across the property.

Her panicked gaze tried to take everything in at once, searching for infrared cameras, or ex-Navy SEALs with night-vision goggles hired to patrol the grounds. But no nets fell on her head Indiana Jones–style. No one called "Get them!" And she didn't trip any invisible wires, because this wasn't an Arnold Schwarzenegger movie. This was reality. And she needed to stay in it if she was going to be prepared for whatever came next.

Where the garden ended, a huge stone patio began. In the center of it stood a three-tiered fountain, but otherwise the area offered very little cover, making her visible from every single window.

Addison's limbs froze as she psyched herself up to

make a mad dash for the house. Once she got there, however, she didn't know what her plan was going to be. But there was still no sign of Felix. She had to keep going.

So she pushed on, darting out of hiding and onto the open patio. Thankfully, the fountain's lively splashes muffled her footsteps and her heavy breathing that was starting to sound more panicked by the second.

Unfortunately, it was also why she didn't hear anyone come up behind her until a hand clamped over her mouth. She cried out in surprise, but the hand pressed tighter to block the sound.

She was dragged to the side, bucking and kicking, now thinking heels would have been a better idea than sneakers; she could have used them as weapons. Still, she kicked at bony shins and jabbed her elbow against ribs.

There were grunts of pain in response, but the person continued to hold her tight. Unable to do anything else, she turned her head and bit the hand covering her mouth.

"Ouch. Dammit, Addy, it's me," Felix's voice hissed in her ear.

She immediately stopped fighting. He released her and she spun around, half-hugging him in relief and half-slapping him at the same time.

"Ouch," he whispered. "What was that for?"

"You scared the crap out of me."

He held up his hand to the dim light filtering through the windows, probably checking for teeth marks. "What are you doing here? I told you to stay."

"I'm not a dog," she hissed back. "I told you I wasn't going to let you go in alone."

"Look, I know you're worried about Princess, but—"

"Don't be so stupid. She's not the only reason I'm here right now." She bit her lip before she said any more. It wasn't the time or the place for a confession; they might be discovered at any moment.

"Look," she finally said. "Safety in numbers, right? You need someone to watch your back. You helped me. Now I'm going to help you get Naia back."

Felix frowned. "But—"

"No buts. The longer you argue with me, the better our chances are of getting busted."

"You're the last person I want to argue with." A shadow of a smirk tugged at his lips. "And sometimes the first person."

Addison stared at him, wondering what that meant. Her heart, which was finally starting to slow, thudded in her chest, so hard she feared even Felix could hear her heartbeat.

Felix held a finger to his lips. "Shhh. Did you hear that?"

"What?" Addison froze, wondering if he really did hear her heartbeat.

He ducked his head down. For a second, she thought he was about to lay his head against her chest, but then he knelt on the ground next to her feet. He leaned in close to a metal pipe running out of the house's brick facade.

Addison crouched down next to him, and they brought their heads closer to listen. Beneath the soft tinkle of the fountain, the breeze rustling the pink and orange zinnias, and Addison's heartbeat in her ears, she could just make it out. The sound was quiet and tinny after echoing its way up the pipe, but there was no doubt about it.

"Barking," Addison breathed.

Felix's eyes ran up the side of the wall, as though he had X-ray vision that could see which part of the house the pipe originated from.

"Alistair wouldn't have all the dogs just running loose inside the house," Addison said.

"No. My guess is the basement."

Addison's eyes widened as she recalled Phillip's

comment from their date. "Or Alistair's famous wine cellar." She suddenly realized Princess might be all right after all, and her body sagged with relief. "That's why I lost Princess's signal not too long ago. She must be too far underground."

"Come on." Felix grabbed her hand. "There's got to be a way in."

"Wait. Over there." Addison pointed to the flowerbed at the base of the house. Hidden behind the colorful zinnias was a low window just above ground level.

Felix wasted no time tearing the flowers out by the roots to expose the window. The remaining orange and pink heads flattened under his weight as he knelt down to peer through the dirty glass.

Addison bent down next to him and looked over his shoulder. "I can't see a thing."

"We'll have to find another way in. This window's too small to climb through."

"For you, maybe," Addison said, already checking to see if the window was locked.

Felix grabbed her wrists. "Now who's being a hot head?"

"We're in this *together,* remember?" she said. "Let me help."

But he didn't let her go. "Then we'll find another way in. *Together.*"

"How?" She waved a hand at the house. "Are we just going to waltz through the front door?"

"I don't know. We'll think of something," he said, not backing down.

They were nose to nose, bickering as usual, only this time when it boiled Addison's blood it wasn't in a way that made her want to shove the crushed zinnias in his mouth. She wanted to shove her tongue in his mouth instead.

She ached to grab him and kiss him one last time, before something happened and it all went horribly wrong. Or maybe before everything went right and they parted ways and never saw each other again.

"May I help you?" a female voice asked from behind them.

Addison and Felix jumped; they hadn't heard anyone sneak up. When they turned around, they were staring up at Penny Peacock. And, more important, the barrel of her gun.

29

Dog Meat

Addison was staring right down the barrel of a gun, and it wasn't a 3D movie. It was real. Too real. She wasn't a ninja, or Arnold Schwarzenegger, or Lara Croft. This wasn't going to be a blank shot at her heart, or red paint that stained her sweatshirt, or fake brains that splattered the walls. It was going to be *her* blood and brains that splattered the bottles of expensive wine behind her and Felix.

Penny's gun hadn't wavered since she took their phones and Addison's keys in the garden. It had remained targeted on their backs as Penny marched them into the mansion, into Alistair's study, through the hidden door behind his bookcase, and down the long wooden stairway into the wine cellar.

Princess's sparkling necklace jingled as she pawed at Addison's leg, stinging the cuts on her shins from the trek through the woods. Her big brown eyes pleaded for attention. She whined, begging to be picked up, to be comforted by her best friend.

Addison's fingers twitched to reach out to her, to scratch her behind the ears and give her a million kisses. But she fought her instincts and kept her hands in the air where Penny could see them, while her brain groped for a way out.

She assessed the dim room lit by a single flickering light bulb above them and a few old wall sconces. Every wall was lined with floor-to-ceiling wine racks full of outrageously expensive wine, probably some so expensive they weren't meant to be drunk. Decades of spilled red wine stained the old hardwood beneath their feet, making it rich with color and aroma.

Wooden barrels were stacked on their sides against the wall beneath the small window. If she had the chance, she could climb them like stairs and escape into the yard, but that would leave Felix to fend for himself. Addison's eyes shifted to the stairs behind Penny, to the only way out of the tiny, cold cellar for both of them.

The gun flinched.

"Don't even think about it," Penny said. "Cozy little place down here, isn't it?" She spoke about the cellar like she was thinking of redecorating it.

Addison thought she could have started with some new hardwood flooring since the old one was currently coated in sticky urine puddles—and worse—from the thirty-five or more dogs anxiously pacing the congested room.

It looked like the floor had been cleaned a couple of times, but the smell lingered, trapped in the raw wood planks. Addison's nose stung with the harsh ammonia smell, overpowering the scent of the wine at times, making her eyes water.

"Nobody even comes down here anymore," Penny said. "Not since Alistair's heart attack. It was the perfect place to keep the dogs. It's nearly soundproof down here."

Her eyes widened with glee. "No one can hear you scream."

Addison gasped, and this time she did risk bending down to pick Princess up. The doxie scrambled into her arms and kissed every square inch of her neck as Addison held her protectively.

"Oh no, don't misunderstand." Penny's expression transformed to one of innocence. "I'd never hurt the dogs." She held a hand over her heart. "You on the other hand"—she waved the gun casually between Addison and Felix—"what am I going to do with you?"

Felix shrugged with his hands still in the air. "Let us go?"

"And let you run to the authorities?" Penny laughed. "I don't think so."

Penny had gone through both their phone-call histories to see if they'd called the police. But of course they hadn't. Addison had sent Zoe a text instead.

Addison wondered what Penny would do if she knew she'd sent the text. If it would prevent her from killing the two of them. It wasn't like she would get away with it if someone knew of their whereabouts, right? Then again, if Penny knew the police were on the way, she might simply kill them sooner.

Addison strained her ears, listening for sirens. Charlotte *should* have told Zoe what happened after they'd left on the lifeboat. Zoe *should* have gotten her text about their exact location. The police *should* be on their way. Was that too many shoulds for Addison to rely on?

"We won't tell anyone," Addison said. "I promise."

"I just want my daughter back," Felix said. "Let me just take her and we'll be on our way." Though he said it like it was a simple business transaction, Addison could hear the desperate fear in his voice.

Penny tapped her chin. "Yes, your mischievous daughter. She was an unfortunate complication."

"Was?" Felix's voice had gone dry and rough, like he'd swallowed sand.

"Don't worry," Penny told him. "She's still alive. I haven't decided on what to do with her. Maybe I'll let her go. Kids' memories are never very reliable. But you, you . . ." She waggled her gun at them again before turning to the swarm of dogs circling her legs. "What should I do, little ones? I can't very well let them go."

Her voice altered, as though she was pretending to be a dog herself—if dogs could talk. A little like Scooby-Doo, Addison thought. Penny ignored Felix and Addison to confer with the show dogs, as though they were coconspirators in her master plan.

She seemed to trust the opinion of one dog more than she did the others: Kingy. The Pekingese still sported Addison's stylish kimono from the night of the cocktail mixer, looking princely among the other dogs that were in various stages of disarray since their dognapping.

Of course the dogs that had been taken from the *Belle* that night still appeared well groomed, full of energy. They jumped around the cramped cellar, unsure of what was going on but excited by all the extra playmates. Colin and Sophie padded over to Addison like it was a regular social call, and Oliver trotted over to Felix like he was checking on his owner before going back to play. The dogs that had been there longer, however, knew the score. They skulked around the gloomy space with matted hair, their long nails clicking on the dirty floor.

Addison could name practically every one of the pets, or at least their owners. There was Baxter, Lilly, Elvis, Precious, Rosie, and a handful of others whose owners had pointed fingers at her at one time or another. And of course there was Oliver and her Princess and even Colin and Sophie who got caught up in this mess. Every one of the dogs that had been taken over the last two weeks, all collected in one place.

Addison was so relieved to find them safe and healthy. Their owners would be overwhelmed to see them. But it wouldn't do anyone any good if Addison and Felix didn't get through the ordeal to tell anyone.

Penny looked so put together. Not nuts at all. She'd changed since the gala into a daffodil yellow pantsuit. Too bright and cheerful an outfit for such a maniacal evil-doer.

"What was that, Kingy?" Penny asked. She listened for a moment, nodding in all the right places and making noises of affirmation.

"Bark," he told her. "Bark, bark."

"Yes, I think you're right."

Felix tilted his head closer to Addison while Penny was distracted, deep in her consultation.

"Keep her talking," he said softly. "Ask her questions."

"What's the point? She's nuts," Addison whispered back.

"She's a total egomaniac. She thinks she's smarter than everyone else to have pulled this off. Just look at her." He nodded his chin in her direction. "She's gloating, but there's no one around for her to gloat to. She wants to tell someone. Anyone. For someone to know how clever—"

"Hey!" Penny screamed.

Marching across the stone floor, she pressed the gun against Felix's cheek. Her mouth screwed up as she dug it in, and his skin puckered under the pressure. Addison could hear the metal scrape against his stubble. She drew a sharp breath.

"I didn't say you could talk," Penny spat.

A noise escaped Addison, but it was incoherent. It took her a few seconds of stuttering to get something, anything to come out. "W-We were just saying how, how clever you were to keep the dogs down here. I mean, who would even think to suspect Alistair when it was his dog that first went missing?"

She didn't know if Felix's plan would work, but she trusted his judgment of people. And what else could they do? They needed to stall for time before the police got there.

"Alistair Yates." Penny said the name like it was a swear word. "All I wanted to do was win. In all my career as a handler, I have never been defeated. My dogs always win." Her eyes widened as though it was a promise, or a threat.

Addison pitied Penny's rivals. She imagined Penny as the type of person Kitty Carlisle had been afraid of at competitions.

Penny pulled the gun away from Felix's face, and Addison's body relaxed until she thought she would melt into a puddle on the floor. She hadn't realized she'd been holding her breath until her lungs ached with the sweet oxygen that rushed in and out of them.

"But it was an impossible win this time," Penny continued. "Alistair was going to destroy my perfect record. All because he couldn't let go of Lilly's glory days." Penny wheeled on Alistair's beagle cowering among the furry group as though it was personally her fault.

She glared at the dog. "You're old. You should have retired two years ago for God's sake. You were lucky to win last year. But Fancy. Oh now there is a star." Penny sighed. "She has a bright future in the circuit. But could I convince Alistair she was ready? No!"

Felix was nodding readily, with an understanding

expression that he'd probably used a thousand times while listening to crazy stories from wingbats like Penny.

"Of course," he said. "It makes perfect sense why you had to take Lilly out of the running yourself. Alistair just wouldn't listen." There wasn't a trace of sarcasm in his voice, and even Addison almost believed his sincerity.

"Exactly." Penny laughed, clearly relieved to have someone on her side. "I would never do anything to hurt Lilly, so stealing her was my only option."

It was just like the bad guys in cheesy eighties and nineties movies, Addison thought. Penny was revealing her evil plan, convinced that she'd already won. But the good guys always got away in the end, after they'd been told everything. Addison had to remind herself that this wasn't a movie though, and in real life the good guys sometimes die.

"But why not just take Lilly?" Addison asked. "Why did you take all the other dogs?"

"Fancy wasn't a sure thing," Penny told her. "She's untested. A virgin to the ring. All those lights, cameras, people. It can be a lot for a first-timer. There was no way to know for sure if she'd win. Especially with so little time left to train before the big show."

"So you took out all the competition," Addison said airily. She was trying to imitate Felix's nonjudgmental tone, all the while thinking Penny was a freaking dog-brained lunatic.

"I made sure to take out all the major players, but I didn't want to be too obvious about it, so I took a mix of red, yellow, and white ribbons as well to throw off the cops' scent. I even ended up with *this* thing." She gestured to Oliver.

Oliver whined like he knew he was being insulted.

Addison nodded. "And by kidnapping Lilly, it took the suspicion away from both you and Alistair."

Penny waved a hand through the air, the one that held the gun, and Addison and Felix stiffened as it passed over them. "Alistair will get over it," she said. "Lilly was past her prime. I did him a favor."

Somehow Addison doubted he would see it the same way.

"And you two were the perfect fall guys." Penny grinned at them like they were two well-behaved dogs. "So naive. You were in the right place at the right time. For me anyway. It was easy enough to sneak the dogs out of the cocktail mixer through the hidden trap doors in the stage floor. Once I got your incompetent assistant out of the way, that is," she told Addison. "I barely even tried to insult the girl and her grooming abilities before she ran out the back door crying."

"And Charlotte helped you load up the dogs at Phillip's party," Felix coaxed her.

"Your boss was very helpful too. He closed up the bar and hid them in there for us until nightfall, after which I shipped them over here to Alistair's."

"How did you get him to agree to it?" Felix demanded, his sympathetic demeanor slipping.

"The same way I convinced the *Belle*'s dog minders to help me out. Everyone has their price. Your boss didn't seem to mind turning a blind eye for a few bucks. Apparently he's built up quite the gambling debt."

Addison could hear Felix's teeth clench. "Joe knew. He knew I wasn't guilty, and yet he had no problem pinning it on me. As long as he kept the heat off of himself."

Even in the dim light, Addison could see the vein on Felix's forehead begin to throb. She jumped in before Felix lost his cool. "But what are you going to do with the dogs?"

Penny considered the odd mix around her. "Find them good homes out of state. Maybe I'll even breed them myself." She paused. Her eyes widened as she turned to the animals. "I mean, just look at all of them." She spread her arms, waving the gun again. "The ultimate examples of each kind. I would have a monopoly of blue-ribbon winners. I could breed nothing but superior dogs. No one could beat them."

"I suppose that's why you've been sleeping with Judge Walter Boyd," Addison said. "To ensure Fancy had his vote. Is he somehow involved too?" She figured if by some miracle they managed to escape, it would be good to know all the details, everyone who was involved.

Penny spun to face her, her left eye twitching. "How did you know about Wally?"

Addison just shrugged. But the mere mention of her robust boyfriend seemed to shake Penny. She swallowed hard, the gun dropping to her side.

"Wally and I share a passion. We are connected through our love of dogs, of perfection." The bat-crap crazy left her eyes, and her expression softened like a schoolgirl in love. "We're kindred spirits."

"Does he know what you've done?"

"Of course not." She grimaced at the very idea of it. "He's too honorable. He wouldn't understand. And he can't ever find out." She gripped her head, the gun still in her hand. Addison silently hoped the gun would go off and blow off her head.

"He'd be furious!" Penny cried. "But it's not like I'm hurting the dogs. They're well cared for." Her eyes filled with pleading, as though she were preparing an explanation for him. Or maybe just convincing herself. "They're okay. See?"

But the dogs didn't look okay. They looked skittish, starved for the freedom and attention that they were so used to getting. The normally mild-mannered, calm an imals paced anxiously in the overcrowded space, growl-ing at Penny, at other dogs, at nothing in particular.

Addison was surprised no fights had broken out among them yet. But then again, even when they were abducted, they had never barked or put up a fight. There were never any signs of a struggle. They always disappeared so quickly and quietly, and now it made sense. As nuts as she was, Penny was one of the best dog handlers there was. She could get a dog to do anything.

Penny shook her head like a dog after a bath. When she looked back at Addison and Felix, her face was stony again. As unreadable as a Keanu Reeves character.

"No," she said firmly. "Wally can't find out. Ever. I can't risk you telling anyone."

Penny raised the gun and pointed it at Addison and Felix. She'd had the gun pointed at them off and on for nearly fifteen minutes—although it felt like an eternity to Addison. Before she'd held it nonchalantly, like a mar-tini glass, like she pointed one at people every day. But now, her muscles tightened with intent, her eyes narrowed with focus, like she meant it.

Addison set Princess down on the ground and pushed her away to safety. Princess just came right back, lean-ing against her leg as if to say they were in it together.

Penny glanced between Felix and Addison as though trying to decide which one to do in first. Addison could feel Felix's muscles tense beside her. Her senses hummed with awareness of his body, his presence, his held breath.

She wanted to move closer, to wrap her arms around him or simply reach out and grab his hand. To feel con-nected to someone, to him, to feel his solidarity and de-pendableness, to absorb his comfort like a sedative into her veins. To get through whatever was about to happen together. But she was frozen to her spot.

In the electric silence that followed, the faint wail of sirens snuck into the wine cellar. Penny must have heard it too because her head whipped to the narrow window near the ceiling.

The pane glowed red and blue. The police had made it. *Thank you, Zoe,* Addison thought.

But was it in time? Would Penny still shoot before they got there? Time seemed to drag like someone hit the slo-mo button.

The wine bottles behind Addison clinked softly. Already on edge, she spun in time to see Felix bring his arm back. A flash of glass in his hand. A bottle.

While Penny was distracted, he whipped it across the room. It flew through the air, cork over bottom, straight for her. But at the last second, she turned back.

It glanced off her shoulder. She grunted and stumbled back. *Bang,* the gun went off.

Felix dove for Addison. He knocked her over and she fell to the floor. She heard him grunt behind her as they landed. Pain exploded in her shoulder and hip as she hit the floor hard.

The dogs were going nuts. But their barking should have been louder, Addison thought. They were muted compared to the high-pitched ringing in her ears.

Addison blinked, feeling a little dazed. Maybe she'd hit her head too.

There was one bark that stood out from the rest, like a voice she'd recognize in a crowd. Princess's deep bark was close by, insistent like a command. *Get up! Get up.*

Addison struggled to stand, but Penny collected herself first. With a hoarse scream, the dog handler whipped the gun around, advancing on Addison and Felix for a close-range shot. Like a snapshot in time, Addison could see the vein in Penny's forehead throb, the hairs up her nostrils as her hooked nose flared with fury.

The dogs barked around her ankles, their growls fierce. Maybe from the gunshot. Maybe from the excitement. It seemed something had snapped inside of them, like Penny's magic over them had worn off.

Princess planted herself protectively in front of Addison, hackles raised beneath her morganite necklace. Lips curling back in a snarl, she tensed like a spring and bared her teeth.

Addison felt the same tension in her own body. The instinct to fight back at odds with the gun pointed at her; it wasn't exactly a fair fight.

Penny's finger wrapped around the trigger. Addison braced herself. Suddenly, Princess lunged at Penny.

As her sharp little teeth sank into the handler's calf, Penny screamed. The gun went off. Addison recoiled, grunting as though expecting an explosion of pain in her chest. But the bullet had gone wide.

Penny tried to kick Princess off, but the doxie clung on. Her little furry body flung back and forth as the handler whipped around wildly in the cramped space, tripping over other dogs. Then Lilly dove for Penny's leg and she dropped the gun in surprise. Together they tagteamed the handler, over and over again, each bite drawing blood through her yellow pantsuit.

Soon the other dogs joined in. They converged on Penny like a pack of wild wolves, barking, biting, chewing, ripping until it looked like one writhing, snarling ball of fur. Those that couldn't find a limb to gnaw on cheered from the sidelines, like *Fight! Fight! Fight!*

Kingy nipped at her ankles, proving he hadn't been on her side at all. But once Oliver and Baxter leapt into the fray, Penny was quickly taken down with a guttural shriek.

Scrambling to her feet, Addison ran for the gun. She reached into the mass of fur. When her hand landed on the cold metal, she picked it up and then held it at the ready. But Penny didn't look like she was going to get up any time soon.

Addison set the gun down; she wasn't going to need it. Then again, she thought, the bad guy always came back for a second round, so she picked it back up.

Princess had ahold of Penny's arm now, gnawing on it like it was a chew toy. Her blonde fur was pink with blood. Oliver drew away and found a new purchase on Penny. This time on her neck.

Addison wanted to look away, but found she couldn't. She watched in horror. The sounds of chewing and licking seemed to fill her ears until she couldn't hear anything else. Bile rose in her throat. Penny had had enough.

"Hey!" Addison yelled. She stomped her feet on the cement threateningly to scare the dogs off; she didn't want to come between them in case they mistook Addison as the aggressor.

A few skittered away, but some of the others weren't ready to give up on their revenge. Raising the gun toward the top corner of the room, she cringed as she pulled the trigger. She jumped as it went off, startling herself as well as the dogs. The gun recoiled, and her wrist shot back with a sharp twist. She hissed at the pain and cursed the movies, which made shooting a gun look so easy.

Most of the dogs seemed to come to their senses and backed off as though in a daze. Baxter, however, she had to pull off by force. She coaxed the beast with soothing words and gentle strokes down his hackled back while steadily tugging him away.

Eventually Penny stopped fighting back altogether. The danger gone, the dogs finally backed off to lick their bloody chops as if nothing had happened.

Penny lay still and pale on the cold floor. The room was so dim, but Addison knew that the dark liquid seep-

ing through the fabric of her shredded pantsuit was blood.
She finally managed to drag her shocked gaze away from
the sight of Penny's body, but from the corner of her eye,
she could see her chest rise and fall. She was still alive.

Dropping the gun, Addison searched the room for Felix among the excited dogs. She found him slumped
against a wine rack, where he'd pushed her out of the way
when the gun had gone off. Beneath his suit coat, deep
red stains seeped through his white dress shirt, spreading across his chest.

Felix had been shot.

30

Play Dead

Addison fell to her knees beside Felix. His bloody shirt clung to his skin. He looked a little dazed, blinking as though just coming around, or maybe she was already losing him.

"Oh God," she said.

Shock kicking in, her limbs seemed to go numb as her body focused its energy on pumping blood to her vital organs, her heart, her brain. Her stupid, stupid brain. The brain that thought it knew better, that had clung to an idea of what "perfect" was supposed to be, to a crazy fantasy she'd invented.

Her brain had ignored her heart's desires, and now it was her heart that was suffering for it. It ached. God, how it ached, like Baxter was making a snack out of it. Yet somehow it kept pumping, and aching, and pumping, and aching.

"Felix," she sobbed. "Hold on. The police are almost here. We'll get you an ambulance."

There was so much blood everywhere, spreading over

his shirt, pooling beneath him. She imagined if her nose wasn't so full of the caustic scents from the wine and the dogs, she'd even be able to smell it. Where were the damned cops anyway?

Oliver wandered over, sniffing at his master. With a whine, he laid his head down on his lap.

Felix gave him a pat, but didn't take his focus off Addison. The look on his face was dazed as his half-lidded eyes met hers.

He must be losing consciousness. She had to stop the bleeding somehow. She wished Piper was there. She would know what to do.

"You're an angel," Felix said.

Her eyes went wide. "Oh my God. You're hallucinating." It didn't take a doctor to know that was a bad sign.

Gripping his shirt, she tore it open. Buttons flew everywhere. She lifted his undershirt and began to run her hands over his bare chest, searching for the source of the bleeding, but all she found was his six-pack and a firm set of pecks. She wished she had more than flickering light bulbs to see by.

She groped him frantically, dragging his jacket off to have a closer look. That's when he winced, hissing in pain.

"Where does it hurt?"

He blinked lazily. "If you wanted to get me naked, all you had to do was ask."

"What? This isn't the time to joke." Tears filled her eyes until she could barely see Felix, much less the entry wound. "You've been shot. You need to conserve your energy."

"Addy. It's okay. I'm okay." He reached for her hands.

"Your hands feel so cold," she said, finding it difficult to breath through the oncoming sobs.

The floor he was sitting on stung her own legs with

chill. It would be warmer upstairs, she thought, but there was no way she was going to be able to drag him up there. "I need to keep you warm." She tucked herself beside him to share body heat.

Princess and Oliver snuggled in close, making a human-dog pile, as if they understood what she was trying to do. Or maybe they just wanted to be petted after their traumatic evening. Colin and Sophie soon joined, also seeking potential petters.

There was so much to say to Felix, so much she wanted to tell him, about her feelings, to apologize for the things she'd said to him, but she worried there wasn't enough time left.

"Addy," Felix said. "It's just a flesh wound."

Her chest shuddered as she bit back another sob. "You don't have to be brave with me."

"No. I'm serious." He took her tear-stained face in his big hands. "The bullet just grazed my arm."

"What?"

Reaching for his shirtsleeve, he showed her a tear in the material. She could see the bright red blood seeping through the fabric around the hole. She touched the stains covering the rest of his shirt, much darker in color.

"But all the blood," she said.

"It's not blood. It's wine. The first bullet grazed my arm as I pushed you out of the way. When I fell, I hit my head pretty hard." He rubbed the back of his head and checked his hand as though expecting to see blood. "I think I blacked out for a few seconds, or minutes maybe. The second bullet hit the wine rack above me." He pointed above their heads.

Frowning, Addison looked up. Wine dripped down from a broken bottle above his head. She hadn't smelled it over all the other scents saturating the small space.

When she looked back at him, he had a stupid smirk on his face.

"Worried much?" he asked.

"Worried" didn't begin to cover it. Sure he'd moved on to Charlotte. He couldn't be Addison's, but she still couldn't imagine a world without him. His gut laugh, and his messy hair, and his stupid band T-shirts. Or a world in which his daughter had to grow up without a father.

After what had just gone down, she wanted to tell him that, to tell him how she really felt. She had fallen for him. Not because she was desperate for any man at all, like Felix thought. She was just desperate for Felix.

But Felix was going to be okay. He wasn't dying on her. In fact, he found her confusion funny. His chest shook with chuckles. He was laughing at her!

Speechless, Addison wound up and punched him in his uninjured arm. "Jerk much?"

He winced but gave a weak snicker. Blinking, he seemed to take in his surroundings for the first time since blacking out. His eyes flitted from the bloody dogs mingling, the gun on the floor, Penny's body.

"Naia," he said. "I need to find her."

"The police must be coming through the gates by now," Addison said.

"I'm not waiting for them." He held out a hand for her to help him to his feet, his face screwing up from the effort. Flesh wound or not, Addison imagined a bullet hurt regardless.

"This place is huge," Addison said. "Where do we start? Naia could be anywhere on the grounds." She glanced over at Penny's motionless body. "And I don't think asking Penny is an option right now."

"We'll split up." He headed for the staircase, stumbling slightly as he grabbed his head.

As though sensing an impending prison break, the dogs rushed to follow him. Addison was nearly knocked over as the pack of purebreds brushed up against her legs in their eagerness to be free. Something small and brown skittered over her foot. She shrieked and backpedalled until she realized it wasn't a rat, but a tiny hairless dog. A Chinese crested.

Once the herd had cleared, Princess was still there by her side. Addison scooped her up and cradled her in her arms. The doxie was shaking, or maybe that was Addison herself. Either way, she held her close, letting Princess kiss her despite the gruesome red stains around her snout. Princess had saved their lives. She was so getting treats when they got home.

"My hero," she told Princess.

In the wake of the fur tsunami, Addison climbed the stairs after Felix. The moment she walked through the hidden door and into Alistair's office, she breathed a sigh of relief—and clean air—as glad as the dogs were to be free of the tiny, smelly dungeon.

"Let's go find Naia," she told Princess. Her legs froze and she blinked, a plan coming to her. "Felix!"

A second later, Felix burst through the door, glancing around the room, like he'd hoped to find his daughter. "What is it?"

"I have an idea. Do you still have Naia's bunny on you?"

"Yeah." He frowned in confusion as he dug into his jacket pocket.

Addison took the bunny and held it in front of Princess's nose. "What's this? Whose is this?" she asked in her excited "You wanna play?" voice. "Is this Naia's?"

Princess sniffed it, snorting as the fuzzy tail tickled her nose.

"Where's Naia, Princess? Where is she?"

Princess's ears perked up and her tail began to whip back and forth. She could tell by Addison's voice that this was a game. And oh, she remembered this game from the park. She liked this game.

Addison set Princess down on the hardwood floor. "Where's Naia? Go find Naia."

Princess took off, barrel chest quivering as she sniffed rapidly, following the stuffed bunny's scent out of the office, down the hall where she circled the Persian rug a couple of times, and then off into the dining room.

Addison and Felix followed Princess through the stainless steel and marble kitchen. The dachshund glanced back at Addison, needing encouragement that the game was still on.

"Come on," she said. "Where's Naia? Go find her."

Addison tried to infuse her voice with cheer, but it still shook with anxiety and adrenaline. She hoped her plan worked, that doxies' noses were as strong as they were famed to be. That it wasn't as stuffed up as hers was from the pungent smells in the cellar.

Princess limped up the stairs with her one short leg, her nose never relenting, as though she chased an invisible trail through the mansion. She followed it up to the second floor, then up to the third, down a long hallway, right to the base of a door. Princess scratched and whined at it, determined to win the game.

Felix grabbed the door handle and pushed, but it wouldn't budge. "It's locked. Stand back."

Addison snatched Princess away and backed up. She watched as Felix took a few steps back. Using his good arm, he rushed forward and threw his weight against it. *Crack!*

Felix grunted and held his breath as he grimaced. He took a few moments to work through the pain. But it wasn't for nothing because Addison noticed a fracture had splintered up the side of the doorframe. He tried once more. This time, he sent it flying open.

Felix charged inside and Addison ran in after him. She didn't know what she'd expected once they'd found Naia, but whatever it was, it wasn't the scene before her.

Naia was perched in the middle of a striped settee with a bowl of chips in her lap and cookies on a gold filigree plate. In front of her, *Toy Story* played on a big-screen TV.

She stared wide-eyed at the door, startled by the noise. As soon as she saw who it was, she cried out, "Daddy!"

If Felix was surprised by the manner in which Penny had kept Naia, he didn't show it. Without faltering, he ran to her and plucked her off the cushion. He crushed her against his chest. "Peanut. Oh, peanut, I thought I'd lost you."

She laughed. "I was in Oliver's house the whole time. I was playing hide-and-seek with Charlotte. She never found me." Naia beamed with pride. The fact that she'd won the game seemed to overshadow everything else.

Penny might have been as mad as the Joker in *The Dark Knight*, but it was clear she'd treated the child well. Addison leaned against the busted doorframe and sunk to the floor in relief and fatigue. The fight was over.

"Well, we found you now." Felix held Naia tight and kissed her hair. "We found you."

31

Publicity Hound

Addison stepped out of Alistair's Seacliff mansion and allowed the cool night air and silence to soothe her frazzled nerves. She shivered slightly from the dewy chill, but she made no move to reenter the house; she was done with answering questions that night. But neither did she head back to her car. She wasn't about to leave until she talked to Felix and Naia again.

Seconds after they'd found Naia, the place was suddenly bursting with cops. Shortly after that, the EMTs arrived, followed by investigators, an identification unit, and animal control. The huge mansion quickly became overcrowded and noisy, filled with so many questions that Addison was suddenly too tired to answer. Felix and Naia had been swallowed up in the frenzy, and she hadn't seen them since.

Drawing up the hood on her sweatshirt, she snuggled Princess's warm little body to her. Together they watched animal control workers reunite the found dogs with their owners at the property gates.

Word about what had happened got around the *Belle* quickly. The moment it docked and the initial questions were asked, it seemed that all the guests had rushed to Alistair's home, led by none other than Holly Hart.

Addison wondered who her sources were, since Zoe would never have given the reporter the scoop. Maybe she had an insider at the precinct.

As Addison watched from afar, EMTs guided a stretcher out the front door and down the sweeping stone stairs. She stepped out of the way and watched it roll past. The supine figure beneath the blanket shifted, and the head rolled to face her. It was Penny.

The famous dog whisperer's hair was matted with her own blood. Claw scratches marred her face, neck, shoulders, and probably everywhere else. She was a mess.

Penny's eyes widened when she saw Addison. "Tell them." Her hoarse voice sounded hollow beneath the oxygen mask. "I wasn't going to hurt the girl. Really. Tell them."

She held out a hand to Addison as she was wheeled past. Addison stepped away from her in disgust, holding Princess closer as if Penny might do something to her even now, while lying on a stretcher and in front of the police coming and going from the house.

But Penny's reach came up short. She looked down and seemed to notice for the first time that she was handcuffed to the stretcher.

Penny was sick and twisted and going away, hopefully for a very, very long time. No hot-tubbing with Judge Walter Boyd, no more dog shows for her. No dogs at all. After what she did, she didn't deserve them.

Addison turned away, scanning the crowd of personnel. She and Felix had saved the day—well, mostly Princess had. Their names had been cleared, and the missing dogs were being returned to their owners. But all she could think of was finding Felix and Naia. To see that they were okay.

A police officer walked out of the front door and down the steps. As he passed beneath the lights, Addison noticed Naia's stuffed bunny in his hands.

Addison grabbed his sleeve. "Excuse me. Have you seen Felix Vaughn and his daughter?"

He shook his head. "Not for a while. I think someone called them a taxi. They might still be here." He pointed to a crowd of well-dressed lookie-loos clustered outside the wrought-iron gates.

"Thanks," she said. "Do you mind if I return that to his daughter?" She indicated the stuffed animal.

"Of course not." He handed it over.

Princess sniffed eagerly at the bunny, but Addison tucked it under her other arm for safekeeping. "Playtime is over, Princess. You did good. You deserve a treat."

Princess barked happily, like *it's about time*.

Addison headed for the property gates. Over the excited chatter, she recognized a high-pitched voice arguing with the officers standing guard. At the front of the crowd, practically trying to squeeze her stick figure through the bars, was *the* Holly Hart.

When one of the officers moved to let Addison out, Holly spotted her.

"Addison! Addison!" She waved her microphone in the air furiously, as though Addison might not see the reporter—as if anyone could miss her. In her other hand, she held the Chinese crested Addison had mistaken for a rat in Alistair's cellar.

Addison did a double take. Holly hadn't been lying. She really did own a dog.

The cops unlocked the gate and cracked it open just

enough to let Addison squeeze through. Once she was on the other side, Holly practically tackled her. She winced as Holly bumped her sore shoulder.

Princess grumbled at Holly in warning and she backed off, holding her microphone and hairless dog up in surrender.

"Addison," Holly breathed. "I'm so glad you're all right."

Addison gaped at her in surprise. She could hear the sheer relief in the reporter's voice and see the worry in her Botox-stiffened face. After how she'd treated her the last time, it didn't make sense. "Holly, I—"

"I was so worried I wouldn't be able to get the exclusive." She flashed her bleached teeth.

Addison let out a grunt and rolled her eyes. That figured. She wanted to tell Holly to . . . well, to do a lot of things she normally wouldn't say. But as tired and as desperate to find Felix as she was right then, she said, "All right. I'll give you an exclusive."

Holly's eyes widened in shock, then settled into their normal conniving slits. "Great. Let's get started."

"But it's not for you," she said. "It's for me. You got that?"

She was only half-listening as she snapped her fingers in the air. "Of course. Of course."

A second later, Hey, You materialized with his camera. As though reading her mind, he placed it on his shoulder and held his eye to the viewer.

Holly held her microphone in one hand and her Chinese crested in the other. By the way she held it, Addison thought Holly might actually have grown attached to the thing. And here she thought Holly was heartless.

Addison tried to rub away some of the blood on Princess's face as Hey, You counted down on his fingers.

Princess wasn't exactly camera-ready. Neither of them were, really, but Addison just couldn't seem to care at the moment. For the first time, her hair was the last thing on her mind.

Hey, You's fingers counted to one and Holly beamed, radiant in her evening gown.

"This is Holly Hart for Channel Five news reporting live from an undisclosed Seacliff mansion for a dramatic show dog showdown," she said, like it was the latest gossip and not a life-threatening event.

"The San Francisco dognappings came to a head tonight on the eve of the Western Dog Show when the infamous puppy pincher struck again. This time, they plucked the pups right off the *San Francisco Belle,* the beloved local paddle wheel boat, while it was cruising the bay. What was worse, they took my own precious Jasmine." Holly kissed her dog's bald, shaking head.

"Thankfully, a dog lover and local fido fashionista was on the exclusive guest list, along with yours truly, and saw the crime in progress. Addison Turner, how were you involved in tonight's events?"

Addison leaned into the mic. "I was attending the gala on the *Belle* when Felix Vaughn and I discovered the dogs were being stolen."

"My sources tell me there was also a little girl taken."

Addison thought it best not to mention Naia's name or the fact that she was Felix's daughter. "The girl was hiding in one of the dog kennels at the time of the theft. All the dogs were then locked in the kennels and loaded onto a lifeboat to get away from the party unseen."

"And you were the only ones who witnessed it?"

"Yes, everyone else was distracted by another boat we'd collided with."

"Coincidence? I think not." Holly cocked an over-plucked eyebrow at the camera. "So what did you do then?" When Holly leaned toward her eagerly, Addison realized she probably didn't know. This was the first time Holly was hearing this part of the story.

"We knew that if we waited for the police, they would get away, so we followed them using a tracking device."

"A tracking device? Did you anticipate this happening?"

"No. My dog, Princess, was wearing a valuable necklace that I've created especially for my Fido Fashion line. Some of the more expensive designs have GPS locators inserted into them, including this one." She held Princess higher so Hey, You could zoom in on the morganite collar.

"You're kidding? That's amazing." Holly actually seemed impressed. Real drama that she didn't have to invent. "So you tracked them down across the city to this Seacliff home using fashion. And they say you have to choose between fashion and function." She gave the camera a cheesy wink.

"When we got here," Addison continued, "we found all the dogs that had been taken over the last couple of weeks. They were being held in the cellar. Before we could free them, however, we were held at gunpoint."

"Oh, that must have been frightening. Was anyone hurt? How did you get away?"

"My"—she hesitated—"friend was injured." It hurt to use the word, but that's all Felix was. All he'd ever be. "But the dogs attacked the dognapper to protect us."

"So the dogs are safe, the child has been rescued, and the dog show is still on, all thanks to Addison Turner of Pampered Puppies." Holly summed up with a dazzling smile. "Make sure to come out and catch the Western Dog Show championships this weekend."

Addison grabbed the mic, resisting Holly's tugs to

take it back. "And don't miss the launch of Fido Fashion on Sunday after the Best in Show is announced."

Holly wrenched the mic back, smiling into the lens. "This is Holly Hart, reporting live for Channel Five news."

"And cut," Hey, You said, and lowered the camera. He opened his mouth to say something else, but Holly snapped her fingers and he shut it again.

"Get some shots of the house through the gate and get a close-up of the owners being reunited with their dogs. Some sweet, tear-jerking crap. Got it?"

Addison could practically hear Hey, You's teeth clench. How he put up with her, she'd never understand. Rolling his eyes, he trudged off to do her bidding.

Holly turned back to Addison. "Thanks for the interview."

Addison's fake TV smile vanished and she glared at the reporter. "Trust me, it wasn't for you. You owed me some positive promotion after the damage you did to my reputation."

Holly gasped as she held a scandalized hand to her chest. "It's my duty to report the news, and you were a suspect."

"Not the only one by far."

Holly held her hands out like *Oh, well.* "But it all turned out for the better. Good guys win, bad guys lose. Your name has been cleared. It's the perfect story. I couldn't have written it better myself." Her mouth puckered as she reconsidered that. "Well, the ratings might have been better if you'd been maimed or killed. But better luck next time, I suppose," she said cheerily.

Addison crossed her arms. "Well, you'd better hope people actually show up for my fashion show on Sunday. Or I'll be calling your producer. I'm guessing this isn't the first story you've embellished on."

Addison turned away, but Holly gripped her arm. "Hold on. Hold on." The reporter laughed, light and clear. Addison imagined she could be quite charming—if you didn't know her.

Holly slid her arm through Addison's chummily. "Well, as a favor to my favorite dog stylist, I will personally host your fashion show. We can call it Holly Hart's Hounds presents Fido Fashion." She ran a palm through the air like she could see the sign now.

Addison yanked her arm away. "How about Addison Turner presents Fido Fashion, as hosted by Holly Hart."

Holly's lips pursed. "It doesn't sound quite as catchy, but I'll do it."

Addison thought the offer was most likely so Holly could boost her ratings on the heels of the breaking story. However, she thought that having a local sort-of celeb host the fashion show could garner a bit of attention.

"Thanks," Addison said.

Something over Addison's shoulder caught Holly's attention. "Oh, there's the detective. I'd better go get an official statement." She waved her microphone in the air. "Yoo-hoo! Detective!?"

Addison watched Holly chase her story through the crowd of onlookers still dressed in their tuxes and ball gowns. Above their heads she could see a mop of ebony hair bob along. She recognized those thick locks instantly.

Her heart clenched at the sight of Felix and her legs automatically moved toward him. She weaved through bodies, both human and furry, standing on her tiptoes to see where he went. When she broke through to the other side of the congregation, she saw Felix headed for a cab parked between a BMW and a Bentley.

His one arm rested in a sling, while the other held Naia. She sagged over his good shoulder, passed out after her long evening. It must have been way past her bedtime. Heck, it felt past Addison's bedtime.

She raised her arm to get his attention, but then she spotted Charlotte following close behind. The server must have come to meet them. She hovered close to Felix, checking on Naia, fussing over her in a motherly way.

Addison found herself slinking back into the crowd. Since the police had arrived, she'd thought of nothing but finding Felix. However, seeing him with Charlotte and Naia, a little reunited family, she suddenly realized that maybe Felix didn't want to see her. That she might be intruding on their reunion.

As Felix turned to say something to Charlotte, his focus locked on Addison like he'd somehow sensed she was there.

Addison waved awkwardly, as though that could encompass *Hey, we nearly died together, but we're still alive. And thanks for saving my life, BTW.*

The hand peeking out of the sling moved in a half-wave, but then it froze and his face suddenly fell. A second later, a hand landed on her shoulder. She jumped and spun, her body geared up from all the action that night. Princess growled, understandably on edge too.

"Phillip," Addison said in surprise. Not surprised to see him there. He'd come to pick up Baxter, after all. She was surprised because she'd nearly forgotten about him altogether in the last few hours.

"Addison, hi."

"Hello," she said distractedly. She glanced back to the road to catch Felix's eye again, but he'd already turned away.

"I'm glad to see you're all right," Phillip was saying. "I just wanted to thank you for rescuing Baxter here."

Addison finally gave up trying to get Felix's attention. He was purposely ignoring her. She looked back at Phillip. "What? Oh. You're welcome." She bent down and gave Baxter a pat on the head. "I'm glad he's all right."

"I became worried when I couldn't find you anywhere after we ran into that boat."

Addison rubbed a hand over her face. Right. The gala. Her date with Phillip. Had that been the same night?

"I'm so sorry. There was no time to explain."

He held up a hand. "Don't apologize. Maybe you can tell me all about it tomorrow over dinner?"

Addison's mouth turned down.

"Coffee then?"

But she shook her head, mostly at herself. Phillip was honestly a great catch. And yay, he wasn't the dognapper—always a bonus. But he just wasn't the guy for her.

"Sorry," she said, pulling a face. "It's a busy weekend and all. I had a great time getting to know you."

He nodded, his perfect lips curling into a sad smile as he took the hint. "Me too."

"Good luck with the conformation tomorrow."

"And good luck with your fashion show." He drew her hand toward his lips and kissed the top. "Good-bye Addison."

As Addison watched the second guy walk away from her that night, yet another hand landed on her shoulder. She squealed in surprise and spun around. Princess growled again before she saw the friendly faces of Zoe, Piper, and Aiden.

Zoe threw her hands up in surrender. "Whoa. Are you two jumpy or what?"

Addison sighed, rubbing Princess's raised hackles comfortingly. "Sorry. It's been that kind of a night."

"I can only imagine." Zoe leaned in for a hug. "Are you okay?"

Piper grabbed Addison the moment she was free and hugged her too—a little awkwardly since she was holding Colin as close as Addison held Princess.

Aiden ducked in for a hug too and Addison received a kiss on the cheek from Sophie who was cradled in his arms. "Zoe said you stole a life raft from the *Belle* and chased after the dogs?"

"What's going on?" Zoe asked. "That brunette, Charlotte I think her name was, said they'd taken Naia."

Addison opened her mouth to explain, but she shut it again. "Everything's okay now. But it's a long story. I'll tell you guys all about it later."

"Ice cream sleepover?" Piper asked with a grin.

Addison batted her eyelashes. "You know the way to my heart."

A wall of snow-white hair bobbed above the crowd, headed in their direction. Kitty Carlisle emerged and came at Addison with a wild look in her bulging eyes. Nestled in her arms, Elvis mirrored her dark, unreadable look.

Addison automatically backed away, but Kitty grabbed her. Addison turned her body to shield Princess and tensed for the worst. She was completely unprepared for what came next. Kitty wrapped her thin arms around Addison and hugged her.

"Thank you," Kitty said. "Thank you for finding my Elvis."

Julia was right behind her, pushing her way past Piper and Zoe. "Yes. Thank you for what you did for my Precious. I thought I'd lost him forever." She bent down to be closer to her cocker spaniel, her midnight blue ball gown trailing in the dirt. She didn't seem to care. "Now that's what I call good service, right Precious?"

"Above and beyond," Kitty agreed.

Other dog show owners gathered behind them, carrying or leading their pets protectively, their leashes choked up so they remained close by their sides. Their faces, which had been tainted with suspicion and allegation for the past two weeks, were now smiling, filled with appreciation and humility.

Rex Harris clung to his pinscher's leash like it was a lifeline. "I'm so sorry we accused you. Thank you for saving Rosie."

Addison recognized Kayleigh, the girl who had clung to Phillip at his fundraiser and had supported Penny's story about her and Felix being partners in crime. "Yes, thank you!"

Addison stood there, shocked by the overwhelming support. "It wasn't just me," she said, when she'd found her voice. "Felix Vaughn and I worked together."

"I heard he was shot," Julia said, with more excitement than concern.

Piper, Aiden, and Zoe all turned to her in varying degrees of shock and horror.

"You were shot at?" Piper asked, or rather nearly screamed.

"Yes, Felix was shot, but he's okay." She added quickly. "And I'm okay," she assured her friends. "I'll tell you all about it later." *When I've had time to process it all first,* she thought.

"I'm just so happy to have Precious back," Julia said. "And in time for the competition tomorrow."

"I don't think Gumball will be ready," the man in the toupee from Phillip's fundraiser said. He rubbed at his dog's snout. "Is this blood?"

"I don't think any of the dogs will be ready in time," Kitty said, assessing the group with a practiced eye.

"So much for this year's conformation. All the likely candidates have been ousted before it's even begun."

Addison took in the competitors as well, but compared to Kitty's taste for perfection, her eye for potential saw things a little differently. "Not necessarily," she said.

"I don't see how they can compete," Kitty said. "They look like a pack of wild animals." Her nose turned up slightly at the sight of her bichon frisé's stained red fur.

Addison laughed humorlessly, shuddering as she recalled the gory scene in the cellar. Kitty didn't know how close to the truth she was. "Well, I just happen to know of a dog spa well versed in specific breed styling for show dogs. And I think the owner might be willing to help out a few special new customers."

"Yes!" Julia shouted. "Absolutely! Can you schedule Precious in?" She hoisted her cocker spaniel in the air, practically thrusting it at Addison to be first in line.

They began to argue over who should go first because their dog had a better chance of winning. There was a chorus of eager requests volleying back and forth through the crowd of dog show enthusiasts.

Addison held her hands up, shouting over the din. "Don't worry! I'll fit everyone in, Pampered Puppies will stay open all through the night if need be."

"But how can you manage all on your own?" Rex asked. "Who gets to go first?"

There must have been fifteen or more owners wanting her services. A single dog could take hours. It wasn't possible to get them all done by the time the show began first thing in the morning.

She scanned the crowd in front of her. "Are there any handlers here with grooming talents?" she called out.

A couple of hands shot up.

"Okay, great. Owners, you'll have to get your hands dirty tonight. We'll need all the help we can get."

Taking out her phone to text Melody for help, she turned to Piper and Zoe. "We'll have to take a rain check on ice cream," she said. "Feel like getting dirty tonight?"

Zoe gave her a saccharine look, full of promise. "You know I like it dirty."

32

Every Dog Has Its Day

Addison sat in her car, staring up at Felix's front door and feeling her chest tighten like her bra was too snug. She wanted to see Felix and yet she didn't. Maybe he wouldn't even answer the door. Or maybe worse. Maybe Charlotte would answer. Or if Felix didn't answer, maybe it was because Charlotte was keeping him busy. It was late after all, almost ten o'clock. Maybe they were already in bed.

But she didn't want to think about that. She'd tortured herself enough over him. Maybe it was best to just slip Naia's stuffed bunny in the mailbox where he'd find it the next day.

Don't be stupid, she told herself. It was just a stuffed animal. She'd hand it over, see they were both okay, and then move on with her life. A life that, only two weeks before, had felt so perfect. Like a blockbuster movie. But now it seemed like the crappier sequel that was banged out on the heels of success but had none of the original cast. It had lost its magic. Its heart. And she knew it was because her heart belonged to Felix.

Her perfect life now seemed empty. Maybe it always had been. Nothing had changed, after all. Except she got a preview, however small, of how full it could be with Felix and Naia in it.

Addison sighed and stepped out of her car. With heavy feet, she climbed the steps to the front door because she knew Naia would want her bunny. She would have returned it earlier if she could have, but she'd worked through the previous night with the help of her friends, the dog owners, and a few handlers.

Bleary-eyed and exhausted, they'd taken the dogs straight to the competition early that morning. Then before she'd headed to the precinct to answer a few more questions, Addison helped those customers without handlers primp and preen the competitors throughout the morning.

Customers. She liked the sound of that. Something she'd thought she'd never see again. Now she had some of the most loyal customers a business owner could ask for. She'd certainly risked enough to get them—as in, her life.

Addison's finger hovered over the doorbell, shaking slightly in anticipation. Before she could chicken out, she pushed it. She heard the muffled *ding*, followed by shuffling inside. Her stomach clenched with nerves. Her heart thudded so fast it felt like a hundred bouncy balls careening around inside her chest. She worried that if she opened her mouth to speak, one might come flying out.

The door squeaked open and Felix was standing on the other side. At least it wasn't Charlotte. The moment he saw her, his dark eyebrows shot up, but he didn't speak until he wiped his face clean of emotion.

"Hi," he said—a little guardedly, she thought.

She gave an awkward little wave. "Hi."

"What are you doing here?"

It was still unclear if he was happy to see her or not. She couldn't read the blank expression or the impersonal tone of voice. Those balls in her chest increased speed. She regretted not going for the mailbox option.

"Sorry to bug you. I just thought Naia might be missing this." Addison practically threw the bunny at him. "But I'm sure you're busy, so I won't keep you long." She took a step back from the door, already fishing her keys out of her purse.

"No, not at all." He reached out to her like he wanted to pull her inside. "Please, come in."

"Really?" She hesitated, poking her head inside, checking for signs of Charlotte; a pair of shoes, a coat. "Are you sure?"

Felix stepped aside and tilted his head in invitation.

She swallowed a bouncy ball and stepped onto the welcome mat, staring at her shoes while he closed the door.

"So how is Naia?" she asked.

"She's good. She finally went to sleep way past her bedtime. She kept asking for bunny." He jiggled the stuffed animal in his hand. "I'm really glad you found it. Thanks."

Felix was being so distant, so unfamiliar, like they hadn't faced death together just the night before. Hadn't spent the last two weeks fighting their attraction. Hadn't ever kissed. Like he didn't know how to make her body, and her heart, sing. But then again, maybe it was because she hadn't looked him in the eye since she arrived.

Forcing her eyes to meet his, she noticed he wasn't wearing his sling anymore. "How's your arm?"

"Good. Good. A bit sore, but not bad." He rolled his shoulder freely, wincing only slightly. "How are you after everything?" He gestured stiffly, like he was having an awkward conversation with a mere stranger.

Maybe that's what he wanted to be. Strangers. Old acquaintances. Addison could be "this girl he once knew." Perhaps that was better, she told herself. That could make it easier to move on. To stop thinking about how he'd saved her life, how easy it was to be herself when she was around him. To stop thinking about his arms around her, his laugh, his charm, and just how much she wanted to kiss him right now.

"I'm fine," she said, finally. "A little tired." She leaned back against the front door because "a little" was an understatement.

"I'm sorry I didn't say good-bye last night," he said. "Or thank you. If that even covers going through something like that with someone." His cool behavior warmed a little. "You helped me save my daughter. You helped me clear my name. I couldn't have done it without you."

"Same here," she said. "Now maybe you'll start getting gigs again. Maybe it's too late for your friend's Irish pub, but there will be another bar, I'm sure."

"Actually. There already is." His face lit up, the rest of the frostiness melting. "Turns out my boss is looking at jail time for his involvement with the dognappings. With all that gambling debt Penny mentioned, he's selling the bar to pay it off so no one is hired to shiv him in jail." He grinned, like the threat of a good shivving was the best possible news. "The bar is up for sale."

"That's great." She smiled. "Yay for shivving."

"And with forty percent of Alistair's reward money for finding Lilly, I'll have more than enough for the down payment."

"Make that fifty percent," Addison said, with a smile. "And that's great. I'm really happy for you."

"Thanks. But what about you? You can use the reward

money to keep your business afloat for a little longer." As their natural connection began to flow again, he seemed to forget his aloofness altogether. It felt so easy to be around him. So instinctual.

"Actually, thanks to our solving the case, business is looking up," Addison said. "The fashion show, on the other hand, might still be a bust." She dreaded finally facing Aiden and telling him his sure-thing investment had become a bottomless money pit.

He pulled a sympathetic face. "Still no reservations?"

"No." She shook her head. "But it's not until tomorrow afternoon. Still a few more hours yet. Things might pick up."

He chuckled, almond eyes sparkling down at her, making her tingle inside and then hurt all over again at the feeling of the loss in front of her. "Ever the optimist. There's the Addy I know and . . ." He petered off. His Adam's apple bobbed as he swallowed. "But surely Phillip will be there. Maybe he has a few rich friends he can invite."

"Phillip?" Her forehead winkled. "I don't think he'll be coming."

Felix gave her a questioning look, and that's when she realized he still thought she was interested in Phillip. That they were dating. The match with Phillip seemed so out of the question to her now, but she'd never actually had the chance to tell Felix, what with the dogs and Naia being stolen from the boat, and being held at gunpoint and all.

"I'm not with Phillip." She wrinkled her nose. "I realized he wasn't for me."

The rest of his strangeness fell away like he pulled off a mask. But he was still hiding some emotion, she just didn't know what it was. "What happened? I thought he was Mr. Perfect."

"He is," she said.

A flicker of that hidden emotion broke through before he suppressed it again.

"He's just not perfect for me," she shrugged. "Anyway. I'm sure Charlotte is happy you're going to buy the bar."

He seemed to take a moment to redirect his thoughts. "She'll definitely have a better boss to work for."

"Well, you'd be more than a boss."

That little crease between his brows appeared. "What do you mean?"

"I just mean . . ." Her throat suddenly felt tight. She swallowed. "I'm happy for the two of you."

"You mean Naia and I?"

"No. You and Charlotte." She struggled to explain herself, feeling heat build beneath her carefully placed makeup. She was so tired and her thoughts were difficult to put into words. "Since you two are starting to date now. You were at the gala together and everything."

He was kind of smiling, but in a very confused way. "I wasn't on a date with Charlotte."

"Well, not technically a date. I know you were really there to investigate but—"

"No," he interrupted. "I mean we weren't on a date."

"But you went there together."

"Because my car was still in the shop. She drove. We're not dating. It's not like that."

Oh God, she thought. They were even more serious than she'd suspected. "When Naia was taken, Charlotte said . . . she said she was going to make a terrible mother."

Felix crossed her arms, and she wondered if she was overstepping the line. It was none of her business.

"Yes," he said. "She meant to her own child. Charlotte's pregnant."

Oh God! They were having a baby. That explained the

rush for getting serious so fast. Maybe they'd even be married soon. Her brain, which had been struggling to keep up with only a couple of hours sleep, suddenly failed her. She leaned back against the door like the news just blew her away.

"Pregnant." The word came out in a rush of breath. "That's . . . great." She tried to sound enthusiastic, truly she did, but it was hard to smile with the tears building in her eyes.

"Our boss found out she was expecting. Joe's notorious for laying girls off when they're pregnant so he doesn't have to pay maternity leave."

Addison scowled, trying to pull herself together. "He can't do that. There are laws to protect her."

"Joe's done it before. He builds up files on everyone, a list of probationary stuff, discipline letters. It's all total made-up bullshit, but whenever he decides he wants to get rid of someone, it looks like he has enough on them to make it legal." He shrugged. "It's not fair. But it's a dive bar. It's not exactly like we have a union."

"That's terrible," she said.

"He's a cheap bastard. She'd worked for him for five years, had earned maternity leave. When he found out she was expecting, he blackmailed her into helping load up the dogs into the van at Phillip's fundraiser. He needed someone on the inside. Said if she didn't do it, he'd suddenly run out of work in the next few months and lay her off."

Addison nodded slowly. "So that's why she helped steal the dogs."

"She didn't think anything bad would happen to them." He stopped and shook his head. "I know that's no excuse, but with a baby on the way and her man recently laid off of his job, I don't envy the position she was in."

Addison noted how casually he called himself "her man." She wanted to condemn Charlotte, but then she thought about what she'd been willing to do to save her own business. And it was just her and Princess. She couldn't imagine the pressure Charlotte had been under to keep her job.

"Well, congratulations," Addison said at last. Trying really hard for that earnest smile. "I'm sure you and Charlotte will be very happy." But those tears were building again, and the last thing on Earth she wanted to do was cry in front of him. She reached for the door handle behind her, getting ready to leave.

"Wait. What?" Felix blinked. He opened his mouth, his kissable mouth, and closed it again. He rubbed a hand over his face and considered Addison for a moment. "*Charlotte's* pregnant. You understand it has nothing to do with me, right?"

"What?" Addison's eyes widened and then quickly narrowed. "How can you say that? You can't just turn your back on her. Take some responsibility, Felix." Her voice rose, but she tried to keep it low as to not wake Naia.

"Addy. Listen to me." Felix gripped her by the shoulders and gave her a soft shake. "Charlotte is pregnant, but not with my baby. She's pregnant by her boyfriend."

She blinked. "Boyfriend?"

"Yes. Boy-who-is-not-me boyfriend." He spoke slowly and clearly so she could understand.

"Not you?" Blink, blink went her eyes. "You're not pregnant? You're not marrying Charlotte?"

"What? No!" He laughed his rich belly laugh. "Where is this coming from? I told you we're just friends."

"B-But the flirting," she stuttered. "And you seemed so close at the gala. And . . . and . . ." She didn't know why she was arguing, like she was trying to convince him he was really dating her, whether he knew it or not. She couldn't wrap her head around it. After everything she'd seen. "What about the night you went to her house?"

Felix grew quiet and still, his hands dropped from her shoulders. Addison bit her lip. She hadn't considered how he'd react to the news before it flew out of her mouth. She'd glazed over that tidbit of information on the *Belle*. Now that she'd reminded him, his gaze narrowed.

"You were following me?" he asked.

She raised her hands, holding off his anger. "I had no idea you'd be there. I know that you insisted Charlotte was innocent, but I just didn't trust her. I felt there was more going on."

Felix crossed his arms and seemed to think for a moment. "Well, I can't blame you. You were right." He sighed. "She'd called me over there and confessed everything that night about her involvement. She was so upset."

Addison's hand was still clasped tightly around the door handle, but mostly so she didn't fall over with fatigue, or surprise. His face screwed up like he worried she was still going to walk out. He laid his hands on the door on either side of her, blocking her there. But she didn't think she had the energy to move even if her brain could catch up.

"But I've never been interested in Charlotte," he said. "Ever."

Addison remembered the embrace she'd witnessed between Felix and Charlotte, the desperation and pleading in her voice as she greeted him at the door. Charlotte had been upset. She needed a friend, comfort. That's all it was. And she'd probably been nervous at the gala. That would explain the clinginess.

"Why did you let me think you and Charlotte were at the gala together?" Addison asked. "Why didn't you tell me it wasn't a date?"

"Why should I have? You were on a date yourself. And, if I'm honest"—his voice softened—"maybe it was because I wanted you to be a little jealous. I know I was." His Adam's apple bobbed again.

"Jealous of Phillip? But it wasn't a date, not really. I knew the night before that it wasn't right. You were right. It was all just a made-up fairy tale in my head. It wasn't real," she said. "I left Phillip's house that night, just after you did."

He straightened at the news. "You did?"

Felix's entryway grew quiet as Addison became silent for a moment, mulling everything over. As did Felix. All the looks she'd imagined between him and Charlotte, all the times she assumed they were flirting. All the misjudgments. Meanwhile, she'd been ignoring something real growing between the two of them this whole time.

"So," she finally said, "I had it all wrong with you and Charlotte?"

His lip curled in amusement. "Yup."

Her shoulders drooped, feeling the weight of all her misplaced emotions. "Just like I had you wrong right from the start."

"Seems that way," he said, his eyes narrowing with some emotion, maybe hesitation. "I suppose I had you and Phillip wrong too."

"I think I had it more wrong than you did." Addison frowned. "I guess I thought that being with someone like Phillip could make life so much easier. That if I lived a life like that, what possible reasons would we have to fight? But then what? We would have had money, but would we have had what it really took to make a relationship work?" As she thought about this—for the millionth time—her eyes drifted sightlessly over his entryway, as though searching for the answer.

Even with everything that had happened over the last couple of days, there wasn't five minutes that had gone by that she didn't reflect on her conversation with her dad, on his relationship with Dora, and what she could remember of her mother. "There's more to life than money," she said to Felix, truly understanding what that meant now that she'd faced the option of having it and chose to walk away for something else—even the remote possibility of it.

"Like what?" Felix asked. She didn't think it was because he didn't know. He wanted to hear her say it.

Her gaze didn't waver as she held his. "Love."

"And is that what you want?" His body seemed to move an inch closer, as though anticipating, hoping for the right answer.

"I think I might have already found it."

That distant stranger who answered the door was gone for good. Her Felix was back, and it seemed there was nothing standing in their way. Not Charlotte, not Phillip, not even Addison's brain. And when he took a hesitant step toward her, there wasn't even space left between them.

Addison rubbed her temples and sighed. "Confusing much?"

"Jumping to conclusions much?" He reached up to her face, his hands hovering over her like he wanted to touch her, but was uncertain of how she felt.

She craved his usual touch: firm, sure, and greedy. She gave him an inviting look that made sure he knew how she felt. "Want me much?"

"Oh so very much." He kissed her. "Much." He kissed her again. "Much." With a softer look than she'd ever seen in his eyes, he held her face. "And you're right. Love is so much more. I believe it can get you through anything. Can get *us* through anything, because I'll stick by you through whatever comes at us. For better or worse. You know that, right?"

Unable to resist, she brought a hand up to explore this sweeter expression with her fingers, this new, unguarded way that he looked at her. "I know. You've already proven that during the last couple of weeks."

"And you've been there for me. And Naia." His eyes creased, as though remembering when he thought he'd lost her.

While Addison had been worried about finding a guy who would stick around through thick and thin, she suddenly realized that he probably worried about the same thing. Hadn't he experienced his own sense of loss, of abandonment by Naia's mother? And like Addison needed him to be there for her, she wanted to be there for him.

"And I always will be," she said.

When Felix kissed her once more, he remained locked there. He explored her mouth, her tongue, slowly, confidently. There was no rush; Addison wasn't going anywhere. Because she knew why she was there this time. It wasn't lust, or curiosity, or a temporary insanity, or because her heart was leading her astray. She was there because she chose to be. Her heart and her brain finally agreed that Felix was *the one*.

Felix swept Addison's golden curls aside, forging a trial of kisses down her neck. "You must be exhausted after the last twenty-four hours," he mumbled against her shoulder.

The vibration of his words against her skin made her lower half clench with anticipation, proving that apparently she wasn't *that* tired.

"Well, I suppose it is way past my bedtime," she teased.

"You do seem tired," he said, with mock seriousness. "Maybe too tired to drive all the way home."

"You're right. It might not be safe." She tried to act cool, but her voice shook, giving her excitement away.

"I couldn't live with myself if I sent you on your way and something happened to you." All trace of teasing humor was gone. His eyes flickered and his breath hitched like he'd never meant anything more in his life.

"I couldn't live with it if you sent me on my way either," she said softly.

"Maybe you should stay here. I could tuck you in." He reached around her, grabbing her butt with a mischievous grin.

She arched against him in surprise. "Tuck away."

Bending down, Felix swept her up into his arms, wincing a little because of his shoulder. He winked at her. "Milady."

She laid a swooning princess hand against her forehead as he carried her up the stairs. "Oh, my knight in shining armor." Maybe there was room for a little fantasy between them, after all.

However, as he carried her down the hall toward the room at the end, her mind didn't wander. It didn't transport her to fantasies of their future, all the possible adventures they could have, imagining them as different characters in new settings. She remained in the moment, because she could think of no better place to be. Besides, who wanted to settle for PG-rated fairy tales when she could have R-rated?

And that was clearly what Felix had in mind as he booted his door open impatiently. A lamp glowed from his bedside table, so she could see the lust in his expression.

With a boyish grin, he suddenly let her go and dropped her on his bed. She squealed before she hit the comforter.

Locking his bedroom door, he pulled off his shirt. The light caught his tanned skin, highlighting every hard dip and swell of his muscles. Holding her gaze, he unfastened his worn jeans, and they crumpled to the floor. He didn't hesitate before reaching for the waistband of his boxers and tugging them down too.

She gasped as Felix was released, and obviously ready for her. A shudder of anticipation coursed through her at the sight of him exposed so unceremoniously, so confidently.

He pounced on her, diving playfully onto the bed. Addison's hands came up automatically, impatient to begin exploring. But as hasty as he'd been preparing himself for her, he slowed down to remove her clothes.

He slid each piece of clothing off her body reverently, like he was opening that Tiffany's box. Her anticipation built with each button he slipped free, each sock he tugged off like it was sexy lingerie.

When he dragged her pants down over her hips, kissing her legs as he went, she suddenly gasped.

"What's wrong?" he asked.

She felt heat crawl up her face. "I, umm, forgot to shave my legs. I didn't exactly anticipate this."

Felix laughed, his breath tickling her thighs. "Addy, I don't care. I don't care about the shaving, and the makeup, and the hair, and the clothes. I prefer you without all of it." He nibbled on her inner thigh, making her squeak. "Especially without the clothes."

As though to prove his point, he tugged off her pants the rest of the way and rubbed his face up her bare legs, his own stubble scratching her skin deliciously.

Ticklish, she giggled and pulled her legs away. Grasping her ankles, he held them apart. His hands were firm and unyielding as his stubble rubbed higher and higher up her inner thigh.

She shivered and squirmed until his stubble tickled between her legs, adding to the soothing sensation of his kiss, his wet tongue, his probing fingers. *Forget R-rated*, she thought, *this is XXX*.

As her body warmed with each kiss, each lick, she struggled to keep quiet. She grunted and gripped the sheets beneath her, twisting them in her hands. When her body began to shake and twitch with pleasure, she turned her face toward a pillow and cried into it to muffle her scream.

Addison was still vibrating with pleasure, coming down from her high, so she hadn't even noticed he'd already put on a condom until he lowered his body on top of hers. She felt his weight, his presence, secure her, ground her. It was as though without him she'd float away like a hot air balloon, drifting aimlessly without direction or purpose for the rest of her life. She would be doomed to look down at the people below, never attached or truly connected to anything.

Felix and Naia could be that connection, she thought. Not tie her down like she'd convinced herself a family would. They could keep her grounded. Anchor her to reality.

Addison laid her palms against Felix's chest, enjoying the sensation as she dragged them down his torso, his abs, his hips, enjoying the security that came with how real he felt, how solid, how firm. Very, *very* firm.

Felix moaned as her fingers curled around that firmness and guided him inside of her, filling her up, like he filled that last remaining part in her life. He filled her

again, and again, and again, until she was stifling her
cries of pleasure against his shoulder and he was groaning into her hair.

Addison knew in her heart that Felix was the one. He
may not have been Prince Charming, and it may not
have been fairy tale perfect. It was better. It wasn't someone else's story, but her own. It was real. Felix was real.
What they had was real.

33

Everybody and Their Dog

The tutus had been fluffed, the fur combed, the jewelry polished, and the lapels pressed. Addison was ready to start the fashion show. Only, was it still a show if there was no one there to *show*?

Twenty minutes remained before curtain call, and the only people on the other side of the closed stage curtain were her father and Dora, sitting front row, center. They'd driven all the way from Linda Mar for the day. Too bad it was just to see Addison flop. So much for her dad being proud of her.

Of course, Holly Hart and her cameraman, Hey, You, were there too. At least the reporter had followed through on her promise to host it. Addison just hoped Hey, You could angle the camera shots so all the empty seats lining the sides of the catwalk wouldn't be caught in the frame.

Since Addison couldn't find anyone willing to volunteer—or even be paid—to help with the modeling, her friends had stepped up to help out. Thankfully they'd all been too busy helping her prep the dogs backstage, so no one knew what was on the other side of that curtain: absolutely no one.

She still hadn't confessed to Aiden just how daunting things were, how much the dognapping scandal had hurt her business. Since her name had been cleared publicly on the news, she'd hoped with every ounce of positive mojo she had left in her that she'd arrive to an audience that afternoon.

But as the minutes ticked down, and the seats remained empty each time she obsessively peeked out, she knew the moment was coming to warn her models and their walkers of what awaited them. It was a huge blow to her ego, but it wasn't from lack of trying her best.

Addison peeked out the curtain for the hundredth time, hoping a ton of people had packed into the room since she last looked thirty seconds before. But all she saw was Holly snapping her fingers at Hey, You.

Her dad held up the pink program for the show while he read it to Dora like it was *War and Peace*. They were holding hands. Addison smiled. It occurred to her that she had no memory of her parents ever showing affection like that, far less in public.

She felt the air shift behind her before two strong arms wrapped around her waist.

"Don't worry," Felix whispered in her ear. "There's still time for people to show up."

Addison couldn't imagine ever being able to worry while in his arms. She spun to face him. "Thanks for helping out today."

He'd unloaded her Mini piled so high with supplies that she'd had to drive with the top down to the venue, even though it had been threatening rain. Then there was the sorting and the organizing—he'd even helped dress Oliver.

"I don't mind," Felix said. "Naia's having fun playing dress up with all the dogs. And I've never seen Oliver look so dashing."

Addison followed his gaze to find Naia arranging a bow tie above Oliver's knitted sweater vest for the casual dress portion of the show.

Addison sighed, trying to look on the bright side of things. "If nothing else, at least Holly Hart's segment will get the show some coverage."

"And no matter what happens," he said, "at the end of the day, you should feel very proud of yourself. You've worked hard to get here." His arms squeezed around her.

She stood on her tiptoes and kissed him. He was right. Things certainly turned out better than they could have. The dogs were safe and sound, back with their owners, her spa was not only still in business, but if all the appointment requests she'd found in her email inbox that morning were any indication, things were picking back up. And out of all the drama, she'd gotten Felix and Naia.

Piper finished zipping up a camouflage jacket on Colin. "What do you think? He looks pretty cool, right?"

Addison squatted down next to him and popped the collar like the Fonz. "Very cool."

"Yeah, and I love this leather getup," Zoe said, escorting a chocolate dachshund named Peanut. "Do you have it in my size?"

Addison laughed when she saw the spicy leather number on the dog. The vest and studded hat bordered on male stripper or S&M.

"You probably already have something just like it," Addison told her.

Zoe grinned devilishly. "You can never have too much leather."

It was at times like this that Addison could see Zoe

missed her old doxie, Buddy. Of course she put on a brave face, but they'd known each other too long for Addison not to notice the sad crinkle next to her eyes, and the way she looked sort of wistful when she stared at all of her friends with their own dogs.

Zoe had only lost him six months before to old age, however, she continued to volunteer at the rescue center religiously because she loved the dogs. Maybe it made her miss Buddy a little less. She'd move on when she was ready, but Addison was just glad Zoe could be involved that day.

Marilyn crossed the stage, calling Picasso to come. He rolled over in his blinged-out ride, sparkling beneath the spotlights. Addison had bedazzled the wheels and spokes of his wheelchair so they glistened as they rolled to a stop in front of her.

He wore a casual jean jacket, with the sleeves pushed up above his little dog elbows. Melody came over and set a pair of tiny sunglasses on top of his head to finish the look.

"I was always a sucker for the bad boy," she said.

Addison assessed the results of all their efforts and took a deep breath. "Well, it's almost time!" she called out. Everyone gathered around. Aiden carried Sophie who was wearing her off-the-shoulder sweater over a flared jean skirt, and Bob brought Princess over in her tutu. Since Addison and Melody would be scrambling behind the stage with wardrobe changes, he'd volunteered to walk Princess down the catwalk.

Naia dragged a reluctant Oliver over to the group. He waddled a little funny, not used to wearing clothes, or being groomed for that matter.

Felix glanced around at the other dogs, which all happened to be doxies. "Looks like you're the odd dog out,

Oliver. Gives a whole new meaning to the term sausage party."

Both Aiden and Bob chuckled at that. But Addison took in the models with a frown. She'd hoped for a wider variety. She had planned an array of outfits, different sizes and shapes for various breeds to show off the versatility of her line. Her "every dog" message wasn't all that effective when the only dogs she had were dachshunds and Oliver—whatever he was.

But it could have been worse, she reminded herself. The show must go on. At least her friends were all there to share the occasion with her.

"I just want to thank you for all being here today," Addison began. "And for all you've done to help me this weekend. I couldn't have groomed so many dogs in a single night without all of you slaving away alongside me. Aiden, thanks for believing in my dream and supporting me. I wouldn't be here without your generosity. And Felix." She turned to her boyfriend, unable to keep the giddy smile off her face. "If not for you, I may not have been here at all."

Felix gave her a look that let her know he'd do it all over again. She allowed that look to fill her with love and support as she found the courage to say the next words. To explain that no one was coming to see the show except for her dad and Dora.

"Unfortunately," she began, "I have to warn you before you go out there that it won't be what you expect."

"Wait! Wait!" A woman's voice cried out.

Addison turned to the backstage door. Julia Edwards swept across the stage with Precious loping next to her, lengthy fur swishing around her legs like flowing skirts. And they weren't alone. Filtering in after her was a long line of purebreds, handlers, and breeders. It was a parade of fur, blazers, and knee-length skirts with sensible shoes.

Julia rushed to Addison, a hand clamped over her chest as she caught her breath. Her wide eyes moved over Addison's gathered friends and the dogs in their outfits. "Are we too late to model?"

The newcomers drew close, staring at Addison in expectation. All of the dogs and owners she'd helped to prepare for the show that weekend had come. In fact, nearly all of the dogs she and Felix had rescued showed up.

Tears sprang to her disbelieving eyes. She dabbed at them, grateful she'd worn waterproof mascara. It took Addison a few seconds to find her voice. "Err, no. No. Of course not. Please, come this way." She gestured to the rack of carefully labeled outfits.

Melody was already flicking through sizes. "I was thinking the gym vest and shorts combo for Precious," she suggested.

"Sounds perfect." Addison began redirecting owners to various racks.

Zoe, Marilyn, and Piper rushed to help—mostly because the men couldn't tell the difference between chiffon and gossamer. Addison was swept up in the rush of getting everyone organized while Princess watched on with a critical eye, barking orders at anyone who would listen.

Snouts up, models! she ordered. *Tails perked! You over there, stop scratching!*

As Addison was doing a head count, she saw Kitty Carlisle's white beehive jostling through the crowd. When Kitty saw her, her eyes bulged. "There you are. Sorry we're late."

"That's okay. I'm so glad you could make it."

"It was my fault. After it came out that Walter Boyd had an"—she glanced around and spoke quietly behind her hand—"inappropriate relationship with you know who, I was asked by the association to be the Best in Show judge this year. Big responsibility, you know. I just couldn't make a decision, so I asked for a few extra turns from the contestants."

"That's great," Addison said, already sorting through the beachwear for Elvis. "Congratulations on the new position. Who won?"

"Precious did," Julia sang. She arranged the blue exercise headband on Precious to match the wristbands. "Didn't you, Precious? Yes, you're such a good boy, aren't you?"

"That's fantastic. Congratulations." Addison felt a bubble of pride that her longtime customer had won.

Rex Harris sashayed through the door with Rosie trotting by his side. "Any room for us?"

"Absolutely," Addison said. "Rosie would be great to start the evening-wear portion." She pointed to the rack on the side. "Oh, and Melody? Can you get Kingy set up with the construction uniform?"

Someone tapped Addison's shoulder, and she turned to find Kayleigh.

"We were just so pleased with the work you did on such short notice. Lionel and I would love to help you out. Oooh, is this cashmere?" She reached out to rub a dress shirt between her fingers.

"Yes. I have it in Lionel's size." She plucked it from the rack and handed it over.

She felt she could barely catch her breath between surprises. Then Alistair Yates emerged from the bustling crowd, Lilly following obediently on her leash. He leaned heavily on his cane, as though weary. Addison imagined it had been a rough couple of days for him too. Or weeks, rather.

"I wanted to thank you for saving Lilly," he said. "I'm

very sorry for the grief I have caused you." By the amount of extra winkles creasing his face, she knew he meant it.

He wasn't a bad man. He'd just been taken in by the wrong person. It's not like Addison didn't have her own fair share of experiences being taken in by liars and deceivers—men, mostly.

"I appreciate that," Addison finally said. "You've had a lot to deal with yourself."

"I'm happy that it's you I get to give the reward money to. You and your friend. I hope it begins to repair the damage I've done to your business." He looked at the chaos around them. "And if you'll have us, we'd like to volunteer for your fashion show. I know Lilly would enjoy it. Today is her last big hurrah, after all."

"You still showed Lilly? Not Fancy, in the end?" Addison struggled to hide her surprise, but her tone must have given it away. Or the fact that she was a terrible actress.

Alistair smiled sheepishly. "I knew Lilly had no chance of winning. Especially after the stress of the last couple of weeks. Maybe she wouldn't have had a chance even if things had gone smoothly. But I just wanted one more year with her. I wasn't ready to let go quite yet. We've been through a lot together."

Addison smiled. That she could certainly understand. "Well, since it's Lilly's big day, I'm sure we can find something special for her."

"Thank you."

The backstage was a whirlwind of activity, silk, rhinestones, and ribbon until the lineup resembled a mixture of breeds, the perfect balance, tails whipping back and forth in anticipation.

It was just how she'd imagined it would be. Not a fashion line just for the elite and rich, but for the everyday dog. Because every dog from Precious to Oliver deserved to be pampered, to feel special, to feel loved like they were so capable of loving their owners and showing it every day.

Holly's head suddenly popped between the break in the curtains. "Are we all ready?"

Addison took a deep breath and cast a final glance at the lineup. "Yes. I think so." She handed Holly the cue cards with new notes scribbled on them in pen. "There have been some changes."

Holly took in the new arrivals. "Good, because we have a full house out there."

"What? Really?" Addison stuck her head out of the curtains.

Holly was right. Practically every seat in the house was filled. She recognized other contestants and even some judges from the dog show. Seated in the front rows were studious spectators with notebooks and cameras at the ready.

Addison nodded to the front row. "Who are they?"

"Oh them? I called a few of my media friends." Holly waved a nonchalant hand, but her self-important smile gave her away.

For a second, Addison was touched that the reporter had gone above and beyond to make the fashion show special. "Thank you."

"Exclusives are only good if everyone wants a piece of the action. I couldn't very well host something no one's even heard of. It would be a waste of a PR opportunity."

"Oh, well"—Addison's smile faded slightly—"thank you anyway."

Holly caught sight of Aiden and gasped. "Oh, Aiden. I didn't know you'd be modeling today." Her breath hitched and released in a sort of shiver.

Apparently Holly's obsession with the CEO was still

going strong, Addison thought. Even though she worked for Channel Five news now, she'd spent years hounding him when she worked at *The Gate,* San Francisco's leading gossip magazine.

Aiden stiffened beneath her undressing eyes. "Sophie is the model." He held up his longhaired dachshund. "I'm just helping out."

"You certainly are model material with that body and bone structure." Holly bit her lip as she ran her gaze down his body.

He shifted uncomfortably, but Addison cut in to end the awkwardness. She clapped her hands. "Okay, time to go."

Holly waggled her manicured fingers at Aiden, but Addison shut the curtains on her before there could be any more delays. She heard a small huff, but then a moment later, Holly's professional reporter voice boomed from the speakers.

"Welcome dog and fashion lovers. I'm Holly Hart. You might recognize me from Channel Five news. I'm your host for this evening, because I too am a fashion lover, and my dates say I can be quite the hound dog." She chuckled at her own joke.

Addison turned to the crowd behind her. "Okay. Everyone ready?"

She got a few thumbs up and some barks.

"Are *you* ready?" Felix asked her.

She gave him a knowing smile. "More than you know."

"It's going to be great." Piper squeezed her shoulder as Addison passed.

Aiden gave her a congratulatory hug. "I knew you were a good investment."

If only he knew, she thought. She tried to ignore the heat creeping up her neck and gave him a brilliant smile. "Thanks."

Outside, she could hear the music amping up and Holly saying, "Let's have a look at the latest in doggy duds."

"Okay Piper, you're up," Addison said. "Good luck."

Piper gave her an excited grin and stepped up. Addison whisked to the side of the stage to peer through the curtain and watch.

As Piper and Colin walked out, Holy narrated. "First down the catwalk—or should I say dogwalk—is Colin. He's is wearing a camouflage jacket that appeals to both the hunter and the city dweller with its hip, urban crossover feel."

The crowd clapped as Piper and Colin took a turn around the catwalk.

"Next up is Sophie," Holly announced. "She's wearing a beautiful cable-knit baby alpaca sweater paired with a jean skirt. The flared skirt allows for easy movement to play in the park while being flirty enough to catch the eye of that poodle you've been after."

Aiden turned around at the end of the stage, and Holly gave him a wink. "And of course there's her owner Aiden Caldwell of Caldwell and Son Investments wearing"— she paused for effect—"well, I'd prefer it if he was wearing nothing at all."

This got a few titters from the ladies in the crowd and a few of the gentlemen. Addison rolled her eyes, but she had to admit that Holly was doing a great job. She knew what the public wanted.

Marilyn and Picasso rolled out on stage to big cheers. Naia was also a big hit when she pranced out with Oliver. She got a few awes and claps, which made her twirl and show off with a cheesy grin. Felix trailed behind, mostly for moral support and to make sure Oliver didn't get overexcited by the crowd and try to take off. Of course, the dog of the hour, Precious, received extra cheers from the dog show fans.

There were more than enough models that most dogs only had to make two changes. And when Princess came out at the end wearing a tiara and a pink ball gown with a train of real flowers, Addison was walking proudly next to her star.

Addison gave a gracious bow for everyone who came that day and a special wave for Dora and her dad who wore proud smiles just for her. She may have imagined it, but it seemed as though Princess gave a magnanimous bow of her blonde head, accepting the praise of her loyal subjects.

Addison turned and waved out the other participants to join her on the catwalk. They each came out one by one with their owners in tow. Addison held out her hands for Felix and Naia to join her front and center. Because she wouldn't have been there if not for them. She beamed at them in silent thanks, since she wouldn't have been heard over the cheers from the crowd.

Felix returned her look, his handsome face filled with love and pride. He was proud of her, of who she was. Just the way she was. She knew in that moment that he'd always be there for her, through thick and thin. The three of them would be a family.

Everything was perfect. Exactly how she'd imagined it would be. No, it was better, because she wasn't living in a fantasy world anymore. This was real life. Her life that she'd built herself. And as Felix took one of Addison's hands and Naia took her other for a final bow, she knew she'd finally found her happily ever after.

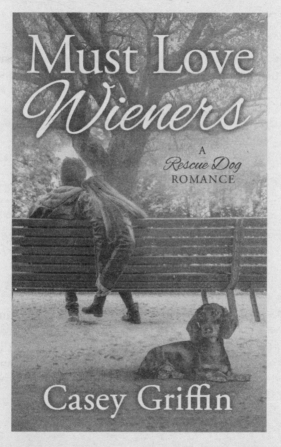

Don't miss Zoe's love story—the next hilarious, heart-tugging book in the Rescue Dog Romance series!

The Wedding
Tail

To be unleashed Summer 2017